TESSA HARRIS read History at journalist, writing for several national newspapers and magazines, for more than thirty years. She is the author of nine published historical novels. Her debut, *The Anatomist's Apprentice*, won the Romantic Times First Best Mystery Award 2012 in the US. She lectures in creative writing at Hawkwood College, Stroud, and is married with two children. She lives in the Cotswolds.

Facebook: Tessa Harris Author

Twitter: @harris_tessa

Also by Tessa Harris

Beneath a Starless Sky

the
LIGHT
WE LEFT
BEHIND

TESSA HARRIS

ONE PLACE. MANY STORIES

HQ
An imprint of HarperCollins*Publishers* Ltd
1 London Bridge Street
London SE1 9GF

www.harpercollins.co.uk

HarperCollins*Publishers*
1st Floor, Watermarque Building, Ringsend Road
Dublin 4, Ireland

This paperback edition 2022

1
First published in Great Britain by
HQ, an imprint of HarperCollins*Publishers* Ltd 2021

Copyright © Tessa Harris 2021

Tessa Harris asserts the moral right to be
identified as the author of this work.
A catalogue record for this book is
available from the British Library.

ISBN: 9780008523848

MIX
Paper from
responsible sources
FSC
www.fsc.org
FSC C007454

This book is produced from independently certified FSC™ paper
to ensure responsible forest management.

For more information visit: www.harpercollins.co.uk/green

Printed and Bound in the UK
using 100% Renewable Electricity at CPI Group (UK) Ltd

This book is dedicated to the men and women of Trent Park, 1942–1945, whose secret work contributed so much to the Allied victory in the Second World War

'Correction does much, but encouragement does more.'
Johann Wolfgang von Goethe, (1749–1832)

Prologue

Munich, Germany

July 1936

Maddie Gresham lay under the bedcovers, fully clothed and barely daring to move in the stifling darkness of a sweltering city night. Beneath the sheets she wore a skirt and blouse, together with a clean pair of white ankle socks. With the back of her hand, she wiped her sticky forehead. She was glowing – ladies didn't sweat – and she wondered how much longer she'd have to endure being swaddled in this heat.

It was madness, she knew. Any sane person would think she'd completely lost her proverbial marbles. But she was seventeen, going on eighteen, and had just thrown off the fetters of her English girls' boarding school. She was two weeks into her summer exchange at the home of her German penfriend, Greta Weitzler, and she wanted to live a little – to push the boundaries. Was that such a crime?

Despite her discomfort, her body remained poised like an animal about to pounce, ready to fling off the covers at the first call. Adrenaline coursed through her veins, but not so much through fear as excitement. This would be an adventure, something daring and undoubtedly frowned upon by her parents' friends at home in England. Mummy, had she been alive, would be quite scandalised. Daddy, on the other hand, and perhaps even Uncle Roly, her godfather, would probably regard what she was about to do as "a bit of a wheeze", like something from *The Girl's Own Paper* that she'd decided to enact in real life. But even though she didn't yet have the key to the door, technically she wasn't a child, either. And this wasn't a fantasy. There were risks, undoubtedly. If they were caught, they could end up behind bars, but the thought of standing up to a bunch of pug-faced bullies and championing an injustice shot a thrill through her entire body. The scent of danger was in her nostrils and she longed to run with it.

The only light – and indeed, ventilation – in the room came from the tiny gabled window in the eaves of the stuffy attic. The smell of mothballs and ginger clung to the air. The usual rasping sounds of arguments emanating from her hosts' bedroom directly below, which either kept her awake or woke her most nights, had subsided. Night, exhaustion, or both, always seemed to bring with it a truce between Herr Helmut Weitzler and his long-suffering wife, Ada.

Maddie relished the silence for a few moments until the bell from the little church round the corner tolled out twelve, then her heart beat even faster. The blood pounded in her ears and a moment later she heard the click of the handle. Nervously, she watched the low attic door open.

'Ready, Maddie?' It was Max, Greta's big brother. His voice sounded muffled in the heat and the darkness.

She didn't say anything at first. Just threw back the covers and jumped out of bed to slip into the soft-soled gym shoes on the rug.

'Ready,' she said, smoothing down the scarf around her head. It was tied at the nape of her neck in a sort of peasant effect. With her single light brown plait – Greta had taught her how to braid like a native – no one would ever guess she was English.

A beam of moonlight hit Max's face. There was a wild look in his amber eyes and his blond hair stood out at angles. He was a good three inches taller than her, but the colours he was wearing made him blend into the shadows. Suddenly she realised her white cotton blouse probably wasn't such a good idea. But then something glinted in the shaft of moonlight from the window and her eye was drawn to his right hand. An ice pick. Max was clutching an ice pick. Before he'd broken his leg in a motor accident and been forced to walk with a stick, Maddie knew Herr Weitzler had been a keen mountaineer. Max sucked in a deep breath before slapping his left palm with the shaft of the pick.

'Let's do this,' he said. He seemed deadly serious.

She nodded and, bending down, retrieved a rolling pin from under her pillow. She'd smuggled it from the kitchen when Cook was fussing over sauerkraut earlier that evening. She held it aloft, like the sword of a warrior about to do battle. Only Max didn't laugh.

They tiptoed along the landing and paused outside Joachim's door. His snores were much louder than usual. They took it as a good sign. The aspirin Max had slipped into his younger brother's warm milk seemed to have achieved the desired effect. There would be no trouble from him. Not tonight, at least.

Down the stairs they crept, past Greta's door. It remained shut. Maddie had hoped her penfriend might still join them, even though she'd already declared she wanted no part in their plans. Like every other young female of a similar age, Greta had been forced to join the League of German Girls, but unlike Joachim, she was not a great fan of the Führer and his cronies. Max had assured Maddie his brother would never betray them, but she was convinced Joachim would hand them over to the Gestapo with a smile on his face. There'd been a few days when she'd thought Greta might relent, especially when she had joined them circling in front of the Feldherrnhalle on her bicycle, refusing to salute the memorial to some failed Nazi coup in a beer hall.

The guards had shouted at them, but all three had pedalled off at high speed. Greta, with her elfin face and long, dark braids, had laughed the loudest then, but any hope that she'd join them tonight was now gone.

'Come on, Maddie,' mouthed Max, at the foot of the stairs. He wheeled his arm to signify his impatience then frowned when he noticed her white blouse. Tugging off his dark green cardigan he thrust it in front of her. She put it on unquestioningly and his hand accidentally brushed against her as he helped her. The shock of his touch took her breath away, but she didn't let it show.

From the peg in the porch, Max reached for his father's raincoat and slipped into it, so that he could hide the ice pick up his sleeve. The belted gabardine was far too large for his slender frame. It looked suspicious on such a balmy night, but at least with the cardigan over her blouse Maddie now felt less conspicuous.

As the latch dropped on the front door, Maddie edged forward and Max pushed her gently in front of him. Together they stepped out into the night, closing the door silently behind them. Once through the front gates, they crossed over the road to avoid rousing the neighbour's guard dog then hurried along the quiet residential street towards the main thoroughfare. Another ten minutes and they would reach the city centre.

They walked in silence for most of the way, Max mentally rehearsing exactly what they had to do and how they would do it, Maddie thinking more about Max than anything else. There were very few people about. Most upstanding Germans were in bed by now. The only ones abroad at this hour were, like them, up to no good, if the Nazis were to be believed.

When they reached the corner of a poorly lit street, Max stopped suddenly. From out of one of the raincoat pockets, he produced a hip flask and thrust it under her nose.

'For courage,' he said. Not that he needed it. He was in his third year of a physics degree at Munich University and, in Maddie's eyes at least, was already very mature and fearless.

Her stomach flipped as she reached for the flask. 'For courage,' she repeated, taking a large swig and promptly spluttering violently as the fiery liquid caught the back of her throat. At home she'd only ever been allowed a single glass of sherry at Christmas.

'Ssssh!' Max snatched the flask away from her and downed the rest of its contents in one.

It was then they heard footsteps: heavy boots tramping on the pavement.

'Who's there?' called a gruff voice from over the road.

They ducked behind a park bench until two storm troopers passed – straight-backed, straight-legged and full of their own self-importance. They were probably not much older than them, Maddie supposed. She knew they had a reputation for being oafish, these bullies who did the Nazi Party's bidding. Ordinarily she and Max could outwit them, but these thugs carried heavy batons, which were more than a match for their improvised weapons.

They carried on to their destination, this time keeping to the shadows. The small square, once home to the city's cattle market, was mercifully deserted apart from a couple of cats lolling on some shallow steps. They knew exactly what to do. In the middle of one side of the square was a large, glass-fronted information board displaying the latest front pages of a particularly unpleasant anti-Jewish newspaper called *Der Stürmer*. Max said that it was a dirty little rag, and no one read it before, but the Nazis were now thrusting it in everyone's face. His mother was Jewish and someone had spat at her as she walked along the street only the other day. Greta was repeatedly called a *mischling*, a mongrel, by some of the girls at school because her dark hair and brown eyes were proof she wasn't entirely Aryan. All sorts of frightful laws were being passed that meant Jewish people were no longer regarded as proper German citizens and Max said he couldn't just stand by and watch his mother insulted. Maddie agreed. It was dreadful to see the poor woman so down all the time, shoulders slouched and eyes often red from crying.

5

They paused for a moment to look at the front page of the newspaper. There was a horrid cartoon image of a Jewish man, his nose all bulbous and mouth pulled into a grotesque scowl. The headline ran: *The Jews Are Our Misfortune.* They eyed each other, then scanned the square behind to make sure no guards were around. With a simultaneous nod they took out their weapons and set to work quickly and methodically, strategically hitting the edges first. After three or four blows with her rolling pin, Maddie had completely destroyed the pane of glass. The crashing sound as it cascaded down onto the stone pavement below was like water flowing over rocks. Max followed on with the ice pick, clawing at the newspaper, tearing it to shreds. Within five seconds it was all over, but there was no time to stand back and admire their handiwork.

'Halte!'

From somewhere behind them, a shout split the darkness.

Maddie's heart flew into her mouth. Max reached for her and together they bolted and hurtled towards a maze of back streets. Hand in hand, they ran as fast as they could. Behind them a stampede of jackboots and shouts from the brown-shirted thugs, in front of them a tangled skein of alleys. But the cobbles were uneven, and Maddie stumbled, her right knee taking the full brunt of the fall. Max juddered to a halt and instantly heaved her to her feet. Wrapping her arm around his own neck, he took most of her weight and together they hobbled into a doorway. Once there, she followed his lead and flattened her body against the door, squashed against his shoulder. His breath was hot on her cheek as he turned to her, trying to steady himself. Seconds later the boots passed, the shouts faded away and the silence returned.

'We did it,' he whispered before his face broke into a beaming smile.

Yes, she thought. *We did something good – together.*

Standing there in the shadows, their hearts drumming against their chests, their eyes met. At that moment they were invincible, and Max suddenly drew her towards him and planted a kiss on her lips. That kiss – her first – was over in a second and yet it gave her the most extraordinary sensation, as if she were travelling in a fast elevator and her whole body was catapulted upwards. He laughed then, and so did she, as if what they had just done was so thrilling that they couldn't hold their happiness inside.

Looking back on it, from that night onwards, something changed between them. Something moved them both so powerfully they would never be the same again. They were riding the crest of a wave and relished the exhilaration of it. When they gazed into each other's eyes they were united in a shared purpose. They could face up to any enemy and together they could beat it. From that night on an unspoken pledge was made and a bond forged, although, of course, at the time, Maddie had no idea that war – and murder – would do everything in their power to break them apart.

Chapter 1

Trent Park, Middlesex

March 1944

The man at the War Office told her to take the Piccadilly Line to Cockfosters then walk up the tree-lined drive for half a mile to the big house. Maddie recognised the place as soon as she saw the magnificent entrance opposite the Underground. Trent Park.

The last time she was there, she had been chauffeur-driven in her father's Rolls-Royce to that magical cocktail party that now seemed such a bittersweet memory of a bygone era. That evening, the magnificent oaks, chestnuts and beeches had all been in full leaf. Now the trees had surrendered to winter gales and were all but denuded of their leaves to show bare, black branches to an overcast sky. But at least there were daffodils on either side of the drive. Nevertheless, she wished she were in a motor car right now. Her Gladstone bag, although only packed for overnight, still felt as though it was full of bricks and her new shoes – a pair of lace-up Oxfords – were letting her down and rubbing against her heels.

The balmy night of the party, she'd been wearing fabulous peep-toed sandals and a lovely yellow silk dress. Now winter, although on its way out, had taken no prisoners, so under her belted camel coat she sported a serviceable woollen suit. A burgundy-red tam sat snugly on her head. She didn't want to look too frivolous, or create a bad first impression. After all, she needed to be taken seriously. At least look the part. Some military personnel, however, obviously had other ideas.

'Once you get to the house, go to the gate, past the swimming pool,' said the sentry when she stopped to ask directions halfway up the drive. She caught him winking at the other guard. 'Then you'll have to get down on your hands and knees and crawl through the doorway,' he told her, obviously taking her for a rookie recruit.

Maddie didn't fall for it, of course. A few years ago, before the start of the war, she might almost have taken the cheeky squaddie seriously. She'd been so naïve. But not now. Not after everything that had happened and, she suspected, everything that was still to come.

'But I couldn't see Colonel McKie with laddered stockings, could I now?' she replied, all innocence, before flashing the sentry a knowing smile. His face fell then, when he heard she had a meeting with the man the squaddies at Trent Park called "the Guv'nor". So, Maddie just carried on up the drive, with an air of confident professionalism while trying to hide the fact that her feet were killing her.

To compound her woes, a few moments later she was confronted by a tradesman's van heading straight towards her, while in between them lay a large icy puddle. The vehicle made no sign of slowing down, or indeed veering to one side to avoid splashing her. A second later it did so with remarkable alacrity, spraying her stockings with muddy water. Whipping round to curse the driver under her breath, she read the gold lettering on the van's side: *Anstruther & Son Gentlemen's Outfitters By Royal Appointment. Savile Row, London.* There certainly wasn't a gentleman at the wheel, she thought. Nevertheless, she ploughed on.

She'd almost made it to the mansion when she paused for a moment in front of it, to take stock. Lifting her gaze, she marvelled at its imposing red-brick façade. The previous owner, Sir Philip Sassoon, had totally transformed the building from an undistinguished Victorian pile into a faux Georgian gem. It was always an honour to be included on his guest list. Her father, Sir Michael Gresham, was high up in the Treasury and a regular invitee. A heady mix of politicians, artists, literary types and film stars continuously passed through the mansion's doors. There was always someone interesting or famous or both to meet. The cocktail party she'd attended was only about three months before war broke out and not long before Sir Philip's sudden death. Charlie Chaplin, George Bernard Shaw and the painter Rex Whistler had been there. She remembered it had taken all her willpower not to ask them for their autographs. The girls at her college house at Oxford were so jealous.

But what a difference five years made. *Sir Philip would be turning in his grave,* Maddie thought, *if he could see what they've done to the place.* The roses that not so long ago tumbled over the ornamental walls had been replaced by coils of barbed wire and joining the tall trees surrounding the immaculate lawns was an enormous, unsightly watchtower. She recalled standing on the terrace at the cocktail party, the setting sun bathing the grounds in a soft glow and the sky turning the same colour as the crimson Manhattan she held in a long-stemmed glass. The memory brought a smile to Maddie's lips, but it didn't last long.

'You, there. Where's your pass?' Someone was shouting at her. To her right, a fearsome-looking sergeant with Eton-cropped hair and a clipboard in her hand broke into her thoughts. 'And you are?' The woman looked at Trent Park's latest potential recruit from her unforgiving shoes up to her red beret. The sergeant herself wore the unflattering garb of the Auxiliary Territorial Service – the women's army – a shapeless khaki ensemble that reminded Maddie of a sack of potatoes.

Without a word, Maddie produced her official pass from her clutch bag and the sergeant's expression changed instantly. Her top-secret clearance was every bit as handy as a magic wand. Almost five years ago, the war had forced her to swap her studies at the Institute of Experimental Psychology at Oxford University to join the staff at a new brain injuries hospital. Her old college, St Hugh's, had been requisitioned by the War Office and become almost unrecognisable. Transformed from a pleasant, airy, all-female college into an all-male hospital, its three hundred beds were occupied by patients with head injuries. They were mostly physical ones, but sometimes mental ones, too. Her tutor, Dr Tobias Baskin, was head psychologist. He'd asked her to follow him to assist with his research into the effects of combat injuries on mental well-being. She'd been honoured to oblige.

Now her life seemed all set to change once more. She'd been "selected" for interview, the letter said. It made her sound a bit like a Beech's Continental chocolate. An odd little man with a nervous twitch and tortoiseshell spectacles had come to St Hugh's and asked her all sorts of questions about her work with Dr Baskin. At the time she'd wondered why he didn't ask the good doctor himself. She rather feared he might be in some sort of trouble, but one didn't like to ask. It was the war, after all. A week later she was tasked to take some tests to assess her "suitability" although she'd no idea what she may or may not be suitable for. She'd then been told to catch the train to London and report to Cockfosters Camp. It was only when she'd arrived at the gates that she'd realised where she was.

'Miss Gresham,' said the sergeant, her tone softening after consulting her clipboard. 'Colonel McKie is expecting you.' She signalled to a timorous young woman hovering nearby. 'Private Briggs, take Miss Gresham to the colonel's office,' she ordered.

Private Briggs, her large eyes peering out from under the peak of her too-large ATS cap, wore the bewildered expression of a fawn. She led Maddie past two more sentries, through the imposing front door and into the mansion. The entrance hall was so stark in contrast to Maddie's last visit. Most of the grand portraits and paintings had been removed and there wasn't a single *objet d'art* in sight.

One set of floor-to-ceiling double doors off the hall opened into a large room with another door on the right. An older woman, also wearing an ATS uniform, presided at a desk. The way her silver hair was cut round her ears made it look like she was wearing a helmet. She peered down her long nose at poor Briggs before realising the girl was accompanying a civilian visitor.

'Miss Gresham to see Colonel McKie,' said the private nervously.

The older woman rose quickly to her feet and replied in a voice as clipped as one of the box hedges in the grounds. 'Ah yes, Miss Gresham. Colonel McKie is expecting you.' Springing over to another door, she took a deep breath, as if she were about to enter some inner sanctum, and knocked.

'Come,' said a deep voice in response.

Colonel McKie rose to greet Maddie. He was an attractive sort, for an older man, she thought: an open face, with intelligent eyes, a well-trimmed moustache and brown hair made darker by a liberal application of Brilliantine.

'That'll be all, Holmes,' he said formally to the secretary who seemed in awe of him. 'Please, take a seat,' he told Maddie, breaking into a broad smile as soon as the door clicked shut. He motioned to the chair in front of his desk on which sat an open file.

'I've been reading about you, Miss Gresham. You've had quite a career.' The colonel glanced at the papers on his desk, and she felt her stomach somersault. 'Deported from Germany, aged seventeen. Now there's a distinction!' He laughed and Maddie smiled uneasily. The experience hadn't been the slightest bit amusing at the time. She still suffered from nightmares about it.

His attention focused on his notes once more. 'So, you've been squirrelled away at St Hugh's for a while now.' She detected a gentle Scottish lilt amid his slightly patronising tone. Not that she objected to being compared with a squirrel, but men, especially military men, sometimes treated her like a child.

'That's right, sir.'

Under Dr Baskin's guidance, she'd been recording altered behavioural patterns resulting from military engagement. They'd been making some interesting findings until, one day, shortly before Christmas, Dr Baskin was suddenly "called away". Since then, she'd only heard from him once. He'd posted a large parcel of notes for her to type. It had taken her an age to transcribe his terrible handwriting, interspersed with his own unique shorthand, but she'd done it nevertheless and returned the typescript to him a week later. But he never acknowledged receipt and, as far as she knew, no one at St Hugh's, nor indeed at Oxford, had heard from him since.

A pipe lay on Colonel McKie's desk. He picked it up and began to stuff the bowl with tobacco from a pouch. 'All those chaps with head injuries. Can't have been much fun,' he mused.

Maddie had never regarded a hospital as the sort of place where one expected to have "fun". Losing part of your brain wasn't really a laughing matter. She just smiled, wishing the colonel would get to the point. Why was she here? Why had someone senior in the Combined Services Detailed Interrogation Centre – *what a mouthful* – requested to see her in person?

'So, you studied for a diploma at the Institute of Experimental Psychology.'

Institute sounded rather grand, but it certainly wasn't. For all intents and purposes, the building looked rather like a vicarage tucked away behind trees on the main road a little further towards the centre of Oxford than St Hugh's. What passed for a laboratory was a single-storey construction at the back, more akin to a gardener's shed than a place of science.

'And you were Dr Baskin's assistant.' The colonel hooked his index finger to pack down the tobacco he'd deposited in his pipe.

'Yes, sir.' He had been doing his homework. Despite its humble surroundings, Maddie felt very privileged to have been offered a position to work under one of the world's leading experts in the field. She typed up Dr Baskin's atrociously written notes – a crash course at one of Oxford's many secretarial colleges helped – and in return she was allowed to assist him in some of his experiments. At the same time, she was studying for her diploma. An outsider might have thought the arrangement rather one-sided. And perhaps it was. But Maddie was simply grateful for the opportunity. She was a woman, after all, as several other academics kept reminding her.

Dr Baskin was never a great talker. Even so, she missed his support and companionship, his fusty tweed jackets with their leather patches at the elbows and his penchant for garibaldi biscuits. He'd always asked her to make tea when she was engrossed in something, but when he'd looked at her intently and said, 'A biccie wouldn't go amiss, either, Miss G,' she'd never had the heart to refuse. And he was such an awfully good listener.

'To hear is to learn. To listen is to care,' he used to say.

McKie's expression suddenly looked grave. Carefully he placed his pipe into a novelty ashtray – in the shape of a rather garish bulldog, Maddie noted – and leaned forward.

She met the colonel's expression with a frown of her own. 'He's all right, isn't he? Dr Baskin? Nothing's happened?'

Clasping his hands on the desk, McKie cleared his throat and said: 'Unfortunately, the doctor is no longer with us.'

'Sir?' Maddie queried. *No longer with us.* Had he gone behind enemy lines? Had the Germans captured him? Surely he wouldn't have deserted.

The colonel shook his head in a sort of melancholy way. 'I fear he's passed away.'

'Passed away? Passed away, where?' An image of Dr Baskin blithely floating by on a cloud sprang to mind.

15

'He's dead, Miss Gresham. He died in his bed. Heart attack,' the colonel told her with alarming finality.

'Oh!' She thought of her former boss with his sympathetic gaze, the way he'd tilt his head when one talked to him. 'Oh, that's terrible,' she blurted. And she meant it.

'Yes, isn't it?' replied the colonel. 'Particularly terrible for us,' he added cryptically. He fixed her with a stare. The look unsettled Maddie. It was as if he were sounding her out – gauging whether she could be trusted. Of course, she'd already signed the Official Secrets Act. (The officer in charge had put a gun on the table and told her that traitors were always dealt with appropriately. She'd thought he was joking as she picked up the pen. Now she wasn't so sure.) But his expression gave her the distinct feeling that what he was about to say might well be on a "need to know" basis.

Maddie, still in shock at news of the doctor's death, remained on the edge of her seat. The atmosphere was so tense she was unwilling even to blink, especially as, if she did, she knew a tear might escape.

'You see, Miss Gresham, Dr Baskin was working for us on a special project.'

'I see,' replied Maddie, suddenly realising she hadn't drawn breath for the last few seconds. So that was why he'd been "called away". He was engaged in something top secret for British intelligence.

The colonel let the news sink in for a moment, then began again in a more measured, almost priestly tone. 'This is a very special place,' he told her, raising his eyes to the ceiling. That word "special" again. From his expression he could have been marvelling at the Sistine Chapel before he switched back down to earth. 'You may have seen all the building activity.' He picked up his pipe from the ashtray once more.

She had. Lots of men were digging holes and erecting makeshift buildings away from the mansion and screened by trees. Offices and accommodation, she'd assumed, but to house what?

'We're playing host to some very important guests, you see,' he explained, popping the pipe stem in his mouth and striking a match.

'Guests, sir?' Maddie had already assumed they wouldn't be Trent Park's usual glamorous set.

The colonel sucked hard, and a puff of smoke rose from the bowl. 'We were originally looking after a few Luftwaffe pilots here after the Battle of Britain. Some U-boat officers, too, not to mention Italians, but over the past year we've had bigger fish to fry.'

'Sir?' Colonel McKie was talking in riddles.

He sighed heavily. 'Things didn't go too well for the Hun in North Africa.'

'No, sir,' Maddie agreed. Along with everyone else she'd seen the Pathé news reports: Rommel's Afrika Korps had lost the fight in the desert thanks to Britain's mighty Field Marshal "Monty".

McKie nodded. 'For a while we've been hosting several German top brass who needed a nice, comfortable place to stay.' He leaned back, smoke now billowing from his pipe.

Maddie's carefully plucked eyebrows shot up in surprise. Was he really implying what she thought he was? Through the smoke she found it rather hard to read his expression. 'At Trent Park?'

The colonel threw back his head and chuckled. 'A hotel for captured enemy generals. It may not be the Ritz, but it's a veritable palace compared with your average POW camp.'

Maddie's eyes opened even wider. 'A prisoner of war camp! Here, sir?'

'Yes. Only the Germans don't know the full story, of course.' He pointed at her with the stem of his pipe. 'The aim is to put the generals at their ease and make them think that we respect them. They're convinced they're going to win the war and we're keen they don't make us suffer too much in defeat. Besides, they believe it's only what they deserve. Superior race and all that!' He barked out a laugh. 'Of course it was Baskin's suggestion originally. Give them what they want: their own shop, the run of the grounds—'

'Their own tailor,' Maddie interrupted.

'Ha, yes, indeed. You saw him this morning?'

'I did,' replied Maddie, recalling his van had almost forced her off the drive.

'So it's a bit like a luxury hotel, but with barbed wire around it. Rather clever idea, don't you think?'

Maddie had to agree. 'Yes. Yes, I do.' The pipe smoke was starting to make her eyes sting.

'But here's the really clever part of it.' He leaned forward confidentially. 'If they're relaxed, they let their guard down and loosen their tongues, and when they do, everything they say is recorded.'

'Recorded?' she repeated. *What on earth can he mean?*

McKie's lips stretched into a broad smile. 'There are microphones in every chandelier and lamp in their quarters. Under desks and in vases.'

'Really, sir? But that's . . . that's . . .' Maddie searched for a word amid the smoke.

'Genius? Yes, it is, if I do say so myself.' McKie let out another chuckle. 'That part, the technical bit, had nothing to do with Baskin, of course, although he was helping us develop our covert interrogation strategy. He maintained we'd get more out of the Germans if we were nice to them.'

In her head she could hear one of Dr Baskin's favourite sayings replaying. 'If you know the enemy and know yourself, you need not fear the result of a hundred battles,' Maddie volunteered. She surprised herself for spouting forth so confidently.

'Quite right,' replied the colonel, suitably impressed. 'And that's where you come in.' Another stab with the stem of his pipe was aimed at her. 'Baskin thought very highly of you.'

Maddie felt the colour bloom in her cheeks. She was flattered. She'd always got on very well with the doctor, even though he seemed terribly aloof for much of the time.

'You know he was working on . . .' McKie began just as the red telephone on his desk started to ring and he abruptly stopped the conversation. 'Better get this. Excuse me,' he said. 'Right ho,' he grunted after a moment. Cupping his hand over the receiver he told her: 'Sorry, Miss Gresham. Military matter. We'll have to speak tomorrow. Holmes will sort you out.'

Maddie thought he made her sound rather like a load of laundry as he flapped a hand towards the door. Nevertheless, she was given the distinct impression that she needed to make herself scarce without further delay.

Walking briskly into the anteroom, she realised Trent Park was no longer the place of leisure and enjoyment she once knew, of house parties and society gatherings. The highly sensitive information she'd just been told meant she now knew something so secret and so vital to the Allied cause that one false move, or one wrong word from her, could put lives at risk and throw the whole of the war effort in jeopardy.

Chapter 2

Back in the anteroom, Holmes made some hurried phone calls.

'A room's been arranged for you, Miss Gresham,' Maddie was told ten minutes later and soon she found herself being ushered into a waiting car. The driver, another ATS private from her uniform, took her overnight bag and deposited it efficiently in the boot before opening the door for her with an enigmatic smile.

Maddie smiled back. There was something about the young woman she instantly liked, a sort of reassuring, sisterly presence in a place where men clearly ruled the roost. A bed in a boarding house in nearby Enfield had apparently been organised, but for how long? Colonel McKie had never actually got round to divulging what her role in his scheme would be, if any at all. Had he just wanted to pick her brains or was Trent Park to be her new posting? For all she knew, she might even be back in Oxford the following evening. She supposed she'd have to wait until tomorrow at their next meeting – Holmes had assured her there would be one – to find out more. Until then, she was feeling rather in the dark.

As Maddie was driven back down the long drive away from the mansion, staring blankly at the bare trees, memories of her first day at boarding school suddenly resurfaced. Her mother had kissed her and told her to be brave, but like now, she didn't feel very brave at all because she had no idea what was to come. Butterflies fluttered in her stomach at the thought of the unknown. Colonel McKie's parting shot was that she must tell no one of their conversation. Of course, she'd had no intention of doing anything of the sort, anyway. She'd already been entrusted with a huge military secret that made small talk look, well, *small*. She pictured the German generals strutting around the mansion, kept in the lap of luxury while hundreds of ordinary families in London had been bombed out of their homes. It wasn't right, but she understood it was all part of a bigger plan – a plan devised by Dr Baskin. He was the reason she'd been summoned. It was up to her to carry on his work.

A heavy weight had just been placed on her shoulders, but it wouldn't be hard keeping the lid on this particular Pandora's box. What would be much more difficult was being normal again, trying to separate the momentous from the mundane.

They were on the outskirts of Enfield. Once a village, it had been swallowed up by London and was now a borough filled with endless houses and factories that made one street look very like the next. But that still didn't deter the Germans, who seemed hell-bent on flattening the whole lot – hospital or home – just to get at the big munitions factories in the area. With over a thousand bombs dropped in air raids on it in the last two years, they were making a pretty good fist of showing their contempt for the place. All the houses had their windows taped up and as many sandbags as sticks of rock in Brighton lined the pavements. Now and again, she'd catch a glimpse of a large patch of rubble where someone's home or place of work once stood; they were ghostly reminders of lives once lived.

As the car turned down another street, Maddie saw the remains of three, or maybe even more houses that had taken a direct hit. What remained of the structures looked like the ruins of an old monastery, while broken timbers stuck out of piles of bricks like jagged teeth.

A gang of boys were busy on the side-lines, picking up what looked like twisted metal and bits of shrapnel – souvenirs of a savagery they seemed to regard as an adventure. One of them, with red hair, was collecting things and putting them in his bicycle basket. Maddie tried to make out their bitter harvest. A pile of broken crockery, from a dresser? Scattered rags that were once clothes in a wardrobe, perhaps, and panels of cast iron from what used to be a cooker, maybe. The detritus of everyday life was broken and mangled and boiled down to this.

On the corner of the junction with the main road, a newspaper vendor, a patch over his right eye, was peddling his daily diet of gloom and doom. Today, however, the placards proclaimed something cheering: *General Eisenhower in London.*

Thank goodness we've got the Yanks, thought Maddie.

'Here we are, miss,' chirped the driver a moment later.

They were just round the corner from the bombsite, in a street of larger, mainly detached houses. The motor car was pulling up outside one of them. A tired wooden sign nailed to the fence read: *Fairview Boarding House.* Maddie thought it would be ironic if she could see the bomb damage from her bedroom window. Two stone lions stood guard on the gate posts, although, by the looks of it, the broken gate had long ago left its hinges, and had ended up in the nearby laurel bushes.

The driver opened the car door and Maddie stepped out.

'I used to pick Dr Baskin up at 0900 sharp. That suit you, miss?' asked the private, handing over her bag.

Maddie took it, at the same time trying not to look surprised that the doctor should have lodged in an establishment that clearly hadn't seen a lick of paint since the last war. 'Thank you, er . . .'

'Paget, ma'am.'

Maddie actually found herself waving off her new friend before she turned towards the boarding house. As she walked up the path to the front door, she noted what was probably a grass lawn had been dug up, presumably with the aim of growing vegetables. The

22

problem was someone's admirable intentions to "dig for victory" had gone awry, leaving only dead leaves and shrivelled tubers in the soil. An old tin bath was propped up against the side of the house and sandbags were piled on either side of the peeling front door. Any hopes Maddie had nursed of just a touch of comfort faded. She knocked.

'Yer . . . s?' A woman in a hairnet and late middle age answered. Speaking through a half-closed door, her eyes were narrowed suspiciously, as if she were not used to visitors.

'Good afternoon,' said Maddie, mustering a smile. 'I believe I have a room booked.'

The woman's expression suddenly changed. 'Miss Gresham, is it?'

'That's right.'

The door opened wide to reveal a dingy hallway smelling of boiled cabbage and cigarette smoke. Just as she stepped inside, a grandmother clock crammed under the stairs, coughed out four chimes.

'Who's goes there?' shouted a voice from a back room.

The landlady raised her eyes to the heavens. 'Our new lodger, Harold,' she called back. 'Nothing to worry about.' She leaned towards Maddie. ''E was on the front line at Passchendaele. He'll never get over it,' she confided, wrinkling her nose.

Not being entirely sure how to respond to the news of this misfortune, Maddie carried on, 'I'm here for the night, I think.'

The landlady rubbed her palms against her flowery housecoat and frowned before consulting a book on the hall table. 'Got you down as permanent,' she replied, sounding as if she was handing down a prison sentence. 'Oh, I see,' was all Maddie could say, recalling she'd only brought one pair of clean knickers with her.

'You're Dr Baskin's replacement, ain't ya?'

'That's right.'

'Shame about him. Such a gent.' The woman ran a sceptical eye over her. 'You're not what I was expecting.'

'I'm sorry,' said Maddie, unsure as to her new landlady's meaning.

'A lady doctor. Well, I never.' She sniffed. 'Still, I suppose they take what they can get these days,' she mused, pivoting on her carpet slippers and leading the way up narrow stairs to the first floor.

Suddenly Maddie understood. The landlady must have been told she was going to be working at the local hospital. That had been Dr Baskin's cover, too. Trent Park – the Cockfosters Camp, as it was called – was off limits. Officially it didn't even exist.

'Well, I . . .' Maddie thought about the man with the gun at her initial interview. He wouldn't have used it, would he? 'I think I'm going to be helping out in the emergency department,' she lied.

'Hum,' the woman grunted, unimpressed. 'Bet it'll still play havoc with your hands,' she replied. 'I always say a dollop of lanolin cream never does any 'arm.'

Maddie was shown to a room at the back of the house. It was small but adequate with varnished William Morris design wallpaper and heavy drapes. Occupying half the room was an iron-framed single bed, topped with a bedspread that had seen better days.

'That's where 'e passed,' commented the landlady in a reverential tone.

'I'm sorry,' said Maddie.

'Dr Baskin. Found 'im, I did. Dead as a dodo one morning.'

The bed suddenly took on a new significance. A sort of shrine. Maddie knew she was stepping into a dead man's shoes, but into his bed as well? That was surely going a bit far. Feeling a little uneasy she replied: 'That must've been terrible for you.'

The landlady nodded. 'It was a shock, I'll be honest. But at least he'd paid his rent in advance.' She suddenly produced a duster from her overall pocket and flicked it at a cobweb hanging from the bed frame.

The rest of the room was home to a narrow wardrobe, a small

chest of drawers which, Maddie supposed, would have to double as a dressing table, and a single wooden chair.

'Bathroom's across the landing. And there's another lavvy out the back, alongside the Anderson shelter. Quite handy really,' she reflected. 'Breakfast at half past seven, tea at six,' the landlady told her. 'No visitors and no men,' she added firmly, as if men weren't real visitors at all, but foreign invaders. 'And here's your keys.' She dropped two into Maddie's palm.

'Thank you, Mrs . . . er . . .'

'Pollock,' she replied.

'Like the fish,' said Maddie, with a smile, rather rashly as it turned out. From the reaction, the remark didn't go down too well.

'Oh and there's no dinner served tonight,' the landlady informed. 'Thursdays is my bingo.'

'Of course,' said Maddie. Landladies were entitled to a regular night off, she thought. She would have to make do with the round of Spam sandwiches she'd made for the train journey from Oxford but hadn't touched.

As soon as the door closed, Maddie let out a pent-up breath. She was grateful to be in her own space, even if it was much shabbier than her room in Oxford. After everything she'd learned she needed to think.

There was a small two-bar electric fire in the room that took coins. She shivered as she undid her suit jacket, then decided to leave it on as she walked over to the window. Long lines of tape criss-crossed the panes and a film of red-brick dust coated the sill. Looking between the diamond-shaped gaps, Maddie's considered the view anything but *fair*. She could, indeed, see the bombsite she'd passed earlier. Hitler was certainly making his presence felt in the borough yet again. After the first Blitzkrieg four years ago, they were calling this most recent wave of bombing the "Baby Blitz". It made the latest killing spree sound almost benign. It was anything but.

A sudden sense of helplessness overwhelmed her as she looked

25

out onto the ruined homes and livelihoods and lives. The same was happening not just here, in England, but in Europe and Asia and Africa. The world had gone mad but never once over the past five years had she ever thought how much easier it would be to let German jackboots march over Britain. There were times, however, like now when she had to admit she did get rather down. When that happened, she'd hear her father's voice in her head. 'Pull your socks up, old girl.' And she invariably did, but now and again she needed something more: something tangible to remind her of what she and all the other Allies were fighting for.

Reaching up towards her neck, she felt for the locket Max had given her – which she always wore under her clothes – and thought of him. She recalled the night of their sixth raid in Munich. It was to be their last. The Gestapo were becoming savvy to their methods. Their escapades had even made the inside page of the Munich newspapers.

'Fools! Vandals!' Herr Weitzler had been sitting at the breakfast table the morning when he'd read the newspaper article. His old leg injury was playing up and made him even more curmudgeonly than usual. 'They should be horsewhipped in public,' he told his Ada. He banged his fist on the table. When the lid fell off the jam pot and clattered onto a plate, the maid almost jumped out of her skin. But Herr Weitzler was unfazed. 'And I, for one, would take great pleasure in wielding the whip myself.' There was no question he meant what he said.

Did he suspect their night-time exploits? Had he rumbled them? Perhaps Joachim had been spying on them. He was always lurking in the shadows, listening at doors. She, Max and Greta constantly had to watch what they said for fear of being reported for their disloyalty to the Reich. She recalled exchanging a wary glance with Max. The pair of them had already planned to go out later that night. It was to be their last hurrah. She was due to leave for England at the end of the week and was determined to go on one more mission. Only it hadn't gone as planned. She could still remember the moment of her arrest as if it were yesterday.

Another shiver coursed through her as she watched the sun set on the devastation beyond the window. The sky had turned a soft gold, silhouetting the mounds of rubble and debris from the bombsite. If she hadn't known its true awfulness, she'd have guessed it was a beautiful hillside in a far-off land, but just then she noticed a small figure had clambered to the top and was standing at the peak, a lone child amid a sea of desolation. The sight made her feel so terribly alone and she found herself welling up with the wretchedness of it all.

Fingering the locket once more, she whispered aloud: 'Oh, Max, where are you?'

Chapter 3

Munich, Germany

August 1938

Herr Weitzler looked grave as he sat behind his desk, his walking stick propped against the nearby wall. His features were set hard, his thin lips unsmiling and eyes narrowed. He had summoned his sons to his study. Greta was no longer counted as his child. She had married a Jewish doctor and now lived with him and their new baby girl, Lena, in Holland, although she may as well have been in Outer Mongolia. To Helmut Weitzler, his daughter was dead.

When the two brothers entered the room, their mother was already sitting crumpled on a chair. She straightened her back as soon as her children arrived, but her eyes were red-rimmed from crying.

'So,' said Herr Weitzler, skewering his sons with a disdainful look. They stood before him, like naughty students before their schoolmaster. 'I have called you here to tell you some important news that will have a great impact on all your futures.'

Max's eyes slid over to his mother as he tried to fight the urge to rush over and comfort her. He wanted to tell her his father's threats would never stop him loving her, but the consequences of his disloyalty, he was sure, would be serious.

Herr Weitzler leaned forward over his desk. 'As you are aware, your mother and I married more than twenty years ago. We were both quite young and I was very foolish. In marrying a woman of the Jewish race, I acknowledge I made a terrible mistake. And now I realise I have been tolerant long enough.'

At his words, Frau Weitzler reached for the handkerchief tucked in her cuff and began to dab her eyes once more. Max pulled back his shoulders, stopping himself from going to her. Mutti had always been forbidden from taking her children to the synagogue and as for circumcising her sons, that was taboo. For all intents and purposes, the Weitzler children were as German as bratwurst and yet . . .

Herr Weitzler's eyes were gliding from one son to the other and back. 'As the fruits of our union, your heritage is polluted. Your Aryan blood is tainted.'

Max bit his tongue. His father had hurled abuse at him many times before, but lately, he'd started calling him a "Jew". Now he knew why, but it didn't make the intended insult any easier to bear.

Joachim, just a little shorter than Max, but with the same blond hair, looked puzzled. He was his father's favourite and felt in a better position to question him. 'But, Vater, surely you don't mean that my blood is tainted, as well?' He threw Max a smug look as he spoke, as if trying to score points off his elder brother.

His father stroked his chin in thought. 'Well that very much depends, Joachim,' he replied.

'On what, Vater?'

Herr Weitzler shifted further forward as if about to take aim before firing a shot. 'On the choice you are about to make.'

'Choice?' It was Max's voice that sliced through the tense atmosphere.

'Yes, Max,' replied his father, his eyes suddenly boring into his eldest child. 'I have decided to divorce your mother.'

A terrible wailing sound escaped from Ada Weitzler's lips at the word "divorce".

Herr Weitzler's own lips, however, twitched into a smile. 'Your sister made her choice when she married a Jew,' he told Max with a shrug. 'Now you must do the same.' He glared at his sons. 'You must choose either to stay with me and enjoy the benefits of my excellent salary and the prestige that comes with my role in the National Socialist German Workers' Party, or to go with your snivelling mother, who will leave this house with what she deserves.' He cast a look of contempt towards his sobbing wife. 'Nothing.'

Angling back in his chair, he waited for his sons to reply and was not at all surprised that Joachim spoke first.

'If you divorce Mutti, will that make our blood pure again, Vater?'

Max looked askance at his brother. He was sixteen. How could he possibly be so naïve? But the remark clearly amused his father.

'Literally, no, my son. But in the eyes of the law, you will certainly be purer, yes.'

Joachim nodded and straightened his back, as if he were addressing one of his superiors in the Hitler Youth. 'Then I choose you, sir,' he barked, like a well-trained dog, without a moment's hesitation.

Herr Weitzler gave a self-satisfied grunt. 'Good, Joachim. You have chosen well.' His glare now switched to Max. 'It will be interesting to see if your elder brother is as wise.'

Max's gaze strayed to his mother's creased face. She suddenly seemed so small and helpless. Ever since the Race Laws had been passed two years before, she'd prayed her husband would protect her, as he swore to do on their wedding day. But these days the Nazi Party seemed his one true love. And now his mother wore her husband's betrayal like a dark cloak that threatened to smother her.

When Max's eyes locked onto his father's, he felt the hatred grow inside him and swell into his chest. For a moment he found it hard to breathe as he struggled to suppress his rising fury. He never imagined it would come to this. His heart was being wrenched out of his chest by his own flesh and blood. Clenching his fists, his body went rigid as he delivered his answer. 'Vater.' He licked his dry lips and looked straight ahead at the wall. 'I would not stay with you if you were the last person on this earth.'

At first his father nodded slowly, as if he'd half been expecting the rebuff, but then he hit the desk with such ferocity that the lid of his silver inkstand rattled. 'I might've known,' he said between gritted teeth, his eyes blazing into his son's defiant face. 'You always were Mutti's little boy,' he mocked before throwing back his head and letting out a mirthless laugh. 'If that is your choice, so be it,' he said in a more even tone. But Max knew it was too much to hope his father would be reasonable. He was right. The next moment, the tirade came.

Suddenly Herr Weitzler leapt up and grabbed his walking stick, raising it high in the air. 'You spineless Jew!' he screamed, banging the stick hard on his desk, narrowly missing Max but sending the desk lamp crashing to the floor. Then, he flung out his arm, using the stick to point to the study door. 'Get out of here and never darken my door again. Out!' he cried, his lips flecked with spittle. With eyes on fire, he turned towards his wife, then back to Max. 'Both of you, you hear! The Reich must rid itself of filth like you. Get out and good riddance!'

Chapter 4

Trent Park

March 1944

'Mind your head!' warned Colonel McKie as they passed under a metal bracket sticking out of the wall the following day. He was leading the way through a sprawling labyrinth of nooks, crannies and rooms that made up a whole netherworld underneath Trent Park. Maddie followed closely behind, descending a narrow staircase into the bowels of the mansion. She ducked just in time, but the near miss made her heart beat even faster. She really didn't enjoy being in such a confined space.

Once home to cellars and stores, where servants busied themselves catering to every whim of Sir Philip and his guests, the basement was now run more like a production line, designed to operate with ruthless efficiency. Everywhere there were engineers, testing the listening devices that had been hidden all over the mansion and its grounds. No sill was safe. No corner beyond bounds. Clusters of wires fed into switchboards like giant forkfuls of spaghetti. The whole set-up looked to Maddie rather like a telephone exchange.

They came to a standstill at the entrance of a small, windowless room with bare brick walls. Six uniformed men sat at wooden tables, wearing headsets and operating some sort of recording equipment. Hanging above the paraphernalia was a single bare light bulb. The sight of it sent a shiver coursing down Maddie's spine. For a split second she was back in custody in a Munich cell. She remembered her sheer terror at the prospect of being interrogated. A sense of panic rose in her chest. It was hard to concentrate on what the colonel was saying, but she told herself she must.

'So, this is one of our M rooms,' said McKie, striding inside.

Reluctantly Maddie followed on behind, looking slightly perplexed.

'M stands for "miked", or "microphoned",' explained the colonel, casting an eye around the space. He picked up what Maddie took to be one of the recording devices from a nearby table. It looked rather cumbersome, like a large hand grenade, or something to be found under the bonnet of a motor car but it obviously did its job. 'These are dash clever thingamajigs. Omni-directional pressure microphones, I believe. They've been placed in several locales where our German guests move freely, so you could say the walls have ears, quite literally,' he quipped. 'And I call these chaps—' he waved a hand at the men seemingly glued to the recording equipment '—our secret listeners. As well as recording everything, they take down anything interesting that's said.'

Pacing over to another table, McKie picked up a large acetate disc. 'It's all recorded on one of these and noted down by our listeners before being taken away for translation. We've got good people to do that . . . Mainly Germans, often Jews, who escaped Hitler. They translate what . . .'

But Maddie wasn't listening anymore. She hadn't been for a while. In her head she was back in Munich, being bundled through a back entrance of one of the grand buildings surrounding the Odeonsplatz, then shoved downstairs to a dimly lit basement.

It was cramped and airless and dark, just like this place. Sweat prickled her skin as fear flooded her body and pressed hard against her chest, making it difficult to breathe. Suddenly stars began to dance in front of her eyes. She felt she might faint. She flexed her toes to stop herself from falling.

'I say, are you all right, Miss Gresham?' Colonel McKie's worried face suddenly presented itself in front of her. 'You look a bit peaky.'

Maddie put her hand on the nearby table to steady herself. 'Yes. Yes, thank you. It's just a little stuffy in here,' she managed to say.

'I suppose it does take some getting used to,' the colonel conceded. 'Let's surface, shall we?' He motioned for her to lead the way out of the cramped room.

They returned, much to Maddie's relief, to the main house and continued with a tour of the reception rooms. 'Our guests are watching a film at the moment. *Mrs Miniver*, I believe, so take a look in here.' He beckoned.

She put her head around the door. It was the billiard room, a large green baize-covered table at its centre. 'There's a microphone under there,' McKie told her. 'And another up there,' he added, pointing proudly to the crown moulding in the corner.

There was also a spacious drawing room with a roaring fire in its grate, an elegant private dining room, a music room, a painting room and, of course, a library. Maddie marvelled at the well-stocked shelves, lined with German titles. She tilted her head to read the spines. Several volumes of Hegel, vied for space with Nietzsche, although Karl Marx was notable by his absence. On a lighter note, there were also nineteenth-century Romantic novels and even some later spy stories, set in the Great War.

Seeing her interest in the books, the colonel smiled. 'Mostly confiscated from the German Embassy at Carlton House Terrace,' he explained. 'We've given them a good home.'

It seemed that no comfort was being spared these captives, apart from, of course, their freedom. They were allowed newspapers and to listen to wireless broadcasts or watch films. 'That way,' McKie explained, 'our chaps can stimulate discussion with the generals and sometimes they unknowingly let slip interesting snippets of intelligence.'

Maddie was duly impressed. 'All rather jolly, isn't it?' he said once they were both back in the comfort of his office in the mansion. This time Maddie was offered, and gratefully received, a cup of tea. Sugar didn't normally appeal, but after her mild panic attack in the basement, she'd made an exception and it seemed to do the trick. Soon she was feeling much better. As it turned out, she needed to be on top form for what the colonel told her next.

As she had toured the rooms in the basement and witnessed first-hand the elaborate – and no doubt expensive – workings of this whole operation, she'd wondered about its ultimate goal. The War Office wouldn't throw money at a project without being convinced of its success. So what was the mission of those at Trent Park? What was driving this whole project? What secrets did British intelligence want these captured generals of the Wehrmacht – the German combined forces – to give up? Feeling the reviving effects of the sweet tea, she plucked up the courage to ask.

'Good question, Miss Gresham. Good question.'

It may have been a good – and crucial question – thought Maddie, but the colonel was showing a reluctance to answer it until he offered: 'Our primary role is to gather intelligence on anything and everything. Advances in technology, plots against Hitler, troop movements, that sort of thing.'

He reels off a catalogue of deadly threats like it's a list for the grocer, thought Maddie.

'So you're hoping your eavesdropping will uncover this information?' Maddie could barely believe the audacity of the plan.

He nodded. 'Amongst other things. Yes. There'll be both overt and covert questioning, of course. Our interrogators will ask the generals questions openly at first, then when they return to their quarters, we know from previous experience they often brag amongst themselves just how much they didn't divulge to us. They let their guard down and that's when we record what they say.'

He laid his teacup back into its saucer, as if considering carefully how much to tell Maddie. 'I'll be frank with you, Miss Gresham,' he resumed after a short pause. 'We're forming a special unit here to deal with matters of the mind: psychiatrists, psychologists and so forth to work alongside the Combined Services Detailed Interrogation Centre. Baskin was recruiting people, but . . .' His voice trailed off to mingle with the lingering smell of pipe smoke.

Maddie felt herself tense. 'Psychologists, colonel?'

Seeing the look of surprise on her face, McKie paused for a moment, then grasped a pencil and began rolling it between his fingers. 'And that's where you come in.'

'I do?'

'We need to get these men to open up. A few can be charming, but most are ruthless and certainly all of them are arrogant. From the transcripts of the prisoners' recordings, you'd assess their mental states, then write profiles of them. We'd like you to continue to help us shape our interrogation strategies accordingly.' He placed both his elbows on the desk. 'Major Herbert Lansley is currently heading up the team. Do you know him?'

Only by reputation, thought Maddie. She'd heard he was a brilliant psychiatrist, but a shy and reserved man. She also knew he'd recently suffered from a peptic ulcer.

'You'd be answerable to him,' McKie carried on. 'But your involvement in Dr Baskin's work puts you in an exceptional position.'

Maddie felt rather flattered. 'So, I would be carrying on his research?'

The colonel hesitated 'I wouldn't call it research exactly. You're the only person who can make sense of his notes, I believe.'

Maddie thought for a moment, recalling the reams of barely legible scrawl the doctor used to produce.

'Yes, I suppose I am.'

The colonel clasped his fingers and twiddled his thumbs.

'We need those notes,' he told her.

Maddie paused. It sounded to her as if he should look for a secretary rather than a psychologist.

The colonel could see she needed a little more persuading. 'The good doctor may no longer be with us—' *that euphemism again* '—but his work lives on.'

Taking a key, he unlocked a drawer in his desk and brought out a file that looked familiar to Maddie. Across the front, the words *Top Secret* were stamped across it in red. Her eyes widened as he slid it towards her, and she recognised her mentor's careless scribbling on the buff-coloured cover.

Tapping the folder, the colonel said. 'This is just one of many.'

Maddie's eyes fell onto the familiar folder. 'And I'm the only one who can decipher the contents.' It had never occurred to her before that should anything happen to Dr Baskin, she was possibly the single person who could read his notes.

Another thought occurred to her. If Dr Baskin had been working on a secret project for the British intelligence service before his death, was she really being asked to fill his shoes? It was a very tall order.

As if sensing her hesitation, the colonel tried to assure her. 'And, of course, you'd be a very valued member of the team, Miss Gresham. We need your unique take on things, you see,' he added, now playing with the teaspoon in his saucer.

'Does that mean you want me to join you officially, sir?' Maddie needed clarity. She hadn't yet been told exactly why she'd been summoned. Dr Baskin's research was clearly of use to British intelligence, but the colonel was still not being completely clear about her own role in all of this. Did he want a secretary or a psychologist?

'Oh dear. I'm putting the cart before the horse, aren't I?' He picked up a pencil and started twirling it through his fingers like a sergeant major's baton. 'As well as being able to transcribe Baskin's notes, you know what makes a man's mind tick, Miss Gresham.' He pointed to his own temple. 'You can help us devise ways to get the most out of our captive Germans – short of thumb screws, of course.' He chuckled. 'And that will be a valuable weapon in our armoury. So, we'd like you to join us.'

'Us?' repeated Maddie. *Who exactly is us?* she thought.

'Forgive me.' McKie leaned forward once more and flashed one of his grins at her. 'We are MI19, responsible for "entertaining" enemy prisoners of war. We're a separate branch of the War Office.'

'I see,' said Maddie, taking a moment to digest the information.

'What do you say, Miss Gresham?' McKie asked, leaning back. 'Will you work for us?'

She really didn't need to give any more consideration to her answer. The work would be hugely challenging, pioneering in fact, and she knew it was of the utmost importance. Information gleaned from these high-ranking prisoners could prove invaluable in the fight against Hitler. She thought of Max, wherever he may be, alive or dead. Of course she'd work for MI19 and she'd do it principally for him and for all those in a similar, desperate situation.

'So, will you, Miss Gresham?' asked the colonel again.

Maddie gave him a tight smile and breathed deeply. There really was no choice to be made. How could she turn down this unique opportunity to help her country? Her participation in this elite, top-secret operation was a given.

'Colonel McKie,' she replied. 'It would be an honour.'

Chapter 5

Paris, France

May 1940

The radio broadcast had sent all of Paris into a frenzy. As soon as news came through on the wireless, Max started to pack the few possessions he'd managed to salvage from his Munich home. Belgium and the Netherlands had fallen to Hitler, and France, it was feared, would be next. For the past eighteen months he and his mother had been living in Paris. But now a dark shadow was being cast over the city of light. Shortly after his father banished them from the family home, but several months before the declaration of war, Max had made his escape from Germany. He'd bought a Volkswagen car from a friend and persuaded his mother, Ada, that the Fatherland had abandoned them, therefore they must abandon the Fatherland.

His widowed aunt, Hannah, his mother's elder sister, had married a French artist and settled in an apartment in Paris thirty years before. It was a long journey, but they made it. Greta was in Holland and Joachim had said he never wanted to see his mother again. There was nothing to keep them in Munich, so

Frau Weitzler sold the few valuable possessions she had retrieved from her broken marriage – a Dresden vase, a canteen of silver cutlery and a Patek Philippe wristwatch – to pay for two transit visas, and reluctantly took to the road with her elder son.

They had not been the only Jews heading out of Germany that winter of '38. Thousands, of course, had already gone, but after the burning and looting of Jewish homes and shops on Kristallnacht, Max knew there was no future for them in their homeland.

Aunt Hannah had written enthusiastically to ask them to join her in Paris and, unlike so many displaced Jews, Max felt very blessed to have somewhere to go. Since her husband, Albert, had passed away last year, Hannah said there were so many jobs that needed doing around the apartment and studio in Montmartre. She also knew of a frame-maker who could use an extra pair of hands.

The old car had struggled on the hills and around the hairpin bends out of Germany and into the Vosges mountains that strad-dled the French border. Germany had not yet been at war, so when they were stopped at the crossing, the guards had been brusque, but allowed them to pass. Max had thought his mother had turned to steel – her body had been so rigid – until he'd driven into France, and it was not until the eventual sight of the Eiffel Tower that she was able to relax and tears of relief flowed from Ada Weitzler's tired eyes.

'*Bienvenue! Willkommen* to Paris!' Hannah greeted warmly, flinging her arms first around her sister, then Max. Like her late husband, she was an artist. Her head was swathed in a bright red scarf and she wore a yellow short-sleeved shirt with baggy trousers. Her long arms were looped with bangles that tinkled every time she moved them, and because she talked with her hands, she was constantly surrounded by noise.

'But you are a grown man!' she exclaimed in wonder at the sight of Max – as childless aunts, who last saw their nephews in lederhosen and eating gingerbread over a decade ago, tend to do. 'Those muscles!' she cried, gripping Max's biceps and looking at her sister. 'I can put those to good use.'

And so she did. For the next few months, life was good. Max worked hard by day in the frame-maker's workshop round the corner to earn money, and sometimes helped to mix paint and prepare canvases in the studio. In the warm spring evenings that followed he was rewarded with hearty ragouts washed down with a glass or two of red wine. There were tarte tartines and petits fours from the nearby boulangerie, and demi-tasses of good espresso drunk on the balcony overlooking the square once frequented by Toulouse-Lautrec. Max's mother – her head now also swathed in a bright scarf – helped her sister with all the domestic chores that had been neglected since her husband's death. She busied herself mending torn tablecloths and pillowcases and planted out pots of bright red geraniums on the balcony and windowsills.

Shortly after arriving in Paris, Max had written to Maddie to let her know he and his mother were safe. As well as telling her about Monsieur Gilbert, the framer, and how he constantly banged his thumbs when he was making frames, so the air around him was permanently blue, he wrote how he wished she could be there. 'You would love all the rush and the colour and excitement,' he said in his letter, although he wasn't sure she'd ever receive it.

That was why, when, last spring, Hannah announced there was a letter for him, Max's first thought was that it was from Maddie. Only it wasn't. He'd recognise Greta's neat hand anywhere. Eager for news, he tore open the envelope where he stood on the balcony. He began to read with a smile, but with every line, his nerves tightened until a look of horror overwhelmed his face.

'What's wrong, Max?' asked his mother, shelling peas into a bowl on her lap as he rushed into the kitchen.

'J . . . Jakub,' he spluttered.

'Jakub?' She repeated the name of her Dutch son-in-law. 'What's happened?' She set down the bowl on the table.

'He's dead,' mumbled Max, the shock stealing his breath. 'He was attacked in the street in Amsterdam.'

'No!' Frau Weitzler's hands flew up to her mouth. 'What will Greta do? And baby Lena?'

'They must come here,' butted in Hannah, eavesdropping from the salon. She joined her sister in the kitchen. 'There is enough room for all of us.'

A look of hope suddenly bloomed across Ada Weitzler's care-worn face. 'Yes. Yes. You must write to her, Max. Oh, my poor love. Tell her to come here.' She bit her lips to stop them trembling and Hannah moved sideways to put a comforting hand on her shoulder.

'Write to her,' repeated Max, as if an invitation to join them in France would answer all Greta's problems. He swallowed down the urge to tell his mother and her sister that such a letter would mean a wasted postage stamp. There was the matter of transport, of money, of crossing borders when Germany constantly threatened to invade the rest of Europe. He would write, of course he would, if only to tell his sister that she was loved and that they were all thinking of her and of little Lena. But in his heart of hearts, he knew that any hope of a family reunion in France was already lost as Germany turned its hungry eyes to the north and west.

Then earlier that day, when they heard Hitler was on the march, Hannah was finally forced to admit that Paris might fall too. But ever the optimist, she said she had good friends in Brittany, in the town of Dinan. They were sculptors and would happily put them up until this "whole mess" was over. So Max, his mother and Hannah would head west, too, just praying that the Nazis wouldn't catch up with them. They would lock the studio and shut up the apartment. But Aunt Hannah was confident they'd be back soon.

'They say the war will be over by Christmas,' Max heard her declare cheerfully, packing crockery in the nearby kitchen.

As he pressed down the catches on his suitcase, he couldn't be so sure.

Where have I heard that before? he thought.

Chapter 6

Trent Park

March 1944

'Welcome aboard, Miss Gresham,' said the Wren officer. She stood to greet Maddie from behind a desk in one of the Nissen huts in the mansion's grounds. Maddie smiled. The naval salutation amused her seeing as they were quite a way from the nearest ship, but the Wren's glossy red lips only twitched vaguely as she extended her hand. 'Third Officer Prudence Havisham. It's my job to see things run smoothly between our two departments – delivering the latest transcriptions, that sort of thing.'

Colonel McKie had apparently instructed Holmes to deposit Maddie there personally, having previously announced he thought she and Havisham would get along "splendidly". Judging by the slightly suspicious expression on the Wren's flawlessly powdered face, however, Maddie wasn't entirely convinced.

'I'm sure that will be most helpful,' she replied, in truth not feeling that sure at all.

Third Officer Havisham was to be Colonel McKie's promised bridge between the secret listeners and the clumsily titled "mental oversight" team. When Maddie had first heard the Wren's name, an image of Dickens's forsaken spinster came into view. But with her expertly applied make-up and the care she'd taken with her flame-red hair, Maddie really didn't think Prudence Havisham need ever worry about being left on any shelf.

Tall and thin and with an air of laconic sophistication, she reminded Maddie more of Rita Hayworth than a typical member of the Women's Royal Naval Service. She was sure her uniform must have been tailor-made as it flattered her figure so well.

In the adjacent office could be heard the clatter of a battalion of typewriters and a quick knock on the door was followed by the appearance of an older Wren with a stack of papers in her arms. She clearly wasn't expecting to see Maddie and faltered a little, but Havisham nodded, and the Wren carried on.

'Latest reports, ma'am,' she said, laying the copies into a wire tray on the desk. Through the half-open door, Maddie could see several rows of young female stenographers. She assumed they were hard at work typing up translations made from the discs of recorded conversations she'd seen in the M Room. The scene reminded her of something her father had quipped when she'd complained about typing up Dr Baskin's notes. 'If the pen is mightier than the sword, then the typewriter must be stronger than the tank.'

At the time Maddie's forehead had creased with a frown. 'Who said that?'

'I did,' he'd replied, chuckling to himself.

She'd thought it a frivolous remark, but now it seemed rather relevant and, given the circumstances, contained a strong ring of truth. Legions of young women were typing for king and country and their work was every bit as important as that of the men fighting on the battlefield.

Once the older Wren was out of the room, Havisham rose. 'I'm to show you to your office,' she said in such a way that told Maddie she was doing so under duress.

Sashaying over to a nearby filing cabinet, Havisham reached for her cap and secured it in place in front of a small mirror on the wall. Once satisfied that her appearance was in order, she picked up a bunch of keys and turned to Maddie once more.

'Shall we?' she said, tugging at her jacket and gesturing to the door.

Outside it remained rather chilly, although a weak sun had broken through the low grey clouds as Maddie was led out of the hut. She followed Havisham down a metalled road, screened by trees, towards a gate in a high, red-brick wall. Just as the Wren was negotiating a large padlock, however, a movement towards the front of the mansion caught Maddie's eye. Seeing her puzzled reaction, the Wren turned to follow her gaze. There were two men, both wearing German uniforms. They were walking casually across the gravel drive towards a wooded area, in the company of a British Army officer. Two soldiers were at the rear.

'Are they . . .?' Maddie began.

'Yes, they are,' replied Havisham, letting the padlock fall for a moment to look. 'A couple of our captured German generals.'

Havisham's heavily mascaraed eyes suddenly slid away from hers, as if she'd just said something she shouldn't have. She resumed her tussle with the padlock.

Maddie watched the men, talking earnestly with the British officer as they disappeared down a path and out of sight. 'But they're . . . well, they look as though they're about to go for a stroll,' she protested indignantly.

'Precisely,' replied Havisham briskly and in such a way that didn't invite any more questions or comments from Maddie.

The padlock finally relented, and the gate opened into a large courtyard. Maddie was ushered through and into an unevenly cobbled area. Havisham was walking quickly ahead, towards a solid Victorian red-brick block. Three steps led up to a small side door, which was duly unlocked in silence.

Maddie now found herself in a narrow, draughty passage with

45

two or three doors leading off it. She supposed this was where the estate offices and stables had been housed in Sir Philip's day.

'Here we are,' said Havisham, opening wide the first door on the left, allowing Maddie to cast a summary glance over the room.

Her initial reaction was one of shock. 'Oh!' she exclaimed. No one had warned her. 'But this must've . . .' Her eyes swept over a fitted bookcase crammed full of volumes that spilled over onto the bare floorboards. A large desk was positioned in the bay of the window, the chair with its back to the light and two filing cabinets sat side by side, but it was the framed photograph that really gave it away: a familiar figure in his mortar board and gown. The Wren caught her looking at it.

'Did no one tell you you'd been assigned Dr Baskin's office?' asked Havisham coolly.

'No. No, they didn't,' said Maddie, making a beeline for the photograph on the desk.

'I would've thought all personal effects would've gone to his relatives,' said Havisham reprovingly, as she reached for the frame.

'Please,' said Maddie, Havisham's hand suddenly freezing in mid-air. 'I'd really like it to stay.' Instead, it was she who picked up the frame to study the familiar image. Dr Baskin had always kept the photograph on his desk at Oxford before he was moved. He was pictured outside the Radcliffe Camera, with his unmarried sister Hester. She was perhaps just a little older than her brother, but very trim with a frizz of grey hair and a twinkle in her eye. Although they'd never met, she reminded Maddie of Miss Marple, the amateur sleuth in Agatha Christie's deliciously devious murder-mystery series.

She laid the photograph back down on the desk and looked around once more, sniffing the air as she did so. The room smelt fusty, too, just like Dr Baskin's tweed jackets. It was as if he'd just left for a moment but would be back shortly to request a cup of tea and a garibaldi.

When she lifted her eyes, on the whitewashed wall opposite

– alongside a poster declaring, rather ironically, she thought, *The Walls Have Ears* – she spotted a helpful map of Trent Park and its grounds.

'It's easy to get lost here,' Havisham commented, following Maddie's gaze.

'I imagine it is,' she replied, realising she was still trying to come to terms with the fact that Dr Baskin was gone.

'But you'll soon get used to it.'

'I expect I will,' said Maddie, unthinkingly, her attention now caught by a green telephone that sat next to a typewriter on the desk.

'That's our hotline,' Havisham said, promptly picking up the receiver to demonstrate. 'Dial 623 and you get through to the M Room,' she explained, but after a moment's waiting and with no sound on the line, she took the receiver from her ear and frowned at it. 'Or you will do when they've reconnected it,' she added with a shrug.

Maddie's brows raised themselves involuntarily at this remark, as if it had suddenly alerted her to her own isolation. *And what if they don't? Who will fix it?* A hundred questions started to pour into her head. Where were the psychiatrists in the team? When would she meet them? Who else was in the building? And yet she had the distinct impression that, even if she knew the answers, Petty Officer Havisham had no intention of sharing them. She seemed so aloof, frosty even. Once more Maddie was reminded of her school days where someone like Prudence Havisham would have been a lofty prefect and she the friendless new girl.

Maddie set down her bag and looked about the room. Her questioning look triggered a brusque reply.

'I'm sure Major Lansley will send someone to brief you on all the details,' said the officer, her tone suddenly softening, as if she sensed the new recruit was feeling a little overwhelmed. Walking over to the door, she shut it firmly behind her. Maddie assumed she didn't want anyone to overhear what she was about to say. When Havisham turned once more to speak, it was in a half whisper. What was more, her icy attitude seemed to have thawed a little and behind her eyes there might even have been a touch of warmth.

'Look, I know this is all a bit much for you at the moment,' she began. *So, she is human after all,* thought Maddie, suddenly heartened. But the feeling didn't last long. 'You're a civilian, suddenly plucked from everything you know, and you've landed on Mars,' Havisham continued. 'It'll be harder for you to adjust to a place like this but let me give you some words of advice.'

Maddie suddenly felt very small again, as if she'd just been summoned to the prefect's study for a good dressing-down.

'You've signed the Official Secrets Act. We all have, and you must learn not to ask questions. If you need to know something you'll be told, and if someone wants your opinion, they will ask for it. Otherwise, say nothing.'

'I see,' was all Maddie could muster, followed by a timid: 'Thank you,' even though she wasn't sure why she should be grateful for a telling-off.

Havisham shook her head. 'I hope you do, Miss Gresham, because some of the most devious, arrogant and ruthless men alive are within a stone's throw of this office,' she said, keeping her tone still low and even. 'And it's our job to discover just what they know and to use their knowledge to our advantage. But secrecy is the key. Without it, we are sunk. We're required to take what we know with us to our graves, if necessary. Just like Dr Baskin.' She flashed a look at the photograph, before returning to Maddie and adding with a twitch of her glossy red lips: 'But you know that, I'm sure.'

An image of a cemetery suddenly landed in front of Maddie's eyes, where every headstone was blank because all the dead had been buried anonymously. Unknown and unsung heroes. What secrets had Dr Baskin taken with him to his grave? But before she could ponder the question, a welcome knock broke into her thoughts.

Havisham whipped round. 'Come.'

The door opened to reveal Private Paget, the ATS driver, standing to attention on the threshold. She saluted.

'Here to collect Miss Gresham, ma'am,' she told the officer breezily.

'Ah, yes,' replied Maddie, suddenly glad of an ally. She turned to Havisham. 'I'm to go back to Oxford to fetch my things.' She was on the verge of explaining her mission to collect her copies of Dr Baskin's notes, but bearing in mind what she'd just been told, she stopped herself just in time. Instead, she said: 'On Colonel McKie's orders.'

Havisham nodded sharply. 'Very well,' she said. But, just as Maddie made her way towards the door, the officer added, rather to her surprise: 'I look forward to working with you, Miss Gresham.'

Maddie stopped short. 'Thank you,' she replied with a tight smile. 'And I with you,' even though she was far from convinced she meant it.

Chapter 7

Oxford, England

The ambulance rattled through the gates of St Hugh's Military Hospital – formerly St Hugh's College – and juddered to a halt in front of the main entrance. Maddie, in the motor car behind, asked Paget to follow and park up as far away as she could. As they drove past, she watched two nurses and a white-coated doctor emerge to supervise the unloading of the vehicle's precious cargo. When the ambulance doors opened, the porters carried out a young soldier on a stretcher, his head swathed in bandages. *His poor mind will need healing too,* thought Maddie.

'Just here will do,' she told Paget, pointing to a large bush that screened a side gate. She really didn't want to be seen by anyone else. Goodbyes were never her thing – a throwback from her boarding school days, perhaps. Colonel McKie's secretary Holmes – she didn't know her rank, and it felt awfully disrespectful calling a woman of her years by her surname – had assured her that all her belongings would be transported to Trent Park. Yet she hated the idea of people packing her personal possessions. 'I won't be long,' she told Paget, slipping out of the car and through the side gate.

Her accommodation was in a former graduate house that lay

in a far corner of the college grounds. Six young women shared a bath and a Baby Belling cooker. She made her way along the gravel path bordered by neglected lavender bushes. On the patio a few men sat in bath chairs, muffled in coats and scarves against the cold; some had their heads swathed in bandages. Fresh air and the great outdoors were regarded as a panacea for most illnesses, but especially mental.

Maddie found it hard to believe she'd left Oxford barely forty-eight hours before. So much had changed for her in that short time. She opened the front door of the house and climbed the stairs. Her small, cramped, unassuming room – with its framed view of Munich above her desk, her disorderly bookshelf and pink candlewick bedspread – was just as she'd left it. She sighed heavily and moved over to the chest of drawers by the window. Bending low she opened the bottom drawer and pulled out a large brown envelope. Much to her relief when she opened the flap, the thick wadge of carbon copies of Dr Baskin's typed notes seemed all present and correct. She'd clipped his original covering letter onto the top sheet. It was written in his usual courteous tone but short and to the point.

Dear Miss Gresham,
    I would be most grateful if you could type up the enclosed notes for me and return them to the above address by next Monday (19th).
    Yours sincerely etc

A pang of sadness stabbed her as she suddenly remembered the doctor was gone. Forever.

Next, she bent low and lifted the edges of her bedspread. Hitching up her impractically tight skirt, she knelt down on her rug, and managed to coax out her old tin trunk to unclip the chrome fastenings. Inside it was almost empty except for a biscuit tin with a colourful image of a windmill on it. All she needed to do was pack it as quickly as she could with her clothes and personal effects. She would have to trust her books to whoever was tasked by Holmes with clearing the rest of her room. But there were some things that were too personal to trust even with her trunk. She reached down and pulled out the tin, hugging it to her chest. After a moment she gave in to the urge to open it. Inside was a bundle of letters she'd tied with red ribbon. She thought it rather silly now, but she'd been seventeen when Max's first letter had arrived, and she'd never broken the habit of trussing them up neatly. His last was on the top of the pile.

Slumping onto her stiff bed, she took out Max's most recent missive. He always wrote in German, in a very distinctive hand that slanted to the right, with curlicues and Gothic flourishes. It was dated August 16th, 1939.

My Dearest Maddie,

Your last letter was such a great comfort to me in these troubling times. As I'm sure you know, the situation in Germany is very troubling. We have had no word from my father or Joachim, but then, I suppose we never expected to.

Maddie recalled how poor Frau Weitzler was in such a constant state of distress during her stay with the family. Herr Weitzler had been told by the Nazi Party hierarchy that he would lose his well-paid job in the civil service if he did not divorce her. Apparently, he didn't seem to have many qualms about consigning his marriage to the scrap heap and abandoning his wife of twenty-two years.

So now my mother and I remain in Paris with her sister, Hannah, at her apartment. Life is good for the time being. However, the situation for Jews grows worse by the day. We are safe, but I fear for Greta and her family in Holland.

She studied the swirl of his handwriting, memorising each letter and the curve of the pen, imagining his gentle hands move across the paper. That letter had been posted in France nearly five years ago, less than a year before Paris was invaded by the Nazis. Since then, there'd been no further word and not knowing whether Max and his mother and aunt were alive or dead was torture. The letters were her lifeline, something to cling to in a sea of uncertainty. Without them hope might drown.

A small photograph slipped from between the pages then; Max's face – serious but handsome – stared out at her with wild, excited eyes and she suddenly saw a flicker of light. Brushing away a stray tear, she told herself to be strong. He was alive. He had to be, because without him she couldn't imagine how she could keep going. Lifting his image up to her lips, she closed her eyes and kissed his mouth lightly before placing it back in the tin and shutting the lid firmly.

Less than twenty minutes later, having flung the contents of her wardrobe and drawers into the trunk to be forwarded to her new lodgings, she was back at the car.

'Everything all right, miss?' asked Paget, seeing Maddie's expression.

'Yes, thank you,' she replied, settling herself into the rear seat once more. 'But I wondered, on the way back, if we might make a stop.'

*

The tower of St John the Baptist church in the village of Stanton St John hove into view thirty minutes after leaving Oxford. Maddie was clutching a bunch of daffodils and tulips bought at a florist on the way. She'd no idea if this was where Dr Baskin had been laid to rest but he'd owned a cottage in the village for many years, so she supposed it might be here.

Leaving Paget in the car she opened the gate into the churchyard and scanned the ground for signs of recent burials. Most of the memorials and urns dated back at least two centuries, but in the far corner were some well-tended graves. An uneven mound topped by scant grass and without a headstone stood out. Three wreaths lay forlornly on top, their petals long dropped, their leaves crinkled and brown.

Maddie moved closer to read the temporary wooden cross with its inscription. It read simply: *Dr Tobias Baskin, May 30, 1888 – January 28, 1944. RIP.* She bent down to add her small floral tribute to the rest then stood back to say a prayer, even though she knew the doctor was a dyed-in-the-wool atheist. Just as she bowed her head, she became aware of someone standing close by and looked around to find an elderly woman watching her.

'You knew my brother?' asked the woman in a slightly husky voice.

Maddie smiled. So, this was Dr Baskin's sister, the one with whom he was pictured outside the Radcliffe Camera. Under a flat beret and wiry hair, she recognised the kindly face and twinkly eyes in the photograph that had reminded her of Miss Marple.

'Yes. I'm Madeleine Gresham. I used to be his assistant at St Hugh's,' she explained. 'I only just heard, or I—'

'Hester Baskin. Tobias's sister,' she broke in, offering her gloved hand and shaking her head. 'There's no need to apologise, my dear. My brother led a very private life, and I couldn't tell everyone, but it's nice of you to come to pay your respects.' Her eyes drifted back to the grave for a moment before she said: 'Not many have. I think it's because of his work.' She paused then leaned closer, dropping her voice to add: 'I'm sure he was involved in something quite hush-hush, you know.'

For a moment Maddie stiffened. Dr Baskin had, indeed, been the keeper of many secrets and now so would she. Did Miss Baskin know about Trent Park?

'Really?' was all she felt appropriate.

The woman shrugged bony shoulders draped in a deep purple coat. 'But now we'll never know.'

There was a respectful pause as both women contemplated the grave, before Maddie said, out of kindness: 'At least he died in his sleep.'

Miss Baskin's wrinkled her nose and switched round to Maddie. 'So I was told.'

Maddie floundered. 'A heart attack, I believe.'

'Apparently,' Hester replied enigmatically. It was almost as if she sounded sceptical. 'They say he had a bad heart, and I know he was under a lot of stress at work.' She tilted her head towards Maddie and smiled. 'One doesn't want to make a fuss, does one?'

Maddie smiled. 'No, quite,' she replied, wondering why Miss Baskin might want to make one in the first place. There was clearly something troubling her. 'I'm so very sorry for your loss,' she said after a moment's pause.

'Well,' Miss Baskin looked sanguine as she cast an eye across the rows of gravestones. 'These things happen, my dear. Bombs or heart attacks, we all end up here in the end.'

On that salutary note, the two women parted, and Maddie retreated to the car. Dr Baskin's death may have been untimely, but her visit had left her rather unsettled. Something about the circumstances surrounding her brother's demise was troubling Hester Baskin, but she remained stoic. In her new role, Maddie feared she would have to do the same.

Havisham's words of warning replayed in her head. 'You must learn not to ask questions.' The only thing she could be sure of as Paget drove her back towards London was that this new Trent Park – the strange and unfamiliar one inhabited by MI19 – was a place of secrets, stealth and subterfuge and it was going to take her a while to get used to it.

Chapter 8

Trent Park

Paget pulled up outside the iron gates of the stable block at Trent Park and unloaded the Gladstone bag from the boot of the car, along with the biscuit tin. The copies of Dr Baskin's notes Maddie kept secure in her bag.

'Will that be all for today, ma'am?' asked Paget.

'Yes,' Maddie replied. 'Yes, I think it will. Thank you.'

She supposed she'd have to catch a lift back to the boarding house, although she had had the foresight to tell Mrs Pollock before she'd left that morning not to save her any supper. What she really needed to do was store Dr Baskin's notes in a safe place and sort out a few odds and ends.

By now it was early evening, so Maddie decided to lock the copies in her own office overnight before asking Colonel McKie where he wanted them stored. She started to head back to her office, just as the stenographers' day shift was coming off duty. The light was fading as dozens of uniformed girls in the khaki of the ATS and the dark blue of the Wrens came pouring out of the Nissen huts. They were all chatting excitedly after a long day at their typewriters. Maddie was about to open the gate to the courtyard when she heard a voice call her name. She held her breath for a moment.

'I say, is it Maddie? Maddie Gresham!'

Maddie turned to see a large young woman bouncing up to her like an over-friendly Labrador. She was wearing the khaki two piece – battledress top and skirt – of the unflattering ATS uniform. Maddie would know that frightfully gung-ho voice anywhere. She also knew it wouldn't be long before there was an outburst of Latin.

'Ruth,' she replied. 'Fancy seeing you here.'

Ruth Meath-Baker had been in her boarding house at school and was potty about the Classics: Latin, Greek and everything in between. Never one to miss the chance to wear a toga, she'd even pepper her everyday speech with Latin phrases, much to everyone else's irritation. Needless to say, it had come as no surprise that she'd gone on to read Classics at Cambridge.

'Salve mi soror mea!' she cried, taking Maddie firmly by the hand. The pretentious greeting was entirely predictable and would normally mildly annoy Maddie, but this time she found it almost comforting to hear.

'I saw you yesterday and thought, it couldn't be you!' Ruth cried– in English.

'But it was!' said Maddie, forcing a smile.

'What are you doing here?' she asked. She broke off, looking terribly serious. 'Or can't you say?'

'I . . .' Maddie floundered before realising her old friend was teasing her.

'All this cloak-and-dagger stuff takes some getting used to, eh!' she said, slapping Maddie on the back. 'Are you working here, now?'

'Yes. Yes, I am,' replied Maddie. 'I only got the job yesterday.' Was it really only yesterday? It seemed like a lifetime ago.

Ruth beamed. 'Splendid, then you must come to the officers' mess for a drink.' She wore the rank of a second subaltern on her sleeve.

'But I . . .' Maddie was feeling tired. No, more than tired, mentally exhausted. There'd been so much to absorb. She was even rather looking forward to going back to her dingy room at the boarding house, but Ruth was insistent.

'It's jolly good fun and there are loads more men than girls, so you'll be in huge demand.' She nudged her old friend in the rib. 'Such a laugh.'

Maddie wasn't really in the mood for frivolity, but Ruth simply wouldn't take no for an answer.

'I've just got a few things to do first,' she replied, giving way. 'My office . . .' She pointed to the stable block behind her.

'I'll spruce up a bit before I come and collect you at, say, nineteen hundred hours?'

Maddie had to work that out quickly in her head. 'Seven o'clock?'

Ruth nodded and patted her on the arm. '*Vide te mox!*'

'Yes, see you later,' Maddie replied, her head swimming after what should have been a perfectly routine conversation. She realised too late she'd made a ghastly mistake. All she really wanted to do was curl up in bed and sleep.

It was almost dark when Maddie stumbled blindly over the threshold into the stable block and felt her way along the wall to her office. The only light came from a faint beam under the door of another room further along the corridor. Leaving her own door open, she made straight for the blackout blinds and drew them down before switching on the desk lamp. Her first priority was to ensure the copies of Dr Baskin's notes were safe. Opening her Gladstone bag, she took them out and, after a short tussle with the sticking drawer, deposited them in her desk. There was a key in the lock, so she turned it and immediately felt a huge sense of relief that she'd just rid herself of one worry.

Glancing back at the open bag, she saw her next priority: the biscuit tin containing Max's letters. The flame of hope – the thought that he had managed to escape France and was still alive

58

– had burned bright at first. Now, five years on, it was starting to flicker. Sometimes, in the early hours, when sleep evaded her, she found herself having to stamp on the thought that Max might be dead. His precious letters were her link to the past and a lifeline to their shared future. She had to keep believing.

Bringing out her silver compact from her clutch bag she studied her face in its small mirror. She looked tired and drawn, but a quick application of powder, followed by a touch of lipstick worked wonders. A dab of Chanel No. 5 behind her ears put a spring back in her step and moments later she heard her old friend's dulcet tones in the corridor once more.

'Hello! *Ave!*'

Ruth looped a congenial arm through Maddie's as they went out into the cold night, as if they'd always been bosom pals. Since leaving school they hadn't actually seen each other for four years and even then, they only met once, by accident, at a mutual friend's twenty-first birthday party. Maddie was average height and weight, while Ruth, on the other hand, was "statuesque" if one was being kind, or "big boned", if one was not. Together they made quite a comical pair as they strode out of the stable yard along a narrow path.

The sky was clear that night and the moon bright; they both knew the Luftwaffe might be waiting to take advantage. The air raids had started up again in late January when the Palace of Westminster had taken a direct hit. Everyone was still alert, but tonight, for the time being at least, Jerry was at bay.

'The officers' mess is in an old cottage in the grounds,' Ruth explained as she ploughed on past thick rhododendrons and privet hedges.

'Didn't Sir Philip's cousin live there after he died?' asked Maddie, remembering a conversation she'd had with her father a while back.

'That's right,' Ruth agreed. 'The old dear had to move out when MI19 got their paws on it. But it's still rather cosy and jolly.'

A minute later a long, low white house emerged from the gloom. Maddie had to admit it did look very homely. Suddenly she felt a little less apprehensive as Ruth went ahead of her to open the front door.

The hallway was quite narrow. Music wafted along it, together with the hum of chatter from somewhere beyond. A passing Army captain with a pint of beer in each hand had to lift them to shoulder-height and flatten himself against the wall to allow them to pass.

'Breathe in, old chap,' instructed another cheerful young officer. He was standing on the threshold of the room where the music and chatter seemed to be coming from. 'I say, who have we here?' he said, looking first at Maddie and then at Ruth. He was quite small and trim, but with a roguish smile.

'Evening, Jock,' greeted Ruth, before turning to her friend. 'Didn't I tell you they were a jolly lot?'

Maddie felt herself blush a little and, scooting past the officer's leer, followed Ruth into the large lounge area. The ceiling was low, and it seemed that two rooms had been knocked together to create a much bigger space. There was a bar at one end and banquettes around the walls, with several small tables in the centre.

Ruth flashed round again, declaring gleefully, 'If we play our cards right, we'll have free hooch all evening.'

Maddie smiled. She could really do with a drink but imagined a free gin and tonic might involve allowing oneself to be chatted up – something she really wasn't in the mood for. The men at Oxford had shown quite a lot of interest, but they weren't her type; either too stuffy or too arrogant. Besides, no one could compare with Max.

Officers clustered around the counter, vying for the bartender's attention. The few women who were nearby seemed to be talking among themselves. Others sat smoking at the tables, presumably waiting for the menfolk to return bearing their drinks.

In the corner of the room sat a big gramophone player and

a young naval officer had apparently taken it upon himself to change the seventy-eights as necessary. He seemed to have a penchant for jazz, which he was playing a little too loudly for Maddie's liking, especially as she'd developed a splitting headache.

'Fruity! I say, Fruity!' Ruth's voice sounded like a megaphone. Maddie turned to see her friend clutching the arm of a slightly tubby Army officer whose uniform jacket was straining at the buttons. 'This is Fruity Boxall,' she said, as if Maddie hadn't already realised. 'He's a real hoot.'

Fruity beamed and with such an introduction Maddie half expected him to tell a joke. None was forthcoming. Instead, his lips twitched into an embarrassed smile, and he offered her his hand.

'Real name's William, but mostly everyone calls me Fruity,' he said rather apologetically, but without an explanation. Maddie wasn't going to be the one to ask why. 'So, you're a civvy, are you?' he ventured.

'Yes,' replied Maddie, realising she could say no more. She supposed the mere existence of a team of civilian psychiatrists and psychologists at Trent Park was top secret, too.

'Isn't she lucky not having to wear this dashed awful uniform?' remarked Ruth, looking down at her khaki jacket as if it were a dirty rag.

'I think it's really rather fetching,' replied Fruity gallantly.

There was a slightly awkward pause – Ruth was clearly not used to compliments – before Fruity volunteered to buy a round of drinks. He clapped his hands then rubbed them together, like a man who wanted to get down to business. 'So, what's your poison, ladies?'

Maddie asked for a G&T while Ruth opted for a half pint of cider.

'Let's go and find a table,' she said.

They bagged a banquette, thankfully as far away from the gramophone as possible, so at least Maddie didn't have to shout to make conversation. They also had a good view of the door, to see all the comings and goings. Even before Fruity had given his order, she spotted the intimidating Wren she'd met who'd warned her, rather bluntly, to keep her own counsel.

'Ah, that's Havisham,' said Ruth, observing Maddie's gaze as she followed the redhead's progress towards a table. She'd undergone a further transformation since Maddie's encounter with her. Her hair was swept up and she wore an even brighter shade of red lipstick.

'Looks like she's heading for a night at the 400,' commented Ruth rather wistfully. 'As soon as she's off base it'll be on with the evening gown.'

The 400, Maddie knew, was a fashionable nightclub in central London. Big bands were a real attraction. As was the fact that the club was located just by Leicester Square Underground. When the sirens sounded, you could pile down the stairs to shelter, which was very handy.

Maddie had only been there two or three times since she'd lived in Oxford. But she had to agree it was the sort of place where one could forget about the war, even if it were only ever for a few hours.

A slightly shorter brunette, also heavily made-up, accompanied Havisham and two men in uniform – one Army, one Navy – trailed in their wake. They pulled out the chairs from the table for the women before advancing on the bar.

'And here comes Fruity,' declared Ruth excitedly, her sights suddenly trained on the portly lieutenant bulldozing his way through the melee of officers, hefting a tray of drinks above his head.

Maddie's attention, on the other hand, had just been engaged elsewhere. She'd caught sight of someone rather familiar. The Right Honourable Flight Lieutenant Edward Fitzroy Windlesham had just walked in. She'd last seen him in Oxford just before he went off to fight in France at the start of the war. At that encounter, he'd treated her to a slap-up luncheon at the Randolph Hotel. She'd agreed to write to him while he was away, and two or three letters had been exchanged. They were friendly, verging on more-than-friendly for his part, which made her think he might ask her out on his return. But she needn't have worried. The following Easter she'd heard on the grapevine that he was amorously involved with some debutante he'd met on leave. After that, communications between them fizzled out.

She'd had no idea he was back in England, let alone at Trent Park. He really was terribly good-looking and very charming. Maddie had always thought he had a look of Cary Grant. With his dark hair and appealing blue eyes, it had even been suggested he could make it big in Hollywood. Rich and with a fine pedigree, no wonder he was a hit with all the debutantes and their mothers during the Season. She'd first met him when they were both auditioning for parts in the Oxford University Drama Society's production of *Much Ado About Nothing*. She went on to play a fiery Beatrice to his equally headstrong Benedick. He was a good one, too, as she recalled.

Maddie wasn't sure what to do. She couldn't even take a well-timed sip of her G&T to avoid possible eye contact. He drew closer, seeming intent on heading for Havisham's party, and for a moment, Maddie thought she'd managed to escape detection, but a couple of feet shy of the table, Fruity bumped into him and the gin and tonic was the resultant casualty.

'Frightfully sorry, old chap,' said Fruity, as Eddie produced a handkerchief and started dabbing his uniform sleeve.

'I say, Fruity, you butter fingers!' called Ruth, leaping to her large feet and loping over. 'Is that Maddie's G&T?'

'I fear it is,' he replied, glancing at Maddie apologetically.

Eddie's eyes followed his and it was then that he saw her. He stopped dead at first, the handkerchief frozen on his sleeve. Then after a moment, he said: 'Good Lord! Maddie. Maddie Gresham!' He hurried forward. 'How the devil are you?'

Maddie felt her face colour. It was too late to take evasive action, so she stood to allow Eddie to touch her lightly on the arm and give her a friendly peck on the cheek.

'Eddie. It's good to see you,' she said, drawing on her acting skills.

'And you,' he replied, smiling broadly. 'What on earth are you doing here? I thought you were still at Oxford.'

'I was until a couple of days ago.' She shrugged. 'But I got a call and here I am.'

A sudden flash of understanding scudded across his face. She'd been deliberately opaque and yet he'd seen right through her reply. Could he be in on the secret, too? Did he know the reason behind her posting?

'Well, that's marvellous. I'm here, there and everywhere at the moment.' His eyes slid sidewards. He was being evasive, and she was treading on eggshells.

'Eddie. Eddie, darling!' Havisham's friend was calling to him, beckoning with her arm.

He heard her and waved. 'Look, I have to dash. But we must catch up, sometime,' he told her.

'Yes,' replied Maddie. 'We must.'

She watched him leave to be swallowed up by Havisham's little party and sat down again.

'Well, well,' said Ruth, her cider now before her on the table. 'You know Eddie Windlesham?' She was clearly impressed. 'What a catch!'

Maddie was slightly peeved. 'I haven't caught him,' she corrected. 'He's just an old friend. We acted in a play together at university.'

Ruth smiled mischievously. 'He trod the boards, did he? I'm not surprised. All the girls in my hut think he's rather a dish and he does play his part frightfully well.'

Maddie frowned. 'What do you mean "he plays his part"?' asked Maddie. But before Ruth could answer Fruity was back.

'Here we are again,' he said, carefully setting down another gin and tonic in front of Maddie.

'Let's have a toast,' proposed Ruth, lifting up her cider. Maddie braced herself for one in Latin and wasn't in the least surprised when it came.

'Dilige amicos!'

'Love your friends,' she translated as Fruity and Ruth chinked glasses first, then with her. 'I'll drink to that,' she added with a nod, while at the same time letting her gaze slide over to Eddie Windlesham. What could Ruth have meant by her remark: *he does play his part frightfully well?* Could it be he was working undercover?

*

It was almost ten o'clock when the drinkers started thinning out and Maddie – after such a long and, quite frankly, almost overwhelming day – was yearning for her bed. Fruity kindly offered to give her a lift back to the boarding house in his trusty Austin 7 and she gladly accepted. She really didn't want to walk in the dark on her own, even if Fairview was only a mile away.

Fruity was very talkative and slightly tipsy, she guessed. Ruth had told her he was an interrogator. 'He gives prisoners the once-over.' A "wolf in sheep's clothing", she'd warned, although right now Maddie found it hard to imagine. He was very chatty and kept taking his eyes off the road every time he asked her a question.

'So, do you think you'll settle in at Cockfosters?' he asked. (She'd been told no one was ever to call the mansion Trent Park.)

'I'm sure I will. Everyone's very friendly,' she replied, thankful his eyes had switched back to the road.

They were driving in the pitch dark with only the moon and tiny slits in the headlamps lighting their way.

'Yes, we're a cheerful lot, by and large,' he replied, throwing her another glance. 'As long as everyone minds their own business and keeps *schtum* it all goes swimmingly.'

But what if they didn't? What if people let slip, or worse still, were ever forced to divulge? This secrets business was going to take an awful lot of getting used to.

Five minutes later, they turned by a telephone kiosk at the junction and into her road.

'Just a bit further down on the left,' Maddie instructed, peering into the gloom.

Fruity slowed down and brought the Austin to a halt just outside Fairview's stately lion gate posts.

'Thank you,' said Maddie.

'All part of the service,' he replied with a mock salute.

He jumped out and was about to open the car door for her when they both heard an engine start up and rev. Before they knew it another motor had swerved away from the kerb up ahead of them. Suddenly it cranked its gears and was heading straight for Fruity. He leapt out of the way, flattening himself against the motor car. If he hadn't managed to dodge back, it would've hit him head-on.

'What was all that about?' asked Maddie indignantly as they both watched the car drive off at high speed towards the main road.

'Not a clue,' replied Fruity, shaking his head and slamming the car door. 'But whoever it was,' he told her, 'they'd been following us since we left Trent Park.'

Chapter 9

France

June 1940

Aunt Hannah was worrying about her late husband's paintings.

'We cannot leave them here for those Nazi swine!' she shouted down from the balcony. 'They do not appreciate good art.'

Max, in the square below, was loading the Volkswagen with boxes and suitcases. He was one of thousands in Paris that day preparing to leave the city or lie low at the very least. Restaurateurs were boarding up their frontages and gallery owners locking away their prized pictures. A few young men were collecting make-shift weapons, preparing to do battle, while some prostitutes were preparing to do good business. Banks were overwhelmed by savers wanting to withdraw their francs. Shops were stripped bare of food. Museum curators hid their most valuable exhibits and fathers wished they could do the same with their young daughters. Entire menageries – chickens, cats, dogs and rabbits – were crated and put onto carts or stuffed into cars, while crying children were treated in a similar fashion.

Max scratched his blond head and tilted it back to speak to his agitated aunt.

'But how can we bring the pictures?' he asked, exasperated. 'You can see the car is already full and that's even before we get in it!'

Aunt Hannah, now joined by Ada, considered the dimensions of the VW from her vantage point above. After a moment she said: 'I have it!' She clasped her hands gleefully. 'You could tie the canvases on the roof!'

Now Ada joined in. 'What a good idea. You could do that, couldn't you, Max?'

'But they are all almost three metres long. Longer than the car!' he protested. His arms were raised, and fingers laced flat on the crown of his head in desperation.

'Just three. That's all I ask,' pleaded his aunt.

'Three?!' exclaimed Max.

'Please, darling,' Ada intervened. 'You know how much they mean to your aunt.'

Max tilted his head even further back, towards the heavens this time. He took a lungful of air to calm himself, drew down his arms from his head, then planted a smile on his face.

'Bring me some rope and I will do it,' he said obligingly, adding under his breath: 'But if they fall off, they fall off.'

*

The exodus from the city was quite biblical. No trains were running, so those lucky enough to have an automobile queued for their share of rationed fuel at the few petrol stations on the outskirts. Those with bicycles loaded them up with bags and bedding and those with nothing simply carried what few possessions they could on their backs in the heat of a June day.

Max's VW joined the queue of cars as they crawled like ants out of Paris. Their slow progress was made even slower by the large canvases on the roof of the car. Eventually, when the traffic

68

started to go a little faster than a snail's pace, the engine struggled to speed up. Six hours after leaving Montmartre, they reached a small town just outside Chartres, where they decided to stop for the night. Little did they know that all the hotels were already overflowing with refugees. They trawled around in the car looking for somewhere in the next town but were having no luck until they stopped outside a shabby guest house on the outskirts. The proprietor, a man with a large moustache and an even larger paunch, asked if the canvases were for sale. Hannah told him firmly '*Non!*' unless he had ten thousand francs to spare.

Max, however, seeing an opportunity, unleashed the top painting of a nude woman to show him. After a moment's consideration, the proprietor pronounced that the model reminded him of his mistress.

'You give me the painting, I give you a room,' he said.

It was a deal, even though Aunt Hannah was very unhappy about it. But at least after sleeping solidly for six hours in a comfortable bed, she woke up in a better mood than if she'd spent the night in the car, or, worse still in a ditch like so many others who'd had no choice. Max, dozing fitfully on the floor, had just been grateful for a roof over his head and access to water.

The following day they set off at sunrise, with hopes of making it to Dinan by noon, but halfway there the car spluttered to a halt in the middle of nowhere. Carrying the canvases and all the other luggage meant the VW had consumed a lot more petrol than normal. The tank was empty.

'Perhaps there will be fuel in the next town,' suggested Max cheerfully, even though he doubted there would be any left.

Fearful of looters, the two women took what few possessions they could from the vehicle. Aunt Hannah was especially reluctant to leave Albert's remaining paintings, but knew she had no choice. It was hot and, although only nine o'clock in the morning, already the sun was beating down.

'At least let's put the canvases in the shade,' Ada said. So Max hefted them from the roof of the VW and slid them underneath the car so that both of them were protected from the full sun.

They began to walk. There was no fuel in the next village. Nor in the next town. They bought the last remaining baguette in the boulangerie and shared it between them. They drank from a stream and filled a discarded beer bottle with water. At Vitré they found a group of about twenty Parisiennes in a café who told them the Nazis were being held at bay by brave French fighters. That cheered them for a few moments, until a hotelier let them listen to his wireless and the shocking truth crackled over the airwaves. The Nazis had swarmed in and Paris had fallen. Max, Ada and Hannah all looked at each other in silence. It seemed as if an earthquake had struck and shaken the very foundations of civilisation. There would be no going back.

Chapter 10

Trent Park

March 1944

Maddie had been ordered to make her way to Hut 6 where the head of psychiatry, Major Lansley, was to meet her in what was called the observation room. Judging from the outside, it looked rather like a car mechanic's shed with its corrugated iron roof and a large sliding door at the front. After she'd passed through security – a smiley Wren at a desk by the front door – she was ushered into a room at the end of a long corridor.

On one side there was a raised dais and a bench, giving those seated a somewhat limited view through a narrow window onto what was ominously known as the interrogation room. (She was assured no instruments of torture were ever employed.) It was just a whitewashed cell, furnished with three chairs on either side of a Formica-covered table, which, she noted with some trepidation, was bolted to the floor. In one corner stood the technical recording equipment, presumably so that anything the prisoner said could be replayed later.

A strong smell – what was that, peppermint? – was the first thing she detected, swiftly followed by the presence of a man, presumably the source of the peppermint. Major Lansley was perched on the edge of a table, looking rather downcast and fidgeting with a small tin in his palm. He was what her father would have called "droopy". His eyelids, his head and his shoulders all seemed to be headed in a southerly direction.

Another man, some sort of military engineer, was fiddling with a complicated-looking piece of equipment covered in knobs and dials in the corner.

'Ah Miss Gresham.' The major stood to shake her hand firmly but didn't smile. 'I'm so glad you're joining us,' he said, before adding quite unexpectedly: 'Like a peppermint?' He thrust the little tin under her nose. 'Works wonders for the digestion.'

Maddie recalled his peptic ulcer. 'I'm sure, but no thank you.'

'As you wish,' he said, a little deflated, then his mouth turned down even further when he said: 'Terrible news about Baskin.'

The major motioned to a chair beside him and Maddie drew it out from the table. She settled herself down just as a tall man in an unfamiliar uniform walked in.

'Podesta,' said Lansley.

Maddie hadn't yet been introduced but had passed the officer in the corridor of the stable block. Along with his height, she'd noticed his very white teeth, and, at the time, thought he had to be American because everyone she'd ever met from the United States seemed to be very superior in the dental department.

'This is Major Podesta, Miss Gresham. He's with US Intelligence.'

The major flashed a dazzling smile and whipped off his cap. 'We're all in this together, Miss Gresham,' he told her. Was that a Texan accent?

'Quite,' she acknowledged.

The major's thick dark hair was parted at the side. He smoothed it down as he addressed the other officer. She already had him down as quite a ladies' man.

'I just came to say something's come up in Washington, so I'm afraid . . .'

'That's not a problem, Major Podesta,' Lansley replied laconically. 'I'm just going over the basics with Miss Gresham.'

The American turned to Maddie and flashed her another smile. 'I look forward to working with you,' he told her, before nodding his head to both her and Lansley and taking his leave.

As the door snapped shut, the major turned to Maddie.

'Better get started I suppose,' he told her, even though she didn't have the foggiest idea what would happen next.

'Almost ready, sir,' the engineer relayed, taking a disc from its sleeve.

Lansley squinted at his wristwatch. 'Very well,' he replied with a sigh, as if he were waiting for someone to join them.

The engineer had been checking the connections on the two sets of headphones on the table and the microphone. Now he reached for a stack of what appeared to be gramophone records.

'Colonel McKie has briefed you, I understand, about our recordings.' He handed her a folder. 'A transcript,' he explained. 'Your German is good, I take it?'

'Yes, sir,' Maddie said confidently, even though she feared it might be rather rusty. There hadn't been much cause to use it for the past six years.

'Our focus right now is to find out all we can about this secret weapon Hitler seems to be developing. The colonel told you about that, too, I assume?'

'A secret weapon, sir?' This was certainly news to Maddie.

Reading the startled expression on Maddie's face, he said: 'I'd better start at the beginning, then.' His cheeks caved as he sucked on his peppermint in thought. 'For a while we've been hearing talk among our German generals of some sort of super weapon – a rocket – that the enemy is working on, but the information we could glean was sketchy. But now,' he continued, settling himself on a chair, 'we seem to have bagged ourselves a rather big prize.'

'Really?' Maddie was intrigued.

'Someone who's been key in the weapons development programme.' He pointed to a photograph on his desk but didn't show it to Maddie. 'Brigadier Josef Hammler. Captured by Special Operations Executive in a joint venture with the Americans. All strictly under wraps, of course.' His eyes dipped to the photograph. 'He has quite a reputation for being a driving force behind the whole project. If we can get him to talk, we'll all sleep easier in our beds at night.'

Her mind was racing now. 'These weapons, sir . . .'

'Types of flying bombs and rockets, we understand. Some of the generals here have been recorded talking about them. They don't need pilots and are fired at targets.'

'But that means . . .'

'Yes, Miss Gresham. Thousands more innocent civilians will be killed if the Germans can fire their blasted weapons across the English Channel. So you see what we're dealing with.'

A shiver ran down her spine. She presumed it would be up to her to produce a psychological profile of this Josef Hammler – to uncover what motivated him to kill so many people in such a cold, calculating and completely dispassionate way. She imagined he would be arrogant and unyielding.

'Surely you don't think he'll talk?' she blurted. But as soon as the clumsy words tripped off her tongue, Maddie realised she must sound very unprofessional.

'As it stands, you're right, Miss Gresham. We've got reports he's proving rather a difficult character.'

'I'm sure,' agreed Maddie. He'd been captured by his enemies and asked to betray his country. Most high-ranking officers would be "difficult" in such a situation, she supposed.

The major continued. 'He's being kept at a holding facility at the moment. The interrogators have thrown the book at him, but without success. That's why they're sending him here. He should be with us by the end of the week, but that doesn't give us much time.'

Time, thought Madeleine. *Time for what?* To read up on what the Joint Intelligence Committee had managed to scrape together on this monster and devise a strategy to make him talk? Without torture, she was certain it would take more than a few days to make his sort sing to the Allies' tune.

The major's head drooped a little, as if readying himself to make an apology, and he sighed. 'You see, Miss Gresham, it seems whether Hammler talks is rather up to you. Colonel McKie has set great store by Dr Baskin's methods, and now he feels it's your job to carry them on.'

'My job?' said Maddie, suddenly feeling very alone.

A huge weight had just dropped from the heavens and landed on her shoulders. It was as if not only was she being asked to fill the late Dr Baskin's shoes, she was expected to climb a mountain in them, too.

Chapter 11

Maddie was relieved to swallow her last Brussels sprout. Like all the others on her plate it had been cooked to a pulp. It was proving quite an achievement to finish the unappetising meals served up at Fairview. She liked Mrs Pollock, she really did, but her mashed potato had even more lumps in it than Dr Baskin's old mattress.

'Enjoy your tea, Miss Gresham?' asked her landlady.

'Lovely, thank you, Mrs P,' she replied, rising to help clear away the plates – something the men wouldn't dream of doing.

They'd been joined that evening by a new addition to the household: a rather spivvy-looking man with a bootlace moustache. Mrs Pollock had introduced him as Mr Clancy, a garage owner from the town whose own home had been bombed out. When she'd walked into the dining room that evening, he'd winked at her, making her feel most uncomfortable, followed by: 'Cheer up, love. It may never 'appen.' Any time soon she half expected him to offer her a pair of nylons on the sly.

Maddie scraped a slick of gravy from her plate to another, before collecting Mr Pollock's and Mr Clancy's. The knives and forks she laid on top, before heading to the kitchen to put the dirty crockery on the draining board, while Mrs Pollock collected the glasses. It was then she had a strange sensation of being watched. She turned but could see no one until she heard a rustle in the corner and lowered her eyes to the cooker to see a little girl of no more than five, crouching down in the corner. Maddie was quite startled at first, but the child didn't react. Peering out from under a fringe of wild curls, she just kept her large blue eyes trained on her. In her arms she held a tatty stuffed rabbit with a stitched-up ear, which she now hugged tighter, as if afraid this stranger might steal it from her.

'Hello,' said Maddie. 'I didn't see you there.' She bent down. 'What's your name?'

Mrs Pollock entered the room then and answered for her. 'Oh, that's Sally,' she replied, depositing the dirty glasses on the draining board. 'Don't mind her. She's been at my sister's for a few days.'

'Hello, Sally,' said Maddie softly, seeing the child's reticence to engage. 'My name's Madeleine, but my friends call me Maddie.'

Mrs Pollock started to fill the washing-up bowl with water. 'You won't get any joy, I'm afraid. She's been like that since we lost our Jeanie in an air raid a couple of years back.' She started to wash the glasses.

'You mean she won't speak?' Maddie had read of trauma causing children to stop talking, but she'd never come across a case herself.

'She's mute,' said Mrs Pollock, matter-of-factly. ''Er 'ouse took a direct 'it. It was a miracle the little thing survived. They pulled her out still clutching Benjy.' She tossed a look at the bedraggled rabbit. ''Is ear was damaged, and 'e lost an eye, but we managed to make him better, didn't we, Sal?' This time she smiled at the child, but still had no response.

'Well, he's a very fine rabbit,' said Maddie, kneeling down, so that her face was almost level with the little girl's. 'How do you do, Benjy?' She held out a hand to the toy then said, 'Do you think I could shake his paw?'

Sally's large eyes darted to her grandmother for approval and when she received a nod, she loosened her grip on Benjy and lifted him up. Slowly Maddie shook the rabbit's paw.

'Pleased to meet you, Benjy,' she said with a smile.

At this, Sally smiled, too.

'Well,' said Mrs Pollock, turning away from the sink and planting her hands on her rather wide hips, 'that's the first time I've seen her do that in a while.'

*

Buoyed up by her small victory, Maddie went to her room that evening thinking about how she could further help Sally regain the confidence to speak. The poor child must have suffered so much. It was bad enough losing your mother – there was no mention of a father, and she didn't like to ask – let alone being trapped after a bomb blast that wrecked her home, too. No wonder the girl was traumatised.

As she lay in bed, pondering someone else's misfortune, her mind wandered further back, as it often did, to Max and to her own trauma suffered that summer. Max had saved the best for last, he'd told her. This time the target he had in mind for their finale, the climax to their wonderfully daring campaign, was the bulletin board by the Feldherrnhalle in the main Odeonsplatz. It was the most heavily guarded area of Munich.

'If we can smash the glass there, in the city's great square, that will be such a major coup,' he'd told her gleefully.

She'd clasped her hands together in delight. 'Yes!' she'd replied excitedly. 'Let's do it!'

'Let's do it!' he'd repeated, and he'd kissed her hard on the lips.

With Max was by her side, anything was possible. In those last few weeks, they were giant slayers. They were both on the cusp of life and the world awaited them. She'd come to Germany to improve upon her already excellent German and had always respected authority before. After all, she'd been brought up a nice English girl, who minded her manners, but Max had taught her that "nice" people needed to stand up for themselves or be bullied just like his poor mother.

For this raid, he'd really prepared well. He'd been on a reconnaissance mission and discovered that the guard at the Feldherrnhalle changed at midnight. That's when they would strike. There would be confusion among the sentries, which they could use to their advantage as they made their escape.

It was the end of August and already the weather had started to change a little. The nights, of course, were drawing in, but there was also a chill on the air as the two of them crept along in the lee of the large buildings and down deserted high streets towards Odeonsplatz. The sky was clear, the moon high and both knew they were taking a big risk, but they felt invincible. Their methods were tried, tested and, to date, successful. Tonight would be no different.

Their target stood at the mouth of the street between the Odeon concert hall and the Palais Leuchtenberg, near the statue of Ludwig I. The old emperor, mounted on his steed, would be watching them no doubt, thought Maddie. There was no one about, apart from the guards surrounding the Feldherrnhalle and the odd stray dog or cat. Just before midnight, the sound of jackboots on the cobbles could be heard as a small detachment of guards marched up to the mausoleum. Now was the time.

Weapons at the ready, the two of them leapt out of the shadows and hacked at the bulletin board, smashing the glass within a couple of seconds before Max clawed at the newspaper with his ice pick.

'Let's get out of here!' he whispered hoarsely, as soon as they'd finished their work. He whipped round and started to run off, but he'd only gone a couple of metres when he realised she wasn't following. She'd paused for a moment, transfixed by the damage they'd done, as if she was making a last act of defiance on behalf of oppressed Jewish people like his mother. The problem was she lingered just a little too long and a split second later they both heard the crunch of glass under foot.

'Maddie,' she heard him scream. But it was too late. A storm trooper clamped a heavy hand on her shoulder and, in that crucial moment, Max faltered, then turned and ran.

Chapter 12

It was a bittersweet moment when Maddie sat in her office and unlocked the filing cabinet drawer. She reached for the battered foolscap folder containing pages of Dr Baskin's notes, opened it up and set it in front of her. The pages were still covered in his nightmarish scrawl. No doubt he would've got round to asking her to type them up, had he lived. She squinted at the spidery letters, before deciding she needed her reading glasses to decipher them.

It was her job to uncover as much as she could about Brigadier Hammler before he arrived at Trent Park and she wondered if Dr Baskin had already come across him. He'd produced psychological profiles on other high-ranking Nazis like Goering and Goebbels, so there was a chance, albeit slim, that Hammler had already been on his radar.

She started to flick through the pages. At first she found it hard to reacquaint herself with the doctor's strange letter F's that looked like S's and the way he sometimes neglected to cross his T's, but she quickly slipped into the rhythm of his prose. About halfway through the pages, her eyes latched on to the word "rocket". She read on, snatching at the next page, then the next, until there, buried in amongst some other names was the one she was looking for – Josef Hammler.

Hungrily, she started to read what the doctor had managed to uncover about the officer's background. She discovered he was a civil engineer but had volunteered to join a rocket development programme in 1941. Since then, he'd so impressed his masters that last year he was promoted to command a special division. His job was to oversee the technical development of the secret weapons programme.

As for his private life, the doctor's notes were very scant. Hammler was married with four children, although nothing more about them was known.

So much for the facts – but then she came to the doctor's psychological profile. It was brief, but nevertheless disturbing. *He is known to be completely driven and will stop at nothing to achieve his goals,* noted the doctor. But it wasn't until she turned the final page that Maddie had to catch her breath. In the margin, her mentor had written a note to himself in capital letters: N.B. DON'T BE FOOLED. THIS MAN IS UNPREDICTABLE. FIND HIS WEAK SPOT.

Maddie shivered. It was as if she'd just heard the doctor's voice from the grave. What she'd just read concerned her, but encouraged her, too. Dr Baskin was telling her that this German, who cared nothing for the lives of thousands, could be broken, not by torture but by psychology.

Armed with this information, she headed to Hut 6 once more, where she was due to report to Major Lansley. She found the psychiatrist waiting for her in the observation room.

'Peppermint?' he asked.

Maddie declined. 'I've been doing some digging, sir. On this Hammler. It seems Dr Baskin already knew of him.' She opened the folder and passed it across the desk to him.

'Well, well,' he muttered, his eyes frowning as he tried, clearly without success, to decipher the notes.

Maddie stepped in. 'The man's clearly educated – a civil engineer with a PhD, but he's also cold and calculating with a complete disregard for human life.'

The major nodded. 'A troubling summary, Miss Gresham. As you know, it was Baskin's idea to allow prisoners to remain tight-lipped in front of our interrogators. They always feel rather pleased with themselves at the end of a session, so they brag to their fellow prisoners about what they didn't tell us. Let us hope the strategy works on him.'

Maddie bit her lip. 'But if it doesn't?'

'We always have the stool pigeons.'

Once again Maddie found herself in strange territory. 'I'm afraid I'm not familiar with the term, sir.'

The major rolled his eyes. 'Did Colonel McKie tell you nothing, Miss Gresham?'

She didn't reply.

Lansley sucked harder on his mint. 'Here we have certain operatives – sometimes trusted captives, sometimes émigrés, often Jews, who pose as officers. They share rooms with the generals, drink with them, ingratiate themselves with them to gain information.'

'You mean they pretend to be German military personnel? Inside the mansion?' She could barely disguise her amazement. 'But surely, if they're discovered . . .'

The major nodded. 'It's dangerous work, Miss Gresham. The risk isn't denied. If they're found out by the Germans, the whole operation will fail.'

'And what about them? What about the stool pigeons' personal safety?' Questions were dropping into Maddie's head as fast as bombs on London in the Blitz.

Lansley's face betrayed his own disquiet. He knew what she was driving at. If they were uncovered, the generals would surely dispense their own form of justice. 'As I said, it is dangerous work.' He shrugged. 'And of course sometimes, when the generals think they can relax, they admit to some shocking things.'

'Shocking things?' repeated Maddie.

Was she imagining it, or had the major's face just turned a little paler? Either way he ignored her question and looked down at his watch, as if he was expecting someone. 'You will be given transcripts of all the relevant recordings we have so far,' he told her. 'But I thought you ought to hear some examples for yourself.' The engineer checked more switches, nodded to himself, then left the room. 'In a moment we're going to listen to a conversation that took place yesterday between one of the generals and Lord Frobisher.'

'Lord Frobisher, sir?' she said, before realising she was making a habit of repeating what the major was telling her.

'Didn't McKie tell you?'

'Tell me what, sir?' It suddenly struck her there was rather a lot Colonel McKie hadn't told her.

'Ah.' He sucked harder on his mint.

Just then there was a knock at the door. 'Come,' said Lansley as the caller revealed himself, sending the major's droopy brows shooting up unexpectedly to reveal his eyes fully for the first time. 'Ah, good timing, Flight Lieutenant Windlesham. Or should I say Lord Frobisher?' For the first time he let out a sort of muted chuckle under his breath. 'Come and meet Miss Gresham.' He motioned the flight lieutenant towards a seat at the table, where Maddie sat with a rather bemused look on her face.

Eddie flashed her a smile. 'Actually, we already know each other, sir,' he said, pulling out a chair opposite Maddie. 'We were in a play together at Oxford.'

Lansley nodded and turned to a very puzzled Maddie. 'So, you're already aware Windlesham here is a fine actor, Miss Gresham, but I'll leave it to him to explain.'

Maddie leaned forward and looked directly at Eddie. 'Please do,' she said.

'It was Dr Baskin who suggested the idea of a sort of welfare officer,' Eddie began.

That sounds just the sort of thing he would have suggested, thought Maddie. *'To hear is to learn. To listen is to care.'*

'A person to enlist the trust of the generals; someone to be their ally, to fight their corner and appear to be on their side. He wanted someone of a similar background and class to them, who could pretend to have sympathy with their cause. They needed to be a fluent German speaker, cultured, educated, and, above all, a good actor.'

Maddie smiled and nodded. 'And you were the perfect candidate.'

Another one of Eddie's smiles sped across the table.

'Well, the strategy is paying off,' said Lansley. 'Lord Frobisher seems to have a certain manner that appeals to the Germans. Makes them open up, so to speak.'

Eddie Windlesham could charm a bird off a tree, thought Maddie.

'And, of course, it helps they've been told he's closely related to the king.'

Maddie's eyes widened.

'They think I have His Majesty's ear,' Eddie said, giving his own earlobe a tug. 'But then I always tell them I was friends with his brother, too, and that we wouldn't be at war if Edward hadn't abdicated, so it's a win-win!'

'How very even-handed of you,' Maddie remarked dryly. Somehow she wasn't in the least surprised that Eddie the charmer, the pin-up with good looks and suave sophistication in spades, had landed such a plum role.

Just then the engineer, who'd disappeared for a while, returned to the room. 'All set, sir,' he told the major.

'Good,' he replied, as the stylus was placed on the acetate disc on the gramophone player. 'This recording was made a couple of days ago, in the library after dinner,' explained Lansley. 'So now we can all listen to what a couple of the German generals talk about when they think no one's listening.'

Eddie looked across the table at Maddie with a frown. 'I must warn you, Miss Gresham,' he said earnestly, 'it doesn't always make for easy listening.'

Chapter 13

France

July 1940

Max screwed up his eyes against the stark, white light of the room. He'd no idea where he was at first but snatches of voices crept into his head. He felt a hand, soft and warm on his, and he wanted to say something, only when he opened his mouth, it was so dry no sound came out.

'You must rest,' ordered the voice that belonged to the soft hand. 'Rest and place your trust in God.'

Was he in heaven? He sniffed the coppery air. There was blood on it. Blood and soap. He was in a hospital and the voices belonged to nuns. He licked his lips.

'How . . . How lo . . .' This time he could form the words, but he couldn't breathe sound into them.

'Two weeks,' replied a higher, sweeter voice. 'You were badly hurt, but a priest saved you.'

The words triggered a memory.

He was running away from the sound in the sky. At first, he'd thought it was made by bees, but then the droning gradually

87

swelled and suddenly it burst into an ear-shattering symphony of death. Ada, Hannah and he had been on the road for three days. Both his mother and aunt were flagging in the searing heat. Ada had terrible blisters on her feet and Hannah kept complaining of a blinding headache. There were others on the road, too, although some had fallen by the wayside. They passed an old man who had just given up. He lay on the verge as if asleep. Only Max knew he wasn't sleeping by the flies that buzzed about him.

After what seemed like miles of flat golden cornfields, fringed by woods, they saw a stone bridge up ahead.

Ada called out. 'A river!' She turned to Max, her face suddenly splitting into a smile. 'We can drink and wash.'

The women quickened their steps, as if the mere thought of fresh water could revive them. They were almost at the river's edge when they all heard the bees, their buzzing growing ever louder. Only Max looked to the sky, shielding his eyes from the glaring light. It took a moment to adjust and then he saw them: fighters. Four, five, six of them. Germans. They were headed straight for them, dropping through the cloudless blue at an alarming speed.

Someone shouted: 'Take cover!' But there was nowhere to shelter except under the bridge and then, in another second, a larger plane dropped its deadly cargo and there was a huge explosion that sent stones and flame and debris hurtling into the air. A curtain of foul black smoke was suddenly drawn across the azure sky. A moment later the machine guns were spitting hails of bullets at anything that moved below. Anyone on the road was a target. Men, women, and children dived into the nearby ditches, but many were mown flat by the giant scythe that swept down from the sky. For the next few moments, the screams were drowned out by the *rat-tat-tat* of the machine guns, until the fighters flew off and left fewer screams in their wake. Now there were mainly just wails and sobs and silence.

With his heart hammering in his chest, Max had flung himself on his stomach. He'd yelled at Ada and Hannah, a little way ahead of him, to get down, but the bridge had exploded before they could, and the debris had showered over them like deadly confetti. It was only when he called out their names through the choking smoke that he realised he had been wounded. A dull pain clenched his side and when he looked down, he saw his shirt was caked in blood. He staggered on, clutching his ribs, trying to staunch the flow, until he stumbled across two bodies. Side by side. Both hit by flying debris. He knew instantly they were Ada and Hannah and he fell to his knees, searching frantically for any signs of life. But there were none and suddenly the searing pain in his ribs didn't matter anymore. It was the agony in his heart that cut deeper than any shrapnel.

The priest must have found him later. Just how much later, Max had no idea. He lost consciousness shortly after seeing both his mother and aunt lying bloody and lifeless on the ground. Once more he tried to gather his breath to speak, from his hospital bed but as he did so, a terrible pain stabbed at his chest.

The sweet voice came closer and through a blur of agony, he saw her lean over him. 'Say nothing,' she whispered.

Sleep drifted over him again and the next thing he remembered was being woken by the sound of shouts and heavy footsteps outside his room. The door wasn't opened gently, but flung wide and two men stormed in. He saw them through the narrow slits of his own eyes before he closed them tight. Gestapo.

'*Heil Hitler!*' The bullet arms shot out. The familiar click of the heels.

'He has not long,' the older nun protested, sliding protectively in front of the bed.

'Papers!' barked the senior officer.

A rustle by his bedside.

'*Voici, monsieur.*'

In the silence that followed Max could hear his heart beating in his ears, and the faster it beat, the more he needed to breathe, but that would show a man struggling to live and he was supposed to be on the verge of death.

'Jean-Baptiste Vallade,' the senior officer read out loud.

'A labourer. He fell from a barn roof,' the older nun informed. 'His family has lived in the city for generations.'

The officer seemed satisfied. 'Very well,' he said, his tone softening. 'Sisters.' A stiff bow and both men took their leave.

More footsteps and the click of the door handle followed, gently this time. Certain the Gestapo were gone, Max opened his mouth to gobble up the air, like a starving child with a piece of bread, but the pain was so intense that he could only nibble at it.

The older nun returned to see him flailing and poured water from a jug to hold a dampened cloth to his lips. The moisture seemed to help and he looked into her lined face, framed by a tight white wimple. He realised then that she had saved his life not just once, but twice; the first time with medical care, the second with a lie.

'Why did . . .?' He couldn't finish his question, but she understood it, nevertheless.

She looked at him for a moment. 'Your papers said you were a Jew, and we know how the Germans treat Jews right now.' She moistened his parched lips. 'We have many deaths here, at the hospital, and sometimes papers go missing or get mixed up.' She tilted her head as if to study his face. 'So, now you are no longer a Jew, but a son of France.' She twitched her lips and gave a Gallic shrug before adding: 'And what's more, for as long as you remain here, you are safe.'

So, for the next few weeks, the young man once known as Max Weitzler remained at the Hopital de St Therese in Rennes. His body may have rested, but his brain did not. Memories of his mother's head tilting back as the bomber dropped its load and the sound of Aunt Hannah's screams would echo in his head for as long as he lived. Once more he had escaped from the Gestapo, just like he had in Munich when he abandoned Maddie, but once more the ones he loved had suffered.

Every day his condition improved. A surgeon had removed a chunk of shrapnel and his cracked ribs were knitting but his punctured left lung had needed longer to heal. Then one day, Max Weitzler had an unexpected visitor as he sat recuperating on the hospital terrace. A young woman posed as an old family friend. The bouquet of fresh flowers she carried came with a proposal. The French had saved his life. Now it was his turn to save others. Would he join the Resistance?

As soon as he was well enough to leave hospital, new clothes and a new hope were added to the false papers the nuns had given him. In return Max would join with the Resistance to help run an escape line for British RAF pilots shot down and stranded in Nazi-occupied territory. He must no longer be a victim. The time had come to act.

Chapter 14

Trent Park

March 1944

Third Officer Havisham, blowing in like a northerly gale, plonked down four buff-coloured files on Maddie's desk and announced: 'So, you're now on the circulation list, Miss Gresham.'

The overnight frost had left the office so cold that her breath billowed out like smoke as she spoke.

'Good morning and thank you,' Maddie returned, in a more measured fashion. She sat shivering in her thick coat, having had to scrape ice from the inside of her window when she'd arrived for work. Quickly she skimmed the covers of the folders; there was one from each armed force – Army, Navy and Air Force. The fourth, she saw as she thumbed through them, contained transcripts of recordings of Hammler made at the detention camp where he was currently being held. Her brief, according to a note from Major Lansley pinned to the transcript, was to study it and devise a list of questions to be asked during the brigadier's initial interrogation as soon as he arrived at Trent Park.

Eager to begin, Maddie shuffled her chair closer to the desk and was about to open the folder when she suddenly became aware that Third Officer Havisham was still watching her. She looked up.

'I'll get onto this right away. Thank you,' Maddie replied, expecting the Wren to leave then.

Instead, the officer lifted her neatly coiffured head. 'I hope you enjoyed yourself at the mess the other night,' she said quite suddenly, a glint in her eye.

Maddie was quite taken aback. 'Yes. Thank you. I did,' she replied briskly, expecting that to be an end to the matter. Only it wasn't.

'Eddie said that you and he were at Oxford together,' continued the Wren.

'That's right,' replied Maddie, quite surprised that Havisham was calling the flight lieutenant by his first name. Not to mention the fact Eddie had discussed their friendship with other people. 'We acted in a play together.'

'So I understand.'

Was that disapproval in Havisham's voice? Or jealousy? Or perhaps even a warning to stay away from Eddie, although Maddie was probably being oversensitive. She was, after all, in a fragile emotional state. News of Dr Baskin's sudden death had rather knocked her for six and seeing an old friend had lifted her mood. But before she could reply, the Wren added: 'I hope you'll come to the mess again. Next time we must make up a party.'

Maddie was slightly unnerved by this sudden thaw in Havisham's Snow Queen act. Nevertheless, she smiled. 'I'd like that very much.'

'Good,' said the officer with a nod. 'Please call me Pru, by the way.'

'And you must call me Maddie,' she replied, still a little shocked at the change in attitude.

Suddenly Pru rubbed her hands together. 'I say, it's frightfully cold in here.'

'Yes, it certainly is,' replied Maddie, also rubbing her hands, unconsciously reinforcing the point.

Pru responded with a muted laugh. 'You can barely hear the girls' typewriters for the sound of chattering teeth in our hut,' she said, suddenly glancing at the empty fireplace. 'I'll see if I can get you some coal.'

'Thank you,' replied Maddie gratefully. Perhaps the formidable Third Officer Havisham wasn't so intimidating after all.

Once Pru had left Maddie got down to work, but her stomach turned over as soon as she looked at the photograph on the folder's front cover. So this was Josef Hammler. She had never studied the face of someone who could be so completely indifferent to human suffering before. Worryingly, he looked almost normal, if rather formidable. His thick, dark hair was slicked back to reveal a high forehead and exaggerated his heavy eyebrows. His thin lips were turned down at the edges and his nostrils slightly flared, making him look as though he had an unpleasant smell under his nose.

Threading a sheet of paper into the roller of her typewriter, Maddie paused to frame her thoughts. It would be her job to produce a set of questions to provoke and cajole this enigmatic, but clearly unscrupulous German. Reaching for the notes she'd made at yesterday's meeting with Major Lansley, she'd just flipped open the pages when another scrap of paper slipped out onto her desk. She picked it up and studied the handwriting. This time the words were perfectly legible. *Maddie, Let's catch up over dinner. How about 7.30 p.m. tomorrow tonight (Wednesday)? I'll pick you up from your digs. Eddie.*

Maddie heard herself let out a girlish giggle. Dinner with Eddie. Her mind flitted to the luncheon at the Randolph at Oxford. She'd enjoyed his company. There was no harm in it, was there? Eddie certainly had lots of female acquaintances. He must take girls out to dinner all the time. It meant nothing. Just two old friends making up for lost years. That was all. Why then, by intending to accept the invitation, did she suddenly see Max's face before her and feel a twinge of guilt?

Chapter 15

Maddie told Mrs Pollock she would be eating out that evening as soon as she came in from work. Her landlady crossed her arms over her flowery overall and said: 'Goin' anywhere nice, are we?'

'I'm not sure, Mrs P,' she replied, although she knew that Eddie wouldn't take her anywhere that wasn't nice, of course. 'I was rather wondering if there's any chance of a bath?' she asked rather gingerly. Bathing was such a luxury these days. But she may as well have asked for a full-body massage. Mrs Pollock shook her head. The two large curlers pinned to her scalp rolled like barrels on a ship's deck.

'Boiler's packed in, Miss Gresham,' she replied. 'You'll have to make do with a lick and a promise.'

Forced to settle for a good wash, Maddie decided to wear her hair in a victory roll updo to disguise the fact it hadn't been shampooed in a week. Once she'd slid into her dress – she may even have lost a few pounds – she stood back to inspect herself in the long wardrobe mirror. Seeing Pru at the officers' mess the other night, made up to the nines, had made her decide to go all out to impress. Her midnight blue evening gown fitted the bill nicely.

It was then that she noticed, lying flat against her milky white skin, just above the sweetheart neckline of her dress, the silver locket. The one Max had given her. The one she always wore. Still looking at her reflection she fingered it lovingly. The thin chain of possibility that he was alive, forged in her mind over the past few years, sometimes wavered but still held. If she ever stopped wearing the locket, that would mean she had lost faith that they would one day be together again. She couldn't give up on him.

Just then, as she turned a little in front of the looking glass, the light from the nearby lamp bounced off the silver, making the locket glint. Her hands flew up to her neck and she clasped it tightly then. It was a sign. It had to be. As long as there was light, there was hope. The locket would remain around her neck.

After that, she popped her lipstick, powder compact and a handkerchief in her evening purse. She admitted to herself it felt odd to be back in high heels, but oddly empowering. A stole would have completed the ensemble nicely but she had to make do with her ordinary coat. Nevertheless, Mrs Pollock seemed impressed.

'Well, aren't you a sight for sore eyes?' she said when Maddie finally came downstairs at twenty-five minutes past seven. Her landlady was just about to serve liver and onions. She held a hot dish in her hand as she walked from the kitchen into the dining room.

'Who goes there?' came a voice from behind her and she turned to her husband. 'It's Miss Gresham, Harold,' she said, switching back to add: 'Looking very stylish, if you don't mind me saying so.'

Maddie smiled, nodding her thanks for the compliment just as Sally appeared. The little girl was still clutching her rabbit.

'Don't Miss Gresham look a proper lady?' said Mrs Pollock, as the child clasped her grandmother's thigh, before suddenly putting the rabbit's mouth up to her ear.

Noticing this development Maddie asked: 'Does Benjy like my dress?'

After a moment Sally nodded coyly, before swiftly covering her face with the landlady's apron.

Mrs Pollock smiled. 'She's taken a real shine to you,' she said.

'Well, I have to her,' replied Maddie, pulling back her shoulders. 'In fact, I think we're going to be the best of friends. Don't you?'

The little girl re-emerged from behind her grandmother's apron to nod.

'You got a key now?' asked Mrs Pollock, rather maternally.

'Yes, thank you, Mrs P,' replied Maddie, returning Sally's smile before looking up once more. She'd been made to feel as if she were about to embark on a great expedition rather than just go out to dinner in town with an old friend.

'And don't do anything I wouldn't do,' chirped up Mr Clancy, popping his well-oiled head around the dining room door.

'Oh Mr Clancy, you are awful,' said Mrs Pollock, tapping him playfully on the arm.

Maddie lifted her chin, bestowed a cheery smile and sallied forth, past her small audience and out of the front door. Thankfully Eddie was already waiting in his open-topped green roadster. She knew she was in for a chilly ride and, as Eddie hurried round to open the door, she suddenly found herself hoping it might be one of those new motor cars with a heater.

'I wasn't sure you'd come,' he told her as he helped her negotiate the low seat.

'Why wouldn't I?' she asked disingenuously.

He returned to the driver's side but ignored her question. Instead, he looked up at the sky. 'Not a star in sight,' he said, placing his gloved hands firmly on the steering wheel. *Nor a heater,* thought Maddie. At least the clouds that had cloaked the sun all day now skulked across the moon, too. The absence of light should hold any roving Luftwaffe at bay.

'Let's hope it stays that way,' she replied, tying a scarf under her chin to keep her hair in place.

Dodging bomb craters and driving on slitted headlights, they made slow progress to the train station, but once on board the 19.52 they found themselves in the West End a little over an hour later.

'Savoy all right?' Eddie asked as Maddie tiptoed over some broken glass strewn on the pavement.

'Yes,' she replied. 'Lovely.' Even a cup of tea at a Lyons Corner House would be heaven right now.

'We can talk there,' he added, as they passed a desolate gap in a row of shops, where once a department store had stood.

When they finally turned into the little courtyard at the front of the Savoy, it was like entering a different world. Here, the war was something going on in a far-off country. Rolls-Royces and Bentleys lined up by the entrance to disgorge their elegant passengers as the liveried doorman saluted.

Once they'd negotiated the revolving door into the foyer, and been relieved of their coats, they entered the dining room. It was alive to the music of chatter and laughter and popping corks; these were the sounds of people who were living for the moment, Maddie knew, and she was about to join the party.

'I'll just need to powder my nose,' she told Eddie, keen to check that her hair had remained in place. But there was another reason, too. The ladies' room was an oasis of calm where she could garner her thoughts. There were lots of scented towels and little phials of cologne and a pink chaise longue if the going got really tough. A matronly woman in a silver dress was touching up her rouge.

Maddie inspected herself in the mirror and was relieved to discover her hair didn't look too messy, all things considered. Nevertheless, she smoothed down wayward wisps and applied another coat of lipstick, even though the first was still perfectly in place.

Her thoughts then turned to Eddie, waiting for her in the dining room. What on earth was she doing with him? This was the young man who, at Oxford, had girls loitering outside the gates of his college, hoping to catch a glimpse of him; they attended lectures in English Literature, even if they were studying Mathematics, just to get closer to him. The young women at Trent Park would be no different. He could have any debutante in his set, in or out of uniform, and probably had, and yet, for some reason, it was her he'd chosen to take to dinner.

As she made her way back to the table Maddie looked around her at the other diners. She was keen to avoid anyone she knew so that her father, or worse still Uncle Roly, didn't receive reports that she'd been "about town" with a young man. She rejoined Eddie at their table in a quiet corner. A bottle of Bollinger sat enticingly in an ice bucket. The waiter poured two glasses.

'To you,' he toasted.

'And you,' she replied.

'To us,' Eddie came back, chinking his glass against hers. That was going a little too far, she thought.

'It's not every day one can spend time with an old friend,' Eddie said. The candlelight made him look even more handsome and he smiled at her with that same disarming smile he always dispensed so freely to women. But she wasn't going to fall for it. Not tonight, at least.

Another waiter handed Eddie a menu and informed them there was no Dover sole, but there was some excellent coley instead.

'The sole was off the menu at the Randolph, as I recall,' Eddie remarked.

She paused. 'Yes. Yes, I think you're right,' she agreed. In any case, she imagined the only "fishing" off the coast of Dover nowadays was for German mines and U-boats.

'Don't you miss it?' he asked, looking up from the menu.

For a moment she thought he was referring to sole. She'd never actually cared for it that much, unless it was served in *à la meunière*, but before she made a complete fool of herself Eddie explained: 'Oxford, I mean. We had fun, didn't we, doing the play?'

She let out a little nervous laugh, grateful for being saved any embarrassment. 'We did,' she agreed, recollecting that the rows they'd had to enact between their characters were particularly amusing. 'I remember the first time I had to slap your face, you almost toppled over.'

He threw his head back and let out a laugh. 'That's right. You clearly don't know your own strength.'

'Luckily, I haven't had to slap many men lately,' she told him, just as the first courses arrived.

'Ah, yes. All those poor, injured soldiers at the military hospital at St Hugh's. I bet they loved you.'

'I like to think I was of some help to them,' she replied, recalling those who'd lost everything yet still managed a smile for her from their sick beds.

'And now you've taken over from Baskin.'

'Yes.' Her stomach flipped every time she was reminded of her new responsibility.

'He was a good man.' His eyes slid away from hers.

'You knew him?'

'Only by reputation,' he was quick to say.

As if he'd caught himself straying into forbidden territory, he changed the subject. 'Do you think you'll go back to Oxford, when this ghastly mess is over?'

'Who knows?' she said with a shrug. More than anything she missed the freedom working at Oxford brought with it. Now her world had shrunk more or less to the confines of Trent Park. At St Hugh's she could stroll around the parks, play croquet on the college lawn, even take out a punt on the Cherwell if she fancied. She remembered guiltily waving Eddie off to war in France while she remained in the city of dreaming spires.

'Was it hell, over in Europe?' she said, shocking herself at her own forthrightness. Somehow, thinking of Oxford, had brought her back to Max again.

'Yes,' he replied without hesitation. 'But I'm here now, aren't I?'

Understanding he didn't want to talk about his experiences, she took a sip of Champagne. They were dancing around conversational topics in some sort of risky ritual. When she lifted her gaze, however, she realised that Eddie had kept his eyes trained on her. She found herself wanting to look anywhere but at him until he said something rather odd. 'Actually, I'm here, but you're not.'

His words pulled her up short. 'I don't know what you mean,' she said, a little tetchily.

'Are you still with that German chap. The Jew?'

His gaze had dropped to the plate of caviar that had just been set before him. It was only when he looked up again and saw Maddie's horrified expression that he realised he'd made a terrible faux pas.

He'd found out about Max at their luncheon in Oxford way back in '39. He'd watched her fingering the locket, just as she was now, and he'd guessed, rather perceptively she thought, there was someone else in her life. When she told him she'd met a special person in Germany, Eddie had immediately jumped to conclusions. He'd leaned back in his chair and said: 'So, he's a Nazi.'

'Goodness gracious, no!' she'd snapped, then relented slightly. Eddie deserved an explanation, so she'd recounted how she'd met Max and how their "little spree" had landed her in trouble with the authorities.

Eddie had looked at her intently then, just as he was looking at her now at the Savoy, only this time he said: 'Have I put my foot in it again?'

Maddie, toying with her melon, sighed. 'I still haven't heard anything from him.'

'Oh dear,' said Eddie, rolling his eyes.

She didn't find his reaction in the least helpful. 'If you must know, he's what they call a *mischling*. Only his mother is Jewish, so in Germany that makes him technically a Jew, too. Quite frankly, it's a dreadful situation.'

He nodded. 'I'm sorry. That was insensitive of me.' He pulled a sort of apologetic face then tucked into his caviar with gusto.

She had suddenly lost her appetite, but watched Eddie continue to eat.

'It is a dreadful situation,' he agreed, wiping his mouth with his napkin.

'Sorry?' She was getting the distinct impression he knew something more.

'The Jews over there. I've been hearing a lot of terrible stories lately.'

He slumped back, allowing one waiter to remove his empty plate while another set down his filet mignon in front of him. A third waiter served Maddie her coley. As soon as the staff were out of earshot, Eddie began shaking his head as he cut into his meat.

Maddie frowned and lowered her voice. 'What sort of stories?'

'Group of chaps from Germany and Austria mainly. Some Czechs and Poles,' he remarked without once looking up at her, as if he were commenting on the food.

Remembering Colonel McKie had mentioned something in the M Room, she laid down her own fish knife and fork. 'What do you mean?' she asked softly, leaning forward. 'They managed to escape?'

'Not many, but a few. Doctors, engineers and all with tales to tell, poor devils . . .' He smiled an inscrutable smile. 'Your fish any good?'

But it was no use trying to divert her. He'd thrown her a crumb of hope. Max might be alive. Max might be among this group of escapees.

'Where are they, these men?'

Wide-eyed, he jerked back his head. 'As it happens, some of them are working in the M Room.'

'What?' Maddie didn't understand.

'You honestly don't expect me to say any more, do you, Maddie?' he asked her disingenuously. 'Not here, at least. Tonight, you're with me. Let's enjoy this evening, shall we?'

'I'm sorry,' she said, looking forlornly at her barely touched fish. 'It's just well . . .' Perhaps she shouldn't have agreed to come out tonight. She clearly wasn't ready for it psychologically. She, of all people, should have realised that.

'I understand,' Eddie said, tilting his head, a sympathetic smile hovering on his lips. 'But, right now, we all need to live for the moment.'

She nodded, then followed his gaze as it suddenly scooted to the far end of the dining room. A quartet – a woman and three men – was making its way onto a small stage, where their instruments awaited them. There was someone else within her view, too. The woman in the silver dress she'd noticed in the powder room seemed to be very interested in her. Maddie was just about to remark on her when Eddie turned back, and she thought better of it.

'Now eat up,' he said with a wink. 'You're going to need all your energy for the dance floor.'

Chapter 16

Even though Maddie did manage to eat a few more forkfuls, talk of Max had left her distracted. Dancing a foxtrot, having to concentrate on avoiding Eddie's toes, was the last thing she felt like doing. He picked up on her reluctance.

'I say, I know a quiet little place just over Waterloo Bridge,' he told her, his voice almost drowned out by a rather cheesy rendition of "There'll Be Bluebirds Over". When he saw her hesitate he added: 'We can talk more there.'

Maddie smiled. 'I'd like that,' she said and together they set off. It was only a short distance from the Savoy to Waterloo Bridge but although Eddie tried, he couldn't find a taxi for love nor money to take them across the river. A red double-decker bus drove past them but didn't slow down at the stop. He suggested they walk. Maddie looked at her best shoes but decided to be brave. If the worst happened and they rubbed the backs of her heels, she'd had the foresight to pack a couple of sticking plasters in her clutch bag.

'It's not far, once we're on the south bank,' said Eddie cheerfully, completely unaware that her feet were already hurting.

They set off, side by side, pocket torches blazing. An icy blast rushed down the Thames as soon as they stepped onto the bridge.

But Maddie thought braving the cold worth it for the view. There were quite a few couples about, strolling leisurely across the bridge, despite the plummeting temperature, seemingly just happy to be out in the open after the recent horrors of the Blitz.

The clouds had cleared to reveal a full moon. It was high and cast its golden glow along a wide stretch of water. The view east was of church spires rising like needles to pierce the blue velvet sky. But it was the silhouette of the great dome of St Paul's Cathedral that dominated them all. While just two years ago London had burned all around it, Wren's masterpiece had stood solid and unflinching.

'What a beautiful sight,' murmured Eddie as they stopped to take in the vista.

'Yes, it is,' Maddie agreed, although when she turned to him she realised he wasn't looking at St Paul's at all, but at her.

'You said the bar was quite close,' she reminded him with an exaggerated shiver. She hoped he'd take the hint and move on.

'Not far,' he assured her. 'It's just . . .' But he didn't finish his sentence because just then his words were drowned out by the great wailing sound of a siren tearing through the calm. They looked at each other. An air raid.

Suddenly the familiar sight of searchlight beams criss-crossed the London sky. Maddie looked up, unable to make out any aircraft, but she thought she detected a distant drone beneath the searing siren.

'Here they come,' said Eddie, facing east, his eyes trained on what looked like giant insects caught in the flares. Then came the strafer fire from the big guns below and flashes as artillery shells burst into the air, perforating it with bangs.

The shock of it all suddenly charged through Maddie, and she felt a surge of energy as Eddie grabbed her by the hand.

'We need to get to the shelter at the station,' he shouted over the sirens, although his voice remained calm. He'd probably been in town during the Blitz, thought Maddie. Londoners were a resilient lot and seemed quite unfazed by Hitler's bombs, whereas she, having spent most of the war till now in Oxford, wasn't used to air raids at all. She was frightened. Nevertheless, she was determined not to let her fear show and managed a stiff smile.

They walked briskly. Now they were joined by other pedestrians who'd also been caught on the bridge. A couple of squaddies and their girlfriends were running. A woman in an evening gown was looking around, as if she'd lost someone. From out of nowhere an air raid warden appeared and began to marshal the gathering crowd.

'Get back!' he shouted, his arms waving madly. 'Get over there!'

A blinding flash lit up the night as the first bomb exploded on the other side of the river. It shook the ground beneath their feet. The sky turned red. The shock wave made Maddie stagger. She looked up to see flames shooting into the air. A second bomb followed almost immediately, blasting the other side. This time it hit one of the buildings by the railway station, sending chunks of masonry hurtling through the air. Some landed on the far side of the bridge. Up ahead, she could see three or four people flung flat to the ground, their arms over their heads as bricks, suddenly turned into deadly missiles, hurtled towards them.

'Let's turn back,' said Maddie, tugging at Eddie's hand, as another dull crump on the other side of the river sent tongues of flame spewing into the sky.

'We're over halfway across. We'll shelter under the arches,' yelled Eddie. He seemed determined to march on, despite bucking the trend. An older man with a briefcase bumped into him as he moved off again with Maddie in tow, and a moment later a youth in overalls shouldered him as he ran in the opposite direction.

It was only after yet another explosion lit up the sky and a shower of sparks narrowly missed them that Eddie broke into a run. He dragged Maddie with him. By now her shoes were digging deep into her heels, making her limp, and she knew she was slowing them both down. Snatching back her hand, she bent low, kicked off her stilettoes and picked them up again.

'That's better!' she cried breathlessly, the stone pavement cold against the soles of her feet. But when she looked up, Eddie was nowhere to be seen. 'Eddie! Eddie!'

Suddenly a woman ran screaming towards her, carrying a bundle in her arms. It was a baby. Maddie had no idea whether it was alive or dead.

'Help me! Help me!' cried the woman.

'I . . . I . . . I don't . . .' Maddie stuttered, as the mother shoved the child under her nose. She reached for her flashlight, but realised she must have dropped it, although in the moonlight she could see blood on the shawl. A policeman came to the rescue then and put a comforting arm around the woman. Maddie was so grateful to him. 'Thank you. Thank you,' she cried, but when she turned around to scan the bridge, Eddie was still nowhere to be seen.

'Eddie!' she yelled again as panic gripped her chest.

Another shuddering explosion split the air. This time much closer. A siren wailed behind her and seconds later she found herself diving out of the way as a fire engine sped over the bridge.

All the while the menacing rumble of bomber engines droned overhead. Yet still she ploughed on, barefoot and gasping for breath, her eyes darting this way and that. She was on her own, but it was too late to turn back. She had to reach the other side. She knew she should be afraid, but there was not time for fear. Then suddenly . . .

'Maddie! Maddie!' A voice came out of the smoke, somewhere from behind. It was Eddie's. Blindly she turned back to follow it, the acrid fumes stinging her eyes, and a moment later she felt strong arms sweep her up. She almost collapsed with relief.

'I'm here,' he said, holding her tight. 'There's no time to get to the shelter at the station. We'll have to stay under there.' He was pointing up ahead.

As the darkness and the smoke threatened to swallow them up,

Eddie shepherded her under one of the large arches by the station. Together they huddled against the sooty brickwork as more bombs rained down, exploding within a few hundred yards of them.

Under the arches Maddie suddenly felt safer, but still not safe. Eddie's body pressed hard against hers, shielding her. The nearby goods depot took a direct hit and flaming debris was falling all around. Clamping her hands to her ears to try and block out the roaring and the crashing, she shuddered with every shock wave. Eddie tried to steady her trembling body by stroking her hair and telling her that everything would be all right, but the smoke was so thick that each of her breaths felt it could be her last.

'One, two, three . . .' Eddie suddenly began.

'What are you doing?' she gasped.

'Counting. It takes your mind off the raid. It won't last forever,' he whispered hoarsely in her ear. So she started to count, steadily, and found it helped her keep calm, almost like a prayer. After every few seconds the explosions grew fainter, until when they'd counted to two hundred and ninety-three, the blasts faded to faint crumps somewhere further down the estuary. The German bombers were jettisoning the last of their load. On the count of three hundred and fifty the all-clear sounded.

'It's over,' said Eddie.

Maddie felt the muscles in his arms relax before he stepped back a little.

'Yes,' she replied, mustering a smile.

'You're shaking.'

She nodded. She was no longer cold, but her subsiding fear had left shock in its wake. 'You're safe now. It's going to be all right.'

He held her close once more and she found herself wishing him not to let her go. But when, after a moment, he did, she lifted her head and looked into his eyes.

'Yes,' she replied. His warmth seemed to have melted the icy grip of her shock. 'I do believe it will be.'

Chapter 17

Maddie sat at her desk the next morning, her head in her hands. It ached. Her feet were blistered, too. And her throat was still sore from the acrid smoke. But she was alive and for that she was truly thankful. She'd no idea how many people had lost their lives in last night's raid over London, but one was one too many. Apart from the Almighty, her appreciation had to go to Eddie. If it hadn't been for him, she could have been trapped under some charred roof timbers or pinioned under a collapsed brick wall. Instead, they'd spent the raid in each other's arms and even though it pained her to admit it, as the bombs fell and they held each other close, something had happened between them. When staying alive was the only thing that mattered, Eddie had been there for her and that had been truly special.

He'd been the perfect gentleman, of course. He hadn't taken advantage of her vulnerability. When the raid was over, they'd still made it to the little bar. They'd both downed stiff brandies, rather than the planned cocktails. But the trains were still running, as most had done throughout the Blitz. They eventually made it back to Cockfosters, exhausted and covered in brick dust, but thankfully both still in one piece, at about four o'clock that morning.

Yet with her gratitude to Eddie, there also came a sense of guilt. When she finally rested her head on her pillow in the early hours, it was Eddie, not Max, she thought about as she dropped off to sleep. Yet earlier in the evening, over dinner, he had given her the hope that Max might still be alive. He'd handed her a thread – a slender one, granted, but a thread, nonetheless. While it brought with it a feeling of optimism it also ushered in a growing sense of unease. If Max was still alive, then she would have to suppress any feelings she might have for Eddie. Last night, as he held her in that archway, as the bombs fell and the buildings exploded all around, he had been her rock. He had been there for her when Max could not be. For that she would be forever grateful.

The sound of a knock on her office door bounced around her fragile skull. It made her wince. It was Pru, looking as fresh and prim as a starched white collar. The briefcase carrying the transcription folders was in her hand.

'Oh dear,' she said, the moment Maddie lifted her head. 'Someone didn't get much sleep last night.'

As the Wren laid the folders down on the desk Maddie noticed she was almost smirking. Did she know she'd been out to the Savoy with Eddie? If so, how?

'No, I didn't,' replied Maddie, opening the top folder. There was no reason to tell Pru how she was caught in a raid with him last night. She made light of her wan appearance. 'And I'm not used to Champagne these days.'

'Champagne,' Pru repeated. 'Was it a special occasion?'

Maddie wasn't expecting her to pry even further.

'I suppose it was,' she replied, reflecting that meeting up with an old friend after such a long time was, indeed, a special occasion. Even so, she said no more apart from a guarded 'Thank you.'

Taking the hint Pru headed for the door and was just about to turn the handle when Maddie called her back.

'Pru.'

'Yes?'

'These transcripts.' She pointed at the folder on her desk. 'Who translates them?'

Pru took her hand away from the handle and turned back with a wry smile on her face. 'They're mainly German refugees,' she said.

Maddie remembered what Eddie had told her at the Savoy. People in the armed forces, like him, looked down on the men who'd escaped from Europe, largely Jews. Men like Max.

'The clever types come to us. Some engineers, physicists and the like and they all speak excellent English.' Pru leaned in conspiratorially. 'Some of them are rather dishy, too.'

Maddie forced a sisterly smile, but unbeknown to Pru, her mind had just been plunged into turmoil. These Germans, these secret listeners and translators were people like Max, thought Maddie. If he were alive, he would be perfect for the role: a native German speaker, with a degree in physics and fluent in English. She felt her stomach clench.

'I hope we'll be getting a few more soon,' ventured Pru. 'Things are really hotting up now and I think a few of them are still interned.'

'Interned?' repeated Maddie.

'Camps on the Isle of Man.'

'You mean prison camps?'

'Sort of,' Pru said lightly. 'Once they're vetted, they undergo thorough training before they come here.'

Maddie's mind flicked to a vision of Max clutching at iron bars.

'And, of course, they need to have the right temperament for the work,' pointed out Pru.

Maddie frowned. 'I don't quite . . .'

'Most of them have been through a lot. They hate Herr Hitler and all his cronies and what they might hear down the wires could be rather . . .' she lifted one of her pencilled brows '. . . shocking.'

'Shocking?' repeated Maddie. Major Lansley had used the same word.

'Yes, you know.' Pru shrugged.

But Maddie didn't know. She could only guess that the Wren was referring to the rumours of mass shootings of Jews in Poland and Czechoslovakia. She'd heard her father mention something about "massacres" to Uncle Roly. Such devastating events were bound to have psychological effects on any "listener" with families or friends in the area.

Maddie nodded. 'Thank you,' she said in such a way that Pru knew it was time to leave. As soon as the officer had gone, she took a deep breath to steady herself. The prospect that Max might still be alive had been fresh hope. It shouldn't be too difficult to lay hands on a list of names of the secret listeners on the off chance that Max might be among them. But for the moment, she somehow had to focus on the task in hand.

The first transcript on the pile was of a conversation between two of the longest-serving captives, Generals Steiger and von Schiller. It took place in the library where the pair were perusing the British newspapers by the fire and was prompted by coverage of recent Allied advances. But she put it to one side so she could concentrate all her efforts on preparing for the arrival of Josef Hammler. After typing out some of her notes, she'd just made herself a cup of strong tea on her desk and had downed a large gulp when the telephone rang on the scrambler phone.

The red light was flashing. It was Colonel McKie.

'Ah, Miss Gresham.' Maddie thought he sounded almost breathless with excitement. 'We've just heard Brigadier Hammler is on his way here. He'll be with us very shortly.'

'Today, sir?' She hoped the colonel didn't hear the panic in her voice.

'I know it's ahead of schedule, but he'll need to be assessed first thing tomorrow.'

'Yes, sir,' she said, relieved she still had another few hours to prepare for his first interview.

'Major Lansley will conduct proceedings, but I'd like you to observe.'

'Of course, sir.' She was even more relieved, knowing she was to observe rather than confront the prisoner.

'As a psychologist, you are more adept at predicting how the subject will react in certain situations so that we can, if necessary, adapt our interrogation strategy.'

'Yes, sir. I see.'

'Good,' continued the colonel. 'I'm sure you can tell me what the man had for breakfast just by looking at his shoes. What!?'

Once again, the colonel laughed at his own joke.

'What this man won't know about this infernal secret weapon won't be worth knowing. So, the questions will need to be angled, but I'm sure you'll think of a way to tease what we need out of him.'

'I'll do my best,' returned Maddie, unable, at that very moment, to see the funny side of this opportunity. It was going to take some skilled questioning to understand the workings of this evil man's mind and persuade him to reveal his secrets. It was a tall order to uncover just what destructive forces Hitler planned to unleash on the British population. Yet right now, everyone seemed to be depending on her. She prayed she wouldn't let them down.

*

At precisely 1600 hours the gates of Trent Park swung open for a military bus. It pulled up outside the main entrance to the mansion. Colonel McKie was there to greet his very special guest.

As a guard opened the door of the vehicle, an officer in German Army fatigues emerged. He straightened himself, lifted his gaze to take in the mansion then tugged at his tunic. A batman retrieved a single suitcase from the back.

Maddie, watching from the wings, thought he looked remarkably composed for a man who'd been snatched from his surroundings and brought halfway across Europe to an enemy prison.

'Welcome to Trent Park, Brigadier Hammler,' McKie greeted.

As was customary when a German general arrived, the colonel offered his hand. Hammler's hand, however, remained at his side for a moment until it was suddenly thrust forward in a salute.

'Heil Hitler!' he exclaimed.

The colonel seemed a little taken a back. 'Yes, well,' was all he said as the newest guest was ushered into the mansion.

The exchange simply confirmed to Maddie what she'd feared from the start. It was going to take a lot more than games of billiards and strolls in the park to turn this fanatical Nazi into a compliant prisoner, let alone make him talk.

Chapter 18

'One more step and you're dead!'

The man's voice boomed from underneath the stairs and a shadow suddenly leapt out at Maddie as her foot reached the second tread. She didn't so much scream as bark out her shock. Her hand clutched at her chest, as she stopped in her tracks.

'Harold! Harold! Stop that this minute.' Mrs Pollock emerged from the kitchen to rein in her errant husband. He'd clearly confused Maddie for one of Kaiser Wilhelm's men. ''Ow many times 'ave I told you not to hide under them stairs?' She turned to Maddie. 'Thinks 'e's in the trenches,' she explained shaking her head and wheeling her husband round to face the kitchen door.

Maddie managed a smile. 'That's quite all right,' she replied, trying to calm herself. Harold Pollock may have meant her no harm, but there was still something deeply disconcerting about the way he'd looked at her, as if he'd happily have run her through with a bayonet if one was to hand. All she wanted to do was go upstairs and shut herself in her room.

'You've remembered it's Thursday?' Mrs Pollock reminded her. 'I'm off in a mo.'

She'd forgotten it was bingo night, but it made no difference if her landlady was out. 'I thought I'd just have a quiet evening. I've got a bit of a headache.'

'As you wish,' replied Mrs Pollock cheerfully. 'There's some tongue in the larder if you feel peckish,' she added, reaching for her coat from a peg in the hall.

Once in her room, Maddie drew down the blackout blinds and wrapped the candlewick bedspread around her for warmth to sit on her bed. She needed space to think away from the pressurised atmosphere of Trent Park, but she'd barely plumped up her pillows when a sudden tapping crashed into her thoughts. Her limbs stiffened. Was she imagining it? Mice scuttling along the skirtings, perhaps? But then it came again. Louder this time. Someone was at the door.

'Who's there?' she called, suddenly fearing it might be Harold Pollock.

No reply.

Flinging off the bedspread from around her shoulders, she hurried over to the door and listened for a moment. Nothing. Gingerly, she opened the door slightly but couldn't see anyone. She looked across the landing. All the other doors were shut, and she was just about to close her own when she saw the fingers of a small hand grasping a jamb.

'Sally? Sally is that you?'

The rest of the hand appeared shortly after, then a scuffed shoe and a dirty-grey ankle sock, followed finally by a little girl, clutching a toy rabbit. The thumb from her other hand was firmly inside her mouth, being sucked voraciously.

'Hello,' said Maddie softly. 'Shouldn't you be downstairs?'

As if on cue, Mrs Pollock shouted up the stairs. 'Sally! Sally!'

'She's with me, Mrs P,' Maddie called back to the landlady, who was now dressed in a blue coat and matching hat.

'Will she be all right with you, Miss Gresham?'

To her amazement, Maddie watched Sally's thumb emerge from mouth as the little girl nodded vigorously. Her eyes were as round as buttons.

'She'll be absolutely fine,' she shouted down, then, looking to Sally for confirmation she said: 'Yes?'

'You behave, missy. You 'ear me?' the landlady told her grand-child, whose large eyes now peered down the stairs.

'I'm sure she will,' Maddie said, smiling. 'Have a good evening.' And she wheeled the child inside her room and shut the door. 'You want to stay with me for a while? That's nice.'

Once in her room, Maddie decided it was far too cold for a child, so she put a match to the two-bar gas fire, and it burst into life, but Sally remained by the door, as if she were anxious about venturing further inside.

Maddie's heart suddenly ached. She longed to hug her but didn't want to frighten her. She willed her to speak, but the words seemed to remain stuck on Sally's tongue. 'Why don't you tell Benjy what you want to say?' she asked.

Sally nodded, her unruly curls flopping over her face as she did so. After appearing to confer with the soft toy, she cast a weather eye over the rest of the room until her gaze settled on a jewellery box on top of the chest of drawers.

'Ah, you want to look at my pretty things,' said Maddie with an understanding nod. She rose to her feet once more and walked over to the chest of drawers. The key to her jewellery case was kept in a little tin box nearby. Taking it out, she opened the lid. A garnet ring – a gift from Uncle Roly – was there, along with her pearl earrings, diamante brooch and matching necklace she'd been given for her twenty-first birthday. She hadn't brought anything of real monetary worth with her – not her mother's jewels – just to be on the safe side. One could never be too careful sharing a house with strangers.

Listen to yourself, she thought. These days she seemed to be regarding everything with a suspicious eye. A sudden tug at the hem of her cardigan made her jump, but it was only Sally reminding her that she was waiting.

'Oh yes,' she said, looking down at her with a smile. 'Where were we?' It had suddenly occurred to her that working at Trent Park with all its secrets and subterfuge, with her unease over Dr Baskin's sudden death and a sense she was being watched, she might easily fall prey to a mild form of paranoia.

Chapter 19

A sense of dread weighed heavily on Maddie's shoulders as she made her way to the observation room to meet Major Lansley. She was first to arrive and began pacing the floor of the narrow room, reading and rereading her notes. It felt almost as if she was preparing to do battle with Brigadier Josef Hammler. Her brief had been clear. This "interrogation" came in the guise of a routine welfare assessment. She was not to say anything, merely observe. Even so, she found herself shaking at the prospect of being in the presence of such evil.

'Well, Miss Gresham, are you ready?' Major Lansley stood at the doorway, his lids hiding half his eyes. Before Maddie could reply, the sound of a lock springing back and a steel door creaking open made her flinch. Turning to look through the window, she saw Brigadier Josef Wilhelm Hammler had just entered the interrogation room.

'Let's take a look, shall we?' suggested the major, gesturing to Maddie to step up to the window. A guard escorted the prisoner inside and asked him to sit. The brigadier wore the grey uniform of the Wehrmacht. He'd been awarded the Iron Cross, according to Dr Baskin's note, although she supposed he'd not had time to grab his medals when he was abducted. Entering the room with a ramrod-straight back and his head held high, he stalked in with an air of superiority. Like so many powerful men, it was clear to Maddie that he loved himself. Such personality types always responded well to flattery.

When he took his seat Maddie also remarked the general crossed his legs as well as his arms. Was he being defensive? Or calm and in control? She was about to find out.

As if reading her thoughts, Lansley countered: 'He's clever. More educated than most of them. But above all, he hates Jews. He was ranting about them on the journey over from France.'

All Nazis hated Jews, she knew. But from the major's expression there was more.

'I didn't tell you before,' he went on.

'Tell me what?'

'Most high-ranking Nazis don't have nicknames. It's usually reserved for those in the SS.'

'But he does?'

'Yes,' replied Lansley softly.

'Which is?'

Lansley kept his eyes trained through the glass on the prisoner. 'The Crocodile.'

'The Crocodile,' she repeated. 'Why?'

He turned to Maddie. 'Because he's got a reputation for being cold, calculating and, quite frankly, deadly.'

This last remark shot a chill through Maddie's veins. She suddenly found herself wondering if the man on the other side of the glass had ever killed someone in cold blood. But by the time she'd stepped on her anger and could focus again, the major had left the room. She watched him through the window as he settled himself on a chair opposite the brigadier. A nod was the signal to the engineer in the next room to start recording.

Lansley glanced at the clock on the wall. 'It's ten hundred hours on Tuesday, March 18, 1944. Major Herbert Lansley interviewing Brigadier Josef Hammler.' There was a sharp intake of breath. 'Good morning, Brigadier.'

The prisoner shot him a disdainful glare but remained silent.

Lansley took out his tin containing peppermints and offered him one. He turned away with a look of scorn.

'Welcome to Cockfosters, Herr Brigadier.'

No response.

'You'll find your stay much less spartan than in your previous . . .' He paused, thinking for a softer word than prison. 'Let's say "camp". Here you will have much more freedom.'

The brigadier remained taciturn, scanning the floor or the walls, but not looking Lansley in the eye.

'I believe your great poet Goethe had a saying: "Correction does much, but encouragement does more."'

Maddie felt the hairs stand up on her arms. It was one of Dr Baskin's favourite quotes, and one he'd clearly applied to his strategy for Trent Park.

A snort then, followed by a sneer, then slowly uncrossing his arms and legs, he replied: 'Goethe also said: "None are more hopelessly enslaved than those who falsely believe they are free."'

This Hammler was indeed clever, thought Maddie. Or at least he thought he was.

Lansley scratched the back of his head, as if not sure how to reply, then said: 'Yes, well. Let's not waste each other's time, shall we? I have a number of questions to ask you about your living conditions and routines. They are designed to make your life here easier, Herr Brigadier. So perhaps you could also make my life easier by answering them.'

The major began his spiel, reeling off from his clipboard. 'Is the food to your liking?'

Silence.

'Do you have enough reading material?'

Another silence.

'What about exercise?'

The silence continued. Hammler simply sat with one leg

121

bouncing up and down, as if impatient for the interview to end. Or was it his mounting anger?

Finally the major asked: 'And do you receive letters from your family?'

At the mention of his family Hammler suddenly seemed to explode. He sprang forward and hit the table with a balled fist, sending the major jerking back in shock.

'I have no family,' he screamed. His face was suddenly livid. It was as if, Maddie observed, a switch had been flicked in his brain. The Crocodile had opened his jaws and snapped.

'Point taken,' replied Lansley calmly, although his rhythm had been broken.

Maddie remembered Dr Baskin's notes mentioned a wife and children, but no more. She wondered if they were still alive.

'Very well,' said the major, relieved that he'd finally reached the end of his checklist. 'Is there anything you would like to make your stay more enjoyable, Herr Brigadier?'

He seemed more composed now. A smile appeared from nowhere, then, and his shoulders heaved in a silent laugh as he pressed a finger to his lips in thought. 'Perhaps,' he said.

'Yes?' replied Lansley.

'Perhaps a woman.'

Surprise shot through the major's voice. 'A woman, Herr Brigadier?'

'Yes,' he replied, a smile hovering on his lips. 'I miss female company you see. It's been a few months and a man has needs.'

Maddie noticed he smiled again then. A sort of unsettling leer. Suddenly her pen began to shake in her hand and an ugly feeling thumped against her chest. She watched the major's reaction. He'd suddenly turned a pale shade of grey.

'Yes, w . . . well,' he stammered in a very English way. 'We'll . . . We'll have to see about that,' was all he could say. Soon after, admitting defeat, he beat a retreat as quickly as he could.

Back in the observation room, Maddie was finding it hard to

remain detached and professional. Watching Hammler had tested all her training, even though she hadn't been face to face with him. The glass window had shielded her. With the exasperation she was feeling right now, it was just as well. She had to remain calm.

'The man clearly has anger issues. Probably verging on a psychopath,' remarked the major back in the observation room. 'Wouldn't you agree, Miss Gresham?'

She nodded. 'Possibly, sir,' she replied. 'He has definite mood swings, and his aggressive behaviour will present problems when he is around the other prisoners, in my opinion.'

'You're right. We'll have to see if he mixes, won't we? I very much doubt it.'

Maddie considered what might make a man so full of hatred: failed relationships, a traumatic event, a combination. She needed to uncover the root cause of his behaviour to use it to her advantage. FIND A WEAK SPOT, Dr Baskin had written. On reflection, perhaps she just had.

Chapter 20

France

November 1942

The Lysander landed at the small makeshift airstrip on the Brittany peninsula in the dead of a November night. The moon was high and the gales buffeting the French coast for the past three days had finally passed. The sky was now cloudless and flame torches marked the landing strip. Nevertheless, the plane was almost half an hour late for the rendezvous. Four men were waiting anxiously in the copse nearby – three Resistance members and an RAF pilot shot down over Nantes three months before.

The Resistance men – all French – were running the Comet Line. Their task was to evacuate shot-down pilots and soldiers back to Britain. It was dangerous work. Many had already been caught and imprisoned, or executed, by the Nazis. Now, with each passing minute the men became more concerned that they'd have to abort their mission.

At the sound of a low hum of an engine in the distance their eyes looked upwards until the noise swelled to a roar. Relief soon surged over their faces as the aircraft touched down and came bouncing to a precarious halt a few metres away. Bracing themselves against the backdraft of the deafening propellers they raced towards the plane's fixed ladder. Only one of them began to climb in.

'Johnson is not 'ere!' yelled one of the Frenchmen up to the cockpit.

'He hasn't made it?' replied the navigator.

'*Non.*'

The pilot glanced back to the wide seat at the rear. If they'd originally planned on getting two airmen out it would be a shame to return with only one. 'Is there anyone else?'

'This chap,' came a shout from halfway up the ladder. It was from the downed flyer, as he pointed to one of the Resistance men. 'We could take him. He's Jewish, God help the poor bugger!'

'Climb aboard!' called the pilot, beckoning to the bewildered man standing below. 'Then let's get out of here!'

There was no time for goodbyes. The man known as Jean-Baptiste Vallade scrambled up the ladder and squeezed himself into the cramped bucket seat at the rear of the aircraft alongside the rescued RAF pilot. The other Resistance men faded into the darkness.

The propeller spun. The engine roared. The cold bit into his legs and hands and he could barely move in the cramped seat, but Max knew he was flying to freedom. It was the best feeling in the world and within three minutes the matt-black Lysander had gained enough height to turn west out over the Atlantic with a course set for England.

*

The rain had been ceaseless since the ferry docked at some remote island off the north-west coast of England – Max didn't know its name – three days before. The crossing was short but rough. Many of the passengers suffered from seasickness and had retched over the side, himself included, as the waves lashed the vessel. He'd only been on the mainland for a few days when he was told he was being transferred. Someone said something about him being an "enemy alien". There'd been a misunderstanding. His papers said he was French, but he'd told the truth to the authorities – that he was really German – and, in the eyes of the War Office, that meant they should treat him with caution. He'd been bundled into a truck and driven to a port. He'd never expected to be banished to another island, but one of the other men, a German like him, told him they were heading for an internment camp on the Isle of Man. The name was foreign to him, but he'd heard of Alcatraz in America and imagined an island prison surrounded by shark-infested waters.

At the port they formed a line and were marched by the guards along a promenade. On one side it was lined with elegant villas, while on the other lay the sea. Another internee told him that before the war they were boarding houses, where holidaymakers based themselves for a week or more sunbathing, walking or playing golf. What a world away that all must seem to the islanders, Max thought, now that the road was cordoned off with barbed wire and the only visitors were ones who weren't welcome. A few islanders had even come out to jeer as the men were marched to the camp. A young woman shouted something angrily as they passed. In her arms she held a small girl who was waving a Union Jack at them. The child made him think of Greta's little daughter, Lena. He wondered what had happened to them.

Max's roommate in the seafront boarding house where they were interned was also a German and Jewish. Ernst Lehmann had not been forced to flee his homeland like most of the other émigrés. He was already lecturing in London when war broke out. He had, however, left his new wife, Rosa, in Germany and his fears for her grew daily.

Max thought of Maddie then and wondered what she was doing. Had she forgotten him? Had she found someone new? Of course she had. She was beautiful and clever. Despite the promise they'd made to each other, she would have moved on with her life. As they lay in their bunks in the darkness that night, listening to the rain that sounded as if someone were hurling handfuls of gravel at the glass, the men's thoughts remained with their loved ones.

'The English have no idea,' said Ernst. 'The horror stories I've heard coming out of the East.'

Max had heard them, too. He found himself pausing out of respect for the thousands of Jews he knew to be dead already. 'I want to fight so badly,' he said finally.

'There is the Pioneer Corps,' replied Ernst after a short silence.

'What's that?'

'A regiment of men like us mainly. The lucky ones who got out. They're not allowed to carry arms, but they can work with their hands.'

Max turned on his side. 'The Nazis make the French do that.' He knew of Frenchmen who'd been rounded up and transported to hellish munitions factories in the East to power Hitler's war machine.

'Ah,' said Ernst. 'But these men aren't slaving for some tyrant. They are working for Mr Churchill and standing up for us Jews.'

'You want to join then?' asked Max.

There was no hesitation. 'What do you think?'

Chapter 21

Trent Park

March 1944

Maddie was working late. She'd decided to transcribe the remainder of Dr Baskin's profile of Brigadier Hammler to see if it turned up any more information that might help in some way. She was tired and anxious and her movements reflected it. Tugging at the cabinet drawer she located the file and seized it with such vigour that she dislodged a piece of paper. The sheet fell slowly to the floor, and she didn't even need to bend down to recognise the familiar shorthand scribble. It appeared to be a note, written in Dr Baskin's nightmarish scrawl.

Intrigued, she picked it up and returned to her desk. As far as she knew, she'd transcribed all of his notes, apart from a few extraneous ones that were filed separately. The top drawer still seemed jammed at the back, nevertheless she managed to open it halfway and extricated her reading glasses – the ones she only needed when she was trying to decipher Dr Baskin's writing – and hooked them on. The date at the head of the paper was January

24, 1944. *Four days before his death,* she thought. What's more, it was addressed to her.

> *Dear Miss Gresham,*
>   *I did not wish to burden you with this, but certain events have recently occurred that have made me think I ought to tell you . . .*

And there the note ended. Not only did it end, but a line also scored through all the script. Dr Baskin had obviously had second thoughts about sending it to her. But what had prompted him to write such an ominous message in the first place?

*

Major Lansley had instructed Maddie to send her initial assessment on Brigadier Hammler straight to Colonel McKie. Sitting in his office, she'd been waiting on tenterhooks for his verdict.

'Well, we knew it wasn't going to be easy,' he concluded, lifting up the thin folder, then slapping it down on the desk again. 'This fellow holds the key to Hitler's secret weapons, Miss Gresham. We know that much.'

He was pacing up and down as he spoke. There was both agitation and frustration in his voice. Then he turned to face her. 'From now on it's all systems go,' he said. 'We need to step up our efforts.'

Just exactly what the colonel meant, Maddie wasn't really sure. Short of pulling out the brigadier's fingernails, which would of course be contrary to the whole philosophy of Trent Park, she saw little else that could be done, apart from applying constant pressure on him and hoping he'd feel the need to talk to his fellow officers.

'Yes, sir,' she said, out of habit. But another matter was troubling her, and she took the opportunity to air her concerns.

'You may go, Miss Gresham,' said the colonel, seeing her remaining standing by his desk.

'Sir?' she said, a question in her voice.

'What is it, Miss Gresham?' By now McKie had resumed his seat. He didn't bother to look up.

'It's about Dr Baskin.'

'Oh?'

Now she had his full attention. 'I found this in his notes,' she said, laying the piece of paper on his desk.

His eyes ran over it. 'I can't make head nor tail of it,' he retorted.

Maddie retrieved it. 'It says he wanted to tell me something.'

'Tell you what?' McKie was clearly irritated.

She paraphrased. 'He says he didn't wish to burden me, but certain events made him think he ought to tell me . . .'

'Tell you what?' he repeated.

'That's it, sir. I don't know.' She shook her head. 'I'm worried he was in some sort of trouble, sir.'

'Trouble? What sort of trouble?' The colonel, as far as she could see, was being deliberately obtuse.

'He wrote the note just a few days before he was found dead, sir. Doesn't that strike you as worrying?'

The colonel made an odd sort of noise, like a growl. 'Dr Baskin had a heart attack. He died in his sleep, as we all would wish to. The matter is closed, Miss Gresham.'

Maddie bit her lip, then said, very reluctantly: 'Yes, sir.'

She had no choice but to drop the subject and return to her office. Her frustration at the colonel's obstinacy was soon put aside, however, when she discovered someone else was already there.

'Good morning, Miss Gresham,' came a voice from what Maddie had always assumed was a cupboard. She was hanging her coat on a hook when she turned to see the closet door open and a familiar figure stepping out of it.

'Private Briggs! Good morning,' she replied.

'I'm sorry if I startled you,' replied the doe-eyed young woman. She was edging towards the desk clutching a file.

'No. Not at all,' Maddie replied, wondering what on earth Briggs might have found of interest in the cupboard. She fixed her with a puzzled look, waiting for an explanation.

'Didn't Colonel McKie tell you, ma'am?' asked Briggs as soon as she interpreted the bemused look on Maddie's face.

'Tell me what?' she asked.

'That I'm your secretary, miss. And that—' she jerked her head towards what Maddie had always thought was a cupboard, although she had never looked inside '—is my office.'

Maddie felt herself breathe in sharply, but she breathed out with a smile. 'That's great news,' she said, genuinely meaning it. 'I can really do with some help. I'm getting rather snowed under. You couldn't have come at a better time,' she muttered, thinking out loud about Brigadier Hammler.

Briggs nodded. 'I know, ma'am. It's getting busy out there.'

'What do you mean?' asked Maddie, moving towards her desk.

'More lads from the Pioneer Corps arrived last night. They went round the back, to the barracks.'

'Ah yes,' said Maddie. Those would be the new recruits; although Briggs could never be told that. As far as she, and most other personnel working at Trent Park were concerned, the new intake was here to help out with the expected influx of German prisoners, carrying out mundane tasks like maintenance and cleaning. They might even have thought that themselves, because their role was so secret. Perhaps this was all part of Colonel McKie's plan to crank up the gears.

'Tea, miss?' asked Briggs.

'That would be lovely, thank you.' A good, strong brew would set her up nicely for the piles of paperwork teetering in the wire basket on her desk.

Maddie assumed her role would be to assess each one of the new recruits in due course and look out for any psychological problems they might experience. She recalled Major Lansley's words when he'd first informed her about the listeners: 'We need these fellows profiled to ensure they're all solid types.'

'Solid types?' she'd repeated.

'Men who can take knocks on the chin and come back fighting.'

The rumours, she'd heard, the ones of mass shootings of Jewish men, women and children in the East – the rumours she couldn't believe at first because they were too awful – were now known to be true. She'd seen the transcripts herself. Some of the German officers talked about the killings over brandy in the evenings, or as they played cards. One or two expressed regret at the deaths of Jews. Several, however, clearly delighted in it; gloating over the way they'd dispensed with human life so efficiently.

The impact of reading the testimonies had been bad enough on her, but for those listeners who'd lost loved ones . . . She knew such devastating events were bound to have psychological effects on any of the men with families or friends who had been slaughtered.

'Yes,' she told Briggs as she stirred her tea, while scanning the paperwork in front of her. 'We're going to need all the help we can get.'

The previous evening's transcripts were at the top of the pile. Opening the file, she pictured the scene as she read the text. In the comfort of the drawing room "prison", Generals von Birkel and Koenig were raking over last year's defeat in north Africa. Both had been furious that so many German generals had surrendered. Maddie smiled wryly as she imagined von Birkel, pacing the room and venting his wrath.

Birkel: I'd rather have blown my brains out than surrender. What cowards! What traitors!

Koenig: Yes. No sense of honour.

That much Maddie already knew. But yesterday's listener's transcript had picked up something much more interesting

– something that could prove to be crucial. Her heart began to race when she realised what she was reading.

Koenig: Have you met Hammler yet?

Birkel: Not yet. And you?

Koenig: No. He's refusing to leave his room. He smashed a chair yesterday. (Pause.) The Crocodile.

Birkel: Yes, I heard they call him that. He has a temper. He did well at Peenemünde.

Koenig: Yes. That's why he was promoted.

Birkel: Ah, yes. The Vengeance rocket.

Koenig: No wonder the British were keen to get their hands on him. He won't talk, of course.

Birkel: Of course not, but it'll be interesting for us to hear from him how things are coming along on that score. There was a rumour about a flying torpedo with an automatic guidance system.

Koenig: Sounds impressive. Just think of the havoc that could wreak.

Both men laughed.

A cold shiver ran through Maddie. It was a warning – a warning delivered in such a chilling and callous way that she had to read it again. *A flying torpedo with an automatic guidance system.* This was it: the deadly secret weapon that Hitler was developing.

The RAF raid on the missile factory at Peenemünde on the Baltic coast the summer before had only been a partial success, Maddie had been told. The listeners had picked up some of the intelligence when two generals had discussed the launch sites. Much of the base had been destroyed but the Germans had managed to salvage some of their deadliest weapons. Colonel McKie said they needed to find out more, then target where the new ones were being built before they could be unleashed over British towns and cities. She remembered his ominous words exactly. 'It's a race against time.'

She looked up from the file. 'A race against time,' she repeated out loud.

'Beg pardon?' said Briggs, standing at the filing cabinet.

Maddie blinked. 'Sorry, I was talking to myself. Leave this with me but I'll need you to type up a memo.'

'Yes, Miss Gresham,' replied Briggs.

Just then the telephone on the desk rang and the red light flashed. It was Colonel McKie. 'I'd better take this alone,' said Maddie, as she picked up the receiver. Briggs retreated into her tiny office and shut the door.

'Ah, Miss Gresham. You've got the latest transcript.'

'Yes, sir.'

'It's the breakthrough we've been wanting. It looks like this Vengeance weapon, this V-1, will soon be unleashed. Let's capitalise on it. I'd like to see a list of approaches to interrogation on my desk as soon as possible.'

Chapter 22

Long Barton Manor, the Cotswolds

The crack of gunfire blasted against Maddie's eardrums and split the freezing air around her as dozens of pheasants soared overhead. As with all arial bombardments, precision was most desirable and to that end several dead birds rained down from the leaden sky. These poor, beautiful creatures were reared to die and not designed to fly far. Yet here were six grown men armed with Purdeys, who even employed beaters to thrash the undergrowth and terrify the birds into flight so they could take pot shots at them. Somehow they called it "sport". It was a very uneven match.

She sat a little way back from the shooting party, out of the biting spring wind, in the lee of a hill. Perched on a shooting stick and trussed up in a sheepskin coat and headscarf, she'd been reluctantly persuaded to watch the ghastly spectacle. This is what it must have been like on the Somme, she mused, only a thousand times worse. She thought of poor Mr Pollock at the boarding house and how the experience had turned him into a volatile wreck, ready to lash out at anyone who invaded his home. Was it really necessary to gun down defenceless animals when defenceless civilians were also being gunned down across the Channel?

If Maddie had known her father was holding a shoot on the estate that weekend, she'd never have come home; she'd have postponed her leave. Long Barton Manor was supposed to offer peace and quiet; a haven away from the pressure cooker that was Trent Park. She'd made the journey because she needed space to think. Colonel McKie had tasked her with finding a way to use the latest intelligence from the generals to make Hammler talk, but she'd just walked into this killing spree.

After the excited dogs had retrieved the dead birds, the carcasses were laid in rows on the ground to be collected and counted. Everyone – the shooters, the loaders, the beaters and two of the hardier ladies who braved the cold – came to inspect and admire the bloody booty.

A few minutes later, the gamekeeper ordered the shooting brake to take the party back down to the manor. The beaters and loaders followed behind the vehicle with the haul, which was to be deposited in the game larder.

Tea was something Maddie knew had to be endured rather than enjoyed. The shooters' wives were local ladies who did "their bit" for the war effort: directing and organising, while occasionally involving themselves in practicalities such as knitting scarves, or writing letters to the troops.

'Maddie, dear, what an unexpected pleasure,' said Lady Pendleton, when everyone had spruced up and assembled in the drawing room for sandwiches and scones by a roaring log fire. 'What brings you home?'

'I took a little leave,' she replied, perched on the window seat in the large bay. She'd rather hoped no one would bother with her if she sat as far away from the hearth as possible.

'Doing your bit, are you?'

Maddie nodded. 'We all must, Lady Pendleton,' she said, tilting her head and coaxing her lips into a smile.

'Quite right,' she said, adding with a barb, 'if one is still single. Georgina, of course, has just given birth to her first child. She and Giles intend to have a very large family.'

Georgina Pendleton, Maddie remembered from her youth, had once played the piano for Queen Mary. Lady Pendleton probably had visions of her daughter producing her very own orchestra.

Mrs Gilbert Hanson and Mrs Oscar Delapole, teacups and saucers in hand, joined in the conversation, which soon progressed to whose daughter was engaged to whom.

'And when might we hear some good news about your own situation, my dear?' asked Mrs Hanson.

Maddie faltered. Talk of marriage always made her beat a hasty retreat. 'Oh, do forgive me,' she said. 'I need to speak to my uncle, urgently.'

Much to her relief, a small, white-haired man had just walked in the room. Sir Roland Fulford was a good deal older than her father. His moustache was waxed to a point at each end, and he very often twiddled it when thinking or if there was a lull in conversation. He wasn't actually her uncle, but her godfather and was something in the civil service, although she hadn't a clue what he did. Someone once called him a Whitehall mandarin, which made him sound like a duck. For some reason, he thought he had every right to voice an opinion about her education and social life. But right now, she felt his conversation might be preferable to the female guests'.

'Hello, Uncle Roly,' she said.

'Ah, my dear Maddie.'

She glanced at the tumbler of whisky already cupped in his hand. 'I'm glad you've got something to warm you up,' she said with a smile.

His shoulders bounced in a chuckle. 'And so have you, from what I hear.'

Maddie was uncertain. 'I'm sure I don't know what you mean, Uncle Roly.'

He twiddled his moustache and drew closer, lowering his voice. 'I heard you were spotted recently.'

'Spotted?' Maddie thought that made her sound like a butterfly or a bird.

'Dinner at the Savoy, eh? In the company of a certain Flight Lieutenant Windlesham.' He touched the side of his nose with his forefinger and winked.

'How . . .?'

'I have my spies, you know,' he replied gleefully.

Maddie felt herself colour as she recalled being surrounded by all those prying eyes sweeping the dining room for the merest whiff of gossip or, better still, scandal. And, of course, there'd been that older woman in the silver dress she'd noticed staring at her. She should've realised that word would get back to the shires.

'We are friends,' she conceded. 'Nothing more.'

He nodded, adjusting his monocle. 'That's all right, my dear. It's high time you settled down instead of having a job. No man wants to marry a bluestocking.' (He said the last sentence as if the words were burning his tongue.) 'Besides, nice girls like you shouldn't be involved in that sort of thing.'

Uncle Roly made it sound as though she were a nightclub hostess or a stripper at one of those sleazy Soho bars. *What sort of thing?* she was tempted to ask, but on reflection, she thought that might be inviting trouble.

'Oh, there's Lady Houghton, if you'll excuse me,' she said, smiling politely, then with no intention at all of speaking to the old dowager in the corner, she left the room. Now that Uncle Roly was *au fait* with her liaison with Eddie, it wouldn't be long before every blueblood, from Cheltenham to Chipping Campden, also knew. The dashing flight lieutenant was, after all, a "good catch" as Lady Pendleton and, of course, Ruth would say. But worse was still to come.

The prospect of dinner loomed and as she applied her make-up in her bedroom, the thought of having to make polite conversation about this year's hunt ball or the reorganisation of the ATS over jugged hare, seemed almost unsufferable. Even more frustrating was the fact that she really hadn't managed to grab more than a half a dozen words with her father since she returned home because he'd been so busy hosting his frightful guests.

From the hall below the sonorous notes of the large grandfather clock struck six, summoning everyone to assemble for pre-dinner drinks in the drawing room.

'Round two,' she muttered to herself, checking her evening gown in the cheval mirror once more.

Proceeding down the oak staircase a few moments later, she expected there to be a steady hum of voices and the odd guffaw from Sir Charles Ashton whose laugh was notoriously loud. But no. All was quiet. She entered the drawing room to find it quite empty and, puzzled, turned to see Mason, the butler, stalking blindly across the hall carrying a decanter on a tray and seemingly unaware of her presence.

'Mason.'

His head turned in her direction. 'Miss Madeleine.' He'd been with the family since she was a child.

'Where is everyone? I thought dinner was at seven.'

'It is, miss. Sir Michael is waiting for you,' he told her with a gracious tilt of his balding head.

Maddie was taken aback. 'Really?'

Mason gestured her towards the study, and she found her father sitting by a cosy fire. He rose when she entered and she saw he wasn't wearing a tuxedo, but a smoking jacket.

'I thought we'd eat in here tonight, darling,' he told her in answer to her questioning gaze.

'But what about everyone else?' She turned towards the door as Mason set down the decanter on a small table beside Sir Michael's winged chair. 'Lady Pendleton and Uncle Roly and . . .'

Her father – a tall, distinguished-looking man with wings of silver hair – smiled. 'One of the perks of being a senior civil servant is that work can always provide the perfect excuse. I cancelled dinner, saying I had a call scheduled with the PM this evening.'

Maddie smiled. 'So, it's just us?' She felt the tension leave her.

'You seem a little on edge, darling. Are you still upset about Dr Baskin?' asked her father.

'What?' Her head cracked up. What had he heard? Had someone been talking?

'Don't look so scandalised, darling. Your letter said that he'd passed away and I know how . . .'

'Sorry,' she said, quickly realising her mistake. She'd mentioned the doctor's death, but certainly nothing about his connection to Trent Park. 'I'm fine – really, Daddy.' She was snapping. At her father. The truth was the circumstances surrounding Dr Baskin's death had unsettled her. Like a stone in her shoe, the doubt had begun to niggle at her. It was playing on her mind, but there was no one she could tell. Colonel McKie had been deliberately terse, so she had nowhere else to turn.

'Come and sit down.' Her father was pointing to the chair opposite him as the butler poked the fire into life once more. 'Just you and me, like old times. Mason will get you a drink and then we can have a good chat over supper. Cook has made you one of your favourites. Shepherd's pie. I thought we could eat it on our laps in here.'

There was something so comforting about nursery food. 'I'd like that very much,' she said, settling herself down and holding her palms to the blaze. 'A sherry, please, Mason.'

Since her mother's death, Maddie had grown much closer to her father. Before, both her parents had been aloof, as she accepted many parents of children born to her class were. 'Seen and not heard,' was a favourite maxim in the household, as she recalled. In fact, her relationship with her mother had been rather like a game of pass the parcel, Mummy being the prize. But in order to reach her, one had to take off the layers of wrapping paper and ribbon that surrounded her to find the real mother inside.

But she'd died, quite unexpectedly, from influenza, before the music stopped.

After that, her father had looked to her for solace, finding in Maddie a sort of soulmate he didn't know existed before. She, in turn, discovered a new ally. As her mother died before she officially "came out" she managed to persuade Sir Michael she shouldn't have to endure the usual tortuous twists of the debutante chicane; that the Season really wasn't for her and she didn't have to go through the rigmarole – or vast expense – of being presented to the king and queen at court. Instead, she gently cajoled him into allowing her to take the academic route. It had proved remarkably easy. Her father had always loved his books and when Maddie was offered a place at Oxford, he seemed genuinely delighted.

'So, I hear you're enjoying yourself,' he said with a wink, as Mason handed her a schooner of sherry a few moments later.

'Ah,' she said. Uncle Roly had already got to him. She'd suspected as much. She waited until Mason had shut the door behind him. 'Flight Lieutenant Windlesham and I went out to dinner, that's all,' she told him. Of course, she couldn't disclose they worked together at Trent Park. That would be breaking the Official Secrets Act. She recalled the man with the pistol.

Sir Michael sipped his whisky. 'As long as you don't end up getting hurt, my darling,' he told her. 'But I suppose you're a fair judge of character.'

She left out a laugh. 'I'm a psychologist, Daddy, so I tend to go deeper than most when it comes to analysing a person's temperament.'

Sir Michael also laughed. 'Touché,' he agreed, raising his glass to her. 'It's just that I know you must find it hard sometimes, as I do, not having your mother around. I miss her terribly. Everyone needs someone to fight their corner, to be on their side. Someone they can count on in times of crisis, even if it's just for a chat, or a walk or the occasional supper to help one relax. God knows, we all need to let our hair down now and again. I just want you to know I'm always here for you, Maddie.'

His words offered the comfort she hadn't quite realised she needed so badly. He was lending her a shoulder to cry on and it came as a huge relief to know it was there. Rising suddenly, she went over to her father's chair and planted a kiss on his forehead, taking him quite by surprise.

'What was that for?' he chortled, rubbing his forehead.

'For being there, Daddy,' she told him. 'I want you to know that I appreciate you.'

Unbeknown to Sir Michael, he'd also just planted the seeds of an idea in her head.

Chapter 23

Trent Park

The main briefing room at Trent Park was a sort of nondescript, whitewashed space in one of the new buildings. It had a low ceiling, and a blackboard ran across half the width of one of the walls. It was also very cold and even though Colonel McKie had ordered a kerosene heater, Maddie's breath billowed out like smoke from the colonel's pipe as she spoke.

As well as the colonel, Major Lansley and Major Podesta had been summoned to listen to her proposal. Eddie was also present. The men sat at a long table in a rather intimidating row in front of her, the lingering scent of peppermint wafting around Major Lansley offering a rather pleasant olfactory counterpoint to the usual pungent tobacco.

'So, Miss Gresham, Major Lansley says you've come up with an interesting strategy to help us not with just Hammler, but for all of the Jerries. We're all ears,' the colonel began, glancing first to his left, then right.

Maddie had prepared well. The idea that had come to her at her home at Long Barton Manor was taking shape. After spending the evening with her father, she'd gone to bed quite early and replayed in her mind their conversation. Something he'd said struck a particular chord. *Everyone needs someone to fight their corner, to be on their side. Someone they can count on in times of crisis, even if it's just for a chat, or a walk or the occasional supper to help one relax.* Thanks to Dr Baskin's revolutionary ideas, those principles had already been applied to the generals at Trent Park. They were all allowed their batmen to look after their needs and already took regular walks in the grounds. They had their own shop for sundry items and received a visit from a tailor, who saw to their uniforms each week. Maddie had recalled her encounter with the van in the drive.

Most people responded well to being shown kindness and consideration, but from reading the transcripts, Maddie had come to the conclusion that some of them regarded five-star treatment as their absolute right. Of course, many wouldn't contemplate the possibility Hitler might actually lose the war. The British were only treating them well because they were afraid of what might happen after a Nazi victory. It's what the likes of von Birkel and Koenig had come to expect from their Trent Park captors. But she suspected their egos craved even more and Brigadier Hammler probably had one of the biggest of them all.

'Their arrogance demands respect,' Maddie told her small audience, 'but they want something else. They want status.'

'Status?' repeated Colonel McKie.

'Yes. As prisoners they've lost their power, so now they long for social acceptance among people they consider to be in their own class. That's why having Eddie play the role of Lord Frobisher, wining and dining them, is proving effective.' She looked at Eddie as she spoke. 'Short of releasing them into the drawing rooms of English society, where they clearly feel they should be, it's the next best thing.'

Major Podesta flashed his white teeth but looked bemused. 'So, what's this about, Miss Gresham?'

Maddie cleared her throat. 'I've come up with a suggestion

designed to extract even more useful information from our German officers and Brigadier Hammler, in particular.'

Podesta, folding his arms, smirked. 'Where's the rack?' he heckled.

'Carry on, Miss Gresham,' urged the colonel, throwing the American a disapproving scowl.

Not to be put off her stride, Maddie stuck out her chin.

'In summary, gentlemen, the addition of female company to interact socially with the generals would make them feel much more at ease.'

Podesta, lighting a cigarette, shook his head and laughed. 'So, what are you proposing? We bug a brothel?'

This remark raised a chuckle from the colonel, too, but Maddie remained stony-faced.

She continued: 'A woman on equal social terms could host dinner parties, organise outings to galleries . . .'

Suddenly she heard Eddie's voice breaking in. She hadn't dared look at him until now, afraid he might be angry with her for going over his head with her proposal. 'Surely you're not actually thinking of showing them the sights?'

Podesta dragged on his cigarette and joined in. 'A trip round the Tower of London might be appropriate.'

'Why not?' she asked defiantly. 'A tour of London, for example, would show them that most of our great landmarks remain unscathed by their bombs.'

'Not a bad idea,' said the colonel with a nod.

Maddie ploughed on. 'All these men have mothers and wives, sisters and daughters and yet many of them have been deprived of female company for several months if not years.'

'I wouldn't be too sure about that,' interjected Podesta once more, with a flash of his white teeth. This time he was ignored. As for Eddie – Maddie didn't dare look at him while she was talking for fear of being turned into a pillar of salt like Lot's wife.

'And do you have any particular ladies in mind for this venture,

Miss Gresham?' asked Colonel McKie.

Maddie took a deep breath. 'Yes, sir,' she replied sticking out her chin. 'I am volunteering to become Lady Frobisher.'

As she scanned the thoughtful faces before her, Maddie thought the silence seemed interminable. Had she overstepped the line? After all, the colonel, Major Podesta and Eddie were, by their very nature, conservative. But she knew that other agencies were using women as couriers, interrogators, decoys and even Special Operations Executive agents. Might MI19 also be willing to take chances and break new ground. This time, had she gone too far?

Major Lansley spoke first. 'From a psychological viewpoint, Miss Gresham has made a strong argument. Many of the generals must miss female company.'

Podesta winked at Eddie and laughed. 'I'll say.'

'Refined female company,' added the major. 'And of course, there's Hammler. The others loathe him or fear him, or both. He's very isolated at the moment. And he did ask Lansley for a woman, as I recall.' Another laugh from Podesta. 'He might respond well.'

The mere mention of the Crocodile's name made the blood rush to Maddie's feet. He would be her biggest challenge, but one she couldn't shy away from. Given time, and persuasion, she believed there was a chance he might talk. She nodded her thanks to Lansley.

By now the colonel had taken out his pipe and was already puffing away, thoughtfully. 'Well, that's all very interesting Miss Gresham, but . . .'

Maddie had been dreading this moment: hearing that small, three-letter word that could destroy her idea. She braced herself for humiliation.

Colonel McKie pointed at her then with the stem of his pipe. 'You really think you could soften them up, Miss Gresham? Use your feminine wiles?'

Podesta frowned as he stubbed out his cigarette in a nearby ashtray.

'Haven't you already assessed some of these guys? Wouldn't they recognise you?' he asked.

'No, major, I haven't. So far I've only watched assessments from the observation room.' She shot a look at Major Lansley who confirmed her statement with a nod.

'Anyone got anything to say on the subject?' asked the colonel. 'Windlesham, you're very quiet.' He aimed the stem of his pipe at Eddie, who had remained remarkably detached throughout the exchange. 'Miss Gresham would, after all, be your wife, so you should have some say in the matter.'

Eddie, who had been sitting rather quietly, Maddie noted, now shifted in his seat and his face, which had been neutral throughout, twitched a restrained smile. 'I think Miss Gresham would be perfect in the role,' he agreed. 'Charming, intelligent, attractive and already duplicitous. A good combination for a spy.'

Maddie wasn't sure if Eddie thought her duplicity was aimed at him. 'I'll take that as a compliment, Flight Lieutenant.'

Colonel McKie leaned forward with an arched brow. 'So, Windlesham, you're saying you'd be happy to take this woman to be your unlawfully wedded wife?' He seemed most amused.

Eddie raked his fingers through his hair. He didn't seem to appreciate the joke. Nonetheless, he looked at Maddie and smiled at her before addressing his remark to the colonel.

'I would be, sir. We could entertain the generals together and put them at their ease. Their guard may come down even more in a lady's presence. I can see a lot of merit in the idea.'

The colonel tapped his pipe on the rim of a nearby ashtray, seemingly satisfied by the arguments for Maddie's new role, but then his expression suddenly changed. 'Really?' he said after a steep second. 'Well, I'm afraid I can't.' He turned to Maddie. 'No offence, Miss Gresham, but I think it's quite a ludicrous idea. Getting information about the secret weapon from Hammler is of course our priority, but it's not women's work.' He turned to Eddie. 'Windlesham, how's Lord Frobisher getting on with him?'

Eddie scratched the back of his head. 'Hammler's going to be a tough nut to crack, sir. Most of the generals steer clear of him, and, as the major said, he keeps himself to himself. From what I can see, he's not mixing. Spends most of his time knocking eight bells out of the punchbag in the gymnasium.'

McKie harrumphed. 'Better that than another man, but we know what he's like. What do they call him?' He narrowed his eyes in thought. 'The Crocodile? Calm one minute, then snapping the next. And I really can't have a pretty young thing like Miss Gresham put at risk.' His frown was now directed at Maddie. 'I could never live with myself if I thought I'd put you in harm's way.'

'But, sir!'

Maddie was shocked at the colonel's attitude, but he stopped any further protest with an upraised hand.

'Lord Frobisher is doing an excellent job as it is, and we don't want to upset the apple cart,' he told her. 'I know you are well intentioned, but what you're proposing would have as much effect as painting the Forth Bridge with a toothbrush.'

Turning his attention to Eddie, he added: 'Keep up the good work, Windlesham. You're still a bachelor and you'll stay that way.'

Chapter 24

Maddie returned to her office still smarting from her humiliation. She should have expected her idea to be rejected. Even though Major Lansley and Eddie had been on her side, she was never going to have a fair hearing. She was a woman. A young one, too. And it was a man's world. She recalled Uncle Roly's words: *No man wants to marry a bluestocking.*

Briggs saved her from her self-pity when she arrived bringing the morning post. Among the boring manila envelopes, Maddie spotted a white one with an Oxford postmark. Intrigued, she opened it to find a letter from an Oxford solicitor informing her that Dr Baskin had bequeathed her a legacy. Naturally, she was delighted with the cheque for one hundred pounds. It was lovely to be remembered in that way by her mentor, but it had also reminded her of the nagging doubts she harboured over the circumstances of his death.

Scanning the letter once more, she saw Dr Baskin's sister had been copied in on it and her address was printed below her own. She thought of the elderly woman with her intelligent eyes and ready smile, who'd first sown the seeds of doubt in her mind. If she wanted to lay her suspicions to rest over the doctor's death, the next step suddenly became clear to her. She should contact Hester Baskin.

*

Wearing a warm wool coat and sensible shoes, Maddie strode purposefully down a blustery Oxford High Street. Her destination was an "olde-worlde" tearoom, which in normal times would be frequented by tourists.

Hester Baskin sat at a table in the corner of the elegant, high-ceilinged room, dressed in sensible tweeds and knitted beret. It had been a month since Maddie had last seen her and the initial twinkle in her eye seemed to have dulled. In fact, she was looking rather pasty and the way she was fiddling with her handkerchief suggested a bad case of nerves.

'I'm so glad to see you, Miss Gresham,' she greeted, watching Maddie seat herself. 'Your letter was most welcome.'

Maddie smiled. 'So was your brother's legacy. And certainly unexpected.'

'Tobias spoke very highly of you,' she said, her bright eyes darting about the tearoom.

Maddie sensed she wanted more than a cosy chat as Hester suddenly turned to her and lowering her voice said: 'I've really rather been at a loss these past few days.'

Maddie, peeling off her woollen gloves, frowned. 'I'm sorry to hear that,' she replied. 'May I ask why?'

A waitress, wearing a Victorian-style mob cap and a long white apron, came to take their order. Both settled on a pot of what passed for Earl Grey but declined the scones offered with it.

'Now where was I?' asked Hester, still flustered. Little beads of perspiration dotted her forehead, even though barely any of the warmth from the coal fire radiated as far as their little corner.

'You were saying how you'd been at a loss,' prompted Maddie.

Hester leaned in. 'Ah, yes. As you know, Tobias's solicitors have been sorting out his estate. He left me his cottage and I've been wondering what to do with it. Last month I finally decided I ought to sell it, but I kept putting off going to clear out all the furniture and his belongings. Then a few days ago, I took the bull by the horns, as it were, and returned to the cottage for the first time since his death.'

Her voice started to crack, and she began to play with her hands. When she lifted her gaze once more, there were tears in her eyes.

Conveniently, the waitress appeared with the tea at this point and allowed Hester to compose herself.

'I'm sorry,' she said, as soon as the waitress left the table.

'Please don't apologise,' replied Maddie. 'You're still grieving.'

At this remark, Hester sniffed and turned to her with a disconcerting look. 'Not so much grief as shock, I'm afraid.'

'Shock?' repeated Maddie, intrigued.

Hester nodded. 'You see, when I entered the cottage, it had been burgled.'

Maddie felt her body jolt with shock, too. 'Burgled? You're sure?'

'Yes,' replied Hester, her small fists clenching forcefully as she spoke. 'A back window was broken, and the place was an awful mess.' She tutted. 'And Tobias was such a fastidious man.'

Maddie nodded, remembering how meticulous he was with his filing and Miss Baskin certainly didn't strike Maddie as a woman prone to histrionics. 'So, you think whoever broke in must've been looking for something in particular?'

'I'm sure of it,' she replied.

'Have you been to the police?'

Hester straightened her back but shook her head. 'Of course, but they told me there's really nothing they can do. They said the break-in might have been weeks ago, and any trail a burglar may have left will be long cold. I even contacted the chief constable – he worships at the same church, you know – but to no avail.'

Reading Hester's troubled expression, Maddie decided she was holding something back. It was clear the police had washed their hands of the matter and the doctor's sister remained unhappy.

'Is there something else you want to tell me, Miss Baskin?' asked Maddie, straining the Earl Grey into both their cups.

'It's just that I know how hush-hush Tobias's work was and I'm rather worried the burglary might have had something to do with it.'

Thoughtfully, Maddie took a sip of tea. 'I understand,' she said. 'I shall certainly contact his former employers with your concerns.' Of course she couldn't tell Hester that she'd filled her brother's position.

'You will?' Hester's eyes lit up. 'I'd be most grateful, Miss Gresham. Thank you.'

They parted half an hour later, agreeing to stay in touch, although Maddie wasn't really sure where either of them could go from there. If the Chief Constable of Oxfordshire refused to investigate Dr Baskin's death further, and Colonel McKie clearly had no interest, Maddie told herself she would have to be more creative in her approach.

*

On the train back to London later that afternoon, Maddie felt vindicated. She knew she'd been right to worry after reading the doctor's note, even though she hadn't spoken about it that afternoon. Hester's mention of a break-in at the doctor's cottage threw a whole new and unsettling light on the affair. Had the doctor really died of a heart attack, or could more sinister forces be at work? To an enemy he might have presented an Achilles heel when it came to keeping secrets. He was, after all, a civilian, lodging away from Trent Park. And if the good doctor couldn't be persuaded to divulge those secrets, things might have taken a turn for the worse.

The train chugged through a cutting near Sonning, plunging the carriage into gloom, but Maddie remained staring out of the window. Her own reflection suddenly stared back at her. It was then the most chilling thought of all occurred. She thought of the times she swore she was being watched or followed. First there was the incident when Fruity's car was followed to her lodgings, then she recalled the woman in the silver dress at the Savoy. There was also something rather dodgy about the lodger, Mr Clancy, too. As Dr Baskin's successor, did this mean her own life was in danger? Right then, the only thing she was certain of was that she wouldn't feel safe until she'd somehow found out exactly was going on. Only then would her own mind be put at rest.

As the train pulled into Paddington and she alighted onto the platform, she couldn't also help but notice a familiar figure in a trilby a few paces ahead of her, stepping down from a carriage. She felt anger clench her chest. This time she was going to get to the bottom of things and find out why she was being followed. Marching up to the man as he walked in front of her, she tapped him from behind and asked in no uncertain terms: 'Just what do you think you're playing at, Mr Clancy?'

Shocked, the man pivoted round to stare at her. 'I beg your pardon?' The stranger scowled. 'You'd better mind your manners, young lady.'

Chapter 25

'Coming to the 400 tonight?' asked Pru, setting down a pile of transcript folders on the desk. It was almost six o'clock and Maddie noticed she was wearing an even brighter shade of lipstick than usual. It made her look quite vampish. Her nails were painted to match. *Colonel McKie would certainly approve,* she told herself wryly. It would be straight out of uniform and on with the evening gown and heels as soon as her shift finished.

Maddie sighed heavily as she opened the transcript folder in front of her. 'No. Not this evening,' she replied with a shake of her head. 'I'm washing my hair.' (*If only,* she thought. It had been two weeks since there'd been any hot water at Fairview.)

Pru gave a little shrug, to signify she wasn't too disconcerted but added: 'It's Fruity's birthday, so there'll be drinks in the mess before we go off. Perhaps you'll join us then?'

But before she replied Maddie looked up with a deep frown furrowing her brow. 'What's happened here?' she asked, pointing at the transcript of the previous evening's conversation between three of the generals. Several lines had been blacked out. They were illegible.

Pru returned to the desk to glance at the page. 'It's been redacted,' she replied in a matter-of-fact voice.

'*Re . . .?*' She was so surprised, the word got lodged on her tongue.

'Redacted. Crossed out.'

'I know what redacted means, but why?' said Maddie, a note of annoyance creeping into her tone.

Pru continued huffily. 'They don't want you to see what's been said. They do that occasionally.'

'They?' repeated Maddie, reminding herself that she was supposed to have full security clearance.

'Colonel McKie, I suppose and maybe one or two other top brass.' The Wren paused, reading the frustrated look on Maddie's face. 'I told you this place was full of secrets. You'll get used to it, that's all.'

*

Maddie continued to work through the ever-growing stack of documents when a knock broke into her thoughts. She glanced at the clock on the wall. It was ten past six.

'Yes.'

A familiar head peered round the door.

'You coming, old girl?' asked Ruth.

Maddie gave her a dazed look. 'Coming?'

'To the mess. Pru said she'd mentioned Fruity's birthday drinks.'

Maddie shook thoughts of Dr Baskin from her head. After the day she'd had, a gin and tonic was very tempting. 'Sorry. Of course,' she replied.

A new coat of lipstick was swiftly applied, together with a dab of scent, and ten minutes later she was in the mess. Pru and her brunette friend – Maddie discovered her name was Pammie – were both looking frightfully glamorous on top as they sipped lukewarm martinis. Eddie was also looking dashing, ready for a night on the tiles. She needed to talk to him and had already decided to act with humility. He may have thought her idea about becoming Lady Frobisher was a good one, but on reflection, she should have cleared it with him first. Arming herself with a stiff drink, she went to sit down near him as he sat nursing a whisky.

As soon as she did, he leaned over to her. 'Are you terribly angry?' he whispered in her ear.

'I was,' she admitted, perching at his side. 'But I suppose I'm more disappointed now. Still, it was only to be expected.' She heaved her shoulders in a shrug.

'You should've told me first.' There was mild annoyance in his tone.

She switched round to face him. 'Why, so you could talk me out of it?'

'Not at all.' He laughed. 'I said at the time, I actually think it's a marvellous idea.'

'Yes, you did,' she conceded.

'And I still do. In fact, some of the generals having been wanting to know if I'm married.'

'I suppose that's only natural.'

Eddie nodded, then licked his lips. 'I just wished you'd mentioned your idea to me first. I could really have backed you up. I agree the generals would benefit from some female company. I've even invited Hammler for a drink and offered to go for a stroll in the grounds. He just won't play ball. He's clearly not interested if it's just me. If you on the other hand . . .'

'It's too late now,' she said, on a long sigh. 'Colonel McKie has spoken.'

Eddie took a gulp of his whisky. 'I wouldn't give up that easily if I were you. Fight your corner.'

She nodded and smiled. 'Thank you, Eddie. I appreciate your support. And besides,' she said as an afterthought, 'McKie thinks I do have my uses.'

Eddie snorted a sarcastic laugh. 'That's good of him.'

'He's asked me to interview some new recruits for the M

Room. I'm going to be working in town for a couple of days. A nice, safe assignment.'

After her proposal to act as Lady Frobisher had been rejected, she'd agreed with Colonel McKie that she would spend a few days in London assessing potential listeners from the Pioneer Corps.

Eddie smiled. 'I'm in town, too. Something for the War Office. Perhaps we could . . .' His eyes suddenly narrowed.

'Yes?' she said.

'Let's meet up for a drink.'

'I'd like that,' she said with a smile.

He smiled at her too – a long lingering one that suddenly turned into awkwardness. 'The air raid . . . I hope you don't think I was too . . .'

She wasn't used to seeing Eddie tongue-tied. He was normally so cool.

'I don't think anything, Eddie,' she broke in. 'You saved my life. That's a fact. If we hadn't made it to shelter . . .' She stared into her glass. She would never admit it to him – she found it hard enough to admit to herself – but when they were huddled together under those arches as the fire storm raged around them, she hadn't wanted him to let go. For a split second she'd wanted to surrender to the moment and longed for him to kiss her, but there was still something in her heart that held her back. She couldn't betray Max. 'Let's just put it down to the situation shall we?'

It was clearly not what Eddie wanted to hear. Nevertheless, he managed to sound cheerful when they arranged to meet in London.

'A drink, then. Good,' he said lightly. 'Until then,' and with that he waltzed off towards the bar to fortify himself before a night at the 400.

*

Later that night Maddie awoke with a fright. Jerking up, her hand clasped at her throat, and she felt for Max's locket. It was still there. She'd suffered another of her nightmares.

Switching on her bedside lamp, she reached for the lined notebook always kept in readiness. Her disturbing dreams were what started her on her journey into psychology. Taking up her pen, she began to scribble frantically while she still held the vivid images in her mind.

I was underground in a labyrinth of cellars. Normally I know I'm back in the cells in Munich, but this was different. (It was then she recalled being first shown the M Room and the sudden feeling of panic that had overwhelmed her.) *I was in the maze of passages beneath Trent Park, and I was looking for Max. Somehow, I knew he was in danger, and I called his name, over and over, but there was no reply. Then I came to a small room, and I looked in. I saw Dr Baskin on a chair. I thought he was asleep but when I went to wake him he was dead. Then I saw Max. He was up against the wall and from out of the brickwork came hundreds of wires, like snakes curling around his body. He screamed my name just as the wires began coiling themselves around his neck and tightening. He couldn't breathe. He was being strangled. Then Eddie appeared at the doorway, and he held out his arms to me and I wanted to run to him because I knew he could help me escape.*

I awoke.

Maddie knew what the dream meant, of course. She didn't need Dr Freud to interpret it. Dr Baskin's note, now safely locked away in her jewellery box, had troubled her, and Max still needed her to believe in him. But then Eddie had come on the scene and offered to take away some of her fear. It would be so easy to run into his arms.

Chapter 26

The long winter seemed to have decided it was time to beat a retreat, or at the very least call a truce. Even though it was still only late March, there was a hint of spring in the air.

'Good morning, Private Paget,' Maddie greeted. Seeing the ATS driver's smiling face always seemed to lift her spirits.

'Good morning, ma'am,' she replied. 'Lovely morning.'

'Indeed, it is.'

Her optimistic frame of mind, she knew, was also down to the fact that she'd been entrusted to move Trent Park's gears up a notch by recruiting secret listeners in London. Any idea she might have harboured about being Lady Frobisher had been swiftly quashed, but she could still do *"her bit"* as Uncle Roly would say.

Maddie was looking forward to escaping the claustrophobic confines of Trent Park for the city. A room had been booked for her in a modest hotel for the next two nights. As they powered down the long drive, it was as if the frothy blossom in the hedgerow and tulips on the verges formed a guard of honour. Spring was making its presence felt despite the madness going on in the world and for a few moments, unfettered by the constraints of protocols and procedures, Maddie dared to dream that one day soon birdsong would drown out the sound of guns. Her eye had just been caught by a particularly lovely purple azalea that had rather taken its chances with the spring frosts to emerge in its full glory when Paget touched the brakes. Switching her head back and onto the drive, Maddie saw a convoy. Two jeeps carrying armed guards were heading in their direction. Behind them a large bus followed on. Paget pulled over into a passing place.

Maddie said nothing as the vehicles sped by, but she knew all about the bus's passengers. Colonel McKie had told her they were expecting a few more captured generals that week. It would mean even more work for her, writing psychological profiles.

Each time she left the gates of Trent Park, Maddie felt slightly strange, like Alice stepping back out of the looking glass. The reality of war stared her in the face as they drove through Enfield on their way into central London. The ruins of homes and the scars left by Hitler's bombs only served to reinforce her determination to beat the enemy. Just then they passed the bingo hall in the main street, the one Mrs Pollock went to every Thursday night. The trouble was a large banner across the main entrance read: 'Closed until further notice.' All the front windows and doors were boarded up.

Maddie looked backwards as the car moved by, just to be sure there was no mistake.

'The bingo hall,' she said to Paget.

'Yes, miss,' she replied, glancing up at the rear-view mirror.

'How long has it been shut?'

Paget frowned in thought. 'I think it took a hit from behind a couple of years ago, miss. Been boarded up ever since.'

If that's the case, then where on earth does Mrs Pollock go every Thursday evening? Maddie asked herself. *Unless of course . . .* It suddenly occurred to her what her landlady could be getting up to in secret. The innuendos and the playful gestures sprang to mind. Mrs Pollock, thought Maddie, might be having an affair with Mr Clancy.

*

Almost an hour later Paget stopped off at the hotel – which was more of a guest house really – to allow Maddie to drop her overnight bag at the reception, before moving on to Whitehall. The interviews were to be conducted in the War Office. Maddie stepped out the motor car to look up at the imposing building. The neo-baroque style was softened by four ornate domes, as if the architect had wanted to add a feminine touch to a bastion of masculinity. Rather than feeling intimidated, Maddie was encouraged. Perhaps there was room for women like her inside, after all.

Even so, it took an age to pass through clearance. There were checks on the front desk, a quick frisk – by an ATS girl – and another, more detailed check of her briefcase before she was allowed into the lift to the third floor.

'Someone will be with you shortly, miss,' she was told, standing at the threshold of a large office.

Left alone she was drawn to the window, criss-crossed by a grille, to savour the view of Horse Guards Parade below.

'Rather magnificent, isn't it?'

The voice from behind, a man's, was clipped but friendly. She turned to see a civilian in a rather baggy suit extending his hand. 'Baldwin. MI5,' he told her. 'Miss Gresham from Cockfosters Camp, I assume.'

Maddie smiled, shaking his hand. 'That's right.'

He was middle-aged with bad dandruff and the vaguely shabby air possessed by some men that a military uniform was so good at concealing. Baldwin pointed to the desk. 'That's where you'll be today. The first lot is already waiting.' He smiled at her in a sort of show of civilian camaraderie. 'Is everything clear?'

'Yes. Thank you,' said Maddie, laying her briefcase on the desk as Baldwin left the room. There was a large clock above the mantelshelf. It was already nine. She knew it was going to be a long day and was half regretting agreeing to meet Eddie that evening. He'd been considerate to her ever since they'd sheltered together

161

during the air raid. The trouble was, she'd felt her attraction for him grow. But it still wasn't love – not on her part, at least. He could never hold a candle to Max.

A few minutes later, the ATS private delivered the list of candidates in alphabetical order. They were nearly all German, apart from a few Czechs or Poles and a Frenchman. For some reason, the prospect of interviewing so many foreign men suddenly unnerved her slightly because it made her think of Max again. What if he was on the list? What if he'd escaped from France and made it back to England to join the Pioneer Corps? Her eyes tore down the sheet as her heart beat faster. Flicking through the first and second pages of typed foolscap, she came to the W's. *Wagener, Weber, Wilder*, but no *Weitzler*. The hope that had sprung up so suddenly inside her was uprooted before it had a chance to grow.

Before she'd begun interviewing, Maddie had already told herself that she wouldn't listen to any personal stories that involved torture or loss or any of the other inhuman things that she'd heard might be happening to Jews at the hands of the Germans. Some of the men, she expected, would have ended up in those terrible factories as slave labourers, working for Hammler on his rockets. But she couldn't allow herself to be guided by emotion. Colonel McKie said he expected the new recruits to hear some unpalatable truths when the generals' tongues were loosened and he didn't want any "cracks" to appear, as he put it.

'Oh, and we're on the lookout for more stool pigeons, too,' the colonel had told her on her way out. 'You know the sort we need. Strong, dependable types who can keep cool heads in tricky situations.'

Easier said than done, thought Maddie. 'Of course, sir,' she said.

Maddie had decided to conduct the interviews in German to put the candidates at ease. The first two men she saw – both Germans – were satisfactory, one from Leipzig and the other from somewhere in Saxony. Their scores on previous psychological tests they'd completed were relatively normal, but neither had displayed much initiative in the other results. When pressed on this, their responses seemed to bear out her initial assessment.

Another candidate had been a political prisoner in a camp, serving a six-month sentence for distributing anti-government leaflets in 1934. He'd taken the first train he could out of Germany, leaving his elderly parents. He was still angry. Too angry, Maddie decided.

At eleven o'clock the ATS private brought in a pot of tea and Maddie perused the next candidate's details as she sipped. She'd reached the L's. *Lehmann. Ernst Lehmann.* According to his records, he was formerly a lecturer in civil engineering at the prestigious University of Göttingen before being sent on temporary secondment to Imperial College at the University of London. He was in England when war was declared.

'Mr Lehmann. Please, take a seat.' Maddie gestured to the chair in front of her as the older man with wavy hair, flecked with grey, and a nose once clearly broken and not reset properly, entered. She looked at his profile.

'So, you are a lecturer in civil engineering.'

He nodded.

'Interesting,' she murmured. On paper at least, Ernst Lehmann might make a good fit for Hammler. There was only one caveat. Academic qualifications were worthless if Lehmann's psychological state was weak. It would take a mentally strong person to withstand the depraved stories the "Crocodile" might share with a companion.

She sat back in her chair. 'Tell me about your family in Germany, Sergeant Lehmann.'

He paused for a moment to fix her with a gaze that made her feel quite awkward. Then he licked his lips – a sure sign he wasn't being completely honest, according to Dr Baskin – before shaking his head.

'I do not have one,' he replied bluntly.

Maddie frowned. She needed to give him another opportunity

163

to clarify what she suspected was a falsehood. 'You don't have a family, Mr Lehmann?'

He shrugged and sat back in his chair. 'My parents both died in the war, the first one. They were Jewish, which unfortunately made me Jewish. I was adopted by a gentile couple, but they were not kind.' He pointed to his crooked nose. 'My stepfather gave me this for my fourteenth birthday, so I left as soon as I could. I've always made my own way in the world.'

'So you are not married and you have no children?'

'Children? No.' He looked up at the ceiling. 'Not that I admit to!'

Humour, thought Maddie. So often used to mask a painful truth.

She met his weak joke with a wry smile, and he hooked her gaze with an appealing look.

'I'm sorry,' he said, raising his hands momentarily then letting them fall into his lap. 'I just want you to know that I have no emotional ties to anyone apart from my beloved country, which has been stolen from me by the Nazis.' This time he pointed to his greying hair. 'As you see, I'm not getting any younger, but I want to help in the fight to win it back and I am so thankful to be given an opportunity by you British to do just that.'

It was a heartfelt speech, and it made Maddie warm to him.

'Thank you, Mr Lehmann. That will be all,' she said.

He lifted himself up from the chair and turned to go, but just before he reached the door he swivelled round again. Fixing her with that same, piercing gaze, he said: 'I only want to help put right all the wrongs.'

There was no doubt in Maddie's mind about the sincerity of his convictions, even if, as she suspected, he wasn't being entirely truthful about his family ties.

'Please wait outside,' she told him, her gaze sliding to the door. She watched him leave before her attention settled back down to her desk. Despite her misgivings, she decided to give him the benefit of the doubt. In the next moment, she found herself writing the word "*Yes*" on Ernst Lehmann's application.

Chapter 27

'I say, you're quite stunning.' Eddie greeted Maddie when they met up at Trafalgar Square under Admiral Lord Nelson's watchful glare.

She knew she wasn't looking her best. Rouge and lashings of mascara could do little to compensate for her rather utilitarian work garb. No, she did not look stunning, nor did she feel it. Yet she still managed a smile. Eddie, on the other hand, was looking extremely dapper with a blue silk handkerchief in the breast pocket of his well-cut suit.

They made their way to a chic Art Deco cocktail bar off Leicester Square, where all the women seemed to be dressed in feathers and sequins and flashing jewelled cigarette holders. Next to them with her hurriedly applied make-up and professional suit, Maddie felt decidedly dowdy, not to mention exhausted.

'How did it go today?' Eddie asked as they talked on plush banquettes over gin martinis.

'You know I can't say,' she replied.

'But you made progress?' he pressed, sipping his martini.

She nodded. 'Yes,' she said, to get him off her back more than anything else. Progress had, indeed, been made. If her plans worked out Ernst Lehmann would make an excellent sounding board for Brigadier Hammler.

'Good,' he said, before suddenly clasping her hand. 'It is lovely to have you in London for a couple of days. I thought tomorrow evening, we could . . .'

Maddie broke him off. 'I'm afraid there won't be a tomorrow evening, Eddie,' she said, turning on the banquette to look at him directly.

'What do you mean? I thought you were interviewing over a few days.'

'I was, but I had a phone call, just before I came here.' She looked around to make sure they couldn't be overhead. Two elderly women in furs were their nearest neighbours. She lowered her voice. 'Colonel McKie wants me back. A couple more prisoners arrived today, and I need to write their profiles as soon as possible.'

Eddie looked puzzled. 'So who will . . .?'

'Major Lansley will take my place.' Then noticing a look of disappointment on his face, she added: 'And I'm sure you've got more than enough to keep you occupied.'

Eddie grinned and gazed into his half-empty glass, an olive on an elaborate stick propped against its rim. 'As Lord Frobisher of Bradstock, you mean?'

She smiled. 'So, you're finally getting to act professionally. I seem to recall you planned to go to Hollywood.'

His mouth turned down at its edges. 'Acting isn't a career for a gentleman, you know. Papa would never approve.'

She noted a certain sadness in his eyes as he spoke. 'Well, I'm sure he'd be very proud of you if he knew what you were doing for the war effort.'

He smiled but shook his head. 'Unless I'm actually bayonetting the Bosch, then I'm a sissy,' he told her. 'My father commanded a regiment on the Somme and calls anyone in intelligence a frock wearer!'

'What nonsense,' she retorted. 'This war will be won with brains, not brawn.'

'I think you're right. The generals were a little hostile to me at first, but the second-cousin-to-the-king routine slipped into a conversation, seemed to start the thaw.' He picked up the stick and demolished the olive whole. 'Now most of them are eating out of my hand. We've had some useful stuff from them in their unguarded moments.' Eddie chuckled. 'Oh, and McKie has asked me to draw up a list of jollies to entertain our guests.'

'That was my suggestion,' she pointed out, rather annoyed.

'I know. It's not fair,' he told her, but then he smiled and said: 'When I mentioned a trip to Hampton Court they got very excited. Apparently, they all think Henry VIII is a hero, don't you know?'

Maddie laughed, as well. Eddie did make her laugh. He helped lift the gloom that had shrouded her for so long.

'Do you know what I also think?' he said, suddenly sliding his hand over the linen cloth towards her.

She dropped her gaze to his outstretched palm as the strains of a romantic tune played in the background and this time without hesitation, she took his hand in hers. It felt warm and reassuring. Then she lifted her eyes once more to meet his. 'What do you think?' she asked, feeling her own pulse race.

'I think it's rather a shame you won't be Lady Frobisher,' he said.

For a second Maddie wasn't sure how to react. She decided to laugh, albeit nervously, aware that Eddie was in earnest. 'Perhaps it's just as well,' she told him flatly. 'I'm really not ready to be anyone's little wifey.' She withdrew her hand, knowing she was being hard-hearted.

Undaunted, he winked at her then. 'We'll see about that,' he said.

After that Maddie really shouldn't have been at all surprised by Eddie's kiss. It was delivered very swiftly outside the cocktail bar and was rather too public. They'd only walked a couple of paces when he suddenly turned to face her, took her in his arms in the middle of the pavement and planted his hot lips excitedly onto hers. He certainly took her breath away and for a moment she was stunned.

As he broke back and looked deep into her eyes, she saw doubt flicker across his face. 'I'm sorry. I . . .'

His impetuosity had come in a rather unexpected rush. She felt slightly in shock. 'I thought I made myself clear, that's all.' She pretended to be mildly offended, even though she'd found she rather enjoyed being kissed so spontaneously.

He nodded. 'I just couldn't help my myself.'

She should have been upset – indignant, even. It was a kiss that she knew might come, but which she'd dreaded for a while, ever since she'd realised she felt something for Eddie.

'I really like you,' she told him. Then again, as if to reassure herself as much as him, she repeated, 'I really do, but . . .'

It was true. When she was with him, she felt more positive, as if she could see the sun coming up over the horizon. Any hope that Max might have been one of the escaped émigrés in the Pioneer Corps was fading fast but still something made her cling on. It was no use pretending. She knew she would have to make a decision sooner or later: to keep true to a ghost of a long-remembered love or start living again. But now was not the time.

Chapter 28

April 1944

It had been a long journey and Max's bones ached. He and seven other men – all German Jews – had been sitting in the back of the truck for what seemed like weeks, but in reality was only three days. They'd left the Isle of Man in driving rain and endured cold winds and freezing nights on the way. Folk songs from the Fatherland had kept their spirits up as the truck bounced and lurched its way southwards on pitted roads. But then something happened. The rain suddenly stopped, the sun came out and for the first time in weeks the circulation returned to Max's freezing hands. At the new camp he was treated more like a soldier than a prisoner. There were interviews. There was training. And when, three months later, he was told he would be moving on again, he no longer felt dread, but excitement. When the convoy finally reached its destination and passed through the high gates of the new camp, he joined in when the men raised a collective cheer. For as long as the war lasted, Max knew his home would be in England.

Jumping out of the truck, he could see a large house beyond the trees. It looked very grand, as if it might be inhabited by members of the English nobility. One of the men even joked it was Buckingham Palace. They'd all laughed at that, until a killjoy had suggested that with its watchtower and barbed wire, it looked more like the Tower of London.

Max guessed this grand building was where he'd be working, although he'd been told very little about what task he'd be undertaking. Shortly after joining the Pioneer Corps, his commanding officer had suggested he take various tests in mathematics and engineering. Of course, he'd passed with flying colours and, shortly after that he'd been called to London for psychological tests and told he'd been accepted – although for what, he had no idea. But with his new role had come new papers and the return of his old name. Finally he could be proud and unafraid to be Max Weitzler once more – a German fighting against Hitler's tyranny. Ernst, who'd first told him about the Pioneer Corps, had also been accepted for a new role, although they'd been separated a few weeks back and he hadn't heard from him since.

Their barracks were in a Nissen hut. Iron-framed beds were ranged in two rows on either side of one long space with a wide walkway between. Each bed had a locker beside it and that was all. The room Max had shared with Ernst on the Isle of Man had been more welcoming.

The men collected their bedding, then went to their assigned beds. Everything was basic, but at least it was relatively dry, and he could count on getting fed, but more than that: here, he felt closer to Maddie. It was as if he had journeyed into her world, the world of porcelain cups and tea dances, kippers for breakfast and parlour games. All the quirky English customs she'd talked about when they were alone together in her attic room, were now at his fingertips. Even if he couldn't quite touch them, he would be near them and that helped him believe he would meet her again.

After he'd made up his bed, he unpacked his kitbag. The first thing he took from it was Maddie's photograph. He'd carried it with him since their last goodbye almost eight years ago. It was dog-eared and faded at the edges, but her beautiful face still shone out of it and her eyes were willing him on to find her. He kissed it before laying it under his pillow.

'Right, men. Let's be 'aving you. Stand by your beds!' boomed a voice.

Every time Max heard the English sergeant major's thundering commands he feared the dead would wake. 'There's a cuppa and some grub waiting for you in the canteen, but you best get your sorry arses back here for twenty-two hundred hours for lights out because you've got a big day tomorrow. You 'ear me?'

'Yes, sergeant,' replied the men in unison.

Max's months in internment had made him come to understand – if not fully appreciate – the English sense of humour. For the first time since he'd made it safely to England, he felt more at ease in this place than anywhere he'd stayed before. He couldn't wait to start work at this Cockfosters Camp – he'd learned its name from one of the other men – whatever he was ordered to do, but nor could he wait to start tracking down his beloved Maddie in earnest.

Chapter 29

In the large briefing room, the newest recruits from the Pioneer Corps were standing to attention as Colonel McKie entered, followed by Major Lansley. There were ten young men in total, mainly German but an Austrian and a Frenchman, too. Many of them had been through hell. Some of them had lost close family, while others had been detained in concentration camps. As Jews, all of them had experienced the sense of menace in Germany that pervaded everyday life.

They sat at desks laid out in rows, like a schoolroom.

'Stand at ease,' ordered the major. 'Please be seated.'

Max sat near the back, his blond hair marking him out from all the other recruits. He and the men had come fresh from the M Room in the basement where, for the first time, they'd been told what role they would be playing in the war effort. They listened attentively as Colonel McKie delivered a brief introductory speech.

'The work you do here will be every bit as important as fighting on the battlefield,' he told them. 'I know you will prove loyal and trustworthy in the fight against the Nazi menace that has already terrorised and even killed many of your families, your loved ones, and you want to express your gratitude to the British for giving you sanctuary. We thank you for that and we gladly accept your help in combatting Hitler and his evil tyranny that threatens the freedoms we all hold so dear.'

The colonel – clearly taking his cue from Prime Minister Churchill, thought Max – had ended his speech on a high note, even though it had limited appeal for his audience, given they weren't British. Exhorting the men to do their bit "for King and country", he passed on the metaphorical swagger stick to two Army officers who addressed their questions about working in the "M" Room. They came thick and fast.

'How do we know which general is speaking?'

'You don't, you just have to get used to their voices.'

'What if there is something we can't hear?'

'Put a question mark.'

'What if they say something we know is really important at the beginning of our shift?'

'Tell your supervisor immediately.'

There was so much to learn, but Max knew he would have to learn it "on the job". He'd heard that training took up to three months normally, but he and the other listeners were being plunged in at the deep end. They would have to learn to swim immediately, or they would certainly sink.

Major Lansley then introduced himself as head of the "mental oversight" team. Max recognised him from the assessments in London.

With ten pairs of eyes trained on him, the major began. 'I am a psychiatrist and I work with a psychologist to devise interrogation strategies for our prisoners. The team is here to help you, too. Some of the things you hear the German officers say, you may find deeply troubling and . . .'

But Max was no longer listening because the major's words had stirred a memory inside him. He remembered Maddie had wanted to be a psychologist. She had been intending to study at Oxford, and although the university didn't run a degree in psychology, there was a new institute she'd hoped to attend once she'd graduated.

He pictured her in his mind's eye that last summer: so alive, so fearless and so excited about the life that lay ahead of her. Had she fulfilled her dreams? Had they come true? Or had war dashed them cruelly on the rocks of despair, just as it seemed to have destroyed his?

Chapter 30

The light flashed on Maddie's scrambler telephone. It was Major Lansley. Did she have a moment? Armed with a notebook, she hurried over to Hut 6 and ventured inside to find the major looking even more hangdog than usual. He was rubbing his temples as he studied a file and barely bothered to look up; he gestured her to take a seat without lifting his gaze.

'Major?' She sat down in front of him.

'Remember the stool pigeon you recently recruited? We paired him with Hammler?'

'Yes. Is something wrong?'

'As you know, Hammler's a loner, so Lehmann's cover is as his batman.'

It had actually been Maddie's suggestion. She reckoned if the brigadier thought he was with someone of a lower rank and detached, he might engage with him better. It was a tried and tested method to gain a powerful person's confidence.

Maddie shifted in her chair. 'I thought it was working rather well,' she said. She'd seen the transcripts. The brigadier seemed quite happy to unburden himself on his attentive batman.

'That's right. You remember Lehmann's originally from Göttingen. He and his wife both worked at the university.'

'His wife?' repeated Maddie. 'He told me he didn't have one.'

The major shook his head. 'I'm afraid he's admitted telling you an untruth.' He leaned forward and tented his fingers. 'And now he seems to be having a spot of bother.'

'Sir? What sort of bother?'

Lansley explained: 'These reports about atrocities we've been hearing – they don't make easy reading. As you'll appreciate, being in the same room as a pompous Jerry when he's bragging about how many Jews he has shot, must make it hard for our chaps to hold their fists, let alone their tongues.'

Seeing the generals relate their horror stories, while painting in oils or drinking their fireside brandies, must, she acknowledged, be causing Ernst and his fellow stool pigeons unimaginable turmoil.

The first accounts she'd read had disturbed her deeply. Since then, there had been more reports from other generals that were equally graphic. Of course, many of them didn't take responsibility for the crimes. Instead, some blamed the SS or rogue soldiers. Anyone but themselves. Some, however, wore their brutality like a badge of honour. The psychological impact of those conversations on paper was traumatising enough, let alone hearing them from first-hand.

Lansley slid a file across the desk to her. It was marked *Top Secret*.

'This came to me this morning,' he told her, lowering his voice.

She opened the cover to see three paragraphs of translated transcript underlined in red ink.

'The recording was made as Hammler was shaving. Read it, if you please.'

Maddie obeyed.

Hammler: I remember once, early on, we went to Göttingen University. There was this Jewess. Beautiful. Firm.

Maddie's eyes snagged on the name of the university. Her head shot up. Before the meeting she'd checked out Lehmann's profile. 'Göttingen, but that's where . . .'

'Read on.'

Lehmann: What happened, sir?

Hammler: I could have forced her, but she was like putty in my hands. I suppose she thought I could save her life.

Lehmann: So, you did? You saved her?

Hammler: I wish I could have, but there was no other way. Our men shot seventy-five thousand Jews there over the next few days.

Maddie sat in stunned silence for a moment. An indescribable wave of despair threatened to overwhelm her. 'What did Lehmann do?'

'Afterwards he went to sick bay. In a terrible state. Of course, the Jewish woman they spoke about wouldn't have been in all probability his . . .'

'But she could have been.'

'Precisely, and in any case, it's likely she was among the seventy-five thousand slaughtered.'

Her heart ached for the man. Swallowing down the desolation she felt inside, she asked: 'Do you want me to talk to him, sir?' The words did not come easily as she suddenly thought of Max. Was he lying dead in a ditch with a bullet in his head, too?

'I think that might be a helpful course of action,' agreed the major. 'He's next door now.'

Ernst Lehmann himself looked pale and distracted as he sat in the interview room when Maddie entered. She sat down opposite him and laid out the typed results of his monthly psychological assessment in front of her. From somewhere she could hear a noise, like an incessant tapping. When she looked down she noticed his left leg was moving continuously.

The routine tests indicated what was evident to Maddie just by looking at the man. He was suffering from a high degree of anxiety. Yet even though it was obvious to her that his duties were taking a terrible toll on his mental health, she had to tread warily. Major Lansley was watching from the observation room.

'How are you feeling, Sergeant Lehmann?' she asked.

Ernst nodded. 'I am well,' he replied.

Her remark was delivered with a smile but met with an indifferent shrug.

His piercing brown eyes pinned her with a look that might have been construed as convincing to a layman, but she knew that it hid something unsettling. 'All is satisfactory.'

'Are you sure?' she asked. 'Because I have heard otherwise. It cannot be easy working for Hammler.'

He licked his lips, as she'd seen him do before. His voice trembled. 'It is not, but I tell myself I am doing it for my Rosa. And one day, at this end of this war, that monster will be brought to justice, won't he?' He wiped away his gathering tears.

'I read the transcripts, too, you know, Sergeant Lehmann. I am aware of what is happening to Jews in your homeland,' she told him.

He nodded. 'I am glad you know, *fräulein*. I hope those in charge know, too, then perhaps they might take action.'

He spoke calmly now and continued to remain placid throughout the rest of the interview, regurgitating what he'd learned in training: to suppress all negative emotions.

At the end of the half-hour session, Maddie thanked Ernst for his time, but had to let him go. There were no concrete grounds to relieve him of his duties inside the mansion. He was doing a good job, gaining Hammler's confidence the way he had.

'I am free to go?' he asked at the end of the interview. 'Hammler has another appointment with the tailor. I do not want to be missed.'

'Of course,' replied Maddie, although she knew he needed a careful eye on him. But as Ernst Lehmann left the Nissen hut and walked back to the mansion, he was unaware that someone else was keeping an eye on him too.

Chapter 31

Maddie walked back to Fairview later that day with Ernst Lehmann's words ringing in her ears. 'That monster will be brought to justice, won't he?' he'd cried, his eyes glassy with tears. She hoped they all would. But it was going to take a lot of hard work, she told herself as she put her key in the lock.

Mrs Pollock shouted up to the landing as soon as she heard Maddie go upstairs.

'Eating in, tonight, Miss Gresham? I've got a nice bit of tongue.'

But Maddie's appetite had deserted her. 'I'm really not hungry. Thank you, Mrs Pollock,' she'd assured her leaning over the bannisters.

Hammler may have been eager to demonstrate how he earned his nickname in the mansion, but Maddie was fully aware the Crocodile hadn't yet opened his jaws about the weapons programme. Every day special agents were sending conflicting reports from Europe about the so-called Vengeance weapon threat, but still there was nothing concrete.

Once in her room, Maddie slipped off her shoes and lay on her bed as the spring light faded. Having Hammler at the mansion had reawakened her memories of her time spent at the hands of a certain SS captain in Munich. She'd just been arrested and was being frogmarched, one arm thrust painfully behind her back, across the huge square. Down steep steps she was bundled and into a nearby building, which she soon realised was some sort of police station.

'Silence!' barked one of the guards, as she protested. She saw the other one was laughing, but that only made her shout louder.

'I am English!' she screamed as a cell door opened and she was shoved unceremoniously inside. Grasping the bars of the small grille in the door with both hands, she called out again. 'I demand to see the person in charge!'

'Shut up and wait for the captain,' the guard growled as he slid the shutter across the grille. 'You have some explaining to do.'

Slumped on the single wooden bench secured to the wall, she'd looked about her and shivered. Despite the high temperature outside, down here, where neither warmth nor light ever penetrated, the place felt like a dungeon. A prisoner before her had scratched something into the brickwork that she couldn't read. A forlorn single light bulb dangled from the ceiling. She wanted to cry but pursed her lips and stemmed the tears to deny her Nazi guards the satisfaction of hearing her sob.

As the minutes passed, her thoughts turned to Edith Cavell, the courageous English nurse in the Great War accused of being a traitor by the Germans, but then she thought of how her story ended – badly – so she tried to think of something else. She had no idea of the time but guessed it must have been after midnight when she heard the clink of keys and the sliding of the grille. She leapt to her feet suddenly, clenching her fists at her sides.

'An English girl?' she heard a voice say outside. She'd learned to recognise the difference between the way the guards spoke, in rough, back-of-the-throat dialects, and the more educated Germans. This man's voice was refined. Suddenly the thug outside her cell turned, stamped his boots loudly and jangled the keys in the lock. A second later an officer – she could tell by his grey

SS uniform – stood before her, inspecting her, as the heavy door clanged shut once more.

'Well, well,' he said, pulling at the fingers of his leather gloves, one by one, in a move calculated to unnerve her. It worked. His chin jutted out as he regarded her contemptuously from under hooded lids. 'I'm told you were caught red-handed, breaking the glass of the bulletin board in Odeonsplatz.'

He gestured behind him to the grille in the door and the guard closed it. Maddie heard laughter in the corridor outside and saw a smile curl the officer's lips.

'So, we have our vandal,' he said, clearly amused. 'An English girl who thinks she can smash her way through our fine city.' She was standing in the middle of the cell, and he began to circle her. 'Well, well. What a very foolish English girl. What is your name?'

Her fear melded with defiance. 'My name is Madeleine Gresham and I'm a British citizen,' she'd replied unwaveringly.

The officer just laughed in her face. He barked out a spontaneous 'Yes! British!' as if that explained everything. But his expression and his tone didn't remain flippant for long. 'You are a guest in our country, Miss Gresham, and yet you treat our possessions with criminal contempt. Is that the way they teach you to behave in England – to show no respect for your hosts and your betters?'

It was as if his remark lit the tinder that had been smouldering inside her for so long. She turned her head to face him. 'Why do you show no respect for Jews?'

The answer came in a slap delivered so quickly and so violently across her face that it knocked her off balance and sent her reeling back to fall on the bed. The shock of it robbed her of her speech. When she put her hand to her mouth, it felt sticky and when she looked at her fingers, there was blood.

'From now on, it is I who demand your respect,' said the officer calmly, towering over her. She noticed a long, raised scar ran from his left ear to his mouth. It moved as he spoke. 'No more talk. Guard!' he called.

Maddie watched in horrified silence as the door to her cell opened and one of the thugs marched in, his arm shooting out in a Nazi salute.

'This soldier here will teach you some manners,' said the SS captain coldly.

The guard's face broke into a leer, as if he couldn't believe his good fortune.

'I will leave you in his capable hands,' sneered the officer, nodding at the guard who held open the door for him to leave.

As she heard the cell door lock, the blood drained from Maddie's head, and she thought she might be sick as the guard took off his cap and flung it eagerly on the bench in the cell.

'What? No!' Horrified, she realised the beast was reaching for his belt buckle. 'Get away from me,' she screamed. 'Get away.'

There was no way she could fight him off and no one to come to her aid. She had to think quickly. Running to the grille, she could see the officer settle down in a chair outside, no doubt to listen to her ordeal to gain some sick, perverted pleasure. The thug's arms tightened around her waist from behind as she clung to the bars, but she kicked out at him like a bucking horse. He grunted in pain as she screamed through the grille: 'Herr Weitzler will hear of this. Herr Weitzler!' Her breath rasped out every syllable as rough hands returned to maul her. Max's father was her last hope. Her only hope.

*

A sudden sound at the bedroom door made her jump. For an instant she was grateful to be brought back to reality, but then the nightmare made her recall Josef Hammler. His horrific admission to Ernst must have reawakened memories of her own trauma at the hands of a Nazi.

Sniffing away tears, she turned her head to see Sally's blonde curls peeping round the door and quickly scrambled upright.

'Sally. Come in,' said Maddie, quickly wiping her tear-stained face with a handkerchief. 'You caught me feeling a bit sad. But now you're here I shall be happy,' she said, holding out her hand towards the little girl. Sally took it. 'Do you and Benjy want to come and sit by me?' Maddie asked, seeing the forlorn rabbit was still in tow.

The little girl nodded and, with a helping hand from Maddie, managed to climb onto the bed, where she settled herself beside her on top of the covers. She was wearing a pinafore dress and in the front pocket she carried a piece of folded paper and two crayons, one blue, the other red. Delving into the pocket she pulled out the paper and presented it.

'You want to draw?' Maddie asked.

Sally nodded and proceeded to open up the folds in the paper. It was only then Maddie realised something was printed on the other side. It looked like a flyer of some sort. She read the wording.

'Does your granny know you have this?' she asked.

The little girl suddenly looked very sheepish and slowly shook her head as Maddie studied the text more carefully with mounting concern. It looked as though she had inadvertently uncovered what Mrs Pollock did every Thursday night instead of going to bingo. Her landlady wasn't enjoying secret liaisons with Mr Clancy as she'd originally supposed but attending regular meetings. She was, it seemed, a member of the Peace Pledge Union, an organisation originally formed to promote peace. Lately, however, Maddie knew its image had been tarnished because she'd read it had been infiltrated by the British Union of Fascists.

Maddie's landlady, it turned out, was a card-carrying pacifist. Or maybe even a supporter of Hitler.

Chapter 32

June 1944

The BBC Home Service broke the news in a special bulletin. It was eight o'clock in the morning and Maddie was just about to eat a spoonful of watery porridge, when it was announced: Operation Overlord had begun.

'My word!' cried Mrs Pollock, busy with bread and dripping at the stove. She hurried over to the set to turn up the volume, just in time to hear the announcer tell Britain that the Allies had landed on the northern coast of France. It was D-Day.

'Oh, Harold!' cried the landlady, hugging her husband. He was seated at the table, a napkin tucked under his chin, yet seemed unaffected by the news. Nevertheless, Mrs Pollock's joy remained unabated. She clasped her hands together before reaching out to kiss a slightly bemused Sally. There was even a hug for Maddie.

'That is good news, ain't it?' she said, wiping her palms on her overall. 'This war could be over soon.'

'It certainly could,' said Maddie. Her landlady's euphoria made her think that she wasn't a supporter of Hitler after all, just a naïve pacifist. Maddie knew the landings were only the beginning of the fight-back and there was no guarantee of success. But seeing

Mrs Pollock dancing around the kitchen, she really didn't want to be the one to rain on her parade.

Rumours had been flying round like midges for weeks. Everyone suspected something momentous was about to happen; *a big push*, someone had called it. They just didn't know how or when.

Three days later, as news of Allied advances reached London, Maddie was summoned to McKie's office. The colonel was standing, his arms clasped behind his back, looking out of the window. He turned and smiled at her, although he wasn't looking as pleased as she thought he might, given the morning's news of the continuing Allied successes in France.

As bidden, she took a seat and listened to what the colonel had to say. He made a few remarks about the landings as he puffed ferociously on his pipe, but it wasn't long before he arrived at the crux of their meeting.

'I've come to a decision, Miss Gresham,' he told her, looking uncharacteristically serious.

'You have, sir?' He was making her nervous.

'With his troops on the run, Hitler may decide it's a good time to use his infernal secret weapon,' he warned. 'This Vengeance rocket, or whatever it's called.'

Maddie acknowledged it was a possibility.

'Our troops are now more exposed to air attack than ever. But Lansley tells me no real progress has been made with Hammler. The man takes meals in his room and barely speaks to the other officers. He seems completely immovable. Happy enough to accept our hospitality but give us nothing about this infernal weapon in return. Threats don't work. They tried those at the holding facility, but it seems he won't cave with kindness, either.'

'No, sir.' She had to agree that on the subject of Hitler's secret weapon, the Crocodile's jaws seemed firmly shut. Hammler was a fanatical Nazi. It would take a change of heart to make him talk. But did she also detect a change in the colonel's tone? It seemed to have softened. She could tell he was building up to something.

Regarding her with an unfamiliar expression which, to her surprise she recognised as humility, he told her: 'What I'm saying, Miss Gresham, is that I was perhaps too hasty when I dismissed your suggestion about a woman's touch.'

Maddie felt her back stiffen and she shifted in her seat. She knew she hadn't used that exact phrase, but she supposed the colonel had got the gist of what she'd been driving at. 'Really, sir?'

He sucked on his pipe. 'Yes, really,' he said, 'although I do have your best interests at heart.' He frowned. 'It's a delicate matter, you see. As I've said before, I fear you might be putting yourself in grave personal danger.'

Maddie felt he was being fatherly towards her, and she knew what he was implying. Any relationship she struck up with this "Crocodile" might lead to him exploiting her vulnerability. She suddenly shivered as the memory of that night in a Munich cell stabbed at her brain.

After a short pause, the colonel looked her straight in the eye. 'I think it's high time we put Lady Frobisher on the case, Miss Gresham. See what she can find out for us.'

Surprise and fear charged through Maddie in equal measure. 'Yes, sir. Of course,' she replied, while at the same time feeling the ten-ton weight already on her shoulders had doubled. Despite her initial disappointment and being made to feel decidedly second-class by the colonel, she suddenly found the thought of becoming Lady Frobisher quite terrifying.

*

'Looks like we've got work to do,' said Eddie later the same day, seated in her office.

He'd behaved in such a gentlemanly way since she'd rebuffed him the other week. He was kind and courteous but she almost wished he'd acted how so many men would've, given the circumstances. It would be so much easier if he'd thrown his toys out of the pram and stormed off. But he hadn't and he was making her life even more difficult by tugging at her heartstrings every time they met.

'Does next Monday suit you?' she asked, her pen poised over her diary.

'Our first outing as husband and wife,' he said, his eyes trained on her. 'At least we've got a ready-made cover story. We met at Oxford acting in a play together, fell in love, broke up, then found each other again.'

Maddie shot him a sceptical look. 'That's not how I remember it, Eddie,' she snapped.

'Oh well, a chap can dream,' he said.

There was an awkward pause, before his gaze suddenly switched above her face.

'What's wrong?' she asked, self-consciously touching her hair.

He reached into the briefcase at his side. 'I hope you don't mind, but I asked the chaps at MI6 to do some more digging into Hammler's background. They came up with this.'

He pulled out a photograph from a file and laid it on the desk in front of her. It was of an attractive woman with high cheekbones and blonde hair. She was probably a similar age to herself, thought Maddie.

'Who is she?' she asked, continuing to study the image.

'Clara Hammler,' said Eddie.

Maddie's head jerked up. 'His wife?' She suddenly remembered reading Dr Baskin's notes.

Eddie nodded.

'And Colonel McKie has seen this?'

Another nod. 'It's what helped him change his mind. He thought if . . .'

'If I reminded Hammler of his wife, he might open up to me.' Her words came out on an icy breath. It was a ludicrous idea, not to mention terrifying.

'Precisely.'

Maddie coughed out a laugh and slumped back in her chair. 'It doesn't always work like that. Seeing someone who resembles her could have the opposite effect. He might even be violent towards the poor woman.' She snatched at the photograph again and looked at it. 'She's beautiful.' *How could he . . .?* she asked herself, thinking of what Ernst had heard about the young woman at Göttingen. She felt sickened. 'What do we know about her?' She gave the image back to him.

'Not much. They lived in Berlin and have four children. But that sort of information could help, couldn't it? Don't you psychology types like to know a person's background?'

'Naturally their past experiences very often shape their character,' she agreed. 'But seeing someone who looks like his wife could turn him even more withdrawn. Violent even. In the case of a man like Hammler – someone powerful and without morals – this is playing with fire.'

'But you won't be his wife. You'll be Lady Frobisher and with other people every step of the way, Maddie. We'll be out in public places: galleries, restaurants. Just what you suggested. And you know McKie wouldn't let anything happen to you.' He looked at her intently. 'Nor would I.'

She shook her head, thinking of Hammler's mood swings and her assault in the Munich cell. 'It only takes a second for a man to strike,' she reminded him.

'At least think about it, Maddie,' he asked her, returning the photograph to its folder. 'It could make the difference between success and failure.'

Chapter 33

In a wigmaker's salon, just off Curzon Street in central London, Maddie sat in front of a large, oval mirror. A copy of the photograph of Clara Hammler was at her side. It had taken a long time to find the right shade and style to match the woman's hair as near as possible. But the wig did not sit easily on her head. Turning this way and that, she studied the Marcel waves and how the light bounced off them. She felt awkward about it. Once again she found herself stepping into someone else's shoes, as she had with Dr Baskin, and they didn't fit her comfortably.

If she could establish some sort of connection with Hammler – in this case reminding him of his wife – then it would be worth it. She owed it to the thousands of innocent civilians at risk to force him to confront what he'd done and the terrible consequences if he remained silent. She doubted a fanatic like him would ever pass on his country's secrets knowingly. But at least she should try and prompt him to open up.

Holding a large mirror to the back of her head so that she could assess the overall effect, a rather effete man whose overpowering cologne made her want to sneeze, had insisted she looked *'divine, like an angel.'*

Colonel McKie had given her a clothes allowance. She'd gone

to Harvey Nichols, and recalling Clara Hammler's style, had opted for outfits that were plain, simple and well cut. Good Nazi women did not dress lavishly.

A pillbox hat with a small net veil – which might even mask the fear in her eyes – also went on the store's account. That, together with a bottle of *Je Reviens. A woman's scent speaks volumes,* her mother would say when Maddie, as a child, watched her admiringly at her dressing table. She'd marvel at the way she dabbed perfume behind her ears. The scent would instantly transport her to a summer meadow, or an exotic palace, depending on her mood.

From now on, whenever Maddie wore her wig and dressed in her new outfits, she was Lady Madeleine Frobisher, Lord Frobisher's charming, but rather bird-brained wife. She would fool Hammler and lull him into false sense of security, making him divulge things he'd never impart to the likes of Fruity Boxall. The plan, on paper at least, sounded plausible. The charade had worked well for Eddie's alter ego. It might work even better for her, although having to deal with the Crocodile would certainly up the stakes.

*

Paget took care of the hatbox and various packages when they arrived back at Trent Park, but as soon as she walked through her office door to find a flustered Briggs, Maddie sensed trouble.

'Oh, Miss Gresham. I'm so glad you're back. Colonel McKie says he needs to see you, urgently.'

Maddie went straight away and arrived at the colonel's office to be met by very serious faces. To her surprise Eddie was there, his blue eyes hard and steely. He rose when she entered the room, but while there was acknowledgement, there was no smile.

'Ah good, Miss Gresham,' the colonel greeted her brusquely. 'You need to hear the troubling news I've just received. Take a seat.' His pipe sat in the bulldog ashtray, but he was rolling a pencil between his fingers.

Maddie looked at Eddie who gave an almost imperceptible shrug as if to say he had no idea what was going on either. The colonel looked down at some notes on his desk.

'Reports are coming through of a huge explosion on the main Liverpool Street to Southend railway line at Bow Viaduct.'

Maddie instantly thought there'd been another air raid. There hadn't been any German bombing missions for a few weeks, although, following the D-Day landings everyone had been primed to expect some sort of retaliation by Hitler. But then she realised from Colonel McKie's pained expression that this could be the payback they all feared.

'What's of particular concern,' he carried on, 'is there was no bomber and no pilot.'

The intake of breath by both Maddie and Eddie was simultaneous and audible. It seemed that the pilotless plane they had been dreading had arrived.

'The Vengeance weapon,' muttered Maddie. She recalled General Birkel's chilling description of it to Koenig. *A flying torpedo with an automatic guidance system.*

McKie nodded and suddenly the pencil between his finger snapped in two. 'As feared, we have a new and even deadlier weapon to contend with than conventional bombs. The missile is powered by a liquid-propellant rocket and when that runs out the whole shebang just falls out of the sky to wreak havoc below. And we're expecting more. The siren only sounded for a few seconds before the engine cut out and it hit.'

Maddie was shaking her head. 'So hardly any time to get to shelters?'

'Precisely,' replied McKie, reaching for his pipe, as if the thought of hundreds more civilian deaths invoked in him a desperate need to smoke. 'This, of course, means we need you to speed up your efforts with Hammler. We know he has detailed knowledge about the rockets' capabilities, and we need to find out more about how they're launched and, of course, from where. Our chaps are doing aerial reconnaissance but they're a bit tied up right now covering for our ground troops on the Continent. Intelligence suggests the launch sites must be along the French coast somewhere, but it's like looking for needles in a haystack. We need to give them some idea of where to search.'

'Of course, sir,' replied Eddie. 'What do you suggest?'

McKie struck a match and held the flame over the bowl of his pipe. 'That Lady Frobisher works her magic right away,' he replied, looking at Maddie pointedly. 'Get Hammler to talk.'

Chapter 34

The next day dawned dull, but dry. At 0900 hours precisely Paget collected her important passenger from just around the corner from Fairview Boarding House. Maddie had managed to evade Mrs Pollock's scrutiny by slipping out of the front door shortly after breakfast, but she still hadn't dared don her wig and or hat. She saved those accoutrements for a lay-by just outside the main gates. Paget had left the usual Humber Snipe in the garage and was driving a decidedly more grandiose Bentley. She let her important passenger use her rear-view mirror.

'How do I look?' asked Maddie, barely able to apply her lipstick because her hand was trembling so much.

'Very stylish, miss.'

'That's what I needed to hear,' she replied, as she gave her nose a final dusting of powder. She mustn't show any sign of weakness.

Paget moved off smoothly and soon they'd passed through the security gates of Cockfosters Camp and glided up the drive to come to a halt in front of the mansion's main entrance. There, the brigadier was standing stiffly in his immaculate uniform and high, polished boots.

This was the day Maddie would finally come face to face with the Crocodile. Brigadier Josef Hammler had loomed large in her psyche ever since she'd read Dr Baskin's reports on him, then watched him foil Major Lansley's questioning with his bull-headedness. At first she'd found him easy to pin down: a narcissist with an ego the size of a Panzer tank. He was a loner, but he still loved himself and thought everyone else should love him, too. But that was before she'd listened to Ernst's shocking testimony. Hearing how he'd looked on as thousands of Jews were shot had made her both hate him and fear him. It would take all her strength to overcome her own feelings and remain dispassionate.

The mere thought of having to shake his hand chilled her to the bone. Knowing he'd been complicit in the killing of inno-cent Jews in cold blood, repulsed her. If their eyes met, would he register her revulsion? If their arms brushed, would he notice her shudder at his touch?

A trip around central London to see the sights was on the schedule; Maddie called it the "depression" tour. It was to focus on the landmarks that had escaped the Luftwaffe bombs and would end at Harrods, where a leisurely browse in the food hall would show the brigadier that, contrary to Goebbels' propaganda, England wasn't starving. She'd previously designed the itinerary to impress and make the German generals think Hitler's *"blitz-krieg"* wasn't quite so devastating after all. Many of them had been hoodwinked into believing their bombing raids had caused little destruction to the capital. But would such a ploy wash with Hammler? She wasn't sure he'd be so easily taken in.

If all went to plan, while the brigadier was distracted Maddie would probe his mental state and see if she could find any chinks in his psychological armour, as Dr Baskin had proposed. Judging on past experience, she feared, however, it would not be that straightforward.

At the briefing beforehand Major Lansley warned her to be careful in Hammler's presence. 'Try and get him talking about his family. That sometimes helps to break down barriers.' Maddie was fully aware that *sometimes* worked, especially in a textbook situation, yet this was anything but. Getting Hammler to open up was a tall order. She would have to play the whole thing by ear. But she was under pressure to produce results and she had to face the fact that she needed to befriend a man who was, in effect, a mass murderer.

On arrival at the mansion, Paget opened the door for Maddie. She disembarked to be greeted by her husband. The introductions were made by Lord Frobisher.

'Darling, I want you to meet Brigadier Hammler.'

For a moment he just stared at Maddie, taking in her face and hair, making her feel self-conscious. As her cheeks began to colour she wanted to turn away, but then she detected a flicker in his features before a smile suddenly appeared and broadened a little.

'Lady Frobisher. Delighted to meet you,' he said.

'Brigadier Hammler,' she said, offering her gloved hand. Something had stirred in him, she could tell, as he took her hand in his. She wanted to turn away from him so very badly to spare herself his gaze, but she forced herself to look at him, hoping the veil over her eyes would offer some protection. *He must not see the fear in them.*

Lord and Lady Frobisher sat on the back seat of the limousine, while Hammler settled himself comfortably opposite them. His back was to Paget and a glass screen was drawn so their conversation couldn't be overhead.

'We're delighted you agreed to accompany us, Brigadier Hammler,' ventured Eddie.

The German smiled and turned to Maddie. 'I only came because you said your wife would be accompanying you, Lord Frobisher,' he replied calmly as they sped down the drive.

Eddie flashed a tight smile. 'And does that make the prospect more enticing?'

'It most certainly does,' he replied, flashing small white teeth at Maddie.

Somehow she managed to hold down the rising nausea to

give a gracious nod. The Crocodile did seem charming, on the surface at least.

*

Paget's route was strictly mapped out. Top of the agenda was Battersea Power Station. 'Still standing despite your pilots' best efforts.' Eddie chuckled. Hammler didn't seem to appreciate the humour although it made Maddie smile, the way his seemingly affable comments so often carried a sting.

In fact, Hammler remained fairly taciturn throughout the journey and seemed completely uninterested in the sights London had to offer. He clearly had other things on his mind. As Maddie stared out of the window, she felt his eyes boring into her. When she angled round and looked at him now and again, he made no effort to turn away. His thin mouth would twitch unashamedly, and she found herself obliged to flash a forced smile in return.

They crossed Tower Bridge and several other bridges, just to prove they were also still standing. Of course, St Paul's Cathedral was as majestic ever, although Paget deliberately steered clear of the carnage wrought by firebombs around Paternoster Row. The Houses of Parliament, too, were looking magnificent in the sunshine.

'Cleopatra's Needle,' remarked Eddie, as they passed the structure, flanked by two bronze faux sphinxes, through the window. 'Your chaps dropped a bomb nearby in 1917, I believe. We still haven't repaired the shrapnel damage on the right-hand sphinx.'

Hammler turned and spoke then. 'Why would you not repair it?' he asked. In person, his voice was cultured and surprisingly deliberate, thought Maddie, compared to what she'd heard on the recordings.

'Perhaps it's a reminder,' she suggested. 'To keep us on our toes.'

It was a sunny day in early July. The pavements were agreeably busy with Londoners going about their daily lives as if they hadn't a care in the world. Hitler was on the back foot. City types with bowlers and rolled umbrellas, servicemen and women on leave, nannies with perambulators, hawkers with barrows; it was as if Colonel McKie himself had choreographed the scenes, thought Maddie. The Allies were, after all, making great inroads into German-occupied territories.

The Bentley stopped along the Embankment to allow the party to stretch their legs. The plane trees lining the road were in full leaf and rustled in the slight breeze.

Paget opened the back door to allow her passengers to disembark. As he was nearest to the door Hammler was first to leave the limousine. Once on the pavement, he turned and held out his hand to assist Maddie. She took it, but felt the bile rise at his touch.

Paget remained by the car as the others stood looking out over the river at London Bridge and St Paul's to their left, with Big Ben on their right.

'So, is this why you brought me here, Lord Frobisher?' Hammler asked. 'To show me that London is still intact? That our Luftwaffe have not done such a great job after all?'

It was the first time he had said anything of note the whole morning. Maddie hid her surprise at this remark. Surely the Crocodile wasn't trying to put the Reich down?

'It'll take more than a few bombs to stop Londoners in their tracks,' she came back – a silent laugh in her voice to lighten the comment.

'I would not be so sure,' Hammler replied, an edge to his voice.

This was the moment. They had to capitalise on it. If he was ever going to talk, surely it would be now? Maddie fired first.

'Oh, you mean the pilotless bomb?'

Hammler's expression registered mild shock. His head tilted back in surprise. 'You are well informed, Lady Frobisher.'

Eddie feigned anger. 'You know you're not supposed to say anything about that, darling.' He leaned in to Hammler. 'They're keeping it very quiet, but just between us, one of your new flying bombs paid us a visit the other night. Didn't hit anything but gave us a nasty fright.'

Hammler arched a brow and smiled. 'So, you can cut off the Medusa's head, but another one will grow in its place.'

'Brigadier, are you saying there will be more?' asked Maddie.

'Oh yes, dear lady. Many more,' he replied.

A barge carrying coal chugged by them, sounding its horn, as they began to walk towards the Houses of Parliament, three abreast with Maddie in the middle. It was an opportunity for a deeper conversation, even though she was dreading it.

'And where do you call home, Herr General?' she asked.

'Berlin,' he replied. 'I fear it did not look as fair as London after your RAF raids.'

Maddie smiled. Their little propaganda trip had obviously managed to pull the wool over Hammler's eyes.

'So how are you finding England, Herr General?'

He smirked, his hands behind his back as they walked. 'I am a prisoner, Lady Frobisher,' he snapped. 'And you ask me if I like my prison?'

'Oh, but you're being treated quite well, aren't you? Given the circumstances.'

Another smile hovered on his lips. 'We are only given what we deserve.'

'One does one's best,' added Eddie, pretending to be mildly offended.

They walked on for another mile in the sunshine, but all the while Maddie felt Hammler's shadow darkening her mood. Finally, she suggested they pay a visit to Harrods.

The food hall was looking as enticing as ever; it was a place where rationing seemed to be something for other people to worry about, thought Maddie. No one here looked worried about getting their two ounces of tea and butter. Apples and pears were piled high. There were strings of sausages and flitches of bacon, too, and the shelves were full of boxes of chocolates and tins of biscuits. Hammler appeared to relax a little and was seemingly impressed. He even bought a box of chocolates.

'For you, Lady Frobisher,' he told Maddie, presenting them to her with a bow. She had to stifle the urge to throw them back at him.

Nevertheless, he returned to Trent Park apparently in a much better mood than when he left. From MI19's point of view, at least part of the mission was accomplished. Hammler had seen for himself that London may have been bloodied but certainly not bowed by Hitler's bombs. Even more importantly, the brigadier was now aware that the new vengeance weapon had finally made its presence felt. His reaction to such news might produce results in the days to come.

At the end of the return journey Paget parked the car on the drive at the front of the mansion by the entrance, flanked by ornamental urns. However, as well as trailing lobelia and geraniums, it was also planted out with a microphone. The device had already yielded interesting comments from the generals after their outings with Eddie as they left the limousine.

*

It was Max's second week in the M Room. From now on he would spend all his day – or night – depending on his shift, in the dingy, airless basement without any creature comforts. But he was doing something. Playing his part in the fight. At last, he felt valued.

As he was still learning the ropes, he wasn't yet entrusted to work on his own. A Wren – Third Officer Havisham was her name – was supervising his training session, while a senior listener, an Austrian, sat at his side.

There'd been a couple of conversations considered worthy of recording that afternoon. Three high-ranking Luftwaffe officers and two from the German navy were discussing Hitler's leadership. A great divide had opened up between those who supported the Führer unquestioningly and those who doubted. But there'd been no mention of the secret weapon. Then, at 16.15 precisely, the Austrian listener sprang into action.

'*Horen!*' he cried. 'Listen up!' Clamping his earphones to his head, he flicked a switch on the recording machine. It was the signal for Max to follow suit. With his pencil poised over the relevant form, he waited to dictate what came down the line.

As a German voice crackled over the airwaves, both men started to scribble. 'It's been a very enjoyable afternoon, Lord Frobisher.' The speaker, a male, was educated and calm.

'Our pleasure, Brigadier,' replied a cut-glass English voice.

The German again: 'And the company of your wife made it all the more pleasurable, Lord Frobisher.'

A woman's voice next. 'I am delighted that you found it such a pleasant diversion, Brigadier Hammler.' Her voice, too, was educated. English upper-class. *Just like Maddie's.*

The pencil suddenly dropped from Max's fingers and the Austrian shot him a dirty look. Aware that his lapse of concentration had been noticed, Max retrieved his pencil quickly and started jotting again.

'Next time we must do lunch,' said the Englishman.

I shall look forward to it, noted down Max. There was the usual clicking of Nazi heels, followed by a name. *Lady Frobisher.* Max imagined the German kissing the woman's hand. He knew these Nazi officers could be so treacherous, casually killing with one hand, while holding a Champagne glass in the other. The thought sickened him.

He listened hard again to the crunch of footsteps on gravel and two seconds later a door opened and shut.

Taking his cue from the Austrian, Max unhooked his earphones and breathed deeply. What had he just heard? Or, more importantly, who?

'That was our most important prisoner, Brigadier Josef

Hammler. The initials BJH for short,' volunteered Havisham. She was being unusually helpful as she cast an eye over Max's notes. Her varnished fingernail pointed to the form. 'It's tricky,' she admitted. 'But you'll soon learn who's who.'

'I hope so,' replied Max, still trying to recover from the shock of the familiarity of the female voice. 'And what about the others, the English man and woman?'

'Lord and Lady Frobisher.'

'Who are they?'

Havisham looked down her nose at him. 'You can't ask questions like that.'

Max flinched. He'd been put in his place, but he still repeated the name in a whisper. 'Lady Frobisher.' It sounded strange on his tongue. 'Do you know her first name?'

Havisham smiled at his remark, even though Max hadn't meant it to be the least bit funny. 'As I said, that's not for you to know, sergeant,' she replied. She reminded him of one of the English nannies favoured by the upper classes in Munich when he was a child. But Max did need to know. He had to find out. That Englishwoman's voice, that Lady Frobisher, had reminded him so much of Maddie's it was uncanny. He knew it was crazy, but maybe, just maybe . . .

The Wren, he saw, was still looking at him hard, studying him, and shaking her head.

'You've got no hope there, Sergeant Weitzler,' she told him, adding haughtily: 'She's way out of your league.'

Chapter 35

'Hammler told Lehmann all about you,' McKie informed Maddie late the following day. The colonel's enthusiasm manifested itself in the ardent puffing of his pipe. 'He seemed quite taken. Good work, Miss Gresham. I suggest you see him again. Soon as you can.'

Maddie suddenly realised she'd been holding her breath as the colonel spoke. She breathed again. Major Lansley had congratulated her, too. Her debut as Lady Frobisher was being seen as a success, but the real breakthrough had been made by Eddie when he'd slipped into the conversation that the new V-1 had launched successfully.

'Did Hammler say any more about news of the rocket?' she asked. She hadn't yet seen the relevant transcript.

'Apparently he brought it up in conversation last night with Ernst. He seemed rather annoyed that it didn't hit central London as intended. So keep up the good work, Miss Gresham,' said the colonel with a chuckle.

*

The next time Maddie and Eddie reprised their aristocratic roles their destination was Simpson's, a fashionable restaurant on the

Strand. Lady Frobisher made her own way there. On arrival Maddie caught sight of her reflection in a large plate glass window as the doorman held open the Bentley's door. Easing out of the limousine, knees and ankles together, she really didn't recognise the person who stared back at her. Had she reminded Hammler of his wife? In his eyes she had detected some sort of reaction, but she couldn't be sure what it meant.

The restaurant was packed. Ever since the government had introduced a law putting a five-shilling ceiling on meal prices, practically every Tom, Dick and Harry could dine out. Simpson's, however, remained rather exclusive. The tables were occupied mainly by men in dark suits, interspersed with a few uniforms. Officers only, naturally. The women all wore expensive outfits and were draped in furs and jewellery. Even though she'd kept her look simple in line what she thought were Hammler's tastes, she knew she still fitted in. In fact, she felt so at home in the restaurant she feared some of her father's friends up from the country might see through her disguise. She had to keep reminding herself that she looked so different it was unlikely any of Lady Houghton's Cotswold coterie would recognise her. At least, that was her hope. And as to the reaction of diners when they saw a German briga-dier in uniform striding through the restaurant to lunch just like everyone else – that would be most interesting.

Hammler was sporting a new Wehrmacht uniform. It had been made by the visiting tailor and he wore it with pride. Lord Frobisher was in civilian dress.

Once inside the restaurant, the maître d' greeted them – he'd obviously been primed – and showed them into a rather special dining room where they sat at a rather special table. Heads had certainly turned on their arrival. For an awful moment Maddie even detected a lull in conversation as dowagers raised eyebrows and lords' jaws dropped. After running such a gamut of shock and disapproval it was a relief when they finally took their seats out of the public's glare.

A waiter brought them menus, along with a bottle of Châteauneuf-du-Pape. When he'd poured out the wine, the sommelier left the bottle on the table. Hammler seemed in good spirits.

'Nineteen thirty-eight,' he read aloud, scrutinising the label.

'Let us hope that the grapes aren't being left to rot on the vines,' mused Eddie. The remark was delivered in a throwaway fashion, even though it was completely calculated.

'I doubt it,' snorted Hammler. 'We Germans love our wine just as much as the French. But ours is far superior.'

Maddie returned his smug smile, but silently begged to differ. The Riesling she'd sampled in Munich she'd considered only fit to rinse her teeth. The brigadier was arrogant and self-opinionated, as were most of his fellow officers, but he seemed to be attracted to her. She felt like a goat tethered to a riverbank, left as bait. How she would manage to eat in Hammler's company, she had no idea.

'You Germans are far superior in so many things, Brigadier,' Eddie replied mischievously, playing the flattery card.

'So, now you are telling me you are an admirer of the Fatherland, Lord Frobisher?'

A trap? wondered Maddie.

Such a question, asked so openly, was a little awkward, so Maddie lowered her voice to intervene. 'As far as I can tell there is much to admire, Herr Brigadier,' she replied, trying to keep her gaze steady as she spoke.

Hammler smiled then, showing his teeth once more. 'Indeed. Your rightful king is a good man and a friend of the Führer. He should never have abdicated.'

'If he hadn't, our two countries would probably have remained close allies, but instead . . .' Maddie had thrown out some red meat and the Crocodile had seized it.

'You are so right, dear lady. As you yourself implied before, it is a tragedy that our two countries are at war.' He leaned in as he spoke, and his look made Maddie uncomfortable.

Just then a waiter came to take their order and Eddie directed the proceedings. Glancing down at the leather-bound menu in his hand he said: 'This place is famous for its roasts, Brigadier. May I commend the sirloin to you?'

Hammler nodded. 'With some of the famous Yorkshire pudding, yes?' he suggested, suddenly cheered by the thought of food.

'Yorkshire pudding, yes, absolutely!' said Eddie before turning to Maddie. 'And for you, darling?'

'You know you always choose for me, dear,' she replied, batting her eyelashes at him. She loathed playing the helpless little lady, but right now it suited her purpose.

'Three soups, two beef and one turbot,' Eddie relayed, then pointing to the Châteauneuf-du-Pape, which was almost empty he asked: 'More wine, Brigadier?'

*

Of course, Brigadier Hammler wasn't aware, as he quaffed wine, ate fine food and enjoyed female company, that almost fourteen miles away, the listeners in the M Room were recording their every word. Microphones had been concealed under their table and in lamps nearby, picking up every sentence and innuendo. One of the listeners just happened to be Max.

He'd been confused when he heard the female voice the other day. It was so unbelievably like Maddie's – or at least how he remembered Maddie's voice. But he judged himself mistaken. His heart wanted it to be hers, but his head told him otherwise. Now, however, he had spent the last two hours listening intently to this woman make polite conversation with a Nazi, – even laugh and flirt with him. This man was his enemy: a fanatic, a Jew hater. He had blood on his hands, and she was in league with him. It was Maddie, all right. He was convinced of it. But not his. This Maddie was not the seventeen-year-old English girl who had stolen his heart in Munich. Now she was a woman – a married woman, too – but she had changed beyond recognition. Those nights they spent smashing noticeboards, risking their own lives for the sake of justice for Jews, clearly meant nothing to her. Everything they'd both stood for in those heady summer days when they were invincible, had disappeared. The bond they had forged was broken, the light extinguished.

Unhooking his headphones, he sat for a moment, dazed and horrified by what he had just heard. His shoulders slumped as he stared silently at the brick wall ahead of him. His past flashed before him: his mother lying dead by the bridge, his pain in the hospital, his shadowy existence with the Resistance and his wretched days spent interned. After everything he'd endured, after all the sacrifices he'd made and the risks he'd taken, the Maddie Gresham he knew and loved was no more. She was dead to him.

'I say, Weitzler,' came a voice from behind. It was his supervising officer. 'Something wrong?'

Max looked up to see the captain's concerned face and lifted a hand towards the recording machine.

The captain nodded. 'Heard something bad, have you?' he asked. 'It's the hardest part of the job for you chaps, I know.' With that he patted Max on the shoulder and added glibly: 'Just got to bite your tongue. Onwards and upwards, eh?'

Right now, however, Max's dream of a future with Maddie had been snatched from him and his heart torn into pieces. His life would never be the same again.

Chapter 36

As it was after the end of Maddie's shift, Paget dropped her back at Fairview once she'd changed out of her disguise. She was relieved to find the house empty – a note from Mrs Pollock told her she and Sally had gone to call on a friend – and Maddie headed straight for her room. Once safely there she threw her blonde wig and hat into the small vanity case she kept under her bed. She really didn't like being Lady Frobisher because of the expectations that came with playing her character. She wasn't a natural spy. Creating a persona that was expected of her as an aristocratic wife, rather than one she really was, made her uneasy. But more than that, when she was in the presence of Hammler – and had to ingratiate herself with him, flatter him, flirt with him – she felt sullied. If there had been any hot water at Fairview, she would have run herself a bath and scrubbed off the feeling of dirt on her skin.

Kicking off her shoes, she lay fully clothed on the bed, staring up at the ceiling. It reminded her of when she used to wait for Max in the attic room in Munich. Then she'd lain under the covers in the sweltering heat, her heart beating so fast that she hadn't even heard Max's footsteps on the landing before he opened her door. But then her memories took a darker turn, as they almost always did. Perhaps it was because she had spent much of the day in the company of Hammler but suddenly, from somewhere deep inside her psyche, she had another flashback.

It was that night once more and she was clutching at the bars of her cell. As the guard approached her, snorting like a bull, she'd screamed Herr Weitzler's name until her lungs burned. When he realised whose name she was shouting, the officer waiting outside leapt to his feet and stalked over.

'*Halte!*' he'd shouted at the guard through the bars. The mauling stopped instantly. 'Weitzler,' he repeated, his gaze intense through the bars. 'How do you know Herr Weitzler?'

She could barely speak. 'I am . . . I am his guest.'

It was as if Hitler himself had given the order as the officer called for the cell door to be unlocked once more. Inside the guard was rearranging his breeches like his own life depended on it.

'Out,' ordered the officer, booting the thug in the rear. He kicked the door behind him.

Now the two of them were alone and Maddie felt her hair stiffen on her scalp. The officer began to circle her once more and the moment tautened like a rope.

'Herr Helmut Weitzler?' he asked.. She nodded silently. 'Well, well,' he said with a smirk. 'Herr Weitzler is, indeed, a well-respected member of the Party. Your mindless actions will be a great embarrassment to him, as they will to your own country, no doubt.'

He was trying to kill her with shame, but she would not be bowed, even though she was dreading Herr Weitzler's reaction when he was told what she'd done. He would be furious, she knew.

'I could charge you. You know that?' His voice was tinged with menace. 'The penalties for what you have done are grave.'

Little stars began to dance in front of her eyes. Thumb screws? The rack? Electric shocks? Beatings? A gallery of instruments of torture paraded through her mind. She was going to faint.

'You've gone very quiet, Miss Gresham,' the officer remarked as he started to prowl once more, his hands behind his back. He was talking to her as he strode from left to right, like a panther about to pounce. 'Perhaps the thought of your punishment has made you realise the consequences of your actions?'

He put his face close to hers so she could smell his rancid breath. She flinched but kept looking straight ahead.

An agonising moment passed before his pacing stopped. Screwing up his eyes as he looked at her, he said: 'I will drop all charges.'

Maddie swallowed hard and tried not to blink. That would be a sign of weakness. She kept her gaze straight ahead, feeling his glare boring inside her.

'I could have you thrown into jail.' He paused. 'But if you say nothing . . .' His eyes darted to the bruise blooming on her cheek. '. . . I will release you, *ja*?'

'Nothing,' Maddie repeated as the relief that was flooding through her body seemed to flush away her strength at the same time. She steadied herself against the cell wall.

'Nothing,' he said, yanking down his jacket in a gesture designed to instil fear in her and, of course, gratitude. He skewered her with a glare. 'I will, of course, inform your Foreign Office about your reprehensible behaviour. You will be deported. You understand?'

Deported. It was a harsh word. A cold, loveless word, but at least it wasn't torture or imprisonment, or worse still, what had so very nearly happened.

Her answer was carried on a breath of relief. 'Yes, sir,' she replied. She was due to leave for home later the following week in any case, but of course not in such ignominious circumstances. The only consolation was her mother wasn't alive. The very notion of her daughter being ordered to leave another country because she'd committed a criminal act would've mortified her.

Marching out into the corridor, she saw the officer pick up his pen and begin to write something on an official-looking form with a swastika imprinted at its head. He beckoned her.

'You will be hearing from your embassy immediately, no doubt. In the meantime, pack your bags, Miss Gresham.' He looked up from his desk and pinned her with a chilling expression as he delivered his withering parting shot. 'Undesirable aliens like you are not welcome in Germany.' And with those words, she found herself dismissed and manhandled once more into a waiting car that took her back to Max's house and the wrath of his father.

*

Maddie looked at her palms. They were wet with sweat. Somehow she needed to put the memory behind her. She was a psychologist. She of all people should be able to find a way of burying unwanted memories and focusing on the good ones, the positive ones. In the textbooks they made it sound so easy but in practice she was finding it much harder. And now every time she was near Hammler, she found herself back in that cell, her skin crawling at the smell of his breath.

210

Chapter 37

'He's taken a real shine to you,' McKie told Madeleine.

The colonel made Hammler's eagerness to start a friendship with her sound more like a schoolboy crush than what it really was. There was threat and menace in the general's tone, and in his eyes and movements. He was a predator. Why was it that men could never recognise one among their own sex?

'So Flight Lieutenant Windlesham tells me,' replied Madeleine, hiding her disquiet.

The colonel chuckled. He seemed to have shrugged off any concern he'd shown for Madeleine when he'd forbidden her to take on the role of Lady Frobisher. Now, however, he was clearly finding the whole charade rather amusing. She knew she would have to steel herself for yet another performance as Lady Frobisher.

*

It was their fourth outing to London with Hammler. On the last occasion – a trip to see Buckingham Palace – he had made his move on her. As they stood by the Victoria Memorial statue, he'd leaned in and whispered in her ear, 'I only come on these ridiculous outings to be with you.'

It had made her feel uncomfortable, but it was a breakthrough, even if it was a terrifying one. She'd responded by sliding her eyes furtively to his and while Eddie was distracted watching the sentries change the guard, she had returned his smile in a way that a married woman should not. Of course, she'd told Eddie about it, and he'd decided it was a chance to take things further.

Hammler seemed in high spirits as they returned from their current trip, by car. He was much more relaxed in their company now, but Eddie thought it was time to exploit the German's feelings for Maddie.

'I have to go away for a couple of days, so perhaps you might like to accompany Lady Frobisher to the theatre, or the opera?' suggested Eddie. 'You'd like that, wouldn't you darling?'

Maddie was sitting next to him, as usual. 'Yes, of course.'

The prospect delighted Hammler and he was positively leering at Maddie as Paget turned into the gates of the main entrance. There had been heavy rain overnight and the grass was looking particularly green, but the road surface was also rather slippery. Without warning, a deer ran out from behind a rhododendron bush and straight in front of the oncoming car. Paget slammed on the brakes and managed to avoid the doe, but she couldn't stop the skid. The car screeched forward and ploughed onto the grass verge before sliding into a nearby ditch. Its passengers pitched before lurching forward. Maddie suddenly found herself flung into the arms of Hammler.

When the limousine finally came to a halt, it had tilted to one side, with its front wheel in the gulley. Maddie, awkwardly pressed against Hammler, was shocked to feel his hand on her leg. She jerked up her head to catch him leering at her. Struggling out of the brigadier's grasp, she shuffled back onto her seat, and righted herself as quickly as she could, smoothing down her skirt. But the whole incident was very undignified and unnerving. She felt quite sullied.

'Forgive me, Brigadier,' she said, straightening her hat, knocked slightly off kilter by the impact.

Hammler smiled, playfully. 'My dear Lady Frobisher, please do not apologise. Are you hurt?'

'No. No, not at all,' she replied quickly.

'You're sure you're all right?' asked Eddie tersely. He seemed to find the whole incident rather annoying.

'Quite – thank you, dear,' she replied.

Meanwhile, a flustered Paget had climbed out of the car to inspect the damage. Luckily, it seemed there was very little, although she knew it would be difficult trying to reverse the vehicle out of the muddy ditch.

Eddie wound down the window when he saw her crouch low beside from the front off-side wheel.

'I'm afraid you'll all have to get out, sir, while I try and shift her,' she told him, standing up again.

'Very well. If we must,' he replied. Maddie wasn't sure if his annoyance was feigned or real. 'Come on, darling,' he said, taking her gloved hand and clambering out first.

The car was resting at a difficult angle and the passengers needed to exit through the nearside rear door onto the drive. Eddie pulled Maddie up the incline and lent a hand to the brigadier.

Once more behind the wheel, Paget restarted the engine and put the vehicle in reverse, to begin accelerating slowly. Mud started flying as the wheel turned and the longer she kept her foot on the throttle, the deeper the wheel sank.

'It's no use!' shouted Eddie, shaking his head as he watched Paget's valiant attempt. 'We're going to have to get it towed out.'

As he spoke a patrol truck appeared up ahead, coming from the direction of the mansion.

'And here comes the cavalry!' called Eddie with a smile, placing his cap on his head.

As it approached, Maddie was relieved to see two soldiers in the cab. She was sure they'd be carrying a tow rope. The truck slowed and the driver wound down the window.

213

''Avin' a spot of bother are we, sir?'

'I'm afraid so. You chaps got a tow rope?'

The driver, a Cockney, nodded. 'Leave it to us, sir. We'll have you out in no time.' He turned to the other soldier seated next to him. 'Come on, Sergeant Weitzler.'

*

Max jumped down from the cab and hurried round the back to retrieve the rope. As part of his training, he'd been ordered to go out on patrol to familiarise himself with the grounds. Slinging the rope over his shoulder, he approached the stricken car, but a few feet short of it, he stopped dead.

'Right then, sir, let's see what's what,' said the Cockney, bending low to inspect the wheel. The side of the car was splattered with mud and the driver was looking very dejected as she stood nearby. But it was the female passenger who'd caught Max's eye. She had her back to him, but he'd know that outline anywhere.

'That's awfully lucky,' he heard her remark to the German officer as they waited together on the drive. He'd sidled up behind her unnoticed and was standing so close she could smell his cologne.

'Yes. Very fortuitous, Lady Frobisher,' replied the German.

It was then that the woman turned, and Max saw her face for the first time. His breath left his chest in a silent gasp. Her hair was blonde, not brown, as he remembered it, and she was wearing fine clothes. They called her Lady Frobisher, but she was Maddie. There was no doubt in his mind.

For a moment he stood transfixed, trying to take in what he had just discovered, wondering if his worst fears really had come true. His beloved Maddie – the Maddie who'd been willing to sacrifice herself for him and the Maddie he'd dreamed of being reunited with all these years – had married an English lord. She'd torn herself away from their special bond and the promise they'd made and moved on. Max suddenly feared his heart would shatter into a thousand pieces right there and then, but the driver broke into his thoughts.

'Where's that rope, Weitzler?' yelled the Cockney. He and Eddie were bending down on the far side of the Bentley, inspecting the damage. They didn't look at Max. But Maddie did.

*

At the call her head cracked up. *Weitzler.* Max's name. She looked at the tall, blond soldier marching determinedly towards the car, and her eyes suddenly burst into flame. Max? It couldn't be. How could it? Her body went rigid, fighting the desperate urge to rush forward and fling her arms around him. He was looking at her, too. Their eyes met for a split second and a bolt of shock sent her body rigid. It was Max all right, but he mustn't say anything; he mustn't give her away. He held her fate in his hands. One word. One look noticed by Hammler and the whole cover could be blown. Nor must Eddie notice anything suspicious. Thankfully, his attention was occupied by the wheel. He never even looked up. She turned her back on Max, even though she realised what he might think.

If only she could tell him why she was here at Trent Park, why she appeared to be cosying up to a Nazi, why she was seemingly married to a high-ranking Royal Air Force officer and a member of the aristocracy. But she could not. Her lips were sealed. For now, at any rate. But a dagger had just lodged in her chest and until she could tell Max the truth, she knew it would remain there.

215

Chapter 38

Max sat by himself at a corner table in the sergeants' mess, nursing a large beer. The air was thick with cigarette smoke and a gramophone coughed out tunes that nobody knew.

A group of men from his hut came in, laughing noisily. The one whose bed was next to his – the Czech soldier – called to him as the others clustered round the bar.

'Eh! Weitzler! Want to join us?'

Max shook his head and sought refuge in his glass once more, trying to numb the sense of betrayal he felt with alcohol. But it wasn't working. Try as he might, he couldn't get out of his head the last time he and Maddie were together: that cruel day when she was forced to leave Germany for good. The memory would stay with him forever. It was what had kept him going through those long, dark days after his father had expelled him and his mother from the family home. Paris had been a brief respite, but then he had lost both his mother and aunt and almost died himself, while internment had been almost unbearable. Yet throughout all the loss and the hardship, was the thought of Maddie and the promise they had made to each other as they waited together in the attic room for the man from the British Foreign Office to arrive. Max wasn't going to be allowed to accompany Maddie to the railway station, but although she was in disgrace, she'd refused to shed tears for her action. She had no regrets about what they'd done, but she'd cried herself dry after she saw how his father had beaten him so cruelly.

As they sat side by side on the narrow truckle bed, he'd pulled out his grandmother's silver locket from his pocket. She had given it to him shortly before she died.

'Close your eyes and open your hand,' he'd told her, laying the locket in her outstretched palm. 'I want you to have this, Maddie,' he'd said.

He heard her breathe in, her mouth making a little circle of delight.

'For me?'

'It's a sign of our love,' he told her, unclasping it. 'Let me put it on you.'

She turned and lifted her hair to expose her alabaster neck and, as she did, he could see her close her eyes at his touch. Once the clasp was secure, he lowered his head and kissed her neck tenderly and she made a soft mewing sound, before turning and pulling him close to her.

'I shall always wear it, Max,' she promised.

'Always?'

'Yes.' She slipped her thumb under the locket and lifted it up to his lips for him to kiss. 'There. Now you will be with me wherever I go. Always in my heart.' And she guided his hand and laid it on her breast. 'Because I love you.'

He'd told her he loved her too and that nothing, and no one, would ever break them apart. He'd believed it then, but not now.

He snorted out a bitter laugh. Promises were meant to be broken and they'd been young and naïve. Even though he'd kept his vow to her, he hadn't really expected her to remain faithful. It must've been hard for her – not knowing if he was alive or dead, stuck in a sort of limbo. It wasn't even the fact that she'd married that hurt him most. He couldn't blame her. She was young and beautiful. She must have had dozens of offers of marriage. No, what cut the deepest was that she was laughing and chatting with one of the very men who'd killed his mother. It was hard to believe that she could betray him like this.

Chapter 39

'Max is alive. Max is alive!' No matter how many times she repeated it, Maddie still couldn't quite believe it. How often had she pictured their reunion? How many times had she dreamed of the day when she'd rush into his arms, and he'd sweep her off her feet and they'd laugh and cry together? Yes, Max was alive and for that she was so grateful, but he'd seen her with Eddie and, worse still with Hammler. If he was, as she suspected, a listener, then he might even have heard her conversations as Lady Frobisher, making small talk with a Nazi who had blood on his hands. He might even believe that she was a traitor. Somehow, she needed to tell him the truth. She would ask Briggs to lay her hands on a list of the names of M Room personnel. She just had to get in touch with him, even if it meant breaking the rules.

She was still in a state of shock early the following morning when, as she was rolling up the blackout blinds in the office, Colonel McKie called. He wanted to see her as soon as possible.

When Maddie arrived at the mansion, she found Eddie had just pipped her to the post.

'Ah, Miss Gresham and Flight Lieutenant Windlesham.' Colonel McKie was puffing away at his desk, signing papers.

With Eddie present, she supposed it was something to do with their performance as Lord and Lady Frobisher.

'Miss Gresham?' The colonel had caught her deep in thought, but she still wasn't expecting the reprimand that ensued.

'Slap on the wrist time, I fear,' said McKie, flinging his pen down on top of the pile of papers and sitting back in his chair, both hands on its arms, as if bracing himself for impact.

'We've done what Hitler and his high command very often do,' Colonel McKie told them. He paused for dramatic effect. 'We've sent our prime minister into an apoplectic rage!'

The PM had heard through the grapevine about their excursion with Hammler and was certainly not impressed.

'On reflection, lunching at Simpson's with a sworn enemy isn't really the best idea in wartime, is it Windlesham?'

'Oh,' was all Maddie could say. She immediately wondered if any of her father's colleagues had been there and spilled the beans to Mr Churchill? They were all so well connected in Whitehall. In all fairness, it wasn't every day in wartime that one bumped into a high-ranking German officer out on a spree.

'So, we were spotted?' Eddie piped up, stating the obvious.

'No one needed to spot you, Windlesham. Hammler must've stood out like a zebra in the Arctic Circle.'

'I suppose he did rather, sir,' mumbled Eddie.

'Yes, he did rather,' replied the colonel, his expression now thankfully more relaxed. 'When I agreed you could take them to luncheon, I didn't mean with half of Whitehall looking on. The PM was on the blower afterwards and I felt the full force of his tongue. Quite frankly, he was outraged that this man should be living the high life while our own people are being bombed by them and surviving on rations.'

Secretly Maddie thought the PM did have a point. 'Yes, sir,' she mumbled.

'Quite, sir,' said Eddie.

'Quite, Windlesham,' echoed McKie, reaching for his discarded pen and turning it in his hands. 'In a nutshell, he's banned all of the Germans from going on jollies for the time being.'

'Ah,' said Eddie.

'I can't say I blame him,' said McKie.

'But I really felt we were making progress, sir,' protested Eddie.

McKie nodded. 'I actually agree, Windlesham,' he replied, before turning to Maddie. 'You two make a good team. But orders are orders, as they say.'

'So do you want us to continue as Lord and Lady Frobisher within Trent Park, sir?' Eddie darted a look at Maddie.

'No need for a divorce just yet.' The colonel chuckled. 'You and Miss Gresham have proved yourselves already. Just make sure you curtail your plans for entertainment for the next few weeks. No more public outings for a while. From now on you'll need to keep your brigadier out of the limelight.'

Eddie frowned. 'That's unfortunate, sir,' he replied, by way of registering a minor protest.

'Unfortunate? Yes,' agreed the colonel. 'But we still need results from Hammler. How about a walk in the grounds next?' He glanced out of the window at the rain that had been incessant since first light. 'When it's not raining, of course.'

Maddie was growing more confident with Hammler. She still loathed him, of course, but she felt she was making progress. He was certainly keen to win her attention, if not her affection. The thought of him made her flesh creep, but she swallowed down her disgust. 'Of course, sir,' she said.

Once out of the mansion, Eddie produced an umbrella and escorted her back to her office.

'You're getting through to Hammler, Maddie. You know that?'

Of course she knew it. That was what she found so uncomfortable. He was no longer trying to hide his attraction towards her. He'd made it very plain.

'Yes, but it doesn't make it any easier for me, Eddie,' she shot back, suddenly reminded of the SS officer in Munich once more.

They were walking side by side. A group of Wrens appeared from one of the huts after finishing their shift but trotted off quickly to their barracks to avoid a good soaking. Eddie lowered his voice. 'I've seen the way he looks at you, Maddie. There's something . . .'

The rain was heavier now, bouncing off the umbrella.

'What are you suggesting, Eddie?' There were limits to how far she was prepared to go.

'I'm sorry,' he said, looking straight ahead of him.

'Remember, he knows I'm a married woman,' she reminded him.

'That wouldn't stop him.'

Maddie knew he was right. 'But you'll be with me on this walk?' She needed to feel safe.

'Of course.'

They had stopped outside her office, and he made sure no one was watching as he touched her arm lightly as they stood under the shelter of the umbrella. 'I wouldn't let anything happen to you, Maddie. You know how much I care for you.'

His smile eased the knot that had been tightening her stomach. 'All right,' she agreed. 'I'll go for a walk with him in the grounds, as long as you're there.'

He grinned and patted her again on her arm. 'I'll get on and arrange it.' He winked again. 'And don't worry. I'll protect you.'

*

Maddie found Briggs watering the potted aspidistra on the office windowsill and suddenly worried she might have seen her and Eddie by the front door.

'Lousy day, miss,' she said, standing back to admire the plant as if it were a work of art.

'It certainly is, Briggsy,' agreed Maddie.

A pot of tea, covered in a knitted cosy, and a copy of the latest transcripts were waiting on her desk. She really had to be the best secretary anyone could have.

'Thank you, but there's something else I'd like you to do for me.'

'Yes, miss.'

'I'd like you to get me a list of all personnel in the M Room, if you would.'

'Right ho, miss,' said Briggs, unquestioningly. 'It should be on file somewhere here. It came the other day.' She turned and delved into the filing cabinet.

Maddie had no idea it would be so easy to lay her hands on a copy, but there it was: a list of all the listeners at her fingertips. She scanned it quickly, her eyes going straight to the last page. To the W's. Finally, there it was. The name she had longed to see on the list of candidates in London but hadn't found. Max Weitzler was well and truly alive, and his name was on an official list to prove it. Now all she had to do was contact him and meet him to explain. But before she could, Eddie suddenly re-emerged unexpectedly, his expression as grim as the weather. This time he was holding a half-soaked folder as rainwater dripped off his gaberdine.

'Last night's transcript,' he said, lunging inside and shutting the door behind him with the heel of his shoe. 'Have you read it?'

Quickly she returned the list of listeners to its folder and squinted at the file he was brandishing. 'No. I haven't got round to it yet.' If she were honest, she hadn't given the transcripts a thought.

'I wanted to get to you before McKie did.' There was a warning in his voice, and she sensed trouble. He threw off his gaberdine and left it to drip from the hook at the back of the door, then sat uninvited at her desk.

'What is it, Eddie?'

'It seems McKie's faith in us was misplaced.'

'What's happened?'

'Hammler has been talking to some of his housemates.'

Maddie tilted her head uncertainly. 'But surely that's a good thing?'

'After our first trip round London it seems General Keiss spoke with him. The newspapers are reporting more V-1 attacks now and he asked Hammler what was going on. Look here.' He swivelled the file round so she could read it and jabbed at the relevant page. Maddie scanned it. It was the M Room transcript of a conversation that had taken place the previous night.

Keiss: So, you must be proud of your first Vengeance weapon, Herr Brigadier?

Hammler: It's a miracle when one makes it over the Channel. But of course, it's just the start.

Keiss: So the new bunker in the north should be fully operational very soon.

Maddie looked up. 'Bunker. Do we know about this?'

Eddie nodded. 'Our agents say it's a launch site in a bunker near the coast at Saint-Omer. We're advancing towards it. But it's not going to be easy to locate.' He nodded at the file once. 'Read on.'

Hammler: You're right. This is just the start.

Keiss: And it is true an even more powerful rocket is yet to come?

Hammler: Yes. The V-2 should be ready to launch very soon. It can travel at the speed of sound.

Keiss: That is impressive. The way the Allies are advancing, your weapon could be our saviour.

Hammler: Let's hope it changes our fortunes.

Keiss: And its accuracy? I've heard the V-1s are sometimes wide of the mark.

Hammler: Who told you that?

Keiss: Lord Frobisher said many of the rockets were landing in the countryside, far from London.

Hammler: Yes. Lord Frobisher seems to know quite a bit. Perhaps he is not to be trusted, General. Everyone wants to be his friend and yet . . .

Keiss: But he can make our lives here much more bearable.

Hammler: Then perhaps you ought to treat him with more caution. If you suspect he is fishing, shut him down.

Keiss: Perhaps you're right. And what about his wife? You are the only one to have met her so far. I've heard she is very pleasing on the eye.

Hammler: She is pleasing, but there is something about her that I can't quite fathom. It seems odd to me that I am the only one to have enjoyed the benefit of her company.

Another general entered at that moment and the conversation ended.

Maddie looked up at Eddie, the colour leaching from her face.

'Oh God, Eddie,' she muttered as her whole body tensed. 'He suspects.'

Chapter 40

Maddie asked Pru to take a message to Max in the M Room on the pretence she needed clarification on one of the transcripts he'd recorded. The Wren had raised a brow when she looked at the envelope. 'Weitzler?' she'd said, as if the name was already familiar to her. She was clearly suspicious, but said nothing.

'Thank you,' said Maddie. If she was found to be on intimate terms with a listener, there could be dire consequences for them both.

On her next day's leave Maddie caught the bus into Enfield Town and began walking towards the George, the pub where they were to meet, as far away from Trent Park as was practically possible. After almost eight years of heartache and suffering, she was finally going to be reunited with Max and she was as nervous as a bride on her wedding night. But this wasn't how she'd imagined it, not how she wanted it to be. She had some explaining to do: first, why she was known as Lady Frobisher and second, why she was in the company of a Nazi. There wasn't even any guarantee that Max would believe her story. Sometimes she found it hard to believe herself.

It was a disappointingly cool Saturday evening in July, although after yesterday's rain at least it was dry. The bus had dropped her outside the cinema, and she was making her way past boarded-up stores and neat piles of rubble swept up on the pavement by diligent shopkeepers. The George was at the far end of the street, but as she drew nearer, she stopped in her tracks. Ahead of her stood a tall young man in civilian clothes. He was smoking a cigarette as he waited on the corner. But it was his hair that gave him away; a white-blond crown that marked him out. Suddenly all the old feelings flooded back; the excitement, the thrill, the sense of being invincible, and she felt an overwhelming need to rush towards him. Unable to fight the urge, her pace quickened until she broke out into a run.

Her arm flew up wildly in a wave. 'Max,' she cried. 'Max!'

Turning towards her, the young man threw down his cigarette, stubbed it on the pavement and walked towards her. Slowly.

'Maddie,' he said when she reached him.

Breathless, she flung her arms around him, but his remained by his sides. She took a step back. She feared he might act this way. It was, after all, understandable after what he'd seen and heard.

Maddie took in his features. He was thinner, his face now gaunt and two furrows above the bridge of his nose made him look as though he wore a permanent frown. His thick hair was cropped at the sides and his skin, which had once glowed with health, was dull. The years had taken a toll on him and mapped his story in scars and creases, but when she read his eyes, she could still see a trace of the old Max.

'Please, Max. I know I have a lot of explaining to do.'

He was studying her intently. 'Your hair,' he said.

When he'd seen her the other day, she'd been Lady Frobisher and blonde.

She nodded. 'A wig, Max,' she told him. 'It was a disguise.' Then, as if she knew how much he needed to see more proof, she suddenly, delved into her blouse. 'Look,' she said. 'Your locket.' His eyes dropped to the silver lozenge. 'I've never taken it off. We did something good together, remember?'

His eyes lit up again, just as they had when he'd first fastened the clasp round her neck all those years ago. 'Yes, I've never forgotten.'

Her breath came out as a juddery sigh of relief. 'Then please, let's go inside and I'll tell you as much as I can.'

The pub had just opened up for the evening and when they entered, Maddie was glad to find there were only two other men sitting by the tiled bar, with their backs to them. One was wearing a grubby raincoat and the other, a bald man, was in a pinstripe suit.

The place had a very Victorian air about it, with lots of dark wood and bare tables. Stale smoke hung in the air and clung to the upholstered seats. Spilled beer made the floors sticky. An old upright piano sat in the corner and yellowing cigarette cards featuring footballers and famous people were nailed onto the upright beams around the bar. It was the sort of watering hole Uncle Roly would call a spit 'n' sawdust.

The landlord, a wily-looking man with a cigarette hanging lazily from his lip and a tea towel over his shoulder, stood at the pumps. He watched Maddie and Max as they entered, but it was only when Maddie said, 'Good evening,' that he actually acknowledged them with a nod of his sleek head.

They chose a quiet corner, away from the bar and Max went to order the drinks: a pint of bitter for him and a dry sherry for her.

'Eight years. It's a long time,' she said on his return. 'A lot has happened. I know it must've been terrible for you and I want to know all about it, but first I want you to hear me out.' Her words came out in a volley, like a round fired from a machine gun, but there was so much she wanted to tell him.

They were sitting side by side and she heard him sigh deeply. 'When I saw you the other . . .' he began, but she put a finger up to her lips.

'Please. Me first, Max.' She'd thought long and hard how she could explain everything to him without breaking the Official

Secrets Act. It wouldn't be easy, but she knew that he would've signed it, too, so she hoped he would respect her glossing over sensitive information.

'You remember I was at Oxford.'

'Yes. I wrote to you there. You got my letter?'

She nodded. 'I treasured it. I still do.' She paused before carrying on. 'I stayed in Oxford to study psychology under a brilliant tutor called Dr Baskin. But then war broke out and he was called away and I went to work at a hospital set up in my old college. Then in February this year, I was contacted by the doctor's former employers. They wanted me to take his place.'

'At Cockfosters Camp?' asked Max.

'Yes. I work there as a psychologist. But I also . . .' She hesitated, aware she could only reveal so much. 'I also fulfil certain other duties that I really can't talk about, Max.' She gazed into her sherry glass. 'That's what you saw the other day with those two men, one of them a German. But I wasn't myself, if that makes sense.'

He reached for her left hand then and looked at her ring finger. 'So, you are not married?'

A weight suddenly lifted, and she smiled with relief. 'No, Max, I'm not.'

'And you are not this Lady Frobisher?'

'No, Max,' she said, almost laughing now. 'I'm still Maddie Gresham and I've missed you more than I can ever say.'

Max laughed, too, then, his whole face lighting up with joy. He flung his arms around her and drew her tight, not caring if anyone saw them in an embrace. 'I've missed you, too,' he told her.

The tears that had threatened in Maddie's eyes began to flow now.

'Don't cry,' said Max, squeezing her tight. 'You are happy, yes?'

'Yes, yes, I am,' she replied, dabbing her cheeks with a hand-kerchief from her bag. 'I was just thinking how mad this whole situation is. You and me meeting in secret, in this quite revolting place, drinking from smeary glasses.' She held up her glass to the

229

light and caught the ghost of a lipstick stain haunting its rim.

'It is mad, but it is wonderful, too. Yes?'

She looked deep into his eyes. 'Yes. Wonderful.'

Just then someone suddenly struck up a tune on the piano so loud that it drowned out her words. Maddie looked around to see the bar had more customers. The tables were filling up, too. Three men in cloth caps, each carrying full pint mugs, exchanged words with the man in the pinstripe suit at the bar. He'd turned round to talk to them. He was bald and wore gold-rimmed spectacles and she thought he looked vaguely familiar. But he turned back to the bar again before she could place him.

The men in cloth caps now came to sit down next to them. One of them took out a pack of cards from his top pocket and started to shuffle. Another lit a cigarette and the third, who rolled up his sleeves to expose a large tattoo, took large gulps of his beer.

'Would you like another?' asked Max, raising his voice over a lively rendition of "It's a Long Way to Tipperary". Maddie nodded and, taking the empty glasses, Max rose to walk over to the bar. At the same time, a couple – the man in Army uniform – entered from the street and the young woman began searching for a seat. To her embarrassment Maddie suddenly realised she knew her.

'Briggsy,' she muttered. She panicked and looked the other way, but it was too late. She'd been spotted.

'Hello, miss,' said Briggs, surprised. She was wearing a fawn cardigan with a chocolate brown cloche hat that accentuated her eyes and instead of scraping her hair back, it fell over her ears, softening her features. 'Not on your own, are you?'

'Oh no,' Maddie shot back, as if any woman worth her salt would venture into a place like this alone, but then she realised too late she'd just implicated Max. 'And you?' She hooked her gaze over to the young soldier at the bar to distract from him.

'That's Derek,' replied Briggs, looking at a brawny squaddie with ginger hair who towered above the bar. 'He's on leave. He only lives in Cockfosters.'

'Is he your . . .?' Maddie had never actually imagined Briggs being attracted to men or vice versa because she'd always thought of her as being too young.

Briggs nodded. 'Yes, we've been walking out for a year now.'

'Have you?' said Maddie, suddenly finding herself trying to guess Briggs's age and putting her down as about eighteen.

There was a slightly awkward pause as Maddie willed Max to take just a little longer at the bar to give Briggs enough time to find herself a table. Luckily, as soon as one became unexpectedly vacant, she took the opportunity.

'Nice seeing you, miss,' she said with a jaunty nod. Out of uniform she seemed so much more confident.

'And you, Briggs,' replied Maddie just as Max turned and started to make his way back through the growing clusters of drinkers.

The men playing cards at the nearby table all looked up as Max returned and eyed him suspiciously. He wore civilian clothes – a cravat and tweed jacket. He stood out among the drab garb of working men. Maddie suddenly felt even more out of place. No, more than that: she felt unease. An insidious resentment seemed to hover in the smoky air between the neighbouring tables.

'I think we ought to drink up and go, Max,' she said just as he set down her sherry. 'It's getting too crowded in here and I've just seen my secretary.'

'Your secretary?' Max shuffled onto the banquette.

'It's all right. She wouldn't say anything, but we can't take any chances.'

'You're right,' Max agreed. Neither of them could risk being reported to Colonel McKie. 'But let's drink a toast before we go.' He raised his glass. '*Prost.*'

'*Prost,*' Maddie replied, before taking a sip. At the same time, she saw the man with a cigarette nudge the one with the tattoo.

The next thing she knew, he was leaning over towards them. 'Only English spoken in 'ere,' he growled.

Maddie suddenly felt her mouth go dry and licked her lips. 'I think we ought to leave,' she told Max.

He frowned. 'If that's your wish . . .'

'It is,' she broke in.

Seeing her pinched look, Max nodded and downed his half pint of beer in one, before rising. Maddie, gathering up her bag and coat, followed suit and headed for the side door, weaving through the knots of drinkers in their way.

Once outside, they found themselves in a dark cobbled alley that ran parallel with the building. The air had a chill to it, but there were no stars and no moon and without streetlights it was difficult to see. Maddie reached for the torch in her handbag. Just as she did, three figures appeared silhouetted at the end of the alley at the junction with the high street. Max saw them first.

'I fear we have company,' he mumbled, peering into the darkness about thirty feet in front of him. He put his arm on her shoulder and wheeled her around. 'This way.' They began to walk fast, but the footsteps behind them were faster. They were being followed and their followers were gaining on them. Suddenly Max grasped her hand, and they broke into a run. For a moment, they were back in Munich, running away from the SS guards. Maddie's heart was pounding in her ears as Max powered on until a shout cracked the night air.

'Oi. You. Jerry!'

He stopped abruptly, pulling Maddie back.

'What are you doing?' she cried, breathlessly, skidding to a halt.

'I need to tell them . . .' He gulped down more breath. 'I'm not their enemy.'

'Are you mad?' she cried. 'Those men don't want to talk. They want your blood.'

'Go. Go on!' Max shouted, and she began to teeter on her heels, but by now the men had caught up and one threw a punch at him. He ducked, but the man with the tattoo waded in and this time, there was no escape.

232

'No!' screamed Maddie. 'You don't understand. He's in the Army.'

But the blow had caught Max on the jaw and sent him spinning against the wall. His head hit the brick hard, and he slid down towards the cobbles, powerless to fend off another punch, this time to his chest.

The other two men crowded in on him as Maddie screamed for help, but it was only then she realised they weren't content to beat up Max, they were tugging at him, trying to pull him back down the alley. He dug his heels in and braced his legs, but it was one against three and he didn't stand a chance.

'Leave him alone!' Maddie cried again, as they began to drag Max towards the main road. She lifted her gaze. Was that a car waiting at the end of the alley?

'Oi! You!' Another shout rent the air. The thugs' heads jerked up to see the silhouette of a large man approaching. 'Get out of it!' boomed a voice. Drawing back a fist and without hesitation, he punched the tattooed yob, sending him reeling down the alley. 'Anyone else?' taunted the voice. The other two didn't reply. Instead, they turned and ran. 'Bleedin' cowards!' he shouted after them before bending down to attend to Max.

Maddie, who'd been flattened against the wall as their attackers fled, hurried back to Max and crouched low.

'Oh, my darling,' she said, shining the torch onto Max's torso, so as not to blind him with the light. She could see there was blood from his cut lip on his shirt and she began to dab it with her handkerchief. At her touch, Max's lids creaked opened, and he grunted.

'Let's get you up,' said the big man, looping his arm under Max's. It was only then that Maddie realised her rescuer was Briggs's beau.

'I'm so grateful to you Mr . . .'

'Gardner. Derek Gardner.' He heaved Max to his feet. 'You get them sorts round here. Bark worse than their bite.' Maddie wasn't

233

sure she could agree with that. ''Ow you feeling?'

Max coughed. 'I'll survive,' he groaned, clutching his chest.

'That's the spirit,' said the squaddie, just as Briggs turned up, flashing her torch. She let out a yelp when the light caught Max's bloodied face.

'You'd best come back inside,' she said, motioning towards the pub door.

'You must be joking,' countered Derek. 'They'd 'ave 'im for breakfast.' He studied Max's face. 'You can walk?'

Max nodded, as Maddie put her arm around him, taking a little of his weight.

''Ow did you rattle their cages, then?' asked Derek with a frown.

'Derek!' Briggs snapped.

'Just curious.'

'There was a misunderstanding,' replied Maddie. 'They thought this gentleman was a German.'

Derek laughed. 'Some people, ey? Although they do say there's Jerries up at Trent Park. Captured ones.' He leaned in closer. 'Best throw away the key, is what I say!'

Briggs tutted her disapproval. 'Honestly, Derek.'

From the look his sweetheart shot him, he realised he was on shaky ground, so he changed the subject. 'Where's home then?'

'With me,' came a voice in the darkness.

Briggs let out a muted yelp as a man in a trilby appeared from nowhere.

'Gave her a fright you did, guv,' snapped Derek, clearly unamused by the man who stood leering at Maddie.

'Mr Clancy,' she said. 'What on earth . . .?'

'You was in my local, Miss Gresham.' She suddenly remembered his garage business was in the area. 'Why don't you get in my motor?' he suggested. He peered at Max grimacing in pain, then added. 'Looks like that fella ain't in any state to walk.'

'Mr Clancy lodges at the same boarding house,' Maddie explained with a sigh. 'Very well,' she said grudgingly. 'We'll take you up on your offer. My friend will get a cab home from Fairview. Thank you.'

Suddenly realising his night out had been brought to an abrupt end, Derek gave a resigned shrug. 'That's it then,' he announced to an equally disappointed Briggs.

'We can't thank you enough, Mr Gardner,' said Maddie as Max, now clutching his jaw, nodded his appreciation.

Derek and Briggs wisely decided to move their custom to a different public house, leaving Maddie and Max to make their way back courtesy of Mr Clancy.

That night was the one Maddie had dreamed of for almost eight long years. How many times had she fallen asleep imagining their reunion, picturing Max's smile, feeling him holding her once again? But the joy and relief she'd felt earlier in the evening had been lost in that dark alley, to be replaced with fear and suspicion. She had a terrible, nagging feeling that tonight's attack on Max wasn't random and spontaneous.

Chapter 41

A taxi returned Max to Trent Park, and he managed to walk unaided back to his Nissen hut. Maddie had cleaned away the blood from his face at her boarding house, but the bruising was very visible. The lights were still on and most of the men were in the sergeants' mess. A few remained in the hut, writing letters or reading. Once he'd signed back in he thought he'd managed to make it to his bed unnoticed. The Czech in the next bed was lying down, his hands clasped under his head. But he opened a lazy eye and when he happened to glimpse the side of Max's swollen face, he jerked up.

'*Kurva!* What happened to you?' asked the soldier, swinging his legs to the floor. Max, his adrenaline still pumping though his body, dived towards him and grabbed him by shirt.

'Not a word, you hear. I tripped and fell, that's all.'

The Czech put both his hands up, signifying surrender. 'All right. You win. I won't say a word.'

'Good,' said Max, giving his shirt a final tug, then letting go.

Returning to his own bed, he carefully stripped off his clothes and shoved them in his locker, before easing into bed.

Despite the pain and exhaustion, sleep did not come easily. As the lights went out and the hours wore on, Max lay on his hard mattress, trying to ignore the springs sticking into his back and the loud snores of his fellow soldiers. But he couldn't ignore his thoughts. His mind went back to Munich, to the time his blood was spilled in his own home.

It was the night of Maddie's arrest. She'd just been returned to the house by a Gestapo officer. Max had been sitting in the dark, loathing every fibre of his own being for leaving her at the mercy of those brutish guards. Each moment, thinking of what she might be suffering at their hands, was torture until there came a bang on the door so loud it must've roused the entire neighbourhood.

His father summoned them to the parlour. They were all in their night clothes. It took Max a little longer than the others to make it downstairs, but he appeared suitably dishevelled in his dressing gown. His mother, white with worry, had her arm around Greta, while Joachim stood beside his father. And there, flanked by two guards was his Maddie. Pale and dejected, she dared not lift her eyes to meet his. The guilt Max felt when he saw her, looking so afraid, threatened to overwhelm him. He wanted to throw himself at her feet and beg her forgiveness for deserting her.

'This English girl says she is your house guest, Herr Weitzler,' snapped the SS captain.

His father scowled. 'She is.'

'And her visit was, of course, cleared with the Party?'

'Of course. What has she done?'

'I fear, sir, she has abused your hospitality and the Reich's. She was caught vandalising an information board.'

His father glared at Maddie, clearly outraged. 'She will be punished.'

The officer nodded. 'Indeed, she will,' he replied, his gaze sliding across to his crestfallen guest. 'Deportation orders will be sent for signatures. Her sort is not welcome in the Fatherland.'

His father blew out of his nostrils like an angry bull. 'No, indeed.'

The captain gave a self-satisfied smirk. His job apparently done, he glanced down at some papers in his hand. Everyone in the room seemed to hold their breath as he nodded slowly before looking up again. Moving closer to his father, he fixed him with an unnerving smile. 'I know you are a prominent Party member, *mein herr,* but I also see you are married to a Jew.'

At that remark, Max's mother let out an odd noise that sounded like a whimpering puppy. She pulled Greta closer to her. His father drew himself up and cleared his throat. 'You are right. I am a member of the Party and a senior civil servant. Unfortunately, my wife is Jewish, but I think you'll find it also says on that document we are privileged. Exceptions are made for us.'

The captain looked down at the papers once more. 'So it does,' he replied, adding with a sharp smile: 'Forgive me.'

There'd been a tense silence as the officer looked everyone in the eye, in turn, before declaring himself satisfied.

'The girl will be escorted out of the country shortly,' he declared finally.

'I can assure you, *Offizier,* she is no longer welcome here,' Weitzler replied, rubbing salt into Maddie's wounds.

Seemingly satisfied, the captain was about to be shown out of the parlour door by the maid when he stopped suddenly as he passed Max. He looked down at his feet. 'Perhaps you should take your socks off to sleep in this heat, young man,' he suggested.

Max had frozen. His father did too, before a nervous laugh escaped from his mouth. The officer responded with a smirk. The tension was broken, and the Gestapo officer continued on his way. As soon as the door shut, however, Max's father gave full rein to his fury.

'Get out!' he screamed at his wife and Greta and Joachim. 'Get out so that I can see where my miserable eldest son really was tonight!'

Greta began to cry, and Max's mother wailed as she dragged her sobbing daughter from the room. Joachim followed swiftly. The door was slammed behind them. Maddie remained, praying the floor would open and swallow her.

'The truth, Max. I want the truth!' screamed his father, sending spittle arcing through the air to hit his son's cheek. 'Horsewhipped!' he cried. 'You should be horsewhipped!'

The threat was enough to spur Maddie into action. Even though he had failed her earlier on, she knew now was the time to come to his rescue. 'It was me. Just me, Herr Weitzler!' she pleaded, but he simply sneered at her.

'I am not stupid,' he hissed. He had already put two and two together and come to the conclusion that his English house guest was aiding and abetting his elder son. He'd deduced they must be responsible for the recent destruction of five information boards in the city. 'You will pay for this,' he growled at Max. Suddenly he raised his walking stick.

Max flinched and his arms shot up over his head, trying to protect himself from the onslaught. Years of obedience meant he would not strike back, but his father's rage was uncontrollable.

'No!' Maddie screamed, lurching forward and tugging at his father's arm. But she was powerless to stop the frenzy of blows that rained down on Max as he cowered below. Suddenly there was blood. The ferrule of the walking stick pierced the skin above Max's eye and crimson rivulets began to flow. Yet still the blows fell until his father found himself exhausted. He collapsed into a chair, panting and sweating.

That night, Max reflected, Maddie had proved herself braver than he had been. He'd deserved to be beaten for abandoning her to the Gestapo, even if it meant he would have been thrown into Dachau had he been caught. Turning on his side, he slipped his hand under his pillow and pulled out her photograph to look at it by the light of the moon as it shafted through the window behind his bed. Yes, she had risked everything for him, just as he would now risk everything to be with her once more.

*

Three days later, Maddie walked into the main mansion as Lady Frobisher, wearing a floral summer frock and a leghorn hat over her wig. Eddie was waiting for her, as arranged.

'You're looking very lovely,' he told her.

She smiled. How could she tell him about Max? It was going to be hard but somehow she needed to break it to him and soon. Over the past few months, she'd grown fond of him, it was true, but reuniting with Max the other day only confirmed that her heart belonged to him and no one else. She couldn't give Eddie any more false hope.

This time, the plan was to take a tour of the gardens with Hammler. Maddie was convinced she needed to get the brigadier to open up about his personal life. But she was also wary. The transcripts had shown him to be suspicious. But, as Colonel McKie pointed out, if her visits were to stop abruptly Hammler would become even more guarded.

A compromise was reached. Today, while they were enjoying the grounds, Lord Frobisher would suddenly be called away at an appropriate time, leaving Hammler alone with Maddie. A guard would, however, remain with them. It was then she would attempt to direct him to talk about his family.

Maddie braced herself as she watched Hammler, dressed in full uniform, descend the main staircase. He suspected her. He would be watching her like . . . She was thinking of a hawk. But, no. He was a crocodile. There would be no warning if he decided to strike.

'How wonderful to see you again, Lady Frobisher,' he greeted. She offered him her gloved hand to kiss, even though every fibre of her being strained away from him.

'Brigadier.'

He flared his nostrils. 'Do I detect *Je Reviens*?' His eyes met hers as he straightened after bowing.

'Yes,' she replied, unsmilingly. The seemingly harmless remark made her quiver.

'The sun has decided to grace us today, has it not?' He gestured to a wedge of light splayed on the tiled floor in the hallway coming through the open front door.

'Yes, we are fortunate,' she agreed, following Eddie outside.

It was edging towards midday and the sun was already high, making it feel very warm out of the shade.

'I thought we could venture down to the moat in the grounds today,' announced Eddie. 'It'll be cooler there. And Lady Frobisher is a whizz at identifying flora and fauna. Aren't you, darling?'

Maddie nodded. 'I wouldn't say I'm an expert, but . . .'

'Nonsense,' insisted Eddie. 'Anyway, let's make a start, shall we?'

The small party headed off towards the far north-eastern corner of the grounds. Eddie led the way, skirting the large ornamental lake, then cutting along a path, past hornbeam hedgerows and black poplars through to a copse.

'Some of these magnificent oaks are more than three hundred years old,' Eddie said, his arms sweeping in an arc. 'This was all part of a royal hunting ground until the eighteenth century.' He was clearly enjoying playing the tour guide, thought Maddie. But her eyes slipped sideways, not to the trees, but to Hammler. She had the strangest sensation she was the one being hunted.

Shortly they came to a stretch of still water. 'Camlet Moat,' announced Eddie. 'A medieval manor house once stood here.' He looked over at Maddie. 'You and your father came here with the owner once, didn't you, darling?'

Hammler switched his gaze to her. 'Yes, King Arthur was said to have held his court here,' she said.

In reply, the brigadier tilted his head. 'On a day such as this one could believe it,' he replied. Once more his look unsettled her.

The secret corner of the estate with its green-topped moat, surrounded by mossy logs and ancient trees, was cool and inviting and still had an air of mystery about it, but with the deep water at her feet, Maddie felt an undercurrent of menace, too. Eddie was standing no more than ten yards away, so why did she feel so alone?

Just then a corporal appeared on the path. 'Sir.' He saluted Eddie. 'Urgent call.'

Eddie turned, an apology on his face.. 'Do forgive me, but it seems I'm required.'

Maddie's stomach lurched. Eddie was leaving her.

Hammler bowed. 'Your wife is in good hands, Lord Frobisher.'

She smiled nervously as Eddie disappeared through the trees. The guard stood at a discreet distance.

'So, Lady Frobisher. I have you to myself at last,' said the brigadier, looking out over the moat. 'I would like to find out more about you.'

Maddie's nerves were jangling, but she needed him to feel relaxed in her company, so she had already decided to humour him. 'There really isn't much to tell, Brigadier Hammler.'

'Oh, but I think there is.' She shot him a look of surprise. 'You don't love your husband, for a start. There is no love in your eyes.'

She turned away from him, trying to hide the panic welling up inside her.

'Please,' he said, touching her arm for a second. The feel of his hand seared through her like a thousand vaults. Her heart was barrelling in her chest, but she needed to remain calm.

'I really don't think . . .' Maddie glanced towards the guard. If she called to him, she could compromise the whole operation.

'Do you really take me for a fool, Lady Frobisher? These outings we go on; I know your husband's game. You take me into London to show me your landmarks are still standing, and your shops are filled with food. All the other generals – the fat Prussians and the old guard Wehrmacht – are taken in by the show. They love your husband's flattery and attention and, of course, his good connections. He is a worthy associate. But this charade doesn't wash with me. I was brought here, to this hotel—' he looked up at the mansion and gestured with his hands '—not because you British have given up on me and decided it's futile trying to make me talk, but because you have changed your tactics.' He flared his nostrils and smirked. 'I remember when I first came here, a major who interviewed me quoted Goethe. He said: "Correction does much, but encouragement does more." I believe that is the game here.'

Maddie had to think quickly. He had seen through the veil of subterfuge. Somehow she needed to divert him. Turning to face him, she said: 'You are right, Herr Brigadier.' Her body shuddered in a long sigh as she spoke. 'I don't love my husband. It was his idea that I accompany you on these outings. He said you had a reputation for being a womaniser.' Hammler laughed then and Maddie knew he was swallowing her line. Colonel McKie's words suddenly jumped into her head. 'He said I should use my feminine wiles on you to get you to disclose your secrets.'

Another laugh and a nod. 'The Vengeance weapons. I've known all along I wasn't brought here just to drink tea and brush up on English culture.' The smile suddenly disappeared to be replaced by a look of resentment that made his lips curl slightly. 'But I'm afraid such tactics won't work with me. I will never betray the Fatherland to you English. Not after how you made us suffer in the Great War.'

His jaw was working furiously now and there was a bitterness in his tone, that snagged on Maddie's thoughts. Of course she knew of the deprivations the defeated Germans endured after the Treaty of Versailles, but there was something more to his pain. Something personal. Then she remembered Dr Baskin's notes.

'Your wife,' she began. 'She is waiting for you back home?'

He turned to her then. 'My wife?' he said, his eyes playing on her hair. 'Yes, you remind me of my Clara.' He gave a tight smile and suddenly lifted his hand to brush her cheek as he studied her face. She flinched and he marked her fear.

'There's no need to be afraid of me, Lady Frobisher. I do not bite.' He laughed then.

She did not. *He must know what they call him,* thought Maddie. 'Yes, you remind me of her, but she is dead.'

Maddie felt her chest tighten. 'Dead?'

'Along with our four young children.'

'I'm sorry. I . . .'

'They were killed in an air raid on Berlin.'

At last, a breakthrough. 'And you blame the English for their deaths.'

He whipped round to face her, his eyes now on fire. 'Of course.'

Just as she was blaming him for the death of thousands of Jews, he held every Englishman responsible for his great loss.

'And that's why you have put your soul into the Vengeance weapon.' Suddenly everything was beginning to make sense. Hammler was a man who'd lost everything because of war, and the rocket project was his own personal way of wreaking revenge. The *Vergeltunswaffe*. But then she noticed he was shaking his head.

'That's where you're wrong, Lady Frobisher,' he told her ruefully.

'I am?'

His reply was whispered on a long sigh. 'I no longer have a soul.' He hung his head down, as if admitting his own moral breakdown.

Maddie saw that his heart was breaking under the weight of his own loss and yet he'd been so heartless and cruel in his dealings with everyone else. He'd suffered the savage pain of loss and yet done nothing to stop it happening to others. He'd witnessed brutality inflicted on hundreds of innocents at Göttingen and simply accepted it. The human psyche never ceased to baffle and amaze her. She even amazed herself as suddenly she felt her own hand reach out to touch Hammler lightly on the arm. Somewhere in her own heart she found a sliver of compassion for him. Yet he'd just told her he had no soul. Like Goethe's Dr Faust, she thought, he'd sold it to the devil.

Chapter 42

Maddie had managed to arrange to meet Max again in secret. She'd suggested Camlet Moat. Her walk with Hammler had reminded her it would be the perfect place as it was so far from the mansion. There was much less risk of them being discovered. She was breaking the rules, but just like the glass they'd shattered on those vile Nazi noticeboards, some were made to be broken.

Skirting the line of trees, she scurried in the long shadows as she moved through the grounds that evening. She needed to avoid being spotted by the security guard in the watchtower. If she and Max were disturbed, she was glad to see they could quickly retreat into the shadows.

The evening was warm, although the August nights were drawing in. She was praying no one would spot her. But someone did.

'Off for your evening constitutional?' The voice came from near the ornamental lake. She switched round to see Fruity Boxall, dressed casually in a checked sports jacket and cravat. He was smoking a cigarette and when he saw her, he threw the stub to the gravel path and stamped it out. 'Fancy some company?'

Maddie emerged from the shadows to move closer but didn't smile.

'I'm sorry, Fruity, I'm walking to clear my head,' she told him, which was partly true. Then she added: 'I'd be no company, I'm afraid.'

His shoulders slumped and he appeared disappointed. 'Bad day, eh?'

Hammler had just vowed never to reveal his secrets. 'You could say that.'

'As you wish.' He nodded and, thrusting both hands in his pockets, returned to looking out over the lake that had turned the colour of burnished pewter in the evening light.

It was hard to imagine him interrogating a Nazi when he always seemed so amenable, Maddie thought. Relieved, she retreated into the shadows once more and continued on her way, half running, half walking until the moat came into view. But, as she scanned the trees, there was no sign of Max. She pivoted around, suddenly anxious that someone might have already discovered their secret. Worries began to creep up on her like ivy on the tree trunks before, when from somewhere behind her, she heard the snapping of twigs.

Turning swiftly, she could see Max's tall figure materialising from the gloom of the woods. She hurried towards him, and he put his arms around her, lifting her off the ground for a moment then swirling her around, sending her giddy. The laughter came then, breaking any awkwardness and she looked at his face. The bruises were still there, but yellow now instead of the livid blue of the other night. His cut lip was healing, too. She touched his cheek lightly.

'Why did they do that to you?' she asked, softly.

'I'm a German. They're English. We're at war. It's natural.' He seemed content with this explanation, even though Maddie wasn't. Those men hadn't just wanted to beat him up. They'd wanted to abduct him and drive him off in that waiting car. And that man at the bar. It had come to her where she'd seen him before. He was the driver of the tailor's van. She said nothing but

246

led Max by the hand to a log at the water's edge.

'I've told you about myself in those missing years,' she said. 'Now it's your turn. I want to know what happened to you after Paris.'

Max nodded and put his arm around her. He thought for a moment.

'It's a long story,' he said.

To hear is to learn. To listen is to care. Dr Baskin's words echoed in her memory. 'I'm listening.'

Max took a deep breath. 'When the Germans invaded, my mother and her sister and I left Paris, like thousands of others. We headed for Brittany, but they were killed when the Germans bombed a bridge we were about to cross.'

She reached for his hand. 'I'm so sorry.' It was inadequate, but it needed to be said.

'I was hurt, too. Shrapnel. I thought I was going to die, but a priest took me to a nearby convent. I don't remember much about the next few weeks, only that I was cared for at this hospital, run by nuns.'

'They saved your life,' said Maddie.

Max nodded. 'They weren't the first,' he replied, knowing how much of a debt he felt he owed her from Munich. 'Nor were they the last.' He pursed his lips. 'As soon as I was strong enough, I joined the French Resistance. They were helping to operate an escape route for Allied pilots shot down over Europe. Your Royal Air Force was running undercover flights to France, but one night an English flyer didn't make the rendezvous. I was given his place.'

'Thank God you made it,' she whispered.

He nodded and lowered his voice. 'In the Resistance I was known as Jean-Baptiste Vallade. So, I came to England as a Frenchman. My name wasn't officially changed until I started work here.'

She straightened her back. 'So that's why I didn't recognise it.'

'What?'

'Your name. On the list of recruits. I was interviewing listeners for the M Room.'

Max nodded. 'From the Pioneer Corps?'

'Yes.'

He paused. 'I had a good friend in the Corps.'

'Oh?'

'His name was Ernst. He was like a father to me.'

She smiled gently, then looked out across the moat once more. 'Tell me about him.'

'He was German and a Jew, but he'd been in London, lecturing, when war broke out.' He looked at Maddie to see her sudden frown. 'What have I said?'

'Nothing,' she replied with a shrug, thinking immediately of Ernst Lehmann, the stool pigeon.

'He'd only recently married and he'd had to leave his beloved Rosa at home at Göttingen. He feared for her.'

Maddie tensed. 'What happened to him?'

'He joined another branch, I think. We lost touch a few months back, although . . .'

'Yes?'

'It's strange, but when I hear Hammler's batman – he sounds so much like him.'

Maddie's heart missed a beat as she pictured Max listening to the secret recordings. What he had just told her sounded too much of a coincidence. Could it really be the same Ernst Lehmann who was now the stool pigeon assigned to Hammler? Yet, even if it was the same man, Max could never know. Telling him would not only mean breaking the Official Secrets Act but could also risk the whole M Room operation.

'These past few years have been hard for us both,' she said, trying to change the subject. 'When I heard news about Dr Baskin . . .'

'You were fond of him, yes?'

'Yes.'

'What is it?'

Max had suddenly noticed a shadow cross Maddie's face.

'It's just, well . . . His death was so sudden, and nobody here seems to being questioning it.' She shook her head. 'I'm worried he didn't die naturally.'

'You're not saying he was murdered?' Max looked shocked.

'I don't know. I can't be sure, but I'm worried that . . .'

'There's nothing to worry about now, Maddie,' he told her, looking deep into her eyes. His hand brushed her cheek before gently cupping her face. 'I'm here now. We're together and *together we can do something good.* Remember?'

How could she ever forget? The light still burned brightly in his eyes – she could see that, as he lowered his head and pressed his lips against hers. It was the moment she'd dreamed about for all those years, so why was she still so anxious?

Chapter 43

Colonel McKie did not look happy. Maddie's report about Brigadier Hammler lay open on his desk.

'Too dashed clever,' he said, pointing at the typescript with the stem of his pipe. 'So, you're saying there's no chance he'll talk willingly?'

Inside Maddie was squirming. She'd always known it would be virtually impossible to get such a fanatical Nazi to disclose the secrets of the Vengeance weapons programme. But she wasn't willing to give up just yet.

'I made some progress, sir,' she offered in her defence. At least now she understood some of the reasons why Hammler had turned from a loving husband and father into a ruthless predator. She knew it wasn't what the colonel wanted, but it was a start.

'So that's it, is it? No more outings to London, then.' He shut the file in disgust.

'He's asked to see me again, sir,' she blurted suddenly.

'What?!' barked McKie.

'Brigadier Hammler wants to see me again, just to talk.'

'So all is not lost?'

'He says he enjoys my company.'

The colonel elbowed the desk. 'Well, well. Does he now?'

Maddie nodded. 'Yes, sir. So, with your permission . . .'

McKie nodded. 'You have it, dear lady,' he said, before adding, rather alarmingly: 'Do whatever it takes.'

*

Maddie arrived back at her office later to find Briggs still hard at work in her cupboard, typing up more notes. She'd stayed late the other night, too, helping sort through some files.

'Why don't you leave a bit early?' suggested Maddie.

Briggs's head snapped up and she beamed. 'Really, miss? That would be nice. Derek's home on leave and he mentioned about going to the pictures tonight. *Gaslight* is on at the Rialto.'

'Well, you wouldn't want to miss that,' replied Maddie with a smile.

She had to admit she was rather envious of Briggsy's trip to the picture house as she settled down to an evening of catching up on the generals' musings by the feeble light of her desk lamp.

As the Allies continued to make inroads into Europe, several conversations between the officers made mention of the treatment of Jews in the East. As more generals who'd fought in Russia and Estonia and Belarus were captured, shocking truths started to emerge, crawling from under stones, coming out from dark shadows. It was as if, in private, they needed to brag to their fellow officers about the atrocities they'd sanctioned, or personally taken part in, and the nightmarish visions they had witnessed.

Ernst was doing an excellent job, gaining the trust of both Hammler and the generals. They spoke freely in front of him, but it still didn't make what was said any more palatable. As soon as she opened his file, her hands began to shake. It wasn't long before she realised her anticipation of dread was well-founded. The words of a conversation between two generals who were captured in Estonia swam in front of her eyes, then reverberated against the walls of her skull.

251

The children were so tiresome. Bawling and screaming the whole time. I'd taken a party to watch one time and there was this small girl – she was probably about three. The noise she made! She just wouldn't shut up.

So what did you do?

I seized her from the guard, grabbed her by the hair and lifted her up. I had no hesitation in shooting her through the head with my own pistol. It made the silence all the more satisfying. (Laughter.)

The tears that had threatened for a while, could no longer be dammed. They sprang down her cheeks in rivulets. She thought of Max, too, and all those other Jewish listeners in the M Room who had lost loved ones or had no idea of their fate. How must they feel having to transcribe these accounts, knowing that their own family may well have fallen prey to such barbarity. What of Greta and her child? Was little Lena grabbed by her hair and shot through the head? Was Ernst Lehmann's wife one of the women the Nazis raped before she fell into a trench, a bullet in the back of her head?

She was still weeping when, from somewhere along the corridor outside, she heard footsteps quicken and saw the door suddenly open. There, on the threshold stood Max.

She leaped up. 'Max! You shouldn't be here. If they find you . . .'

He shook his head. 'I had to see you. It was me who took down the words myself.'

'Oh!' Her hands flew to her face.

'I had to force my mind to freeze.' His voice trembled as he spoke. 'It wasn't my hand that held the pen. If I'd thought about it, I couldn't have taken down those words. I had to blank out the images as I listened to the vile things they said.' She took his hand in hers and laced her fingers through his. 'It was only afterwards that I started to shake and feel the cold inside me turn even colder,' he said. She laid her head on his shoulder and he started to stroke her hair. 'I knew when you read the transcripts, they would upset you. I just came to see if you were working late.'

That same feeling she had before in Munich – the feeling of being understood, that wordless perception that seemed to exist between them – flooded her body. 'Oh, my love,' she whispered, and her shoulders heaved in a great sob. 'How could they, Max? It's not human.' As the tears still burned behind her eyes, she searched his face for an answer.

Slowly he shook his head, as his own eyes glistened. 'You should know that by now, Maddie. They don't feel or care about anyone else. They love no one but themselves and the Reich.'

She nodded at his remark. Max was so perceptive, but what he didn't know was that it was her job to find out what exactly had turned Hammler into this monster and use the information to MI19's advantage. She broke away from him and wiped her eyes with her now-sodden handkerchief then tucked it back into her sleeve.

'Come,' said Max. He sat on the floor, his back against the wall, and patted the space next to him. She slid down to join him, settling herself with her legs out in front of her, laying her head on his shoulder. Exhaustion had overwhelmed her in a great wave, and all her strength, both physical and emotional, had ebbed away. There, they sat, their backs to the wall, side by side in silence, lost in their own tangled thoughts.

Maddie spoke first. 'It is evidence,' she blurted after a moment, her voice suddenly finding strength. 'They must be brought to justice. The recordings are evidence of their vile. They can't be destroyed.' She knew that after a month, the discs were wiped clean and reused.

Max was silent for a moment before he began: 'I shouldn't—' He stopped abruptly.

'You shouldn't what, Max?' She turned to face him.

He looked down to regroup his thoughts, as if he had just spoken out of turn then said: 'I know I shouldn't tell you this, but we have orders to label recordings like those with an "A".'

'A?' she repeated.

253

'For atrocities. They are some of the worst crimes committed by man, Maddie, and they will be used in future trials.'

Maddie's pent-up breath suddenly escaped. 'You mean some of the generals will be brought to justice.'

'That's what we've been told.'

'Thank God. That's good news,' she said, squeezing his arm.

'Yes,' he added thoughtfully. 'There is purpose to our work.'

She nodded, then nestled her head on to his shoulder once more. 'They can't be allowed to get away with this, Max,' she whispered. 'History will judge them.'

For a while Maddie and Max sat in silence on the office floor. Just being together was enough until their peace was shattered when the main door slammed. They looked at each other. A man was singing, something like an off-key ballad, and a woman was telling him to be quiet.

'You'd better hide,' said Maddie, as Max got to his feet. 'In there.' She pointed to Briggs's broom cupboard as the singing drew closer.

'There'll be bluebirds over . . .!'

'Ssssh, will you?' said the woman.

Max opened the door to the small office and shut it just as the door to Maddie's office burst open. Standing on the threshold was a very drunk Eddie Windlesham, a bottle of Champagne in one hand. The other was on Pru's shoulder, helping him to remain upright.

'There you are, you beauty!' he cried, as soon as he saw Maddie. A large pink lipstick stain was imprinted on his cheek and his bloodshot eyes were almost the same shade.

'You're drunk, Eddie,' she told him. She was in no mood to play games and had never felt less like a beauty in her life.

Pru, almost as merry, but far more sensible, pulled a face. 'That's no way to greet him,' she pouted, staggering under his weight.

'It's getting late, Pru,' Maddie said, casting a disapproving eye at Eddie. 'You need to get his batman to put him to bed.'

'I'd rather go to bed with you,' he piped up.

Maddie shook her head, hoping Max hadn't heard that last remark.

'Don't be so ridiculous, Eddie,' she reprimanded, moving towards him, about to push him and Pru out of the door. But before she could something caught Eddie's eye and he seemed to sober up in an instant.

'You've got company, haven't you?'

Maddie tracked his gaze to Max's uniform beret. He'd left it on the desk. Her stomach clenched.

'Someone must've left it by mistake,' she shot back.

It was too late. Eddie broke free of Pru and lunged for the beret. He picked it up to inspect it.

'Well, well. An other-ranker.' He smirked. 'Consorting with the riff-raff now, are we, Maddie?'

'What!?' Eddie's arrogance appalled her. 'Why, you . . .' All the rage and the helplessness that she'd felt earlier on in the evening suddenly bubbled up inside her and erupted like a volcano as she hurtled forward and slapped him hard on the cheek. Pru cried out and rushed to Eddie's aid, as he rubbed his face, but he shrugged her off, his eyes still trained on Maddie.

'Touched a raw nerve, have I?' he chided, suddenly sounding completely sober. Just then the door to Briggs's office opened and Max emerged. Shock shot across Eddie's face just as clearly as if he'd been slapped again; there was an unnerving recognition as he eyed Max. 'Well, well. What a turn-up for the books!'

Maddie was confused. 'You two know each other?'

Max suddenly saluted and stood to attention, keeping his gaze straight ahead.

'My God, Maddie, who'd have thought?' said Eddie as he moved closer to Max and peered at his face. Maddie could see the cogs of his mind visibly working up a jealousy as he realised what was going on. He turned to her, his eyes on fire. 'So, this is *your* German?'

Suddenly all Maddie's defences had been breached. She was powerless against his officer's rank. 'This is Sergeant Max—'

Eddie broke in. 'I know who he is, Maddie. He's one of the men I risked my life for in Brittany running an escape line with Special Air Duties. Isn't that right, Sergeant? As I recall the last time we met you went by the name of Vallade.' He was glowering at Max, his eyes reduced to slits as he skewered him with a look.

Suddenly it dawned on Maddie. Eddie's "here, there and every-where" when they first met in the mess after all that time and his secret role in intelligence made perfect sense.

He switched back to her. 'Have you told him about us?'

'Us?' she repeated, whipping round to see Max's reaction. He opened his mouth in shock, but no sound came out. Then he turned to her with a frown.

'There was never really an "us"; she told Eddie on the defensive. 'We were just good friends.' That wasn't strictly true, of course. She thought of the kiss on the pavement and how it had made her feel happy and slightly giddy. But she'd also feared Max was dead.

'Come on, Maddie,' Eddie mocked. 'That night at the Ritz when we swayed to the music and I felt your body . . .' His eyes were closed, and he was holding out his hands, as if imagining they were around her waist and running up and down her back in a grotesque mime.

'Enough, Eddie!' she yelled, but still he ranted on.

'I love you, Maddie. You must know that. I want you to be my wife. I can offer you everything a woman could ever want: security, money, even a title.' He glared at Max scornfully. 'What can he offer you? A Jew without a penny to his name.'

Max flinched at that remark and, if Maddie had not intervened, might even have landed a punch on Eddie.

'No, Max!' she cried, and she saw his balled fists unclench.

Eddie was goading her, trying to make her doubt her own feelings. She couldn't deny there had been something between them and if Max hadn't come back into her life, their relationship would, possibly, have gone further. Now it was clear to her she'd had a lucky escape. In truth Flight Lieutenant Windlesham was as arrogant and opinionated as the German generals.

By now Eddie's features had stiffened, too, as if all the effects of the alcohol he'd drunk had been flushed away to leave him sober and cold. He tugged at his uniform jacket. 'I could report you for this, Miss Gresham,' he said formally. The fire in his eyes turned to ice. 'You know it's an offence to consort with a non-commissioned officer. And if you've been passing secrets . . .'

'How dare you suggest that!?'

Maddie steadied herself against the edge of the desk. She felt light-headed but she had to be strong. The silence around her thickened like blood as, taking a deep breath, she finally heard herself say: 'If you do, then they will no longer let me work with you. There will be no more Lady Frobisher.'

Eddie was quiet for a moment before he barked out a laugh. 'You're a wily one, Maddie. I'll give you that. Miss "Butter-wouldn't-melt-in-her-mouth". Miss "Goody Two-shoes". Who'd have guessed?'

Pru, silent until now, watching the drama play out before her, looped her arm through Eddie's. 'Let's go,' she told him, steering him towards the door.

But he was determined to take one last parting shot before he went. His mouth turned down as he fixed Max with a look of sheer contempt to tell him coldly: 'I should've left you in France to be shot by the Nazis.'

Chapter 44

Maddie stamped out her fury on the walk home. *How dare Eddie speak to Max like that?* He'd shown himself to be little better than Oswald Mosley and his right-wing louts. A little over an hour later, Maddie left the office, too. By now there was a slight chill on the evening air, and she returned to Fairview at dusk to find the kitchen door closed and an argument in full flow behind it. Mr Pollock's voice was raised and then what sounded like a slap led to immediate silence. It wasn't the first time she'd heard the couple have a row lately. Perhaps Mr Pollock's condition was growing worse, but she didn't like to say anything. A moment later, her landlady appeared at the door, her palm nursing her cheek. She hadn't expected to see Maddie.

'Oh, Miss Gresham. Silly me,' she tittered. 'I just walked into a cupboard door.'

'Are you all right?' asked Maddie. It was a stupid question, but she felt something needed to be said.

'Clumsy, that's all.' She shrugged, then changing the subject, she said: 'There's a plate of bread and cheese with a tomato, if you'd like it.'

Maddie forced an awkward smile, but she'd suddenly lost her appetite. 'I ate at work, thank you, Mrs P,' she replied.

As her landlady scurried out through the back door, Maddie retreated upstairs. A shaft of late sunlight pooled on her rug. She walked over to the window to catch the last of the sun's rays before it was time to pull the blackout blinds. The children were still playing on the bombsite opposite and the boy with the red hair rode up and down the road on his bicycle. She sighed heavily, feeling the weight of all the secrets she carried on her shoulders and decided she would have an early night. As she turned away from the window and approached the chest of drawers, she realised something was amiss. The key to her jewellery case, which was normally kept in a little tin box, was in the lock. Her heart stopped at the sight. Had she left it there? Had Sally been playing with it? Or had Mr Clancy been rifling through her box? With a trembling hand, she opened it, took out the tray on top and saw, much to her relief, that Dr Baskin's note was still there, where she had left it.

Troubled by the incident, it took Maddie a while before she turned out her light, but another age until sleep finally came because her head was in such turmoil. If Eddie reported her relationship with Max, a reprimand from Colonel McKie would surely follow. Or worse. She could be disciplined and ordered to leave Trent Park in disgrace, just as she had been banished from Munich.

She was still awake when a loud buzzing sound filled her ears. At first, she thought there might be a fly in the room and sleepily tried to bat it away. But then reality hit her and exploded in her brain. Sitting bolt upright she flung back the covers to rush over to the window. Pulling up a corner of the blackout blind she looked out towards Trent Park, her heart pounding in her ears. It was a clear night. The jagged skyline was silhouetted against a glow in the east. The dawn perhaps? Or maybe a fire? Then suddenly she caught sight of it through patchy cloud, coming from the south-east. A dart? A bullet? A bright dot ahead of a spear of vapour. A missile. It was whizzing along the horizon so fast that she could barely register the horror as the sound came closer and closer.

Soon the window frames rattled and the high-pitched screech grew so loud that Maddie thought her head would burst. Then, just as suddenly, a dreaded silence descended. Where was it? She scanned the horizon – the clouds thin and wispy – then she saw it again, shearing through the sky, dropping like a lead weight over to the north-west over Trent Park. Her hands flew up to her mouth as she held her breath and saw the sky light up in a blinding flash.

Pulling on her raincoat over her nightgown and slipping on her brogues, she ran across the landing to the stairs. Sally was standing, terrified, in the corridor, being comforted by Mrs Pollock.

'One of them doodlebugs, was it?'

'Yes,' cried Maddie, flying down the stairs. 'I think it's hit Trent Park.'

She ran to the end of the road and turned towards to the gates, anxiety clenching her chest. If the bomb had hit the mansion, she would be able to see the flames from the main road. But all was dark and silent. Her fears for Trent Park were unfounded. The missile must have hit further over on the Chase and landed on the grassland where there were no houses. Her breathing steadied. It was a false alarm.

*

Despite only grabbing a few hours' sleep after the explosion Maddie made it to work on time. At the gates she flashed her identity card then asked one of the sentries if he knew where last night's doodlebug – as Mrs Pollock called the rocket – had fallen. He told her he'd heard it had just clipped the edge of the park and exploded on the outskirts of town.

'Any casualties?' she asked.

The squaddie shrugged. 'Dunno, miss.'

Once in her office, Maddie hung up her mackintosh – rain showers were expected – and pulled up the blackout blinds. The clock on the wall said a quarter past nine. She decided to wait until Briggs appeared before making any tea and went to the filing cabinet. She was just looking out some old notes she needed when she heard footsteps along the corridor and a moment later the door swung open.

'Morning, Briggsy,' she greeted breezily, as she seized upon the desired file.

'Morning, Maddie,' came the reply.

It was Pru. She stood in the doorway looking resplendent in her uniform, hair immaculate, lips blazing, nails manicured to perfection and a folder under her arm. There was no trace of a hangover.

'Pru!' Maddie was surprised to see her.

There was an awkward pause then, as if both of them knew what the other was thinking but couldn't say it out loud. Pru filled the gap when she looked down at the folders in her arms and said: 'Briggs didn't come for this today, so I thought I'd bring them.' She set down last night's transcripts on the desk.

'Thank you.' Another pause.

'I say, did you hear that rocket come over last night?' asked Pru, obviously trying to iron out the creases that had appeared in their friendship.

'Yes. It woke me up.'

'Me, too. I hope it woke the Germans, as well. They deserve a taste of their own medicine!'

Maddie leaned forward with a new conviction. Pru was skirting round last evening's row, but it needed to be addressed. It was now or never. 'About yesterday,' she said, coming straight to the point.

Pru's mouth suddenly plummeted at one corner. 'Rather ghastly, wasn't it?'

'Yes. Yes it was. Have you seen Eddie this morning?'

Pru pushed her tongue to the side of her cheek, then said:

'Ah. No but he did tell me how sorry he was just before I left him last night.'

Maddie tightened her lips into a line then said: 'Hmmm. Well, I'll look forward to hearing his apology in person,' she replied.

Pru smirked. 'Good luck with that,' she said, turning to leave. But Maddie called her back.

'Thank you, Pru,' she said.

'For what?' asked the Wren.

'For not letting on that you knew about Max and me.' She was sure Pru had guessed there was something between them after she took the note to the M Room. Nor had she had a chance to explain her relationship with Eddie to Max. She hoped he would understand.

Pru smiled. 'We girls have got to stick together,' she replied with a shrug. 'Eddie can be most frightfully pompous. Besides, he needs to know he's not the only good-looking fellow on the base.' And on that note she flounced out and shut the door behind her.

Maddie's smile at Pru's parting shot soon turned into an open-mouthed sigh, however, as soon as she looked at the folder in front of her. She was still feeling groggy after her bad night's sleep. Leafing through the transcripts, though, it appeared she hadn't been the only one woken by the V-1 coming over the previous night. The generals had been disturbed from their slumber, too. The arrival of the weapon that exploded less than a mile away from the mansion even seemed to boost some of their moods.

'That is a mere calling card,' one general had told another, in the drawing room. 'If the British think the V-1 is ghastly this will come as a big shock. From what I've heard, this must be the V-2.'

Fear rippled down her spine as she read the alarming words. The Allies might be making progress in Europe and on target to retake Paris, but their victory was by no means assured. The RAF raid on Peenemünde had only stalled the onslaught of the vengeance weapons while D-Day got underway. It hadn't stopped them all together. These new, even more destructive missiles could turn everything on its head once more. London was again in their sights and the capital city of England could be completely destroyed on Hitler's whim. If only she could get Hammler to open up.

Just then she heard footsteps coming along the corridor. She'd supposed it was Briggsy before realising they were heavy and purposeful. They belonged to a man.

'Sir,' she exclaimed when Major Lansley knocked and entered the office without ceremony. She stood up.

Lansley nodded but from his severe expression she could tell he wasn't making a social visit. He closed the door behind him.

'How can I help, sir?' she asked, trying to sound positive, but with a mounting sense of dread. She gestured to a chair. Lansley sat down slowly and deliberately, positioning his cap thoughtfully on the desk, as if trying to frame what he was about to say.

'I'm afraid I've got some rather bad news for you, Miss Gresham.' He looked up, his expression even more melancholy than usual.

'Bad news?' repeated Maddie. 'What sort of bad news, sir?'

Lansley cleared his throat. 'It's about Private Briggs.'

'Has something happened, sir?'

The major nodded. 'I fear so. Last night's rocket attack. She was . . .'

Shock pinned Maddie to her chair. She really didn't hear anything else. She knew what dear Briggsy would have been doing: walking back from the cinema with Derek. They would have been arm in arm, chatting about the film, or maybe even their wedding plans.

'Miss Gresham. Miss Gresham. Are you all right?' The major's voice suddenly drifted back into her consciousness. 'I'm so sorry.'

She looked at him, trying to stem the tears that stung her eyes. 'So am I,' she replied. 'So very sorry.'

'Perhaps you'd care to take the rest of the morning off,' he suggested.

She shook her head. Through the blur of her mounting grief, she saw last night's transcripts on her desk. 'No thank you, sir. That shan't be necessary,' she replied. Now, more than ever, Hitler's weapons of vengeance needed to be destroyed. Somehow she had to get through to Hammler.

*

Briggs was dead; Eddie would say Maddie was being irrational, but it was almost as if the brigadier had killed her with his bare hands. Now she could understand better how he felt towards the English. It was personal and it was visceral. Despair had flooded her body, but she mustn't let it drown her. She had to carry on as normal. Choking back her grief as best she could, she prepared to meet Hammler.

Once more dressed as Lady Frobisher, she met him in the grounds with a guard at a discreet distance.

'I have looked forward to today, your ladyship,' he told her.

'So have I,' she lied. It was hard to concentrate on making polite conversation when any sympathy she had felt for him the other day seemed to have died along with Briggs.

'I thought we could walk in the rose garden,' she suggested.

As they moved off, Hammler looked up at the mansion. 'It is a fine building,' he remarked.

'Yes. It is. It used to be famous for its parties. All sorts came here. Playwrights, poets, politicians. Even the Duke of Windsor.' She was finding it hard to make small talk.

Instead, she walked quite quickly, concentrating on her steps to blank out her grief. Soon they came to the rose garden. A second crop had just come into bloom and the air was filled with a sweet scent.

'These roses remind me of my own garden back in Germany,' he said, sniffing a bloom. 'My wife was the real gardener, of course.'

At the mention of his wife, Maddie looked at him. His

vulnerability had suddenly resurfaced. The first time she'd seen it, she had reached for him and shared some of his pain. Now, however, after what had happened to Briggs, she couldn't suppress the urge to take aim and fire.

'So your wife was a creator and you are the destroyer, Herr Brigadier,' she said. She intended to wound.

He seemed shocked rather than hurt. 'I am the preserver of the Reich,' he replied. 'I want to keep our German way of life that is threatened.'

'So, you not only threaten, but also kill those who get in your way, even if they are completely innocent?' she shot back. The simmering anger inside her was about to boil over. She had to keep it in check, or she might explode.

Hammler seemed surprised by her barbed question, but he countered it with another. 'Are you feeling quite well, Lady Frobisher?'

It incensed her. She shook her head. 'Since you ask, Brigadier, no. I am not. Someone very dear to me was killed last night.' She stifled a sob. 'She and her fiancé were hit by one of your Vengeance rockets.'

Hammler was silent for a moment, giving Maddie space to compose herself. She took a handkerchief from her bag and dabbed her eyes.

'I am sorry,' he told her as they walked on.

But his words only inflamed her. She hadn't planned to be like this. She'd told herself to be professional – to separate her personal feelings from her duty. But all her good intentions had crumbled under the weight of her own raw sorrow. 'Sorry? You say you're sorry? Have you any idea how hollow those words are right now?' Her voice was raised and filled with rage and the guard who had been shadowing them came nearer.

'Please, Lady Frobisher,' said Hammler. He reached up to touch her, but she circled her arm to fend him off. 'Don't you dare touch me!' she cried. 'You told me you didn't have a soul. Well, you don't have a heart either,' she told him, tears streaming down her face again. 'You're nothing but a cold, calculating murderer in my eyes.'

Hearing Maddie's outburst, the guard stepped forward.

'See the brigadier back to his quarters,' Maddie told him.

'Yes, ma'am,' said the soldier.

Maddie watched Hammler being led off to the mansion. She felt herself shaking with fury, but she was angry with herself as well as with him. What had she done except make matters worse? Nothing could be achieved by her outburst. He'd probably refuse to see her again.

She was on the verge of giving way to private tears when the crunch of tyres on gravel made her turn. It was the tailor's van, driving towards the mansion's back entrance, the bald man with gold-rimmed spectacles at the wheel.

Chapter 45

As Maddie walked towards the mansion early the next morning, she was giving herself a pep talk. She told herself it was no use giving in to grief and that any anger she felt about Briggs's death would best be channelled into bringing the enemy to account. But her thoughts were suddenly interrupted by the sound of the siren from the watchtower. It could only mean one thing: a prisoner had escaped.

From out of the Nissen huts men began to pour. Engines started up and guards took up stations around the perimeter fence. She hurried inside for her scheduled meeting with Colonel McKie.

Major Podesta – his golden tan now faded after almost a year in England – and Major Lansley were already in the colonel's office when Maddie arrived. An ATS girl had just brought in a tray of tea and the vibration from the alarm was so powerful it was making the crockery rattle.

At the same time Colonel McKie strode into the room. 'Missing prisoner!' he yelled over the ear-shattering sound. 'Believed to be somewhere in the grounds.'

A minute later the searing sound stopped just as quickly as it started. The prisoner must have been found and everyone in the room breathed a collective sigh of relief. Everyone apart from Maddie.

'Do we know who it is, sir?' she asked.

'Not yet.' The colonel shook his head. He was interrupted by the ringing of the phone.

'Good God!' he said. 'I'll be right over.' Slamming down the receiver, he rose.

'Sir?' said Podesta, expecting to be briefed.

The colonel took a deep breath and his thick brows simultaneously dipped in a frown to deliver the news. 'They've got him,' he said.

'Good show,' responded the major.

'Actually no,' replied the colonel. 'He's dead. Found hanged in the woods.'

Major Podesta's lips stretched awkwardly over his white teeth. 'Ah!'

'Did they say who, sir?' Maddie asked, her voice thick with dread.

McKie fixed her with a sombre look. 'No.'

Everyone knew the gravity of the situation. If the dead man were one of the Wehrmacht generals being held captive at the mansion, the matter would go to the very top and there would be hell to pay. In any case, there'd clearly been a terrible breach of security. Churchill would be furious and McKie would be in the firing line. The entire operation that had thus far reaped such rich intelligence rewards, not to mention cost a vast sum of money, would be thrown into jeopardy.

'He's up by the obelisk,' McKie told them, depressing a button on his telephone. 'Holmes,' he addressed his secretary. 'Get me a car and an ambulance, right away.'

'You'll need me, too, sir,' Maddie prompted. She may have been speaking out of turn, but she wanted to make sure her fears were unfounded. Her experience with head injury patients, some of them psychotic, meant that she was familiar with formal procedures, especially when it came to suicides.

The colonel's moustache twitched, and he looked down his nose at her. 'It'll be no sight for a woman.'

268

Once again, Maddie was forced to swallow her feelings. 'You forget, sir,' she replied calmly. 'My background was at a military hospital.'

McKie narrowed his eyes. 'Very well, Miss Gresham,' he conceded with a nod. 'You, too, Podesta and Lansley.' His gaze jabbed at both men. 'But the fewer people who know about this, the better.' Grabbing his peaked cap from a stand by the door, the colonel marched out of the office, with Maddie, Lansley and Podesta in tow.

Two soldiers in the search party had found the body, dangling from the bough of an oak. Both men were still in the guardhouse and McKie ordered them to travel back up to the obelisk in the ambulance. Maddie asked to accompany them. She could tell the younger one was in shock; he was shaking violently and crying.

'I'll see to him, sir,' she said as she helped the soldier, draped in a standard-issue blanket, into the ambulance.

A small detail was arranged to join the colonel in another vehicle and together they set off in convoy. The ground was wet from heavy rain earlier in the day and to avoid the prospect of getting stuck in muddy ruts, the cumbersome vehicles had to travel on the gravel paths up to the monument.

As soon as they arrived, the older soldier led the colonel to the edge of the trees, leaving the younger one in the ambulance. Maddie, Lansley and Podesta followed close behind.

'Right. I want this whole area cordoned off!' McKie ordered. He turned to the sergeant who led the search party. 'Now show me the body.' He was pointing with his swagger stick towards the trees.

They made their way up the slope and into the trees and all the while Maddie kept telling herself there was nothing to fear. Her father's voice echoed in her ear. 'Pull yourself together' and 'Chin up!' They were expressions frequently heard on hospital wards, too. She had to be strong.

Just a few paces into the woods Maddie caught sight of the dead man and her throat tightened. The corpse was swinging by a rope from a thick bough. Every time the wind blew, the bough creaked. She couldn't stomach the sight at first, preferring to remain a little way behind from the others. Major Podesta overtook her to join the colonel as he stood in front of the dangling body, his face raised towards the head. His expression was unclear from such a distance, but Maddie knew she needed to satisfy herself that the dead man was, indeed, one of the German prisoners of war and not Ernst or Max.

Her legs faltered for a few steps before somehow managing to carry her to up to the corpse. She braced herself for the moment of truth. She'd seen a hanged man before in the hospital grounds, and while the case had been unpleasant, she had dealt with them professionally. This time she feared it might be different. Filling her lungs with a deep breath, she steeled herself to look up at the dead man. This time the shock seemed to paralyse her limbs, as if the roots of the trees were wound round her legs, anchoring her to the spot. This time she was mesmerised by the face of the man hanging from the bough. It was white and twisted, but she still recognised it. There was no mistaking the grey, wavy hair and the skewed, once-broken nose.

The sound of her own laboured breathing filled Maddie's ears before a yelp of shock escaped from her lips. Her stomach lurched and everything around her began to spin. She closed her eyes to blink away the horror but when she reopened them, Podesta was staring at her: a cold, hard stare that was full of contempt for showing emotion.

The colonel, his hands behind his back, was now circling the body as it remained dangling from the branch. She saw McKie lower his gaze to the leaf litter on the ground.

Maddie caught up with the men and moved closer to the corpse herself. It was then that she noticed something odd – something out of place. She noticed Ernst's hand was badly swollen.

Major Podesta sidled up to him again. 'Suicide?' she heard him ask.

'Most likely,' agreed Lansley.

She saw the colonel prodding the ground with his swagger stick and beckon the two officers. They leaned in and he said something she couldn't quite hear. Once again she was being excluded.

'But what if it wasn't suicide, sir?' asked Maddie, breaking up the little huddle. 'What if someone in the mansion found out Lehmann was a stool pigeon?'

It seemed so obvious to her and yet Colonel McKie almost laughed the notion out of court. 'Ah, Miss Gresham,' he said, as if he'd forgotten she was there. 'You recruited Lehmann, didn't you? He was having problems, as I recall.' He lifted his eyes to meet Lansley's, rather conspiratorially, thought Maddie. 'I don't think there's any question. The man took his own life.'

Maddie persisted. 'But you will ask for a post-mortem, won't you, sir?'

Podesta skewered her with a black look. 'We're at war, Miss Gresham.'

The colonel nodded. 'Quite right. The coroner has enough to do without investigating such an obvious death.'

Maddie took a breath. There was no easy way to say what she felt she had to. 'What if he was murdered, sir?'

McKie scowled. 'You have evidence. Motive?'

Maddie felt her heart race. 'I can't be certain, but his hand is injured. Surely murder is a possibility?' she pleaded.

McKie cleared his throat and straightened his back. He shot a glance at Ernst Lehmann as three soldiers struggled to cut down his body from the branch.

'Very well, Miss Gresham. I will order an autopsy.' He gave her the cold shoulder then, turning instead towards Podesta. Maddie knew she wasn't supposed to catch the look the colonel gave the American or hear him mumble: 'We shall see.'

Chapter 46

Maddie arranged to meet Max at the moat again. This time in the twilight. They'd hadn't seen each other since Eddie's outburst. So much had happened in the past few days, that it felt ages since she was in her office with Max. But as soon as she saw him, standing by the moat, his head bowed deep in thought, she understood the encounter with Eddie was still fresh in his mind. They hadn't spoken since, and she feared he was still hurting. She had some explaining to do.

'You've always been the one, Max. Believe me,' she said, stepping closer to him. 'I was going to tell you about Eddie. I just . . .'

He put his arm around her but was silent for a moment until he said: 'I know you would have.'

She lifted her face to kiss him then, but before she could he asked: 'But how many more secrets have you kept from me?'

Of course there were other things – so many other things – that she couldn't tell him. But she came back unapologetic. 'We have both signed the Act, Max.'

'Yes, we have.' He cupped her face in his hands. 'I'm sorry.' He raised his head and looked out onto the water where the harvest moon shone like a golden disc on the surface. 'It's just that sometimes I feel like I'm going to explode.'

She understood what he meant. She ached to tell him absolutely everything, to unlock her heart and let its secrets spill out. But when the personal impinged on the professional, when the lines were blurred, it made life so difficult. Secrets needed to be kept when there was so much at stake. But there was one secret that broke her heart to have to share with him.

'Your friend Ernst,' she began. 'Ernst Lehmann, yes?'

Max looked at her wide-eyed. 'How do you know his . . .'

She sighed. 'I recruited him. He was here.'

Max's face lifted in a wide smile. 'Here?' He scratched the back of his head. 'I knew it was his voice. I just knew it.' He pivoted in a half circle, then returned to the same spot. 'Can I see him?'

Maddie shook her head. 'No, Max. I'm afraid you can't.'

Slowly he began to nod his head, a look of disappointment darkening his face. 'He's in another branch. You can't tell me. I understand.'

The secret listeners knew nothing of the existence of the stool pigeons. It had to remain that way, but she knew if she had let Max talk to his old friend when Ernst was struggling mentally, he could have offered both comfort and support. But this was war, and it was cruel and she was about to tell Max the cruellest thing of all – that she believed his friend had been murdered.

'There's something else, isn't there?' said Max, reading her expression. 'What is it?'

'The alarm, this morning,' she began.

'An escaped prisoner. But they recaptured him, yes?'

Max had swallowed the official line.

'No, they didn't have to recapture him.' She felt an icy shiver course down her spine. 'He was dead.'

'What? I don't understand.'

Maddie shook her head. 'There never was an escaped prisoner, Max. The man was a double agent, working on the inside. He was found hanged.'

The silence between them suddenly filled with the horrific realisation.

'Not Ernst! No!' Suddenly he clamped his hands over his mouth. He turned left, then right. 'He killed himself? He couldn't take it anymore. The stories. The massacres. Rosa! That was it, wasn't it? Wasn't it?' His voice was raised now, as his words flooded out in a raging torrent, and Maddie worried a guard might hear him.

'Sssh, Max. Listen please.' She held his arms to his sides. 'I don't think Ernst killed himself. I think he was murdered.'

'What?' The furrow between his brows was as deep as she'd ever seen it.

In her mind, Ernst Lehmann had been tortured before he was killed. Men with broken fingers couldn't hang themselves.

The heel of Max's hand went up to his temples in disbelief.

'But this is England, not Germany!' he cried.

Clamping her hands on his arms she wheeled him round to face her. 'I think Ernst was murdered and I think Dr Baskin was, too, and if I'm right, then there's a killer inside Trent Park.' She flung out her arm in the direction of the mansion. 'I think someone is trying to find out what secrets Trent Park is keeping, but without success. And that can only mean one thing.'

Max's face, so contorted by shock and grief, was deadly serious now. 'That they may strike again.'

274

Chapter 47

The clue had been there all along. Two days after Ernst was found dead, Maddie had been in her office, rereading some of Dr Baskin's notes, trying to find anything else on Hammler's past that could be used to get him to open up, when she'd needed her spectacles. Once again she'd found the drawer jammed, but this time had been determined to free whatever was stuck at the back and obstructing the runners.

Using a paper knife, she'd prodded around a bit until she managed to dislodge the offending object. She was amazed to see it was a small book of fabric swatches: a selection of grey, blue and brown fabrics all pinkered at the edges. She turned the book over to look at the back. It was then that she saw the label. It read: *Anstruther & Son. Gentlemen's Outfitters. Savile Row, London.*

She remembered seeing the van arrive at the end of her last encounter with Hammler. The tailor – the man who'd nearly run her over on her first day at Trent Park – had been behind the wheel. A quick check with Holmes showed that Ernst had a fitting with the tailor the day before he was found dead. So now she had established a link connecting the two victims. Dr Baskin and Ernst had both seen the tailor.

Luckily Maddie had a day's leave. It was her father's birthday and a table in his favourite restaurant had been booked for dinner that evening with Uncle Roly. But first she had a mission to undertake. She just needed to pluck up enough courage. She was neither a spy nor a sleuth and yet she felt compelled to uncover the truth about the deaths of both Dr Baskin and Ernst, and Anstruther & Son, gentlemen's outfitters, by royal appointment, was where she needed to turn next.

Maddie had stuck to her routine that morning. She didn't want to arouse any suspicion, just in case someone might be trailing her. She'd pulled a cloche hat down over her ears – Lady Frobisher's blonde wig would have made her look too obvious – and worn a plain coat to blend in as far as possible. Just before she reached the gates to Trent Park, however, she doubled back on herself and took the underground from Cockfosters. She changed at Finsbury Park just to throw anyone who might be stalking her off the scent and took a taxi from Bank to Piccadilly Circus. A stop at Fortnum & Mason to buy her father a birthday gift made a pleasant diversion before a brisk walk to Savile Row. A moment later Anstruther & Son, gentlemen's outfitters, by royal appointment, lay directly ahead of her. But she didn't go inside the shop. Instead, she slipped into a café opposite and took a seat that gave her a clear view of the whole of the street.

The café was a favourite haunt of wives who waited for their husbands to be measured up and fitted out at one of the many tailors on the row over a chocolate éclair or two. A matronly woman in a light blue dress and little toque hat sat on the other side of the room. She seemed vaguely familiar. Maddie looked away, thinking she might be someone who knew her father.

Maddie ordered a pot of Earl Grey and proceeded to train her eyes on the shop opposite. She didn't really have a plan, just a hunch that this respectable-looking tailor's establishment was in some way connected to two deaths. She resolved to wait and observe, although she wasn't exactly sure what she was looking for – only that when she saw something significant, she'd know.

When the tea arrived, she proceeded to settle down with a copy of the latest Agatha Christie novel for appearance's sake, as she waited for whatever it was that might or might not happen.

Two cups of tea later, however, she became aware of someone standing by her table and heard a familiar voice.

'I say, Maddie, what on earth are you doing here?'

Eddie stood glowering at her, in uniform and clearly unhappy.

'It's my day off,' she protested, shutting her novel and looking up at him. 'I might ask you the same thing.' She looked about her, half expecting to see one or two of the German generals in tow.

Eddie sat down opposite her, his eyes gliding sideways, before he laid his cap on the table and fixed her with a scowl. 'I don't know what you're playing at Maddie, but this isn't a game for debutantes, you know.'

She slumped back in her seat, as if he'd just kicked her. A game for debs? So, this was what he really thought of her. 'I'm sure I haven't a clue what you're talking about,' she said, reopening her book.

He reached over and, rather rudely, snapped it shut again. 'This isn't a novel.' His gaze dropped to sneer at her Agatha Christie. 'It's real life and it's serious and it isn't for girls.'

She opened her mouth to object but garnering a disapproving look from two other tea drinkers, she thought twice about causing a scene.

Eddie continued. 'Whatever you're doing, stop it now. I warn you, Maddie, you're playing with fire.'

'There's no need to get so het up, Eddie,' she told him. 'As I said, it's my day off and I thought I'd do a little shopping.' She glanced at the small beribboned package from Fortnum & Mason she'd picked up on the way. 'My father's birthday present.'

Eddie sighed. 'You're incorrigible,' he told her as he moved to stand up. 'As soon as you've finished your tea, you need to get out of here. Do you understand, Maddie?' He spoke through clenched teeth so as not to draw any more attention to himself.

'Go and get your hair done, or buy some underwear, or whatever you ladies find to do, but just don't be anywhere near here. You understand?'

'Perfectly,' she replied, lifting her gaze to his.

'Good,' he said, tugging at his tunic and, repositioning his cap he walked out of the café, disappearing down the road and out of sight.

Eddie hadn't exactly created a scene, but he'd raised a few hackles. As soon as he left, she felt the eyes underneath neatly plucked brows still on her and her face flushed. She asked for the bill and as she waited for it to arrive questions crowded into her head. What was Eddie doing there, in Savile Row? What did he know of the comings and goings at Anstruther & Son? And how on earth had he known she was there?

Her eyes swept the tearoom. The woman in blue with the toque hat must have left a while back. It was then she remembered where she had seen her before. At the Savoy. The woman in the silver dress in the powder room and staring at her across the dance floor. Surely, she wasn't being followed.

Maddie paid the bill and left a sixpenny tip. She made a quick enough exit, yet despite Eddie's stern words, she remained defiant. He had no right to dictate how she should behave. She was determined to keep watch on the tailor's, and she could still achieve her goal by browsing in store windows up and down the street.

It was shortly before two o'clock when Maddie left the café. She needed to remain as inconspicuous as possible while keeping an eye on Anstruther's. She'd turned to face a shop display opposite, so as not to be noticed. But as she studied the headless mannequins modelling blazers and cravats, she also noticed a reflection in the plate glass window. She froze as she watched a middle-aged man in a trilby and grubby raincoat sprint up the steps to the tailor's; it was one of the men who'd had his back to her at the bar of the George. Surely that wasn't her shell-shocked landlord? She would wait until she saw him reappear because she

278

needed to convince herself, let alone anyone else, that the man she just saw entering Anstruther & Son really was the person she thought he was.

Feeling uneasy, Maddie loitered a little longer until, less than five minutes later, the man re-emerged from the store, only this time he was accompanied by a short, bald man with gold-rimmed spectacles. She recognised him immediately as the driver of the Anstruther's vehicle. He muttered something, nodded and returned inside the shop while the other man looked first right, then left, before proceeding to descend the steps to the pavement below. She switched back quickly to her headless mannequins before setting off in pursuit of the man in the trilby.

He was walking at a brisk pace and soon turned left into Cork Street. She kept a reasonable distance, the blood pounding in her ears. But she couldn't lose him. He stopped for a moment at a junction, looking around nervously. Making sure he wasn't being followed, no doubt. Simultaneously Maddie took shelter under the awning of a milliner, ostensibly seeking inspiration for a forthcoming social engagement. A moment later he moved on and she moved with him, in the direction of Clifford Street. He turned the corner, but when two seconds later so did she, she'd lost sight of him. A woman with a poodle on a leash crossed the pavement in front of her, followed by an elderly gentleman with a walking stick.

Maddie craned her neck, then caught sight of him a good fifty yards further up the street. She needed to catch up and quickened her pace, but so did her quarry. He turned again. This time into Burlington Arcade, where the famous liveried beadles were standing guard on either side of the entrance to the renowned shopping mall. He passed between them and so did she, but just as she did so, the Agatha Christie novel, which she'd been carrying under her arm, dropped to the arcade's tiled floor.

'Miss!' called one of the attentive beadles, bending down to pick up the book. But his cry had alerted the man. He turned to see her snatching the novel from the beadle's outstretched hand. Seizing the moment, he pivoted and doubled back. This time he wasn't walking ahead, but hurriedly towards her, fixing her in his sights. The tables were turned, and Maddie turned, too. But now she broke out into a run. Much to the amazement of the beadles, she dashed out of the arcade the way she had come and took a right towards Old Bond Street. She didn't stop for breath until reaching Asprey's on the corner. Looking round her, gasping for air in what Uncle Roly would no doubt say was a most unladylike manner, she checked her hat in the jeweller's plate glass window. It was then, to her horror, she caught sight of him again crossing the street towards her. Once more she bolted, scurrying along the narrow pavement uphill towards New Bond Street.

The junction with Bruton Street was busy with traffic: cabs and bicycles mainly, but buses, too. A red double decker was approaching, heading east in her direction, but she knew she had to take her chances. Gulping down a deep breath, she dashed into the road and bounded onto the pavement on the other side. The horn sounded and at first she thought the driver was angry with her, but a half second later there was a terrible thud and a scream from a passer-by. Maddie turned just in time to see to her absolute dismay, none other than Mr Harold Pollock disappear under the wheels of a Number 22.

Chapter 48

Somehow Maddie made it to the restaurant on time although she was still in shock, feeling light-headed and trying hard to hide her trembling hands. She'd gone straight to her father's house in Belgravia afterwards – she didn't hang around for the police to arrive at the scene of the accident – and had drawn herself a long, hot bath to slough off the terrible sense of guilt she felt. Was Mr Pollock dead? Perhaps she should have waited to find out if he'd survived because now the remorse was setting in. At the time panic had taken hold and she'd just wanted to escape. But what if he was dead? It would be her fault. Conversely, if he hadn't been chasing her, he'd still be alive. She thought of poor, peace-loving Mrs Pollock. She would have to face her when she returned to Fairview tomorrow. What should she say? Should she tell her landlady that her husband was injured, or worse, while chasing her? And *why* was he chasing her? Or rather *how* was he chasing her? Harold Pollock was supposed to be a victim of shell-shock, a former soldier traumatised by the trenches, fit neither for war nor work. It must all have been an act.

The questions and confusion played round and round in her head as she scrubbed at her skin, but still the regret remained. It was going to take more than hot water to cleanse her of her demons. Two large sherries helped a little. They certainly made it easier to pretend she was in a party mood even though in her mind chaos reigned.

Maddie arrived at Chez Victor in Wardour Street to find Uncle Roly waiting at the table. He rose, pecked her on both cheeks, and complimented her on how "fabulous" she was looking. Sometimes she thought she could put a paper bag over her head, and he'd still pronounce her "gorgeous".

'No Daddy?' she asked, depositing her small gift on the table.

Sir Roland shook his head, then perked up and, with eyes on the door, began nodding. 'Here he is!'

Maddie's father strode over to them. 'Sorry, I'm a bit late. Apparently, some chap got caught under the wheels of a bus on Bruton Street earlier. Traffic's still snarled up.'

'How awful,' mumbled Maddie. Should she ask if he knew any more about the victim?

'But you're here now. And happy birthday, old chap,' exclaimed an exuberant Sir Roland.

A more subdued Maddie reached up to kiss her father. 'Yes, happy birthday, Daddy.'

As Sir Roland ordered Champagne, Sir Michael looked around the dining room and smiled, as if he were glad to be back in a favourite haunt.

'Did I ever tell you this is where I proposed to your mother?' he asked Maddie.

'Yes, Daddy. Every time we come here,' she said, patting his hand.

She loved the place, too. A *chanteuse*, accompanied by a small band, crooned a syrupy French ballad that immediately transported her to Paris. Silver platters were held aloft, steaming soup was dispensed from tureens and toothpicks were set on the tables.

As the waiter popped the Champagne cork and filled their glasses, Maddie and Uncle Roly raised their glasses.

'Many happy returns, old chap,' toasted Sir Roland.

'Yes, many happy returns,' said Maddie, even though she was in anything but a celebratory mood.

*

They left the restaurant around eleven o'clock and parted with Sir Roland on the junction of Ebury Mews where he had a *pied-à-terre*. Maddie and her father walked on to Eaton Square.

'Fancy a nightcap?' he asked, clutching the bottle of Napoleon brandy that Sir Roland had given him as a birthday gift.

'Why not?' said Maddie with a smile, even though she really didn't like brandy in the least. It would help her numb the pain she was feeling inside.

'Let's have it in here, shall we?' said her father, opening the door to his study a few moment later.

It was Maddie's favourite room, one lined with books and home to comfortable winged chairs on either side of an ornate mantelpiece, where she'd often wiled away a rainy day as a child in the school holidays.

Her father took out two cut glasses from the drinks cabinet and poured the brandy as Maddie sat down in one of the chairs, casting her eye over the titles in the nearby shelves. Her father was always buying books and she was keen to see his latest acquisitions. On this occasion her gaze settled on a volume with which she was particularly familiar: Freud's *The Interpretation of Dreams*. She reached for it as her father advanced with her glass of brandy.

'I didn't know you'd become interested in psychoanalysis, Daddy,' she remarked flicking though the pages backwards until she came to the flyleaf and, to her shock, instantly recognised Dr Baskin's handwriting.

'I need to be able to keep up in the conversation with my clever daughter,' he replied, handing her the brandy.

'*Sweets dreams. Tobias,*' she read aloud. 'You knew Dr Baskin?'

Her father eased himself into his chair. 'No, I didn't. That's Roly's copy. I need to give it back to him.'

Maddie's eyes widened. 'So he and Uncle Roly were old friends? I'd no idea.'

Sir Michael nodded. 'Oh yes. They went way back. Cambridge. Both scholarship boys. I think that's why they bonded.' He took a sip of the brandy, then held the glass up to the light to study the amber liquid. 'And of course, you have Roly to thank for getting you that assistant job.'

Maddie, mid-sip, spluttered. 'I'm sorry. What do you mean?'

Her father shrugged. 'I suppose I shouldn't say really, but it was Roly who had a word with Dr Baskin to take you on.' He smiled at her. 'What else are godfathers for?'

She wasn't sure whether to laugh or cry, but she was erring towards the latter. She'd always thought she'd been awarded the job as Dr Baskin's assistant on merit. She'd had all the right qualifications and had beaten three male candidates fairly and squarely. Now she was hearing it was nepotism, pure and simple.

'But only a few weeks ago at the shoot, he was telling me no man wanted to marry a bluestocking. He was positively hostile to my career.'

Another laugh from her father. He obviously didn't grasp how momentous this news was to her. 'You know Roly, darling.' He took another sip of brandy. 'He's very much "do as I say and not as I do".' He tilted his head then. 'And he really is very fond of you – you know that.'

Fond or not, she felt duped. No, worse than duped, betrayed. Her studies, her degree counted as nothing in the scheme of things. Sir Roland Fulford had pulled strings on her behalf. It made her feel like his puppet.

Chapter 49

Eddie didn't even bother to knock when he blustered into her office first thing the following morning. As she'd travelled in from Belgravia, she only just made it to work on time. The journey had been torture. Not only because the train had been packed but because of what she knew lay waiting for her at the end of the line. She'd no idea how she was going to face Mrs Pollock, let alone little Sally. And now she'd barely hung up her jacket before Eddie flung down a copy of the last night's newspaper. 'Look at this!'

Maddie forced herself to focus on the copy of yesterday's *Evening Standard. Man badly injured by bus,* ran the report at the bottom of the front page.

'Do you know anything about this?' Eddie asked.

Maddie was silent for a moment as the headline blurred in front of her tear-filled eyes. He wasn't dead. Mr Pollock was alive. She slumped back on to the corner of her desk, relief surging through her whole body.

'Well?' snapped Eddie. 'I told you to leave Savile Row and now a man is badly injured in hospital. What have you to say, Maddie?'

'He was following me,' she admitted.

Eddie raked his hand through his hair and turned away from

her. 'You have no idea, Maddie. You need to keep your nose out of MI19's affairs.'

'I need to . . .?' Maddie felt her fury suddenly return. 'I'm supposed to be a member of MI19, remember? But no one tells me anything. Perhaps if they did, I wouldn't have to find out things for myself.'

'Keep your voice down, will you?' Eddie told her. 'We don't want Podesta down the corridor poking his nose in. This is strictly an internal matter.'

'What is, Eddie? Are you going to tell me what is going on?' She narrowed her eyes as she looked at him, her trust ebbing away. 'My landlord is lying badly hurt in hospital and I'm expected to return to my lodgings tonight and pretend to his wife that I'm shocked when she tells me he's had an accident.'

'That's precisely what you'll do, if you don't want to be locked up for ruining everything,' Eddie hissed. His face had turned red with the effort of trying to rein in his rage.

'Locked up?' she repeated. 'You're threatening me?' She could barely believe what she was hearing.

His silence spoke volumes before he began shaking his head. 'McKie's livid about what you've done. You need to be careful.'

Maddie's head was spinning. She walked to the window in silence and looked out as she gathered her thoughts. Spooling back to the tailor's in Savile Row where this terrible episode began, she tried to salvage what she knew from the wreckage that surrounded her. After a moment she asked: 'This must be to do with Dr Baskin's death.'

Eddie closed his eyes then opened them with a rueful smile. 'You know I can't answer that, Maddie.' He looked away and brooded in silence for a moment, studying the poster reminding everyone the walls had ears. 'There are things you don't know, Maddie. Things you can't know.'

There were things he couldn't know, either. Like the way she gave in to her emotions and lost her temper with Hammler.

Nevertheless, she felt like a fly caught in a trap. She realised she'd walked into a spider's web of intrigue as soon as she joined Trent Park. Each action seemed to have a bearing on another and without knowing how each thread was connected it was very difficult to gauge which one to break in order to untangle herself.

'I'm sorry that Mr Pollock has been injured, but unless I know what's going on I cannot be held responsible for my actions,' she protested.

Eddie growled and raked his fingers through his hair. Harold Pollock seemed important to him and to MI19. But what was the connection with Dr Baskin? When she'd come straight out with the question it was as if she'd just opened Pandora's box and Eddie had thrown himself down on the lid.

'Surely you don't expect me to tell you?' he said, his voice dripping with disdain. 'You've done enough damage, without doing any more. Just stay out of it, Maddie.' And with those wounding words, he stalked out of her office just as angrily as he'd arrived.

*

Pru was the last person Maddie wanted to see that afternoon. Last night's transcripts had already been delivered as usual, so she was rather bemused to see the Wren, a large envelope in hand, standing at her desk.

'Colonel McKie said I was to personally see you got this,' said Pru, handing her the package.

Maddie was curious and began inspecting the official-looking envelope immediately. 'Thank you,' she told Pru, unsure for a moment as to whether she would take the hint and go.

As soon as the door was shut, Maddie got to work in earnest with her paper knife. Slitting the top of the envelope, she took out its contents. It was the post-mortem report on Ernst. Her eyes raced down the type-written text, taking in various tell-tale details she'd seen so often when dealing with suicide cases at St Hugh's.

Words like *ligature* and *asphyxiation* leapt out at her. The fact that Ernst had two broken fingers was put down to his suggested difficulty in lashing the rope to the tree. The blood pumping in her ears grew louder as she turned the page to read the verdict.

SUICIDE.

She was still trying to make sense of it when there was another knock on her door. Her heart sank when she saw it was Major Lansley. The hang-dog expression on his face rarely ever changed so it was difficult to read the nature of his visit, but she thought it safe to assume he was the bearer of bad news.

Glancing at her desk he said: 'You've seen the post-mortem report.'

'Yes, sir.'

'And you're not happy with it?' His voice was even, as if Maddie's disagreement with the verdict was a given. He sat down uninvited.

Maddie felt her shoulders lift and fall in a sigh. 'No, sir. I'm not.'

'Hmmm,' he replied. He may as well have said "too bad," or "so what?" Just like they did to Miss Baskin when she raised her concerns over her brother's death. Things were being *swept under the carpet* – another expression of Uncle Roly's. And Maddie didn't like it.

'I'm here to tell you some news,' he said. His voice was lighter, as if he was keen to draw a line under the post-mortem.

'Oh?'

'We've found a replacement for Lehmann. He's undergoing training now, but he came from the M Room, so he knows what he's walking into.'

Even though the office was warm, Maddie suddenly shivered. 'A new stool pigeon to be batman for Hammler?'

'Yes. Important job, albeit rather onerous. It broke Lehmann, so we can't let the same thing happen to the new chap.'

He was staying firm over Ernst's death. She tried to hide her frustration. 'And do you have the name of this new chap?'

Lansley consulted the file he'd placed on Maddie's desk. 'Yes, here we are. Weitzler. Max Weitzler,' he read aloud. 'It was all very rushed, of course, but I had time to do a quick psychological assessment and he seems a good sort.' He shut the file and looked at Maddie. 'I say, Miss Gresham. Are you quite well? You've turned rather pale.'

But Maddie hadn't heard the major's question. The news that Max was the new stool pigeon in Hammler's suite came as a huge shock. Her mind was suddenly plunged into chaos. Why hadn't Max told her? Was he afraid she would have dissuaded him? Of course she would have. He would also have been breaking the Official Secrets Act and now he'd entered the Crocodile's lair. If Ernst had been murdered, as she still suspected, then Max was in grave danger.

Chapter 50

Mrs Pollock looked up from her chair at the kitchen table as soon as Maddie walked in. Her eyes were red-rimmed and her face even puffier than normal. A black bruise from her "bump" in the kitchen the other day was now clearly visible on her cheek. At the sight Maddie felt sick with guilt.

'Thank goodness you're back, Miss Gresham,' she said. 'Something terrible's happened.'

'Oh no,' replied Maddie, feigning ignorance, but knowing exactly what the "something terrible" was.

'My Harold got knocked down by a bus. In 'ospital, he is. Lucky to be alive.'

Maddie sat down next to her. 'I'm so sorry. How dreadful.'

Mrs Pollock nodded. 'They say he's unconscious and he's broke both legs and an arm. It'll be months before he's mended. If he ever is.' Her forlorn voice dissolved into tears and Maddie felt compelled to put her arm around her.

'And Sally?'

'With my sister.'

Maddie was relieved that at least she didn't have to worry about Sally as well.

'Where did the accident happen?' she asked. She needed to get

290

some clarity around Mrs Pollock's own knowledge. How much did she know about her husband's secret activities? Had he been lying to her as well, or was she aware of whatever he was up to?

'In town, near Bond Street,' she replied.

Maddie frowned.

'He left the house without you? But you always said he wasn't safe to be on his own.' *Danger to 'imself and others,* as she recalled her landlady saying.

Mrs Pollock nodded. 'It's all such a mess. I told him.' She was shaking her head. 'I said it was a bad idea.'

'What was a bad idea?' pressed Maddie. Her landlady was on the verge of revealing what was really going on.

She fingered her mug thoughtfully. 'Harold and me, well, we're both conchies, you see.'

Maddie took in a deep breath. *Conscientious objectors.* It was a relief to hear the information straight from Mrs Pollock's own lips. Of course, she knew about her landlady's membership of the Peace Pledge Union, but she'd no idea that Harold Pollock was also a conscientious objector – even though it appeared his pacifism didn't extend to his home life.

The landlady carried on: 'He'd done his bit in the Great War and didn't want to go through it all again.' She shook her head and looked at Maddie as if pleading for her understanding. ''E was nearly forty-two anyway. A month later and 'e wouldn't have been called up. So, he put on this act, see, so he wouldn't have to join up.'

'He pretended to suffer from shell-shock?'

Mrs Pollock nodded, keeping her eyes on the table. 'Then after our Jeanie got killed early on in the Blitz, I had to agree with 'im.' She lifted her gaze. 'We both thought what's the point? It's all senseless, this killin', ain't it? Innocent people blown to bits and little ones like Sal left orphans.' She was staring straight at her now and opening up with such conviction that Maddie thought her own heart might break. 'When Harold's mum died and left us this place, we thought we'd have a fresh start, make money from lodgers. And now . . .' Her look bounced around the four walls that surrounded her. 'After this, God knows what will become of us.' Her hands flew up to her face then and she began to sob once more. Maddie put a comforting arm around her.

Now was not the time to probe any further, she thought. Harold Pollock had become a casualty of his own personal battle with his conscience. Many questions remained to be answered. Had he followed her because he was afraid she'd inform the authorities he'd dodged conscription? Perhaps, but it still left the question of what he was doing at Anstruther's in the first place. But as long as he remained unconscious, there would be no answers. Maddie would let the matter rest for now, but there needed to be a reckoning. In the meantime, as she sat with her arm around her distraught landlady, it occurred to her that she had just added another secret to the many others she had to keep.

Chapter 51

Max, now wearing the uniform of a Wehrmacht batman, glanced around the room in the mansion. The suite was large and comfortably furnished. A cupboard, drawers, a table and chair, a comfortable sofa, a cheval mirror and a single bed. Another door led through to what he assumed was a sitting room.

There hadn't been enough time for the usual, in-depth training, he'd been told when he volunteered to take Ernst's place. His selection, coming as it did at such a critical time, had come as a great relief. It meant he could turn his grief into action. He was taking Ernst's place as Hammler's new batman, captured near Paris. All the generals had their own personal valets, so none would pay him much attention. As long as he kept his commanding officer's boots polished and drew his bath for him, he could move seamlessly among them and no one would suspect a thing.

Hammler's personal possessions were arranged neatly on the dressing table: a hairbrush, pomade, hand mirror, cologne and a photograph of a woman. He moved closer. With her blonde, wavy hair, she looked very like Maddie when she was in the role of Lady Frobisher. He was wondering if the similarity between the two of them was just a coincidence, when he heard loud voices and footsteps. Hammler entered the room, dressed in a singlet and shorts and drenched in sweat from boxing a punch bag in the gymnasium. Wiping the back of his neck with a towel, he suddenly stopped dead in surprise. Max immediately stood to attention and saluted.

'Ah, so you must be the replacement.'

'Yes, sir. Sergeant Weitzler reporting for duty, sir.'

Hammler continued to rub the back of his neck with the towel. 'Do I detect a Munich accent?'

'Yes, sir.'

He nodded and flung his towel to the floor. 'Shame about the other man. Suicide is such a sign of weakness.'

Up until that point Max had been standing to attention with his eyes on the wall ahead. Now they darted to Hammler, his face still flushed from his working out with a punchbag. He hated him already.

The brigadier turned to look in the mirror above his chest of drawers. Jutting out his chin, he inspected it, running his hand along his jawline.

'You were captured in France?'

'Yes, sir.' Max had been given a rudimentary cover story, but at least he knew northern France well.

Hammler was now wiping the sweat from his face with a napkin. 'They let us listen to radio reports, you know. We are abreast of the situation in Europe. You'll find the mood is mixed. There are officers in here who have already surrendered and those who are putting all their faith in the Vengeance rockets.' He sighed as he patted his cheeks, then glanced at Max's reflection in the mirror. 'But there is just one who knows the true picture,' he added with a leer.

'Sir?' said Max with a frown.

Ignoring Max, Hammler shrugged and flipped the napkin over his shoulder. 'But enough,' he said. 'I'm sure we'll get along well enough as long as you do as I ask.'

'Sir,' responded Max.

Hammler's eyes settled on an envelope lying on the chest of drawers. 'Oh and see that the letter is delivered, will you?' he said. 'I'm going for a lie-down.'

'Yes, sir,' replied Max, moving forward to reach for the letter. But when he saw the name on it, his heart missed a beat. The envelope was addressed to Lady Frobisher.

*

Lorries laden with rubble from homes destroyed by yet more missiles rumbled along the road as Maddie walked back to Fairview that evening. She ignored their noise and the trails of dust they threw up. She was deep in thought. The Vengeance rockets were leaving death and destruction in their wake and there seemed little she could do about it. They were being made in underground bunkers and fired from movable launchers, that much was known, but the Allies were still searching for them blind as they advanced through France. So many lives could be saved and yet the man who had the power to stop all this death and destruction was at Trent Park and refusing to talk.

Now Max was in the mansion, perhaps he might pick up something the microphones did not. She feared for him though. He wasn't even given proper training and that put him at even more risk. He was exposed and he was vulnerable.

Up ahead lay Fairview with its grand lions. At the sight she picked up her pace a little when she noticed the tailor's van parked outside the drive. Mrs. Pollock was stepping out of it. She slammed the door just as Maddie arrived alongside and watched as the driver sped off in the opposite direction. Maddie watched, too. Behind the wheel was the bald man with the gold-rimmed glasses.

'Miss Gresham,' greeted Mrs Pollock as she turned round to see Maddie standing behind her. 'I've just been to see Harold in hospital,' she explained. 'He's awake.'

Maddie forced a smile. She was glad he wasn't dead, truly she was, but she was worried what he would say about her when he started talking again. 'That's wonderful news,' she managed.

'Yes, ain't it just?' replied the landlady, even though Maddie didn't detect much enthusiasm behind the statement.

'Has he said anything?' she probed as together they walked to the front door.

Mrs Pollock sounded tetchy, her neck lengthening like a curious hen's. 'Said anything?'

'About the accident. How it happened.'

The landlady's neck retreated into her shoulders again. 'No. No, he didn't. He's broke his jaw, so there'll not be much gabbing for the next few weeks.'

They were walking side by side up the path, past the withered vegetable seedlings, to the front door when Maddie decided she had to ask. 'That man,' she said. 'The one who gave you a lift.'

'Oh him,' Mrs Pollock replied, making more of an effort to sound cheerful this time, even though Maddie couldn't see her face to read her expression. 'He's a friend of Harold's. Works at one of them posh tailors in Savile Row.' Then she added: 'Why do you ask?'

'I just thought I'd seen him somewhere before, that's all.'

Her suspicions were confirmed. The tailor had regular access to the mansion at Trent Park. He'd been there the day Ernst went missing and he'd had dealings with Dr Baskin, too. She needed to get word to Max and quickly.

Chapter 52

Maddie stormed past Holmes and straight into Colonel McKie's office.

'Wait, miss, please!' the hapless secretary called after her, but Maddie was determined and not even Holmes could intimidate her anymore.

The room was full of smoke and the colonel was writing at his desk. As soon as he saw her, he flung down his pen, sat back in his chair and laced his fingers over his stomach.

'Miss Gresham,' he greeted her. 'Any more progress with Hammler?' he asked before she'd had time to catch her breath.

'Not yet, sir.'

The colonel's look was quizzical. 'Why the rush then? Please tell me you've found out more about the V-2?'

Maddie steadied her breathing. 'No, sir. I'm afraid I haven't. It's about Sergeant Weitzler.'

'Weitzler? Isn't he the new stool pigeon?'

'Yes, sir. I'm worried he may be in grave danger. We need to get him out of the mansion.'

To her shock, the colonel didn't seem at all worried. 'You've proved you're a good actress, Miss Gresham, but don't you think you're being a little melodramatic?'

Maddie gulped down a lungful of air, trying to compose herself. She mustn't lose control, even in the face of such pomposity. 'I've reason to believe that Sergeant Lehmann's true identity was discovered.' She took another breath. 'I think the generals' tailor killed him.'

The colonel chuckled infuriatingly. 'But you've seen the post-mortem report, Miss Gresham. You know Lehmann committed suicide. You saw the state of the man. He hanged himself.'

Maddie bit her lip. 'I know the report said that, sir, but I have reason to believe the tailor might be some sort of German agent.'

It was suddenly clear to her from the way his thumbs began circling each other as he clasped his hands, that Colonel McKie was rapidly losing patience.

He considered his next move for a moment then said: 'Leave that sort of thing to the intelligence branch, Miss Gresham. Stool pigeons are in constant danger. They are fully aware of it. You keep your own hysteria in check and just stick with the psychology. Yes? I've got more important things to deal with.'

He took a deep breath and glowering at her, seemed to have second thoughts. 'I suppose you ought to be told.'

Maddie frowned. 'Told what, sir?'

'As if matters couldn't get any worse, there was talk last night between the generals.'

'Talk? About what, sir?'

'Not only do we have the V-1s and V-2s to contend with, a V-3 is expected within the next few weeks.'

'A V-3,' repeated Maddie.

'A super weapon. This'll dwarf the other two. Make the others look like Roman candles. It can fire six hundred shells per hour. It's the largest artillery weapon ever built, and London is its target.'

For a moment Maddie was silent as the enormity of what the colonel had just told her sank in. She said nothing. Simply nodded.

'You may go,' the colonel told her.

She was being dismissed. No, worse than mere dismissal. She

was being ridiculed. Colonel McKie wouldn't take her seriously. He may as well have just patted her on the head and told her to run along. He had more important things to worry about than her "hysterical" claims. But his patronising attitude only fired her up.

Dr Baskin had been murdered, she was convinced of it. So too had Ernst and, if her theory was right, Max's life was at real risk. If the tailor had discovered Ernst was a stool pigeon, then he would strongly suspect his replacement to be one, too.

A grim-faced Holmes was holding the door open for her to leave, as if she were a naughty schoolgirl.

'Oh and Miss Gresham,' the colonel called.

She wheeled round. 'Yes, sir.'

'On no account are you to contact this Weitzler in the mansion, you hear me? This operation will not be compromised by your fanciful whims.'

Maddie arrived back at her office, the anger still coursing through her veins, when she saw a letter waiting on her desk. She looked at the address on the envelope. Written in a bold Gothic hand it read *Lady Frobisher*. She guessed who'd sent it and as she slit open the envelope and saw the signature on the bottom, she knew she was right.

Dear Lady Frobisher,

I have been deeply troubled since our last meeting. I was sorry to see you in such distress after the sudden death of your friend and your refusal to accept my condolences was completely understandable. I was very insensitive, and I trust you will accept my sincere apologies.

I very much hope we can meet again soon.

Your humble servant,

Josef Hammler

Maddie let out a bemused laugh. The man had some nerve. It seemed her unplanned outpouring of anger over Briggs's death had touched him in a way that so much else hadn't. She hadn't meant to cry in front of him or vent her anger at him, but clearly some sort of connection had been made. It was as if, for the first time in many years, he was showing empathy for another human being. Of course she would meet him again and she would put the time to good use.

Her phone rang.

'Maddie?' Eddie's tone was wary.

'Am I forgiven?' she asked. After the other day she knew she needed to pretend to eat humble pie.

A sigh down the line. 'You're still my wife, so I suppose so.' If he was acting the long-suffering husband, she would take advantage. 'And that's why I've called.'

'Oh?'

'The generals want to meet you.'

'What?'

'They've seen you about and know you've been coming on the odd jaunt with me. They want you to go for tea in the mansion.'

A muted laugh from Maddie now.

'What's so funny? I'm in there a lot – drinking with them and playing billiards – so it's high time you joined me. Surely it's not such a silly idea?'

A pause. With the V-3 looming over the horizon, she supposed anything was worth a try to get more intelligence. 'What does McKie say?'

'He wants us to go ahead.'

'Then it's decided.'

'Let me see.' She imagined Eddie checking his diary. 'Shall we say three o'clock tomorrow. I'll make sure we have scones and jam.'

'Excellent,' said Maddie and she put down the receiver with renewed hope. Now perhaps she might be able to get a warning to Max after all.

*

A guard opened the double doors into the generals' drawing room allowing Lord and Lady Frobisher to make their grand entrance. A select group of officers had been invited to tea and was waiting to greet them. Maddie had made sure Brigadier Hammler was also present.

'Gentlemen, I am delighted to introduce to you my wife, Lady Madeleine Frobisher,' said Eddie, beaming.

The officers – there were six of them, all in uniform, including Hammler – stood in line to shake Maddie's hand and bow stiffly.

'A pleasure to meet you.'

'We have heard so much about you.'

'Enchanté.'

Then it was Hammler's turn to greet Maddie.

'Brigadier,' she said, holding out her gloved hand. She was uncertain how he would react, but he took her hand and kissed it, his eyes playing on her face a little longer than they should. This time she didn't withdraw quickly. The connection was there. She could sense it. She could look him in the eye and not be repulsed. Perhaps he sensed that. She'd uncovered a reason that partly explained his calculated hatred. It was not an excuse, and his redemption was still a remote possibility, but at least now she could understand his visceral desire for revenge. Much to her surprise, she suddenly found herself wanting to dive far deeper into this crocodile's depths to help him find his humanity again.

'I hope I am forgiven, your ladyship,' he told her in a low voice.

Forgiveness? How could he ask for forgiveness from her when he should be seeking it from the thousands whose deaths were on his hands?

'Yes, Brigadier,' she said softly before shaking the hand of another general.

The arrival of waiters hefting trays of tea and plates of scones caused a ripple of excitement among the generals. They all took their places around a long, low table to be served.

'Your husband looks after us well,' remarked one of the older

301

generals, who sported a large moustache, to Maddie.

'I'm glad to hear it,' she said. 'I understand the theatre outing was a great success the other night.'

Another officer, a younger major with a softer face, flapped out a snowy white napkin and laid it across his knees. 'It was an excellent play. *Pygmalion*. You know it?'

'It is one of my favourites.'

The polite banter continued in the same vein. There was some talk of royalty and English sport, and now and again Maddie would flash a glimpse at Hammler to catch him watching her, a bemused look on his face. There was, however, no sign of Max.

Maddie was growing anxious. She knew she needed to make a move. She hoped to find him in Hammler's suite. Halfway through her cup of tea and growing increasingly on edge, she deliberately made her fingers slip from the handle of the teacup. Milky liquid spilled onto her skirt, and she leapt up immediately to see a stain the size of a tea plate.

'Oh, gentlemen, I'm so sorry. I'll have to go to the bathroom,' she gushed, frantically wiping her skirt with her napkin.

A waiter, standing nearby, volunteered himself to show her the nearest one. The generals stood en masse as she exited the room, leaving Eddie puzzled. He could tell the spill was engineered, but to what purpose he wasn't quite sure – until that is, he suddenly remembered Max Weitzler was the new stool pigeon. He gripped the arms of his leather chair. Tea at the mansion had seemed like a good idea at the time. Now he wasn't so sure. Maddie was up to something, all right, but if he went to check on her he'd only draw attention to himself by getting involved. It was simply up to him to hold the fort and keep the generals engaged.

The bathroom was down a narrow passage that led off the landing. The waiter pointed to it. Maddie pretended to head towards it, then doubled back. She knew from a plan of the mansion from the M Room exactly where Hammler's suite was located – on the other side of the main landing. Peering round the corner, she could see the coast was clear and walked briskly towards the room. She would tell Max about the tailor and how she suspected he was connected to the deaths of both Dr Baskin and Ernst.

The suite was easy enough to find and standing outside, she put her ear to the door. She frowned. There was an odd sound coming from it, a sort of muffled cry. Something wasn't right. Without bothering to knock she opened the door to find Max lying barely conscious on the floor. A cord was around his neck.

'Max!' She rushed to his side, loosened the cord and bent her ear to his mouth. He was still breathing and his eyes flickered open. But as she looked in horror at the bruising round his neck there was a sudden movement behind her. Glancing back over her shoulder she saw a figure flash past her. Even though she only caught sight of him for a split second as he dashed out of the room, she knew for certain it was the bald tailor with the gold-rimmed glasses.

The startled waiter, by now standing outside, looked on. 'See that he's taken care of,' ordered Maddie as, leaving Max on the floor, she rushed after the tailor. By now he was running across the landing and down the narrow passage towards the bathroom. Maddie followed just in time to see him disappear down the back service stairs. Kicking off her shoes, she went after him.

'Wait!' she called. 'Wait!' – even though she knew he wouldn't get very far.

The service entrance to the basement was blocked off when the M Room was created. Even if the generals had decided to explore the mansion, they would never have been able to reach the M Room or even know of its existence.

Once at the bottom of the stairs, Maddie fumbled for a light switch but could find none. Running footsteps echoed along the passage, then another sound. Maybe the tailor had reached the end of the corridor – the one that led nowhere – and was punching or kicking at the wall. Even if he was trapped, she was still on her own. If only she'd raised the alarm upstairs, when she'd had the chance. There were half a dozen armed guards above her head, but none of them could hear her if she called for help. At the end of the passage, too, behind a wall, lay the basement and the M Room. Within the width of two bricks there were people who could come to her aid and yet they were out of reach.

The only natural light came from a narrow window way up in the wall above the stairwell and the tiles were uneven, but gingerly she managed to make progress. The footsteps had stopped now, but she still thought she could hear something. The hiss of steam pipes overhead? Deep breaths? Or was that the sound of her own blood pounding through her ears?

'I know you're down there,' she called, trying to hide the fear in her voice as she edged along the wall. 'It's a dead end. You're trapped, so you may as well come out.'

As she picked her way further along the passage, her eyes began to adjust to the gloom and suddenly she saw the end up ahead – a blank wall that had been bricked up. But of the bald tailor there was no sign. Confused, she picked up the pace, her heart knocking against her chest. Three steps. Four. Then a tug at her neck and an arm under chin, yanking her back.

'No!' she screamed as she felt herself being dragged along the passage like a rag doll, her feet barely touching the floor. The walls, the floor tiles – everything began to swim before her eyes. It was all happening so fast she couldn't think straight. Suddenly she was back in the basement cell in Munich. The smell. The confined space. The terror. She was clawing at the man's arm as it tugged at her neck, but her strength was deserting her. A thin sound, like a stifled yelp, tapped the darkness until she realised it was coming from her own lips, clamped shut by the arm under her chin.

A German voice burst through the silence. Angry. Authoritative. Familiar. '*Halte.* Leave her!' Her heart knocked against her chest. The Gestapo officer? Was she back in the Munich cell?

Suddenly a beam of torchlight lanced the darkness. But who was holding the torch? Her rescuer, or her killer? She was facing the wall, but in one movement her attacker tossed her in front of him so that the light from the torch blinded her and something hard and cold pressed against her throat. Still unable to move her head, she blinked her eyes then lowered them to her throat to see the glint of a pair of scissors.

'Leave her,' repeated the German voice. She recognised it now. Hammler.

Had he really come to her rescue? A man responsible for weapons that were killing men, women and children in their thousands?

She could hear her attacker's breathing; it came hot and hard against her neck. She felt the scissors, too, digging deeper with each breath.

'It's no use. It's over,' Hammler told him.

A prick of steel pierced her skin then and she closed her eyes. This was it: the moment of her death. But then there was a cry and she felt herself catapulted against the wall. Her skull collided with it, and she slid down to the floor on her knees, the pain on the side of her face so intense that she was only vaguely aware of shouts and a scuffle nearby.

Another cry. Then a visceral gurgling sound, followed by footsteps running back up the stairs. Managing to open her eyes, she peered towards the stairwell to see a man lying on the tiles, something sticking out of his torso. Crawling along the floor on all fours, she reached him. It was Hammler, blood blooming from the front of his tunic; a pair of scissors was lodged in his chest.

'No!' she cried, her fingers hovering over the scissors, the blood flowing fast now, pooling on the floor. His eyes half opened and he grabbed her hand. 'I'll get help,' she said.

Lifting his gaze, he tried to focus on her face and opened his lips to speak. 'Clara?' he whispered.

She looked at him for a moment, but said nothing, as if her silence was comfort enough.

Up above a door slammed and footsteps hurtled down the stairs once more. Then came the sound of a fist on skin, followed by a cry as a body barrelled back down to the bottom, a pair of gold-rimmed spectacles tumbling behind. A moment later there were more footsteps and she suddenly felt gentle hands reach for her as she huddled in the darkness. Another voice now, one that called her tenderly by her name.

'Maddie.'

Chapter 53

The Cotswolds

September 1944

With Paget behind the wheel, the London suburbs were soon far behind them, and they were speeding through the undulating countryside of the Chilterns. Past Oxford they went, then out to the familiar landscape of the Cotswolds. The road looped round the edge of a small town then rose steeply through a wooded valley until it opened out onto the vast expanse of common with its huge, unfettered vistas. The sun was bright in the late September sky, turning the River Severn into a ribbon of silver below.

Maddie wished she could share the view with Max, but she assumed he was still at the mansion. There had been no communication between them since Hammler's death. Colonel McKie had forbidden it. He'd been snatched away from her yet again, just as they'd renewed their love. But she prayed they'd let him see her again before too long. Thanks to Max, the tailor had been arrested and was now in custody, but like everything else at Trent Park, the whole incident was shrouded in secrecy. None of the generals had known what was going on beneath their feet. They were told that Hammler had been transferred to another prison. That was all. The invisible walls of the impenetrable fortress remained unbreeched.

Just why the colonel wanted to see Maddie at this remote location instead of in his office at Trent Park, however, remained a mystery. What was he about to say that couldn't be said in his office?

In another mile a huge aircraft hangar loomed into view like some giant Neolithic barrow on the horizon. The common land was fenced off at this point and a long ribbon of concrete striped the cut grass. The military vehicle stopped at high wire gates. They were at an airbase.

Paget had a brief exchange with a guard and on his signal the gates swung wide open. He saluted as they drove into the compound and along a track towards the hangar. It hadn't rained for two weeks, and dust clouds billowed in the vehicle's wake until it came to a halt by the huge construction. One airman directed the car to stop beside it, and another opened the door for Maddie.

Her curiosity was still simmering, but confusion was now taking over as, on leaving Paget, she was led by an airman through the vast space of the hangar. Just then, from seemingly out of nowhere a familiar figure appeared.

'Eddie?' she called before correcting herself. 'I mean Flight Lieutenant Windlesham.'

Eddie, dressed in full uniform, shot the airman an embarrassed look. 'I'll take it from here, corporal,' he said.

'What's going on?' Maddie asked as she felt his arm at her elbow, pushing her along.

'You'll find out soon enough,' he told her in a low voice. 'This way,' he said, gesturing her into an office at the side. 'Wait here.' He pointed to a chair.

She balked. 'When will you tell me what's going on, Eddie?' she snapped.

'All will be revealed,' he told her enigmatically, signalling to the seat once more. 'Please, Miss Gresham.' He left the room.

She couldn't sit down. Wouldn't sit down. She was too full of nervous energy. Her whole body was like a coiled spring. Just as before her raids with Max in Munich, she was poised to pounce like an animal. She looked about her. The small office was incredibly utilitarian with charts and posters on the wall. One of them pictured a pilot giving the thumbs-up sign as he sat in a cockpit. *Wings for Victory* read the caption and above that *Let's Go*. Maddie only wished she could.

A moment later she heard footsteps, then a door handle clicked. She turned as Colonel McKie entered, followed – much to her surprise – by her godfather, Sir Roland Fulford.

'Uncle Roly! What on earth . . .?' His presence, coming completely out of the blue, unnerved her.

'All will be revealed in due course, Maddie,' Sir Roland told her rather stiffly. Eddie had said something similar, but her impatience was getting the better of her.

Colonel McKie, his face grimly determined, marched round the desk to take a seat. Sir Roland followed behind and sat down beside him.

'Please,' said the colonel, urging her to sit. 'I'm sure you're thinking we owe you an explanation.'

'I am anxious to know what's going on,' she agreed, adding 'sir' as an afterthought, just to show courtesy.

'Of course you are, Miss Gresham.' He twitched a tight smile. 'And that's been the problem, hasn't it?' He tented his fingers on the desk.

Maddie was puzzled. 'I'm sorry. I don't understand.'

The colonel shook his head. 'You're a clever young woman, Miss Gresham, and you've done sterling work for MI19, but your eagerness to question and probe, has quite frankly been rather a thorn in Trent Park's side.'

Maddie opened her mouth, then snapped it shut in surprise.

McKie cleared his throat and elbowed the desk. 'I'll start from the beginning, Miss Gresham,' he told her.

Please do, she thought. She cut to her godfather, searching his face for some sort of explanation.

'I'm in intelligence, my dear. MI5,' he told her, almost apologetically. 'There is absolutely no way I could be seen at Trent Park.'

Maddie's eyes opened wide in shock. She shook her head. She'd wondered why her godfather had never mentioned he was good friends with Dr Baskin. Now she knew that all the while he was leading a double life.

'As I was saying,' the colonel resumed. 'We knew the Germans would always be trying to discover exactly what went on at Trent Park. From the generals' letters home, the enemy was aware our prisoners were being treated royally. While most of the officers thought we were being nice because we feared reprisals after a German victory, the Nazi regime itself suspected our motives. Of course, they were right to think we weren't entertaining them out of the goodness of our hearts, and they were eager to find out why.'

'Naturally,' ventured Sir Roland.

McKie paused, as if his voice was snagged on barbed wire; there was a look of guilt on his face.

And then it came. The admission, rushing towards her like a freight train. 'You were right, Miss Gresham,' the colonel said forcefully. 'We think Dr Baskin was murdered.''

At last, the truth. She wasn't suffering from mild paranoia. All her fears and suspicions were true.

'I knew it,' muttered Maddie, through clenched teeth. But there was more.

'He did die in his bed. Of a heart attack, as I told you,' explained the colonel. 'But we fear it was brought on by shock and trauma.'

'Shock and trauma?' repeated Maddie.

The two men swapped uneasy looks. 'Yes, you see he'd been tortured beforehand, Miss Gresham. His fingernails . . .' The colonel looked down at his hand and flinched, as if imagining the pain. Maddie swallowed down a horrified gasp.

The colonel carried on: 'The Germans wanted to know exactly what was going on behind the scenes. They knew from the generals' letters home that their treatment here was exceptional and guessed we were after something in return for our hospitality. They just didn't know what. Obviously they'd no idea about the M Room, and that the prisoners were constantly being caught off-guard and disclosing secrets vital to help us win this war.'

Maddie recalled the doctor's hurried note to her: the one he'd never sent. He must've harboured fears he was being stalked. 'But we don't believe Dr Baskin gave any information away,' Sir Roland said swiftly. 'That's why his home near Oxford was burgled afterwards. He wasn't meant to die, or at least not before he'd given away our secrets.'

The colonel continued. 'After that we naturally needed to flush out his killer. And you were the perfect candidate.'

'What?' Maddie suddenly smelt a rat.

'We have to level with you, Miss Gresham,' said McKie, grabbing a pencil and rolling it between his fingers. 'You were always central to our plan.'

Sir Roland stepped in. 'We needed to get our ducks in a row to uncover Baskin's killer. After you did your country proud as a youngster in Munich, I knew you had pluck. You were made for the role.'

Maddie felt her mouth open in amazement. 'So I was the bait?' She couldn't believe her ears. Surely her godfather wouldn't have knowingly exploited her?

'More of a honeypot, my dear,' said Sir Roland, with a quick shake of his head. 'We knew you'd want justice for Dr Baskin, just as we did. We helped each other to achieve that goal.'

So she had been a puppet and Uncle Roly, together with the colonel, had been pulling her strings. Admittedly knowing she'd helped bring the doctor's killer to book, went some way to soothing it, but her treatment still rankled. All the colonel's talk about caring for her safety had, in fact, been a smokescreen. His apparent concern for her was little more than a sham.

By way of an apology Sir Roland explained: 'The whole Trent Park operation was threatened. It just couldn't be compromised at any price. Without your input, my dear, MI19 could have been scuppered.'

Maddie was still trying to comprehend the situation. 'So Harold Pollock killed Dr Baskin?'

'Yes.' Sir Roland nodded. 'You brought him out of the woodwork for us.'

'Baskin died a hero,' added the colonel, as if that fact should be compensation enough for his loss.

Sir Roland continued. 'Pollock was a hired thug, recruited by a German agent at a so-called Peace Pledge rally to do the Nazis' dirty work.'

'So, the Peace Pledge Union *was* infiltrated by Fascists?' Maddie asked, thinking of Mrs Pollock's worthy, but misguided intentions.

'Yes, not long after the war started,' broke in Sir Roland.

'And the tailor at Anstruther's was a German agent.'

Colonel McKie nodded. 'Werner Huber is his name. Better known as Vernon Hubbard, a tailor at Anstruther's.'

Maddie thought immediately of the bald man with the gold-rimmed glasses. 'He killed Ernst Lehmann, didn't he? He suspected he was a spy in the camp. He must've seen him coming out of Hut 6 just after I interviewed him.'

She'd seen the tailor at Trent Park the day before Ernst was found dead. He'd probably strangled him in the mansion, just how he tried to kill Max, then strung him up in the grounds to make it look like a suicide. As she suspected, Ernst fingers were broken in the struggle to free himself.

'You are a clever girl,' said Sir Roly. 'When the military police raided Huber's flat, they found a wireless. As we suspected, he was sending uncensored information to Germany.'

'So that's why you were so keen that all the generals got fitted by this tailor. Were you feeding them misinformation that they could pass to him?' said Maddie.

'Precisely. Why do you think so many of those benighted missiles missed their targets and ended up in the middle of nowhere? We gave out false information about where the rockets landed, so Jerry thought their co-ordinates were wrong and adjusted them accordingly.' He paused and shook his head. 'But we never expected Huber to commit murder. He'd got Pollock to do his dirty work before. He guessed we were keeping close tabs on Hammler and came to suspect Ernst, then Max.'

'Our good idea rather backfired,' said Sir Roland. 'And Hammler's death certainly didn't figure in our plans. That was very unfortunate. He tried to play the hero a little too late and paid the price. But now our German spy has been persuaded to see the error of his ways, so to speak.'

'They all do, in the end,' agreed McKie.

'I don't understand,' said Maddie.

'When we told Huber he faced the death penalty for murder and being a Nazi spy, it concentrated his mind wonderfully. He's on our side now,' explained Sir Roland.

'So that's why you trailed me?' Maddie thought about the woman at the Savoy and the tea room.

'We did that to protect you, Miss Gresham,' the colonel told her.

Protect me? thought Maddie, biting back her frustration. She thought of the redacted transcripts, too. Perhaps a few of the generals were in on Werner Huber's game. Even the enemy, it seemed, knew more than she did. There was a fine line between being protected and being patronised – being kept in the dark. Just like her alter ego, Lady Frobisher, her male superiors considered her incapable of making her own decisions.

Eddie knocked and entered the room just then, saluted and stood by Colonel McKie.

'And we saw a great opportunity to exploit that knowledge,'

continued McKie. 'Now that Huber has changed sides, we can get him to knowingly send the enemy false co-ordinates about where their infernal rockets have hit, so more of them will land away from our towns and cities.' His smile shrank then as he fixed Maddie with a particularly serious look. 'But, above all, the secret listeners of Trent Park have not been compromised.'

Maddie took satisfaction from the colonel's words – she really did – but there was something, or rather someone, she needed to hear about before she could fully share in the success of the operation.

'And Sergeant Weitzler?' she asked. 'Where is he?'

Colonel McKie read her anxious expression and dipped his head at Eddie who made for the door. This time when the flight lieutenant opened it, Max walked through.

'Max!' Maddie cried, leaping up from her seat. She lurched forward towards him but remembered just in time to prevent herself flinging her arms around him in front of the others. Max's face registered relief, and he managed a smile, but he stopped abruptly and stuck out his chin. She suddenly realised he was standing to attention. He saluted the colonel.

'Stand at ease, Weitzler,' said McKie.

'So, Maddie, it's a satisfactory end to a rather tortuous operation to keep our secrets safe,' said Sir Roland.

'And it must continue,' added McKie.

'Sir?' Maddie, still trying to digest what she'd just learned, was disheartened to find there was more.

'Perhaps you'd like to explain, Weitzler?' the colonel suggested.

Maddie's gaze switched to Max as he inhaled deeply.

As he looked at her directly, she could see his eyes blaze when he told her: 'I shall remain in the mansion until we find out where the launch sites are.'

Her heart suddenly sank, knowing they wouldn't be able to see each other for goodness knew how long. But then the colonel remembered something.

'I almost forgot,' he said, delving into his briefcase. 'Sergeant Weitzler found this among Hammler's personal effects. It's addressed to you.'

Puzzled, Maddie took the sealed envelope from McKie's hand.

'Open it, please,' urged McKie.

It was dated 19th September, 1944.

'But that was . . .'

The letter was written on the day of her visit to the mansion. Hammler must've intended to give it to her before she left. Only he'd never had the chance. Maddie read it aloud.

Dear Lady Frobisher,

Although my last letter did not receive a reply, I was heart-ened by the fact that you are to make a visit to the mansion today. I am very much hoping this means you have accepted my apology for my reprehensible behaviour, and we can move on.

As I told you, I have enjoyed your company at our previous meetings. Despite the circumstances, I have found great solace in our brief discussions. The most recent will, however, stay with me. My work has caused you, and a great many people, a huge amount of pain. I can see that now. As you said, I needed to avenge the death of my own family by killing others, no matter how innocent. Thanks to you, I am beginning to realise revenge is a fool's game. There are no winners.

To this end, I will be sending details of V-2 launch locations on the French coast to British intelligence. I will also tell them that the RAF destroyed the V-3 rocket launch site near Calais in a raid last year. Your Tallboy bombs penetrated the under-ground bunkers. They rendered the V-3 practically inoperable.

I once told you I had no soul. Perhaps I do, but it was lost along with my family. Maybe I just need to find it again. I very much hope you will help me in my quest.

I look forward to our next meeting as friends, not enemies.
Josef Hammler

There was silence for a second at the enormity of what Maddie had just read. This was the information they'd wanted; the purpose of the mission; the reason why Lady Frobisher existed and now she held the prize in her hands. Just when she thought Hammler had taken his secrets to the grave, he had spoken to her from it.

Colonel McKie was first to react. 'But that's incredible news.'

'By Jove, yes!' agreed Sir Roly.

Maddie felt a surge of – what was it? Relief? Pride? She wasn't sure. Perhaps it was fulfilment. Hammler – the Crocodile, the predator, the calculating mass murderer, complicit in the deaths of thousands of innocent people – had made an effort to seek absolution after all. And he had done it because of her. Of course his one honourable deed didn't cancel out the fact that he had been instrumental in destroying countless lives. He was still a mass murderer. But his admission that Hitler's dreaded V-3 rockets no longer posed a threat to Britain came as a monumental relief. A crushing threat had just been lifted from the country, allowing a glimmer of hope to re-emerge once more.

Maddie was about to acknowledge the praise from the colonel and her godfather. After all, it seemed it was her outburst that had made Hammler change his mind and spill his secrets. But then she suddenly realised they weren't congratulating her at all, but themselves. It was as if her role in the operation to get Hammler to talk had never existed.

'Great work, McKie,' said Sir Roly, patting the colonel on the back.

'Absolutely marvellous, sir,' chimed in Eddie.

'Better tell Whitehall the good news straight away,' said McKie, picking up the telephone.

Amid all the excitement and the self-congratulation, Maddie lifted her eyes towards Max, still standing nearby. At least she could share this moment with him.

Catching his gaze, she whispered: 'We did something good, Max.'

He returned her look. 'No,' he replied, with a soft smile. 'You did something good, Maddie, and you did it on your own. No one can take that away from you.'

Chapter 54

Trent Park

October 1945

Maddie looked out of her office window on a dull autumn day as she rubbed the gold band of the tiny diamond solitaire on her left hand. After McKie and Uncle Roly had revealed all the double-dealing and subterfuge that had gone on behind the scenes, the colonel had exercised his discretion and given her and Max twenty-four hours' leave.

'Use it how you will,' he'd told them. 'As long as you're back at Cockfosters Camp by 1500 hours tomorrow.'

They were both in a state of shock. It was hard trying to take in everything they had just learned, so the next day was heaven-sent. At last, they could be alone together, and each second had been cherished. Over the years, their love had been like a single strand of silk threading its way through both their stories. Now that it was finally joined, Maddie knew it wouldn't break.

They spent their first night at Long Barton Manor and as they lay together Maddie, propped up on her elbow, felt her way over Max's body, exploring it by moonlight. It was the first time she'd seen his bare torso and the scars from the shrapnel wounds ran down the side of his chest like train tracks. She traced them with her finger, thinking of the pain he'd endured in France. She began to kiss his naked chest, lingering over the scars, as if she too, wanted to share in his suffering. But suddenly he clasped her hand and she looked into his eyes.

'Maddie,' he said.

'What is it, my love?' she asked, sensing the urgency in his voice.

'Maddie,' he repeated, his gaze dissolving into her own. 'When this war is over, will you marry me?'

They'd stopped off in Oxford on their way back to Trent Park and spotted the ring in a jeweller's window. Max had bought it on impulse and gone down on one knee to slip it on her finger. But that was the last time she'd seen him. He'd returned to the mansion as a stool pigeon the next day and she was back at Fairview with Mrs Pollock. The landlady had been interviewed but found to be completely ignorant about her husband's treachery. And as for Sally, when the little girl saw Maddie for the first time in a week, she had taken her completely by surprise. 'Maddie!' Sally cried as she threw her arms around her. It was almost two years since she'd uttered a word. Both Maddie and Mrs Pollock had shed tears of joy. The scene even made Mr Clancy – now rather more than a lodger at Fairview – well up.

Six months ago Maddie had heard Max had been posted away – somewhere in Europe – to help deal with the aftermath of the death camps. She'd seen the horrific footage of what the Allies had found when they liberated Bergen-Belsen and Dachau and her thoughts went out to Greta and Lena, as well as to Max. He would have to keep strong in the face of such unimaginable devastation.

VE Day had come and gone. Mr Churchill finally declared victory in Europe in May and the huts and fences on Cockfosters Camp had been festooned with Union Jacks and bunting.

Everyone was smiling at last, everyone apart from many of the generals, of course – and Maddie.

Ruth, Pru and Fruity had all tried to persuade her to go with them into London for the celebrations, to Buckingham Palace. Ruth had stood like an excitable Labrador on the threshold of the office, champing to get away from Trent Park for the day. 'It'll be such fun. They say the king and queen will come out,' she'd panted.

Maddie had forced a smile and lied. 'I'd love to, Ruth, but there's still so much to do. The war may be won, but the battle with paperwork continues!'

Ruth laughed. 'The battle with paperwork!' she repeated. 'Very good. Yes.' She lifted a finger. 'Well, you know where to find us, if you change your mind.'

'Have fun!' Maddie had replied, even though she really had no appetite for partying. Of course, it was wonderful that Germany had finally surrendered unconditionally, but without Max by her side the celebration seemed hollow. When so many were still suffering across the English Channel and the horrors of the concentration camps were so raw in everyone's minds, it didn't feel right to join in as long as Greta and her child were missing somewhere in Europe, most probably dead.

Now she was watching a forgotten garland of bunting flap forlornly from a fence in the autumn breeze. No one had the inclination, or the energy, to take it away. Operations at the mansion were being scaled down. Several staff members had already been transferred to other duties. The Union Jack colours of red, white and blue, festooned everywhere over summer, were now faded and washed out. They looked how Maddie felt, especially after hearing the news.

Colonel McKie had told a select few about the decision from "on high", as he'd put it, raising his eyes heavenwards. But there was nothing remotely uplifting about what he said. Maddie was crushed by his words, as was everyone else in the room. It came as a hammer-blow to them all. None of the Germans' transcripts – the transcripts that told of atrocities, of how their troops and, in some cases, how they themselves had raped, tortured and murdered victims, thousands of them Jews – would ever see the light of day. These transcripts they'd worked so hard to obtain – and in the cases of Dr Baskin and Ernst, even lost their lives for – couldn't be used in any future trials of Nazi criminals. No justice would be done, and the very thought cut Maddie like a knife. Instead, most of the brutes would be transferred to other Allied camps for "re-education" or sent back to Germany, escaping any punishment for their vile deeds.

Maddie and the others were told the recordings of the generals' revelations would reveal Britain's intelligence methods and compromise future operations. She recalled Max telling her how the secret listeners marked discs with an "A" to signify an account of an atrocity. Now, such information would have to remain top secret for as long as they all lived. Their work had been too important to the war effort ever to be revealed.

A knock at the door came then. It was Eddie.

'I've come to say goodbye,' he said.

She walked from the window towards him, with tears in her eyes.

'Do you know where you're going?'

'Whitehall. I'd rather get back to flying of course, but . . .' He shrugged, so she finished his sentence for him. 'It's out of your hands.' *Just like everything else,* she thought. *We're all just pawns in the government's game of chess.*

'And you?'

Her eyes slipped down to the boxes. 'Lots of tidying up to do, but we have to be out of here shortly. After that who knows?'

She caught him looking at her ring. 'And Weitzler?'

'He'll be back soon,' she replied vaguely.

He smiled broadly. 'I expect an invitation to the wedding.'

They both laughed then. It hid the pain of parting.

'Let's keep in touch, Lady Frobisher,' he said, suddenly taking both her hands in his and squeezing them. A peck on the cheek took her by surprise. 'I'm sorry you were kept in the dark, but it was fun being married to you.'

She smiled at that, even though she'd long ago realised being married to Eddie for real would have made her feel rather like a general at Trent Park: a captive kept in luxury.

As soon as Eddie left, Maddie went to her desk and pulled out Max's last letter. In that familiar Gothic script of his, he'd told her he was well and busy and that he hoped to be home soon, although just how soon was anyone's guess. He also said he had registered Greta and Lena on the Red Cross list of concentration camp survivors. *If they are still alive, I will find them,* he wrote. Once again, his words were the only things that offered her hope, just as they had all those years ago in the dark days as war broke out.

*

The posters and maps had all been removed from the walls, the framed photograph of Dr Baskin and his sister stowed away. The filing cabinets stood empty, their contents all catalogued and packed into cardboard boxes. They were arranged in a neat row on Maddie's office floor waiting to be taken to . . . She'd no idea. They might even be burnt for all she knew. Piled on a bonfire and set alight. No one outside Trent Park would probably ever know of their existence.

She'd been kneeling down, pasting labels onto the boxes, when a wave of bitterness and sorrow swept over her. The thought of the transcripts lost forever to posterity, and the men and women of Trent Park obliterated from history, threatened to drag her down. It would have overwhelmed her, too, had she not heard footsteps coming down the corridor. Assuming it would be a soldier, ordered to remove some of the boxes, she sniffed away her

322

tears and readied herself to direct him. Only she was mistaken.

She certainly wasn't prepared for the person she saw. Her visitor was, indeed, a soldier, but she was still taken completely by surprise.

'Max!' she cried, leaping up from the floor. 'Max!' She flung her arms around him. He was still wearing his khaki uniform and was just as she'd remembered him when they parted, only this time the tears that flowed were of happiness. 'I've missed you! I've missed you so much!'

Releasing her arms from around his neck, he looked at her lovingly. 'I've missed you, too, my darling Maddie.' There were tears in his amber eyes, too now, but there was also light, as if a thousand candles had suddenly been lit.

'What is it, Max?' she urged. 'Tell me?'

He beamed at her. 'I have brought someone special to meet you.'

'What? Who?' Her mind was a whirlwind.

His finger shot in the air. 'One moment!' he cried, and he disappeared through the door to reappear a heartbeat later.

'This is my someone special,' he announced, holding the hand of a small girl. Maddie thought she couldn't have been more than eight years old. Her elfin face was framed by two dark plaits and her torn coat was hanging off her painfully thin frame. Her skin was sallow and her legs were like sticks, but despite all the signs of terrible hardship, she managed a weak smile. And the smile was Greta's. She was the image of her mother.

'This is Lena.'

Maddie didn't need to be introduced. 'Lena! Of course!' She rushed forward and, with outstretched arms, bent down to hug the little girl. As tears of joy streamed down her face, she drew both the child and Max close to her. It was then she heard him whisper: 'Greta is gone. We are her family now.'

A terrible, aching sorrow hit Maddie then as she kissed the top of the little girl's head. Greta, her dear friend, had perished in a death camp, so now Maddie would gladly take her place and give Lena all the love her heart could hold. 'Yes, Max, we shall be a family,' she said softly.

For as long as the three of them were together, there would be no more sorrow, no more pain. Only love and good memories of those they'd lost along the way. After everything they'd all endured, Maddie knew it would be up to her and Max to find their own happy ending. And in that moment, as she held him and Lena so tightly, the hurt of the past seemed to melt away, and something told her the light they'd left behind was about to burn brightly once more.

Author's notes and acknowledgements

For decades the true story of Trent Park, a mansion just outside London, remained buried in the London Public Records Office. Tens of thousands of 'Top Secret' transcripts lay gathering dust among the archives until they were declassified in 1996. It was a German academic, Professor Sönke Neitzel, together with the social psychologist Harald Welzer, who first highlighted the importance of these astonishing papers after rediscovering some of their explosive contents. Professor Neitzel's book, *Tapping Hitler's Generals*, published in 2007, is a must-read for anyone interested in this little-known aspect of the war.

In my own research I've discovered that not even local residents had any idea what was going on in the stately home that was literally on their doorstep during the years 1942–45. Unbeknown to everyone apart from a very few, the mansion which once hosted Hollywood stars and royalty alike, became a luxury 'prison' to dozens of high-ranking German officers. These prisoners were allowed many freedoms, including an on-site shop where they could buy sundries, walks in the grounds, the regular services of a Savile Row tailor and even excursions into London. (And yes, they were even wined and dined at Simpson's, much to Churchill's annoyance.) But all this came with a catch. British intelligence did, of course, have an ulterior motive. They wanted to gain access to the secrets of the Nazi war machine. Unbeknown to the Germans, their conversations were being secretly recorded by microphones hidden in every room at Trent Park – in light fittings, under windowsills and even in bushes outside. Those recordings proved very revealing, furnishing the Allies with vital intelligence on a vast array of subjects including troop movements, technological advances, codes and ciphers, gunnery, unit organisation, tanks, the morale of the German and Italian people, oil supplies, and very importantly the V-1, V-2 and V-3 vengeance weapons.

Most shockingly, however, the transcripts have also provided us with a true insight into the horrific attitudes held by many German military personnel towards Jews. Some of the secret recordings are so disturbing that even when paraphrased, as I have done in the novel, they remain a damning indictment against the Germans involved. To this day, these fascinating papers are still being examined and revealing even more. In fact, some historians rank the importance of this intelligence second only to that of Bletchley Park.

Although this novel is peopled by completely fictious characters, I have taken some inspiration from those known to work at the mansion. While Madeleine (Maddie) Gresham is entirely my own creation, it's known the Combined Services Detailed Interrogation Centre employed a team of psychologists and psychiatrists to help monitor prisoners. The identities of these men (and possibly women) have not yet been uncovered, although, in 1941, Henry Dicks joined the British Army as a Specialist Psychiatrist and may well have worked at Trent Park. I felt the field was ripe for fictional treatment.

The character of Max is an amalgam of several of the listeners who worked in secret at Trent Park. Most were Jewish émigrés who had escaped from Nazi Germany prior to the start of the war, although there were some British-born listeners. They worked under the most secretive conditions, having signed the Official

Secrets Act, and many went to their graves never having divulged their wartime role to their families. A few of them did, however, break their silence many years later and to them we owe a huge debt of gratitude. Fritz Lustig was one such 'secret listener.' He was based at Latimer House, one of two other mansions that housed German and other Axis POWs. Although he never worked at Trent Park, his testimony, his BBC videos, and his interviews in national newspapers have left an invaluable legacy for historians. (Sadly, he died in 2017.) He married another German refugee, Susan Cohn, who also worked in intelligence, in 1945. Their son, Robin Lustig, is a former BBC journalist, and I am most grateful to him for providing me with invaluable insights into his father's life and work. Another secret listener, Eric Mark, passed away as I was writing this novel in 2020, aged 97. He was the last known remaining listener.

There was also a welfare officer at the mansion who doubled as a British intelligence officer. Under the name Lord Aberfeldy, he pretended to have Nazi sympathies, and, with his fluent German and affable manner, he managed to lull the generals into a false sense of security, so they unknowingly divulged useful information.

There were also 'stool pigeons', or undercover interrogators planted among the German officers in the mansion. One of them was Ernst Lederer, grandfather of the comedian Helen Lederer, who is now a Trustee of Trent Park.

Many of the incidents I fictionalise in the novel really happened. Maddie's brush with the Nazis in Munich is based on the experience of debutante Sarah Norton who, as a sixteen-year-old, was sent to the city to learn German. She was caught vandalising an anti-Jewish newspaper displayed in a glass case and sent home to England. Maddie's arrival at Trent Park was inspired by an account from Diana Quilter, who served there in the First Aid Nursing Yeomanry, or FANY, as it was known. Both women are featured in Anne de Courcy's hugely entertaining non-fiction book *Debs At War*, published by Phoenix.

St Hugh's College, Oxford, where I studied History, was requisitioned, and became a military hospital specialising in head injuries during the war. The women undergraduates were moved into alternative accommodation.

Of the intelligence gathered at Trent Park, perhaps of greatest significance was information relating to the German 'miracle weapons', particularly the V-1 flying bomb and the V-2 ballistic missile, which killed so many civilians in the later stages of the war. But it was purely by a stroke of good fortune that an RAF bombing mission unknowingly damaged the V-3 rocket development site so badly that the weapon could no longer reach Britain. For more information on the German super weapons, I recommend *Hitler's Secret Weapons of Mass Destruction* by Michael Fitzgerald.

In my research I would like to thank so many people, not least my husband Simon, whose determination for me to see this novel through, despite the many obstacles put in its path, was an inspiration throughout.

Trent Park's Senior Historic Advisor, Dr Alex Henry, has fact-checked this manuscript for historical errors pre-publication. He has provided invaluable support and expert knowledge and I can't thank him enough for his time and patience. His book *War Through Italian Eyes*, is highly recommended for those interested in the Italian POWs who passed through Trent Park and the other CSDIC (UK) bugging sites during the Second World War.

Some facts, such as the layout of Trent Park during the war years, remain classified. As far as the workings of the mansion are involved, thanks here are due to Jasper Stiby, who shared with me his (as yet) unpublished research on: 'Trent Park: The Appropriations of an English Country House'. For an excellent overview I recommend 'A Concise History of Trent Park', by Alan Mitellas. There will, however, be the occasional intentional diversion from the facts for the purposes of the story. Unfortunately, because of the secret nature of the subject matter, there may also be a few other factual inaccuracies, which will be entirely unintentional and purely my own.

My heartfelt thanks also go to Julia Pascal of the Pascal Theatre Company, whose 2012 project, *The Secret Listeners*, shone a light on the little-known events at Trent Park during the Second World War. Her book, *The Secret Listeners*, is a wonderful potted history of Trent Park during the war years. Researcher Sally Mijit, and journalist and author David Keys, have also given me their time and encouragement. My thanks go to them, as well as to members of the Facebook groups Enfield Past & Present in Photos and Winchmore Hill & Palmers Green Memories.

I would also like to thank my editor, Belinda Toor, who once again has been a huge source of encouragement and support to me. Her skill, kindness and understanding have been unfailing.

As I write, a housing estate is being built in the grounds of Trent Park; however, a new museum located in the mansion, which will include some of the original rooms inhabited by the German generals, is taking shape. The aim is to create a world-class visitor attraction to highlight the vital role played by the listeners who were behind some of the most important intelligence discoveries during the Second World War. It is planned to open its doors in 2023 and will, hopefully, be a fitting tribute to the men and women of Trent Park who played such an important part in the Allied victory but who remain such unsung heroes. Find out more at https://www.trentparkhouse.org.uk

Tessa Harris, England, 2021

Keep reading for an excerpt from
Beneath a Starless Sky . . .

Prologue

Munich, Germany

1940

Tilting her silver head towards the gramophone player, the old woman listened to the shellac seventy-eight crackle into life. As the needle scoured out the music, Fred Astaire's voice rose, crooning from the grooves. *Dancing in the dark, dah dah dah dah dah* . . .

A smile twitched her lips. It didn't matter that she couldn't understand the foreign lyrics. Fred Astaire, in his white tie and tails, would scoop her up in his arms and whirl away all her thoughts of despair.

Outside, the city slept under curfew. The only distant sound came from armoured trucks and lorries that rumbled relentlessly along the main highway, taking men and machines to war. Inside, in her dark and damp apartment, its windows blacked out, the old woman was left rocking in her one remaining chair. All the others had been burned in the *kachelofen*, the huge, green tiled stove in the corner.

Dancing in the dark, dah dah . . . The song was a welcome distraction from contemplating her own mortality. It made her think of her daughter. Of happier times. Lilli had given her reason to hope; slipping out of Munich unremarked by the authorities just two days before, she'd left behind the travel papers for her and her granddaughter. The plan was to escape to Switzerland with the little girl, asleep now in the next room. They would both be safe there – safer – until Lilli returned. But nothing seemed to go to plan in war.

When the music's blue notes made the melancholy return, the old woman stroked the black cat on her knee. It was better fed than her.

Starvation could be the possible cause of her death, and if not starvation the cold – if she made it to winter. Or, of course, she might even catch diphtheria from her little granddaughter. That was the most likely cause at the moment. The child had been suffering for several days, although her fever had broken a while back and there were signs of improvement, she still remained weak. Now, however, the old woman herself was feeling a little flushed, her throat was sore and her old bones ached even more than usual.

There was, of course, another way she could meet her end, although she constantly tried to push it out of her mind. They could come for her. Some of her friends had already gone and she doubted she would ever see them again. When faced with the thought of either starvation or hypothermia, diphtheria seemed much more preferable. Dying in a camp would be the worst, but however death came, she prayed it would be quick.

As it happened the old woman was spared the indignities of nearby Dachau and at least her end, when it came, was swift, if rather brutal. She was fortunate, too, in that she was alerted to her executioners' approach before she actually saw them.

When they came that evening, their heavy tread echoing up the stairwell and their thick voices bouncing off the walls, she would not have heard them over Astaire's serenade at first. But the cat did. It heeded them all right and leapt off her knee. In the few seconds between being alerted to her killers' advance and their knock, the old woman knew exactly what she had to do.

Scrambling into the bedroom as fast as her creaking legs would carry her, she lifted the child from the bed where she slept. In the bathroom there was a small chest where towels and sheets were kept. She laid the little girl on one then covered her loosely with the rest.

The pounding fists and the shouts that followed a second later were momentarily silenced as, nervously, the old woman opened the door. When she saw the four of them – an army officer and his three soldiers – standing there, smelling of leather and gun metal, she tried to swallow down her fear, but it caught hold of her throat and snagged her voice.

'Yes, sir? How can I help you?' she asked, feigning innocence, as if she had no idea what could possibly have brought these men to her door.

The officer was short and stocky with a long, raised scar on his face, as if someone had drawn a line in pencil from his left cheekbone to his jaw. Another smaller one marked his chin. His eyes were obscured by the peak of his cap when he spoke.

'Where is she?'

'Who?'

'You know who, you old Jew. Search the apartment,' he ordered.

His men stormed in. They split up: each stomping into a room. The old woman could hear wardrobe doors opening and slamming, drawers flung to the floor, china smashing on the tiles. *As if my daughter will be hiding in a vase*, she thought to herself.

While his men were wreaking havoc in the other rooms, the officer's eye was caught by the gramophone player. The disc was crackling incessantly as it pirouetted on the turntable. Stalking over to it, he lifted the stylus and grabbed the record to read the label. The old woman remained still, watching the fury march across his face. Suddenly he jack-knifed his leg and cracked the disc in two across his knee, cursing loudly.

'Fred Astaire!' he cried, flinging the shards to the floor. 'Records are *verboten*!'

One by one the soldiers returned from their forays shaking their heads. Again, the officer narrowed his eyes. 'You have one more chance. Where is she?'

The old woman also shook her head. 'I don't know who you mean,' she replied.

Without a word, the officer reached into his holster and pulled out his Luger. An image of the old woman's daughter filled his vision. He'd always wanted to possess Lilli Sternberg ever since he'd first set eyes on her all those years ago. There'd been something maddeningly mesmerising about her. She'd driven him frantic with desire, yet whenever he'd come within reach of her, she'd slipped his grasp. Once again, the intelligence had come through too late. She'd be in Lisbon by now. With the former King of England and his American wife. If he couldn't have what he wanted, her mother must pay. Even before the old woman had time to react, he pulled the trigger. An ear-splitting crack filled the space between them. His victim clutched her chest, made an odd gurgling sound and fell. Death did, indeed, come swiftly for her, as she had hoped.

The silence that followed the shot didn't last long. It was pricked by a needle of a cry coming from one of the rooms.

'What was that?' growled the officer.

His men froze, their heads switching involuntarily towards the thread of high-pitched sound. Without warning the door from the bathroom was opened by some unseen force. Hands were clamped around rifles on high alert until, from out of the room, dashed a black cat. It leapt over the crumpled body that lay on the threshold without stopping to sniff the pooling blood, and darted straight past the soldiers and down the stairs.

The officer cleared his throat, re-inserted his Luger into its holster and tugged at his jacket. As he worked his jaw in silent rage, he cast a final glance around the room. What the old woman had said was true. Her daughter wasn't there. His bird had already flown. In his gut he had known it before he came to the apartment looking for her and shot her mother instead. Lilli Sternberg was long gone.

Ten years earlier

Chapter 1

Munich, Germany

1930

Smoke. Not just the smoke from a stove. It tingled in her nostrils. This smoke smelled different. Acrid. Harsh. Lilli Sternberg's quickening heart sounded an alarm as she rounded the corner into Untere Grasstrasse. When she lifted her gaze to the rooftops, she saw the sparks of a thousand fireworks join the stars to fill the black sky.

Fire. Suddenly cries cut through the cold air and a man careered past her at high speed. Before she could move out of the way, he clipped her shoulder and sent her spinning. She staggered back against a wall. Shaking the shock from her head she heard someone nearby shout a warning and she looked up just in time to see a blazing beam hurtling towards her. There was no time to react. It crashed to the ground just a few metres away. She screamed. And then she saw more flames.

'Get back! Get back!' yelled a fireman.

'My father. The tailor's shop! Is it . . .?' But her cries were lost in the confusion.

At least two shops along the street were alight, tongues of orange flame licking clean the bones of the bunched-up buildings lining the narrow street. There may have been more ablaze, but the firemen were keeping onlookers well back. Just before her way was barred, Lilli thought she could make out a few men forming a human chain along the street. They were passing buckets from the water hydrant at the end of the row.

The heat was starting to sting her hands and face. She decided to retreat, narrowly avoiding the shower of molten sparks exploding across the cobbles. The roar of the blaze filled her ears and the thick smoke seemed to suck the breath from her lungs, making her cough.

The flames had already risen to the upper floors. Shattered glass from windows carpeted the narrow road below. A fire engine blocked the street and a solitary jet of water arced up through panes, dampening down the blaze and making it hiss in protest. Lilli could tell some of the adjoining shops were beyond saving. Was her father's workshop one of them?

Lilli felt her legs melt beneath her. Already exhausted from hours of rehearsals with Madame Eva at the *Académie de Danse,* her feet were badly blistered, too. But she knew she needed to return home as fast as she could. She was worried about her father. What if he was inside his shop when the fire started?

An icy blast whipped around her legs and ripped through her lungs like a knife as she ran. Despite her pain, she struggled through the back streets of Giesing, stopping now and again to catch her breath and swallow down the agony in her feet.

Past the old doors plastered in posters and the boarded-up shops she went until she came to the run-down apartment block she called home. The stairs up to the fourth floor seemed even steeper than usual. The shock of what she'd just seen weighed her down. She felt sick with worry with each step that she took. What if her father had been stitching with the sewing machine? He wouldn't have heard the crackling flames. He had a cold, too.

It would have taken him longer to smell the smoke. For the first time in ages she found herself praying to a god she didn't believe existed. *Please, let him be safe.*

As she reached the first landing something darted out in front of her. She veered to avoid it, only to realise it was Felix, the block's black cat.

Just then a child's voice called down. 'Well, if it isn't the movie star!' A small face squeezed between the spindles of the staircase. 'Did you know your vati's shop is on fire?'

It was Anna Kepler, the dentist's daughter, an eight-year-old who often spied on people on the stairs. Her teeth were held back by steel braces. Lilli only wished her tongue could be. Angrily, she powered up the last remaining flights of steps, barging past the girl, cursing under her breath to burst into the apartment, gulping for air.

'Vati! Is he here?'

Her mother, Golda, was sitting hunched on the threadbare sofa. Wrapped in a shawl, she was cradling a cup of coffee in both hands.

'Oh Lilli!' cried Golda. 'Praise be!' A plump hand reached out to grasp her daughter's. Lilli rushed to take it, the room filling with the stench of acrid smoke in her wake.

Their neighbour, Frau Grundig, the one Lilli called the Ram because she wore her braids coiled around her ears, was by her mother's side.

'At last!' cried the Ram. 'It was a good of you to turn up,' she mumbled sarcastically. She disapproved of Lilli, suspecting her of fooling with boys when she told her parents she was at the academy.

'I'm sorry, Mutti, rehearsals ran late and Madame Eva . . .'

'Madame Eva! Madame Eva!' mimicked the Ram.

Ignoring Frau Grundig's taunts, Lilli turned to her mother. 'Vati! The fire! Where's Vati?' she croaked.

'He's safe, praise be,' replied Golda, raising her eyes heavenwards. 'The Almighty took care of him.'

341

Golda was a heavy woman, with large, dark features. Like a sturdy piece of mahogany furniture, her frame was thick and serviceable. She moved in a cloud of resignation. Fire, flood or famine: because she believed they were God's will, she accepted them all without complaint. Her daughter did not.

'I came as soon as I could but . . .' The words still struggled to escape Lilli's gritty throat. She was careful to avoid the Ram's gaze as she spoke. It was true that she'd been kept late rehearsing *Giselle*. She'd been chosen to dance the leading role in this year's gala performance. But if her parents ever found out she also worked as an usherette at the cinema after classes some evenings, she'd be in deep trouble.

'Where is he?' Lilli asked, her dark eyes searching the room.

'Seeing what the Almighty will let him save,' replied Golda with a shrug.

Leon, Lilli's younger brother, sat by the *kachelofen* in the corner, feeding logs to the hungry giant stove. He was four years younger than her, but he had the mind of an adult. He said little, but thought a lot, preferring to bury his dark head in books rather than play sport. Up until then he had been content to watch events unfold, but he suddenly broke his silence.

'You put too much faith in the Almighty, Mutti,' he told his mother, finally prising himself away from the big stove.

'Leon!' Frau Grundig took it upon herself to scold him, too. 'If he were my son . . .' she began, but she was childless and everyone else's child, it seemed to her, behaved badly.

Golda lurched forward in her chair. 'Leon! Wash your mouth out with soap and water!' she cried.

Leon skulked across the room, his hands thrust deep into his pockets, his eyes cast down. Golda slumped back into her seat, shaking her head as she watched her son leave.

'He's angry,' she muttered on a long sigh.

Lilli agreed. She looked on politics as something that happened to other people, like being run over by a bus. Leon, on the other hand, thought all his family's problems were caused by politicians, who stirred up hatred against them. Her brother would not act. Not now at any rate, but Lilli feared that the day would soon come when he and his synagogue friends would do something foolish.

'The people who did this . . .' Golda carried on, staring into her coffee.

'People?' butted in the Ram. 'You think the fire was started deliberately?' Frau Grundig leaned forward, her ample bosom bulging over the top of her old-fashioned dirndl. A scandalised look puffed out her face. 'How do you know?'

Golda shot a savvy glance at Lilli before she replied. 'We can't say for sure but . . .'

'I'm afraid we can,' came a voice from the doorway. Jacob Sternberg stood bowed on the threshold, covered in soot. For an instant he reminded Lilli of the actor in the new American talkie *The Jazz Singer*, whose face was painted black. Her father gave a resigned shrug.

'A star with the word "*Juden*" was daubed on my shop door the other day,' he told them.

'Oh!' Frau Grundig's hands flew up to her face in an exaggerated show of empathy. 'Who could do such a thing?' she asked disingenuously. She knew as well as her neighbour about the recent spate of arson attacks on Jewish premises.

Golda stemmed her tears. Lilli could tell her mother wanted to cry, but, as ever, her pride ensured she did not. 'The usual thugs, with nothing better to do, I suppose,' was all she would say.

'The fire service was already there when I arrived,' Jacob told his small audience. 'They did their best, but . . .' His voice trailed off in defeat.

'They have their work cut out tonight,' butted in Herr Kepler. He was the dentist from the third floor. He stepped into the apartment uninvited, an unlit pipe clenched between his uneven teeth.

'What do you mean?' asked Jacob, wiping the soot from his spectacles with a handkerchief.

'The synagogue is ablaze, too.'

'How can this be?' asked the diminutive Frau Kepler. She'd followed behind her husband, making the sign of the cross as she spoke.

An annoyed Frau Reuter piled in, too, with one of her four small children on her hip. All the commotion had apparently woken her little ones.

Despite the difficult circumstances, Golda suddenly remembered her duty to her visitors. 'You will take coffee?' she asked the Keplers and Frau Reuter.

'My children have been woken up,' Frau Reuter replied testily, jiggling her infant on her hip, as if it was patently obvious she did not have time for a coffee.

Before the others could answer, however, the sound of heavy footsteps echoing up the stairwell brought a halt to the conversation. Lilli was only relieved that Leon was out of the room when the door was flung wide. Herr Backe, in his brown storm trooper's uniform, a swastika band on his left arm, paused on the threshold to survey the gathering. For a moment there was an uneasy silence. None of the residents liked the lodger who shared the Sternbergs' apartment.

'*Sieg heil!*' he barked suddenly, raising his right arm in an abrupt salute. An arc of spittle went flying through the air.

A few months ago, the gesture had made Lilli giggle. Now she and her mother swapped uneasy glances. He was as a cuckoo in the nest and a buffoon, but, as her father pointed out, he was the one whose rent money was putting much-needed bread on their table. They were wary of him and his ways, but they put up with him. Only Herr Kepler responded with a half-hearted salute that was more of an embarrassed wave. The others bobbed their heads in reply.

'Herr Backe,' acknowledged Jacob.

By day Hans Backe was a bank clerk, but by night, after attending one of his weekly National Socialist Party meetings, he seemed to transform into someone quite loathsome.

'Frau Sternberg. Herr Sternberg.' The lodger returned the greeting before pivoting on his heels towards his room. His uniform made him look bigger than his cheap clerk's suit did, thought Lilli. She hated him.

Everyone waited for the sound of the door to click shut, but the damage was done. The unwelcome interruption seemed to bring the gathering to an early close, as if a shadow had just passed over the room. No one knew what to say – not safely – so the Keplers, Frau Grundig and Frau Reuter just smiled politely, and did what any good German citizen would do. They bid the Sternbergs 'Guten Nacht' and left.

Dear Reader,

We hope you enjoyed reading this book. If you did, we'd be so appreciative if you left a review. It really helps us and the author to bring more books like this to you.

Here at HQ Digital we are dedicated to publishing fiction that will keep you turning the pages into the early hours. Don't want to miss a thing? To find out more about our books, promotions, discover exclusive content and enter competitions you can keep in touch in the following ways:

JOIN OUR COMMUNITY:

Sign up to our new email newsletter:
http://smarturl.it/SignUpHQ

Read our new blog www.hqstories.co.uk

🐦 https://twitter.com/HQStories

f www.facebook.com/HQStories

BUDDING WRITER?

We're also looking for authors to join the HQ Digital family!
Find out more here:

https://www.hqstories.co.uk/want-to-write-for-us/

Thanks for reading, from the HQ Digital team

**If you enjoyed *The Light We Left Behind*,
then why not try another sweeping historical
fiction novel from HQ Digital?**

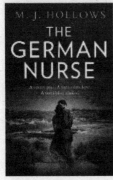